Limerick County Library

30012 00556080 9

The Royal House of Cacciatore

Passion, power and privilege...

Three passionate novels!

WITHDRAWN FROM STOCK

*In February 2008 Mills & Boon bring
back two of their classic collections,
each featuring three favourite
romances by our bestselling authors…*

THE ROYAL HOUSE
OF CACCIATORE

by Sharon Kendrick

featuring

The Mediterranean Prince's Passion
The Prince's Love-Child
The Future King's Bride

FROM BOARDROOM
TO BEDROOM

His Boardroom Mistress
by Emma Darcy
Luca's Secretary Bride
by Kim Lawrence
Hired by Mr Right by Nicola Marsh

The Royal House of Cacciatore

by
Sharon Kendrick

THE MEDITERRANEAN PRINCE'S PASSION

THE PRINCE'S LOVE-CHILD

THE FUTURE KING'S BRIDE

LIMERICK
COUNTY LIBRARY
WITHDRAWN FROM STOCK

◎™ MILLS & BOON®
Pure reading pleasure

DID YOU PURCHASE THIS BOOK WITHOUT A COVER?

If you did, you should be aware it is **stolen property** as it was reported *unsold and destroyed* by a retailer. Neither the author nor the publisher has received any payment for this book.

All the characters in this book have no existence outside the imagination of the author, and have no relation whatsoever to anyone bearing the same name or names. They are not even distantly inspired by any individual known or unknown to the author, and all the incidents are pure invention.

All Rights Reserved including the right of reproduction in whole or in part in any form. This edition is published by arrangement with Harlequin Enterprises II B.V./S.à.r.l. The text of this publication or any part thereof may not be reproduced or transmitted in any form or by any means, electronic or mechanical, including photocopying, recording, storage in an information retrieval system, or otherwise, without the written permission of the publisher.

This book is sold subject to the condition that it shall not, by way of trade or otherwise, be lent, resold, hired out or otherwise circulated without the prior consent of the publisher in any form of binding or cover other than that in which it is published and without a similar condition including this condition being imposed on the subsequent purchaser.

® and ™ are trademarks owned and used by the trademark owner and/or its licensee. Trademarks marked with ® are registered with the United Kingdom Patent Office and/or the Office for Harmonisation in the Internal Market and in other countries.

Harlequin Mills & Boon Limited,
Eton House, 18-24 Paradise Road, Richmond, Surrey TW9 1SR

THE ROYAL HOUSE OF CACCIATORE
© by Harlequin Enterprises II B.V./S.à.r.l 2007

The Mediterranean Prince's Passion, The Prince's Love-child and
The Future King's Bride were first published in Great Britain by
Harlequin Mills & Boon Limited in separate, single volumes.

The Mediterranean Prince's Passion © Sharon Kendrick 2004
The Prince's Love-child © Sharon Kendrick 2004
The Future King's Bride © Sharon Kendrick 2005

ISBN: 978 0 263 86118 1

05-0208

Printed and bound in Spain
by Litografía Rosés S.A., Barcelona

THE MEDITERRANEAN PRINCE'S PASSION

by

Sharon Kendrick

WITHDRAWN FROM STOCK

MILLS & BOON
100 YEARS
of pure reading pleasure.

100 Reasons to Celebrate

We invite you to join us in celebrating
Mills & Boon's centenary. Gerald Mills and
Charles Boon founded Mills & Boon Limited
in 1908 and opened offices in London's Covent
Garden. Since then, Mills & Boon has become
a hallmark for romantic fiction, recognised
around the world.

We're proud of our 100 years of publishing
excellence, which wouldn't have been achieved
without the loyalty and enthusiasm of our
authors and readers.

Thank you!

Each month throughout the year there will
be something new and exciting to mark the
centenary, so watch for your favourite authors,
captivating new stories, special limited
edition collections...and more!

Sharon Kendrick started story-telling at the age of eleven and has never really stopped. She likes to write fast-paced, feel-good romances with heroes who are so sexy they'll make your toes curl!

Born in west London, she now lives in the beautiful city of Winchester – where she can see the cathedral from her window (but only if she stands on tiptoe). She has two children, Celia and Patrick and her passions include music, books, cooking and eating – and drifting off into wonderful daydreams while she works out new plots!

Don't miss Sharon Kendrick's exciting new novel *The Greek Tycoon's Baby Bargain* out in May 2008 from Mills & Boon® Modern™.

CHAPTER ONE

IT WAS just a dazzle of white set against the endless sapphire, but the sun was blinding her too much to see clearly. Ella's eyes fluttered to a close in protest. Maybe she had imagined it. Like a person hallucinating an oasis in the desert, perhaps her mind had conjured up an image on the empty sea that surrounded them. Some sign of life other than the birds that circled and cawed in a sky as blue as the waters beneath.

'Mark.' She croaked the unfamiliar name through lips so parched they felt as if they had never tasted liquid before. 'Mark, are you there?' She racked her brains for one of the women's names. 'Helen!'

But there was no answer, and maybe that wasn't so surprising, for the throb, throb, throb of loud music from the lower deck drowned the sound of her feeble words. She could hear the muffled sound of girlish, drunken giggling drifting upwards. She moaned.

How long? How long since she had drunk anything? She knew she ought to go and get some water, but her legs felt as though they had been filled with lead. She lifted a heavy hand to try to brush the weight of damp hair that flopped so annoyingly against her cheek, but it fell uselessly to her side.

5

LIMERICK COUNTY LIBRARY

She was going to die. She knew she was.

She could feel the strength slowly ebbing from her body. Her ears were roaring and the weak flutter of her heart beat rapidly against her breast. Her skin was on fire, it was burning…burning…burning…

Below, the cool, darkened interior of the cabin beckoned to her enticingly, but an instinct even stronger than her need to escape the sun stopped her from giving in to it. Down there lay chaos, and no chance for escape, but at least here on deck someone might see her.

Her eyes began to close.

Please, God, let someone see her…

His dark hair ruffled by the breeze and his strong body relaxed, Nico stared at the horizon, his eyes suddenly narrowing as the flash of something on the horizon caught his attention.

A boat? Where there should be no boat? Here in the protected waters on this side of Mardivino? His mouth tightened. Modern-day bandits? Seeking access to the tax haven guarded so jealously by the super-rich? The island had a long history of being beseiged by bounty-hunters and their modern-day counterparts—the paparazzi—and his face darkened. Where the hell were the Marine Patrol when you needed them?

But the devil-may-care facet of his character made his pulse begin to race with excitement. Ignoring—almost relishing—the potential danger to himself, he reached for the throttle and his jet-ski sped forward, roaring in a spray of foam towards the stricken craft, which bobbed like a child's toy on the waves.

As his craft approached he could see a figure lying on the deck, and as he drew alongside he could see that it was a woman and that she appeared to be sunbathing. Tawny limbs and tawny hair. Slim and supple, with the tight lushness of youth. It took him precisely two seconds to assess whether or not this was a ploy and she the decoy. It was an age-old method he had encountered before; it came with the territory he inhabited.

But she was not sunbathing. Something was very wrong—Nico could see that from her slumped and unmoving pose.

Moving swiftly, he secured his jet-ski and jumped on board, his stance alert and watchful as he scanned the deck for a brief moment and listened intently. From a distance he could hear the loud beat of dance music, but the woman appeared to be alone on deck.

In a few strides he had reached her. Bending over, he turned her onto her side, blotting out his instinctive first reaction to the way her magnificent breasts rose and fell beneath the skimpy jade-green bikini top she wore.

She was sick.

Assessingly, he ran his eyes over her. Her breathing was shallow, her eyes tight-closed and her skin very pink. He laid a brief exploratory hand on her forehead and felt the heat sizzling from it. Fever. Probably sun-stroke, by the look of her.

Urgently, he shook her. *'Svegli!'* he ordered, but there was no response. He tried in French. *'Reveillez-vous!'* And then, louder, in Spanish. *'Despierte!'*

Through the mists of the dream that was sucking her down towards a black numbness Ella heard a deep voice urging her back to the surface, back towards the light. But the light was hurting her eyes and she didn't want to go there. She shook her head from side to side.

'Wake up!'

Her eyes flickered open. A face was looming over her—its hard, handsome features set in a look of grim concern. A dark angel. She *must* be dreaming. Or dying.

'Oh, no!' he exclaimed, and levered her up into his arms, supporting her head with an unmoving hand as it threatened to flop back. 'You will not sleep again! Do you hear me? Wake up! Wake up now, this instant. I demand it!'

The richly accented voice was too commanding to ignore, but Ella was lost in the grip of a fever too powerful to resist.

'Go away,' she mumbled, and she felt a cold terror when he lowered her back onto the deck and did just that—left her all alone again. She gave a little whimper.

Nico went below deck and the noise hit him like a

wall. He stood for a moment, studying the scene of decadence that lay before him.

He could count five people—three men and two women—and all of them were in advanced stages of intoxication. One woman was topless and snoring quietly on the floor, while another gyrated in front of one of the men like a very poor lap-dancer.

Only one of the men seemed to notice his arrival, and he raised a half-empty bottle of Scotch.

'Hey! Who're you?' he slurred.

Nico gave him a look of simmering fury. 'Are you aware that you're trespassing?' he snapped.

'No, matey—I think *you're* the one doing that! This boat I paid through the nose for, and—' The man pointed exaggeratedly upwards. 'The sea is free!' he added, in a sing-song voice.

'Not here, it isn't. You're in forbidden waters.' And, turning on his heel, Nico went back up onto the deck. He slid a mobile phone from his back pocket and punched in a number known to only a very few, which connected him straight to the Chief of Police.

'*Pronto? Si. Nicolo.*' He spoke rapidly in Italian.

There was a pause.

'You want that we should arrest them, Principe?' asked the Capo quietly.

Nico gave a hard glimmer of a smile. '*Si.* Why not? A night in jail sobering up might teach them never to put themselves nor others in danger again.' But he stared down thoughtfully at the girl, for she was not drunk; she was sick.

He bent down and shook her gently by the shoulder. Her eyes fluttered open, dazed and green as spring grass.

Through the haze of her fever she saw his strength—a rock, a safe harbour and her only means of escape. 'Don't leave me,' she begged.

The raw emotion in her voice made him still momentarily but it was an unnecessary appeal for he had already made up his mind. 'I have no intention of leaving you,' he said tersely, and scooped her up into his arms before she could protest.

Her arms clasped tightly around his neck, she slumped against his chest like a rag doll in an unconscious attitude of complete trust. He gripped her tightly as he manoeuvred her onto the jet-ski.

Most men would have struggled to cope with a woozy female, but Nico had been born to respond to challenge—it was one of the few things in life that invigorated him. A small smile touched the corners of his mouth as he set off for the shore.

He was always trying new thrills and spills, but this was the first time he'd ever rescued a damsel in distress.

CHAPTER TWO

COOL dampness rippled enchanting fingers across her cheeks and Ella let out a small sigh.

'Mmm! S'nice!'

'Drink this!'

It was the voice that wouldn't go away. The voice that wouldn't take no for an answer. The voice that had been popping in and out of her consciousness with annoying frequency. A bossy, foreign voice, but an irresistible one, too.

Obediently Ella opened her lips and sipped again from the cup she was being offered, only this time she drank more greedily than before, gulping it so that the water ran in riveluts down her face, trickling over her chin and startling her out of the hazy fog that engulfed her.

'That is better,' said the deep voice, with a touch of approval. 'Take some more still, and then open your eyes properly.'

Befuddled, she did as she was told—only to find herself even more confused. For there was a man standing over her—a man she didn't recognise.

Or did she?

She blinked up at his face and something peculiar

11

happened to her already unsteady heart-rate, for he was utterly spectacular.

His chiselled features gave his face a hard, auto-cratic appearance, but a sensual mouth softened it. Narrowed eyes were fringed by blocks of dark lashes and his hair was jet-dark and wavy, and slightly too long. He looked rugged and powerful—familiar and yet a stranger. His skin was golden and olive and glowing—as though it had been gently lit from within. His was the face that had drifted in and out of her fevered sleep, coaxing and cooling her. A dark angel. A guardian angel.

So she had not been dreaming at all. Nor, it seemed, had she died.

Still blinking in consternation, she glanced around her. She was in a room—a very plain and simple room, containing little more than a small wooden ta-ble and a couple of old chairs. On the floor were worn floorboards, the walls were wooden, too, and she could hear the roar of waves. It was cool and dim and she was lying on a low kind of bed, beneath a tickly-feeling thing that was too thick to be a sheet and too thin to be a blanket. Her hand slithered inside.

She was wearing nothing but a man's T-shirt!

The last of her lethargy fled in an instant and fear galloped in to take its place. Clutching the coverlet, she sat up and stared at the man who stood over her, his dark face shuttered and watchful. Was she certain that she wasn't dreaming? Who was he, and what was she doing here?

'Would you mind telling me what the hell's going on?' she demanded breathlessly.

'I think…' There was a pause. He watched her very carefully, like a hunter with his prey held firmly in his sights. 'That I should be asking you that very same question.'

Her heart was pounding like a piston. His voice was soft and rich and accented. And accusing. When surely, if there was any accusing to be done… Beneath the coverlet she ran an exploratory hand down over her body, as if checking that all her limbs were intact. And not just her limbs…

Nico watched her. 'Oh, do not worry,' he drawled. 'Your virtue is intact. Or at least as intact as it was when you arrived.' Though God only knew what she had been up to with the band of drunks on board that boat.

Ella tried to will her stubborn memory into gear, but it was as if her brain had been wrapped in cotton wool. Something told her that she must be grateful to this man, but something about his dark masculinity was suddenly making her feel very shy. More than shy. 'What's happened?'

'You have been sick,' he explained, but his eyes lost nothing of their glittering suspicion.

She looked around for signs that she might be in a hospital, but there was nothing remotely medical or sterile about the place. In fact, there were grains of sand on the floorboards, and a wetsuit lay coiled in a heap like a seal skin. Some of the cotton wool cleared. 'Where am I?'

'Ah! At last! The traditional question. It took you long enough to ask,' he observed, arching imperious eyebrows that shot up into the ebony tumble of his hair. His dark eyes fixed her with a lancing stare.

'I'm asking now.'

The eyes narrowed, for he was unused to such a response. 'You don't know?'

'Why would I bother asking you if I already knew?'

Unless, he pondered, she had her own separate agenda, and there was no way of finding out, not until she was properly recovered. Not when she was still…

Nico turned away from her body, its outline undisguised by the T-shirt, its firm curves spelling out a temptation that would have stretched the resolve of the most holy and celibate of men—two things of which he had never been accused.

For hours she had lain there, her tawny limbs and hair flailing as she thrashed and cried out, hot with fever and lost in the strange world of delirium. And he had bathed her. Sponged her down. Fed her with water and sat with her during the long, lonely hours till dawn.

It had been a new sensation for him—having someone reliant and dependent on *him*. She had been as helpless as a wounded animal, and that very help-lessness had brought about a protectiveness he had never before experienced.

Until…

He had been smoothing the damp hair away from her sweat-sheened skin, murmuring words of comfort, when she had suddenly called out in alarm. And when he shushed her she had sat up, the sheet falling from her. The T-shirt he had hastily flung on her had man-aged to both conceal and reveal—and the hazy hint of glorious rose-tipped breast beneath had been en-chanting beyond belief. He had tried to move away but she had lifted her arms and clung onto him with the terrified and irresistible strength of someone who was lost in a nightmare. And she had been close. Oh…so…close… Far too close for comfort and sane thought.

His body had sprung into instant and unwilling re-sponse as she'd pressed closer still. Nerves stretching with unbearable tension, he had stared down into her eyes—the most green and startling eyes he had ever seen—but they had been clouded and vacant. Whomever or whatever she was seeing, it certainly was not him.

'Lie down on the bed!' he had ordered harshly, in English, and the still-dry lips had puckered into the shape of a parched flower before much-needed rain fell onto it.

Some men would have thought—why not? *Taja*

ch'e e rosso, as the Romans sometimes said. To have taken advantage of what was so beautifully on offer might have been an option, but Nico was of different blood from other men. Even if his hadn't been an appetite jaded by what had always been given to him so freely, he could not have countenanced making love to a woman unless she was in total command of her senses.

He stared down at her now and saw that the wild, febrile light had left her eyes. He felt a small tug of triumph, for she had been in his charge and now she was recovered. 'Are you hungry?' he asked unexpectedly.

His words made Ella focus, not on the extraordinary situation in which she found herself, but on the needs of her body, and she suddenly realised that her stomach felt empty and her head light as air. Hungry? She was absolutely starving!

'Why, yes,' she said, in surprise.

'Then you must eat.' He began to move away, as if he couldn't wait to put physical distance between them.

'No—wait!'

He stilled at her words, a bemused expression on his lean and handsome face. How long had it been since someone had issued such a curt order? 'What is it?'

'How long have I been here?' she questioned faintly.

'Only a day.'

Only a day? *Only a day!* She shook her head again to clear it, and strands of memory began to filter back. A boat. A boat trip taken with a bunch of people who, it had turned out, knew nothing of basic maritime law or safety. Who had proceeded to drink themselves into oblivion. And a man who had invited her—who had clearly thought that a woman should pay the traditional price for a luxury weekend.

She screwed up her nose. What had his name been?

Mark! Yes, that was it. Mark.

Her eyes now accustomed to the dim light within the interior of the room, Ella turned her head slowly to look around.

'Where's Mark? What's happened to him?'

Nico's mouth hardened. Had 'Mark' been on her mind when she had pressed her body so close to his? Or was she the kind of woman who was naturally free with her body?

'By now—' he glanced at his watch '—he will just about be released from jail.'

'Jail!' She stared at him in confusion. 'How come?'

'Because I informed the local police of their trespass,' he informed her coolly.

'You've had him put in *jail*?'

'Not him,' he corrected. 'Them. All of them.'

Ella swallowed, suddenly fearful. Just where *was* she? And who the hell was *he*? 'Isn't that a bit over the top?'

'You think so?' His voice became filled with contempt. 'Putting the trespass aside—you think it acceptable for people to be drunk in charge of a powerful boat? To put not only their own lives in danger, but those of others? And that includes you! What do you think might have happened if I hadn't come along?'

Something in the stark accusation of his words made her feel very small and very vulnerable. 'L-look, I'm very grateful for everything you've done,' she said, in a low trembling voice, 'but would you mind telling me exactly what's going on? I don't—'

He silenced her with an autocratic wave of his hand. 'No more questions. Not now. Later you will ask me whatever you please and I shall answer it, but first you must eat. You have been sick. You are weak and you are hungry and you need food. You will have your answers, but later.'

Ella opened her mouth to object, and then shut it again, realising that she was in no position to do so. And even if she had been she simply did not have the strength. He was right—she felt all weak and woolly with the aftermath of fever.

Yet surely she wasn't expected to just lie here, helpless beneath the cover, while this handsome, dominant stranger told her what she could and couldn't do? But what was the alternative? Did she just leap out of bed, feeling strangely naked despite his T-shirt?

He turned his head to look at her and saw the fleeting look of vulnerability that had melted away her objections. Only this time he had to force himself to respond to it. Before it had been easy. While she had been sick he had been able to be gentle with her, as he would have with a child. But now that she was awake it was different. And suddenly not so easy. For she was a beautiful, breathing woman and not a child.

Almost without thinking Nico rebuilt the familiar emotional barriers with which he habitually surrounded himself.

'You wish to wash, perhaps?'

'Please.' But she noticed that his voice had grown cool.

He pointed to a curtain at the far end of the simple room. 'You'll find some basic facilities through there,' he said. He pulled a fresh T-shirt down from an open shelf and threw it onto the divan.

'You might want that,' he said. 'All your stuff is still on the boat and your bikini is hanging outside. I washed it,' he explained, amused to see her look of barely concealed horror. Was she afraid he was expecting her to change in front of him? Then clearly she had no memory of how her T-shirt had slithered up her naked thighs as she had thrashed around. Of how *he* had played the gentleman and slithered it right down again. 'Don't be shy—I'll be outside.'

Don't be shy! Ella watched him disappearing through the door, caught a dazzling glimpse of blue as it opened, and heard the hypnotic pounding music of the waves.

She was obviously in some kind of beach hut—but *where* exactly?

She stared at the closed door and half thought of running after him, and demanding some answers. But she was too weak to run anywhere, and she was also naked, sticky and dusty. Surely she would be better placed to ask for explanations once she was dressed?

Never had the thought of washing seemed more alluring, though the sight that greeted her behind the curtain was not terribly reassuring. There was a sink, a loo, and the most ancient-looking shower that Ella had ever seen. It didn't gush, it trickled, but at least it was halfway warm and there was soap and shampoo, too—surprisingly luxurious brands for such a spartan setting.

Basic it might have been, but Ella had never enjoyed or appreciated a shower more than that one. She washed all the salt and sand away from her skin and hair, and roughly towelled herself dry, then slithered into the clean T-shirt that fortunately—because its owner was so tall—came to mid-way down her thigh. It wasn't what she would call decent, but it was better than nothing.

He was standing by the small table, dishing out two plates of something she didn't recognise, the scent of which made her empty stomach ache. He had left the door open and Ella discovered why the sound of the waves was so loud. It looked directly out onto the most glorious sea view she had ever seen in her life.

Pale, powdered sand dotted with shells gave way to white-topped sapphire waves that glittered and sparkled and danced and filled the room with light. But the room seemed suddenly to have kaleidoscoped in on itself, for all Ella could see was the dark power of the man who was silhouetted against the brilliant backdrop outside.

Now that she was on her feet she didn't need the T-shirt as an indicator of just how tall he was. She could see that instantly from the way he towered, dominating the small room, making everything else shrink into insignificance. His hair was dark and ruffled, tiny tendrils of it curling onto the back of his neck. She felt an odd, powerful kick to her heart as he looked up and slowly drifted his eyes over her.

'My T-shirt suits you,' he mused softly.

It was an innocent enough remark, but something in the way he said it, and the accompanying look of approbation in his eyes, made her feel all woman. She could feel her breasts tingling, and the soft, moist ache of longing. It was a powerful and primitive response, and it had never happened to her quite like that before.

Filled with a sudden feeling of claustrophobia, and unsure of how to deal with the situation, she walked to the open door and breathed in the fresh, salty tang

LIMERICK
00556080
COUNTY LIBRARY

of the air, staring at the moving water in silence for a moment.

'Beautiful, isn't it?' came his voice from behind her.

Composing her face into an expression of innocent appreciation, Ella turned round. 'Unbelievable.' And so was he. Oh, he was just gorgeous. 'That…that smells good,' she managed, in an effort to distract herself.

'Mmm.' He had seen the perking breasts and the brief darkening of her eyes and he felt himself harden. 'Come and eat,' he said evenly. 'We could take our food outside, but I think you need a break from the sun. So we'll just look at the view from here.'

But Ella didn't move. 'You said you would give me some answers, and I'd like some. Now. Please.'

Nico gave a slow smile. The novel always stirred his blood, and it was rare for him to be spoken to with anything other than deference. 'Questions can wait, *cara*, but your hunger cannot.'

His words were soft, but a steely purposefulness underpinned them. As if he were used to issuing orders; as if he would not tolerate those orders being disobeyed. The scent of the food wafted towards her and Ella felt her mouth begin to water. Maybe he was right. Again.

She went back inside and sat down at the table.

'Eat,' he said, pushing a plate of food towards her, but it seemed the command was unnecessary. She had begun to devour the dish, falling on it with the fervour of the truly hungry.

He watched her in fascinated silence, for this, too, was a new sensation. In his company people always picked uninterestedly at their food. There were unspoken rules that were always followed. They waited for him to begin and they finished when he finished. It was all part of the protocol that surrounded him—and yet for all the notice she took of him he might as well not have been there!

She ate without speaking, unable to remember ever having enjoyed a meal as much. Eventually she put her fork down and sighed.

'It's good?'

'It's delicious.'

'Hunger makes the best sauce,' he observed slowly.

There was red wine in front of her, and he gestured towards it, but she shook her head and drank some water instead, then sat back in her chair and fixed him with a steady look. His eyes were as black as a moonless night and they lanced through her with their ebony light.

'Now are you going to start explaining?'

Nico found that he was enjoying himself. He had played the rescuer—so let him have a little amusement in return. 'Tell me what you wish to know.'

'Well, for a start—who are you? I don't even know your name, Mr…?'

There was a pause while he considered the question. It seemed sincere enough, although the Mr tacked onto the end could have been disingenuous, of course. Was it?

'It is Nico,' he said eventually. From behind the thick dark lashes that shielded his eyes he watched her reaction carefully, but there was no sign of recognition in her emerald eyes. 'And you?'

'I'm Ella.'

Ella. Yes. 'It's a pretty name.'

'It's short for Gabriella.'

'Like the angel,' he murmured, letting his eyes drift carelessly over the pale flames of her hair.

It was that thing in his voice again—that murmured caress that made her conscious of herself as a woman. And him as a man. A man who had seen her sick and half-naked. But he was the angel—a guardian angel.

'Where am I?' she asked slowly.

Now his expression became sceptical. 'You really don't know?'

She sighed. 'How long are we going to continue with these guessing games? Of course I don't know. One minute I was on a boat—and the next I'm in some kind of beach hut, eating…' She stared down at her empty plate. Even the food had been unfamiliar, just as he was, with his strange accent and his exotic looks. Disorientated, she found herself asking, 'What have I just eaten?'

'Rabbit.'

'Rabbit,' she repeated dully. She had never eaten rabbit in her life!

'They run wild in the hillsides,' he elaborated, and then, still watching her very closely, he said, 'Of Mardivino.'

'Mardivino?' She stared at him as it began to sink in. 'Is that where we are?'

'Indeed it is.' He sipped from a tumbler of dark wine and surveyed her from eyes equally dark. 'You have heard of it?'

It was one of the less-famous principalities. A sun-drenched Mediterranean island—tax haven and home to many of the world's millionaires. Exclusive and remote and very, very beautiful.

'I'm not a complete slouch at geography,' she said. 'Of course I've heard of it.'

Authority reasserted itself. 'You were in forbidden waters. You should never have ventured onto this side of the island!'

She remembered Mark and one of the others blustering about navigation, and then they had started hitting the bottle, big-time. She remembered how frightened she had been, how she had stood on deck for what seemed like hours and hours, the blistering sun beating down on her quite mercilessly. She shivered. 'But we were lost,' she protested. 'Genuinely lost!'

'Yes.' He didn't disbelieve her. Off Mardivino's rugged northern coast there were rocks and rip tides that would challenge all but the most experienced sailor. No one would have been foolish enough to deliberately put themselves in the danger in which he had found them. So why had they?

His eyes bored into her. 'Those people with you…'

'What about them?'

There was a long pause. 'One of them is a journalist, perhaps?' he questioned casually.

'A journalist?' She screwed up her nose. 'Well, I don't know any of them that well, but none of them said they were journalists.' She met his eyes, which were hard and glittering with suspicion. 'Why would they be?'

'No reason,' he said swiftly.

But Ella heard the evasion in his voice and stared at him. Nothing added up. She stared at him as if seeing him properly for the first time. His clothes were simple, but his bearing was aristocratic, and there was something about his appearance that she had never seen in a man before. Something in the way he carried himself—an arrogant kind of self-assurance that seemed innate rather than learned. Yet he wore faded jeans and a worn T-shirt…

He had brought her to this beach hut, where the shower dripped in a single trickle and yet the soap and shampoo were the finest French brands. She frowned. And he had called her *cara*, hadn't he?

'Are you Italian?'

He shook his head.

'Spanish?'

'No.'

'French, then?'

He smiled. 'Still no.'

Words he had spoken came back to her. 'Yet you speak all three languages?'

He shrugged. How much to tell her? How long to continue this delicious game of anonymity? How long *could* he? 'Indeed I do.'

'And your English is perfect.'

'I know it is,' he agreed mockingly.

This time she would not be deterred by the soft, seductive voice. Ella leaned across the table, challenging him with her eyes. 'Just who exactly *are* you, Nico?'

CHAPTER THREE

THE strangest thing was that Nico was really enjoying himself. It was like a game, or a story—the one where a prince disguised himself as a beggar and no one recognised him.

For a man whose life had been composed of both light and dark fairy tale aspects, it was a new and entertaining twist. And if he told her...then what? Nothing would be the same, not ever again. Her attitude towards him would change irrevocably. No longer would she speak to him as if were just a man—an ordinary man.

When he was a little boy, had he not sometimes wished to be made 'normal', just for the day? And even when he had been at college in America, doing his best to blend in, people had still known of his identity. It had been inevitable—security had arrived before he had, to make the place fit for a prince.

And since when had he been asked to make an account of himself? To explain who he was and his place in the world?

Never.

He leaned back in the wooden chair. 'How does a man define himself?' He asked the question as much of himself as of her. 'Through his possessions? His achievements, perhaps?'

Ella gave him a bemused look. 'Are you incapable of giving a direct answer to a direct question?'

Probably. In the world he inhabited he was never asked a direct question. Conversation was left for him to lead, at whim. It was forbidden by ancient decrees for others to initiate it. When he spoke people listened. He had never known anything else, had accepted it as the norm, but now—with a tug of unfamiliar awareness—he recognised that total deference could be limiting.

'I am Nico,' he said slowly. 'You know my name. I'm twenty-eight and I was born on Mardivino—a true native of the principality.' His eyes glittered. 'So now you know everything.'

'Everything and yet nothing,' she challenged. 'What do you do?'

'Do?' His eyes glittered. How could he have forgotten that in her world people were defined by what they did for a living?

'For a living?'

'Oh, this and that,' he said evasively. 'I work for a very rich man.'

That might go some of the way towards explaining things. Maybe that was why he seemed so impressively self-assured. Perhaps he had picked up and now mirrored some of his rich employer's characteristics, as sometimes happened. That might also explain the extravagant soaps in the bathroom—he might be the recipient of a rich man's generosity.

Ella gestured towards the humble interior. 'And is this your home?'

There was a pause. 'No. No, I don't live here. It's just a place that belongs to my...employer.'

'And the jet-ski?'

'You remember that?' he questioned.

The food and the shower had worked a recuperative kind of magic, and more fragments of memory now began to filter back. She recalled being clasped against a firm, hard body and the comforting, safe warmth of him. Then fast bobbing across the water, with spray being thrown against her fevered skin.

'Kind of.'

'What about it?' he asked carelessly.

'Is it yours?'

Inexplicably, he felt a flicker of disappointment. Would that matter, then? A top-of-the-range jet-ski was a rich man's toy. His habitual cynicism kicked in. Of course it would matter—things like that always did. You were never seen for who you were but what you owned and what you possessed. Take away the trappings and what was left?

'No,' he said flatly. 'It's just something I use when I want to.'

'Well, I hope I'm not going to get you into trouble,' she ventured.

His cynical thoughts began to crumble when she looked at him like that. So...so *sweet*, he thought. So scrubbed and so innocent. So utterly relaxed in his company and now worrying about his welfare! And when had anyone ever done *that* before?

Now that it was dry, the tawny hair was spilling in profusion over her shoulders and face, but not quite managing to disguise the lush swell of her breasts. The aching in his body intensified as he imagined himself running the tips of his fingers over their heavy curves. 'No, you won't get me into trouble,' he murmured. 'I suspect he wouldn't have minded rescuing you himself.'

The words were flirty, and almost imperceptibly something in the atmosphere changed and then intensified. A blurry sexual awareness that had been there all the time was now brought into sharp focus. Ella felt the warm tongue of desire licking its way over her skin and the heated clamour of her response. She found that she didn't dare look at him—and yet where else was there to look? The room was so small, and he was so…so…

She swallowed, her mouth as dry as the sun-baked sand outside. 'Maybe I should think about getting home,' she said quietly.

Nico had watched her body tense, and then seen the wary look that crept into her eyes. He forced himself to steel against the demands of his hungry body, aware that he could frighten her away. Because sex was easy. He could get sex any time he wanted. But not a unique situation like this. And what would sex be like with a woman who *didn't know*?

'Not yet.' His dark eyes on her face, he took a mouthful of wine. 'You still haven't told me anything about you.'

'Well, you know my name. And I'm twenty-six and I was born in Somerset.' Her eyes mocked him. 'So now you know everything about me, too.'

'Everything and nothing.' He echoed her sardonic words. 'And what of the men on board—one of them is your lover, perhaps?'

Ella found her cheeks colouring. 'You can't just come out and ask me something like that!' she protested.

'Why not?'

'Because I thought we were sitting here having a polite conversation, and that sort of question breaks all the rules!'

'A polite conversation?' he murmured. 'Oh, I think not, *cara mia*. When a man and a woman talk together there is always an internal dialogue taking place. What you say is never what you're really thinking, deep down.' *Or else I would be telling you that I want to feel your naked body against me, to taste your tongue as it licks against my lips and hear your cry of startled pleasure as I thrust into you that sweet first time.*

His murmured words increased her wariness, but heightened the sensation of tense expectation, too. Surely by now she should be itching to get away? Not finding her eyes drawn to the luscious curve of his lips, to the hard, clean lines of his body, and thinking how magnificent he must look when he was naked.

His voice interrupted her thoughts. 'So?' he persisted silkily. 'You wish to rush away to the jail-house to greet one of them?'

'Ugh—no, thanks!' Ella shuddered. 'None of them is my lover, nor ever would be. Mark is just someone I met through work.' She bit her lip, remembering how trusting she had been. 'He invited me along to join some friends of his for the weekend, only I arrived to discover that his idea about how we were going to spend our time together differed somewhat from mine.'

'So what happened?'

'I made it clear I wasn't interested in him, and that's when he decided to make love to a bottle of whisky instead.' She pulled a face. 'They all did.'

'And did he hurt you?' he demanded, his expression darkening.

Ella shook her head, taken aback by the sudden hardening of his voice. 'No. I stayed as far away from them as possible. Then they started to drink more and more, and no one seemed capable of taking charge of the boat.' Her voice trembled a little. 'That's when I started to get frightened.'

He remembered the way she had clung to him on deck, and the gut-wrenching effect of the little whimper of protest she had made when he had left her. The way she had weakly gripped onto his hand as if he were her lifeline. Playing rescuer to a woman could evoke some very powerful and primitive feelings, he recognised—feelings he was unfamiliar with, which were given extra potency by her ignorance of who he really was. And that, too, was a rare sensation.

He knew he wanted to make love to her, but he couldn't do it now. Not here. Making love to a woman on his own territory was always fraught with difficulty. And he had no wish to shatter her trust in him, nor to abuse his position. When he took her to bed it must be on equal terms. And in order for that to happen he must get her back to England with as little fuss as possible.

'You want to go home?' he asked suddenly.

His question took Ella off-guard, and she hoped her expression managed to mask her disappointment. What had she been expecting? To stay here indefinitely, in this beautiful place, with this strong, handsome man who had saved her? Alone like Adam and Eve—with the inevitable outcome of sexual discovery?

She fixed her mouth into a wobbly kind of smile. 'Well, I suppose I'd better.'

He heard her reluctance, and that only heightened his appetite. But, as he had already told her, hunger made the best sauce...

He slid a high tech-looking mobile phone from the back pocket of his jeans. 'I'll arrange it.'

He went outside to get a signal and she could hear him talking in a low, rapid voice in Spanish. Then he came back inside.

'We can be airborne within the hour.'

She was unable to hide her bewilderment. 'That soon? But my ticket is from Nice, and that's miles away.'

'We'll be travelling by private jet.'

Her frown deepened. 'How come?'

Again, his eyes pierced her with their brilliant light, but he was enjoying this sensation of anonymity far too much to break it. And besides, he wasn't telling a lie. He was merely presenting the truth in a slightly different form.

'My...employer,' he elaborated casually, 'is an exceedingly rich and generous man. And I'm a qualified pilot,' he added. 'So I can fly you home.' There was a pause and his dark eyes captured hers in their ebony crossfire. 'That is, of course, if you trust me to fly you home safely, *cara*?'

He had rescued her from the boat and ensured that she did not spend a night in the cells. He had cared for her while she thrashed around with fever—what was there *not* to trust?

And when he called her *cara* like that...

'But can you just get up and go like that? Won't your employer mind?'

'Not at all. I have to do some business myself in England, and I can do it this week just as easily as next.'

She saw the gleam of anticipation that had lightened the night-dark eyes, the slow smile that had irresistibly curved his lips, and she could feel the erratic beat of her heart.

'It's very…sweet of you,' she said.

The question *why* hung unspoken on the air.

He shook his head very slightly. It was a very English description, and one that had never been applied to him in his life. 'Sweet? No, *cara*—it is something much more fundamental than that.' He suddenly became aware of the irony of his words. 'You see, I find that I'm just as susceptible to the lure of a pair of dazzling green eyes and a pair of petal-soft lips as the next man.'

Ella felt the heat rise in her cheeks. It was most definitely an overture. And what was she going to do about it? After all, what did she have in common with this all-action foreigner—with his jet-ski and his pilot's licence and his ability to rustle up a delicious one-pot meal in the most basic surroundings? Who lived on a remote island far away from her world…

A shadow of a smile had flitted across the hard contours of his face. 'Maybe you'd like to have dinner with me back in England?' Breakfast would have been his meal of choice, but that would inevitably follow.

From the crashing of her heart against her ribcage someone might think that she'd never been asked out for dinner before—but quite honestly that was the way it felt. As though every invitation up until that moment had been a rehearsal for the real thing. And

Ella found herself smiling at him with lips that she had never considered to be petal-soft before, but that now parted like a flower.

'Why, thank you,' she murmured. 'I'd like that.'

CHAPTER FOUR

IT'S ONLY a dinner date, Ella told herself.

So why did she feel so jumpy? Why were the hands that smoothed the dress down over her hips so clammy and her lips so cool and pale? She rubbed a slick of lipgloss on them and stared at herself critically in the mirror.

The silky black dress gleamed against the curve of bottom and breast, contrasting provocatively with the tiny covered buttons that ran in a demure line from neck to knee.

The spiky black sandals made the best of her legs, and her only adornment was a matching velvet choker at her neck, inlaid with jet as dark and glittering as Nico's eyes.

For the umpteenth time she glanced at the clock, nervously tugging at the hem of her dress, her mind skipping back over the extraordinary events of the last couple of days, which had culminated in Nico flying her home on a private jet.

Ella had spent the flight sipping on a fruit cocktail and looking around her with a sense of disbelief. Whatever Nico's boss did for a living, he must be enormously successful at it to own a plane like that.

She had glanced yet again to the cockpit, to see

Nico sitting in front of a radar screen lit up like a Christmas tree, his fingers caressing the joy stick as if it was a woman's body, and she had shivered, unable to prevent herself. There was something decidedly sexy about a man who could fly a plane—but there again, she'd never met one before!

'Here you are. Home,' Nico murmured as he came through into the cabin after a successful touch-down, his eyes shining.

When he flew a plane he always felt filled with a wild kind of exhilaration—it was the same when he sailed, or climbed, or dived deep to explore the beautiful coral reefs off Mardivino. Some people called it living dangerously—he just called it living.

'Thanks,' Ella said steadily, praying that he'd meant his offer of dinner. 'It was a brilliant flight.'

'So when am I going to see you?' he drawled. 'Tonight?'

It nearly killed her, but Ella shook her head. A woman should never be *too* available—everyone in the world knew *that*! 'No, not tonight, I'm afraid. I have masses to catch up on.'

He raised his eyebrows. 'Cancel it,' he said arrogantly.

Their eyes clashed. That was what he was used to, she recognised. Easy come, easy go. Well, if he wasn't prepared to wait even a day, then he was wasting his time.

'Sorry,' she said coolly. 'I can't. I've been away

and I need to catch up on work. See what's been happening in my absence. You know.'

With an effort he hid the little flicker of irritation and shrugged. 'Sure. So…when? Tomorrow night—or will you be busy then, too?'

She heard the sarcasm in his voice. 'Tomorrow will be fine,' she said steadily, but the small victory of holding out only increased her sense of apprehension.

She wasn't dealing with the kind of man she normally came into contact with—Nico was different, and not just because he was foreign and heart-stoppingly gorgeous. He flew planes and plucked women to safety from lost boats. He was, she recognised, a true alpha male, with the corresponding appetites, and she hadn't run into enough of them to be quite sure of how to deal with him…

'Give me your address,' he said. 'I'll come and pick you up around eight. We'll go somewhere local—unless you'd rather meet up in London?'

Ella's mind raced. London would throw up its own problems—like getting back late after dinner and him suggesting a hotel. And she had never been the kind of woman to fall into bed with a man on a first date. Slightly appalled at the progression of her thoughts, Ella shook her head. 'We have a lovely restaurant, close to where I live. I'll take you there.'

At just after eight Nico jammed his finger on the doorbell, the scent of flowers drifting in the warm, heavy air towards him. Summer roses flowered in profusion around the door of her cottage—which looked as pretty as a picture you might see on an old-fashioned box of chocolates.

He felt a sense of vague detachment, as if he couldn't quite believe where he was or what he was doing—a million miles away from his usual world and all its restraints and rules.

The door opened and suddenly he could barely think straight, for she looked utterly sensational, wearing a clinging black dress that made her body look as if it was coated in liquorice. And he could lick it all off...

A slow smile curved his mouth. '*Ciao*, Ella,' he said softly.

Ella stared at him and words just refused to come—because... Oh, he really *was* gorgeous.

On Mardivino she had been captivated by his powerful strength and his spell-bindingly good looks, but now those qualities were somehow increased a thousandfold. Maybe it was seeing him away from his natural habitat—like plucking an exotic flower and placing it in a suburban garden.

His height made the proportions of her rose-covered porch resemble a doll's house, and next to him even the softly brilliant colours of the garden flowers faded into insignificance. His skin gleamed faintly olive, and he was wearing soft, cool linen through which the hard, muscular power of his body was startlingly evident. His dark eyes gleamed with brilliance, and here, under a gentler English sun, he looked almost indecently alive—as though any other man in the world would look like only half a man next to him.

Her heart began to thunder erratically and her mouth dried to sawdust. 'Hello, Nico.'

It occurred to him that she might have been doing her homework on Mardivino and that things might already have irrevocably changed. Did she know? He stared at her closely but her eyes showed no indication that she found out. He raised his eyebrows in lazy question. 'Hungry?'

She felt as if food would choke her—but that was hardly the most diplomatic thing to say before a dinner date. 'I...I hope you like the restaurant,' she said breathlessly, for his warm, virile scent seemed to be running heated fingertips over her skin.

He smiled with satisfaction, enjoying her response. The unspoken question was already answered in his mind—for the wide-eyed look of pleasure that made her green eyes sparkle like emeralds convinced him that to her he was still just 'Nico'.

'You look very beautiful,' he said softly.

Oddly enough, his flattery had the reverse effect to the one she suspected he wanted. It brought her to her senses. Made her see things for what they really were, and not how she would like them to be. She was not beautiful—she was reasonably attractive on a good day.

'Mediterranean men are always better at giving

compliments than their English counterparts,' she observed coolly.

'Which might explain why Mediterranean women are more gracious at accepting them,' he countered wryly.

Oh, if only she could rewind the clock and play that scene again! Was she going to ruin the evening before it had even started? She gave him an apologetic smile. 'You're right.'

'Shall we try again?' he mocked, curving his lips into a smile. 'You look very beautiful.'

'Thank you.'

'You're welcome.'

Her heart pounded. When he looked at her like that she wished... She wished he would pull her into his arms and kiss her. She wanted to touch her fingertips to his cheek, as if to assure herself that he was flesh and blood and not some figment of her imagination. But she stopped herself.

'Would you...um, would you like a drink first?' she asked. 'Or shall we just get going?'

She was like a lioness protecting her den, thought Nico, and clearly nervous about letting him set foot over the threshold! He had never had to play by the rules of other men before, and now he was beginning to see the disadvantages.

He shook his dark head, recognising the need to get her on neutral territory. 'No. Let's go and eat,' he said.

It was too warm for her to need a coat or wrap,

and they walked side by side down the village street, which was washed amber with the light of the sun. An old man was in his front garden, dead-heading his roses, and he smiled at them as they passed.

'Beautiful evening, isn't it?'

'It's gorgeous,' said Ella, stealing a look at Nico's hard, dark profile.

The restaurant was nestled into a crook of the high street, right next to the church. It was small, and run by an enthusiastic amateur, but word had spread about its fresh, seasonal food, and in high season it was nearly always full and notoriously hard to get a booking. But on fine nights they put more tables out on the terrace and down onto the lawn beyond, and to-night was one of them.

Ella saw a couple of women turn their heads and stare hard at them as they wended their way to a table beneath a chestnut tree. Maybe she shouldn't be surprised—Nico *was* exceptionally good-looking, and he really *did* stand out in a crowd. And there weren't exactly many Latin hunks strolling round the streets of Greenhampton!

'You must order for me, *cara*,' he said firmly once they had sat down, handing his menu straight back to the waitress.

'What do you like?'

'Everything. I like everything.' His eyes were steady as they rested on her face. 'I have very catholic tastes.'

Oh, heavens... Ella was aware of a sudden wave

of helpless longing as she was caught in the soft ebony light from his eyes. It was as if a man had never looked at her before—though when she stopped to think about it no man had—not with such an undeniable message of sensuality. Yet his silent flirting did nothing to detract from his cool air of self-possession, which seemed so at odds with his warmly Latin exterior.

She ordered asparagus and prawns and chilled Montrachet, unable to miss the unmistakably flirtatious glance the waitress slanted at him—though to his credit he didn't react in any way.

The sky was a pale Wedgwood blue, softened with apricot edges from the sun. In the distance could be heard the sporadic sound of birdsong and the occasional rattling brush of crickets. Nico had deliberately sat with his back to the other diners, and now he drank a glass of wine and expelled a long, low sigh as he felt all the tension leave his body.

'That's good wine,' he murmured.

She looked up. 'I know it is.'

He laughed, and captured her eyes. 'So, have you lived here a long time?'

'About three years. I went to university nearby and liked it a lot—but it wasn't until I knew what I wanted to do that I put down roots.'

He ran the tips of his fingers reflectively around his chilled glass. 'I don't really know anything about you,' he observed.

'No.' Ella laughed. 'Maybe it's because of the peculiar way we met.'

Her phrase had the slight resonance of permanence about it, and made him slightly wary—until he reminded himself that women had a habit of making every new encounter sound as though it was a contender for the *Romeo and Juliet* stakes. And if he wanted her—which he did—then surely he should indulge her?

He sipped his wine. 'So tell me about yourself.'

'Well, I studied History at university.' She drew a deep breath, then told him about leap-frogging from job to job, about never quite feeling any real satisfaction in her work and being unable to settle to anything, until one day an American cousin of hers had complained that it was impossible to discover the 'real' England—that everywhere was just a plastic Ye Olde Teashoppe-type experience. Foreign visitors wanted to see places off the beaten track, places of historic interest and wonderful gardens that weren't completely overrun by day-trippers with cameras.

'So you saw a gap in the market?' he guessed.

'Absolutely. I sourced all the best small castles and country houses and found comfortable non-chain hotels. I went looking for simple restaurants—ones like this—the kind of places you wouldn't normally get to hear about. I took a loan from the bank, founded the Real England Tour Company, advertised on the Internet and the business has just taken off. I've even got someone working with me now.'

'Wow.' His eyes gleamed. 'I'm impressed.'

'So that's me.' Ella put her elbows on the table and, leaning forward, rested her chin in her hands. 'What about you?'

They both watched in silence while the waitress put their food down in front of them. They stared at it as if it was an unwelcome intruder.

Nico ate a prawn, more for convention than hunger's sake. 'Actually, I work in tourism myself—but in a different kind of way.'

'Really? Like what?'

'Well, it's complicated. It would take hours to explain.' And he didn't have hours. Not to spend on talking. He leaned towards her and the faint scent of lilac drifted to him. 'Let's not talk about boring stuff like jobs, Ella. Because on a night like this the stuff we aren't saying is deafening us—can't you hear it?'

She stared straight into his eyes, feeling herself beginning to melt, knowing what was coming next and both scared and longing to hear it. 'Stuff like…like what?'

'Like the fact that I have waited just as long as it is possible to wait and now I want to kiss you. And that if we order any more food it is going to be completely wasted because I would prefer to take you back home, where I can kiss you in private.' His dark eyes glittered unrepentantly as they lingered on her lips. 'Shocked?' he drawled.

'Not shocked, no,' she said slowly, because his

words had scraped sharp, jagged fingernails over her senses, leaving her raw and aching.

There had been men she had wanted before, of course there had, but never like this—with a wave of longing so powerful that it seemed to have punched out all her breath and heartbeat and sense and reason. She shook her head again.

'What, then, if not shocked?' he murmured.

His eyes caressed her and she could feel the warm, honeyed throb of her blood urging her on, compelling her to tell him what she really wanted.

'Impatient, I guess,' she said huskily, and swallowed.

His eyes narrowed, her reaction taking him momentarily by surprise—but the unexpected was a very potent aphrodisiac. He withdrew a wallet, peeled off several notes and threw them down on the table.

'This was supposed to be my treat for all your help,' Ella protested.

'Shut up,' he said softly.

'And you've left far too much,' she commented as he stood up.

'Then it will be a pleasant surprise for the waitress, won't it?'

She hoped he could afford it—that he wasn't making an expansive gesture just for the sake of impressing her. But then he was putting his arm around her shoulders, and his fingertips were brushing against her bare skin, and all she could think about was his touch.

They walked breathlessly into the street, and as

soon as they were out of sight of the customers he pulled her hard against him, choosing a darkened alcove where they could not be seen—like a college boy who wanted to get intimate without ruining his bachelor reputation.

It seemed to have taken a long time to get here, but at last she was in his arms, and he was kissing her, and she was kissing him back, and suddenly things began to spin out of control.

CHAPTER FIVE

'NICO!' Ella gasped as his lips drove down on hers, shocking and cajoling them into an instant, yielding response.

'*Si? Che cosa?*' he whispered impatiently, circling his hips against her and hearing with triumph yet another gasp.

'We can't do this!' She closed her eyes as he blatantly pressed the rock-hard cradle of his desire against her. 'Not here!'

Nico stilled. She thought he was going to take her there? Unzip himself and pull her panties down and do it up against a wall? His desire rocketed almost out of control and he pulled his mouth away and closed his eyes, trying desperately to steady his breathing.

'Let's go,' he bit out.

He took her hand and Ella let him, in such a daze that it might as well have been *his* village, not hers, as she blindly mirrored his footsteps until they arrived back at the cottage.

Her hands were trembling so much as she tried to unlock the door that he took the key from her. Once they were inside the hall, he turned to her, lifted her chin and stared down into her troubled face, creasing his forehead into a frown. 'What is it?'

'What must you think of me?' she breathed.

Ah! He hid a smile. He knew this game. Women wanted sex just as much as men did, but nature made them need to dress it up as respectable—if sex could ever be described in such a way.

'What do I think? I think you are very beautiful, *cara*, and I want to make love to you very much.'

She pulled away from him, her eyes dark with hunger—but years of conditioning was hard to get rid of in just a couple of short hours. She pointed towards the kitchen. 'Maybe…maybe I should make us some coffee?'

For a moment he was incredulous. She had been in his arms, just seconds away from instant surrender, and now she was distancing herself? It was unknown—and unheard of! A pulse beat deep in his groin. If he moved towards her again and touched her would she have the strength to repeat her actions? He thought not.

But something stopped him, and it was more than the unimaginable idea that she might hold firm in her resolve. No, once again it was the tantalising prospect of experiencing what other men must encounter every day of their lives. Having to fight for what they wanted.

For once the playing field was equal, when usually all the odds were stacked high in his favour. Had he not wondered over the years what it would be like if a woman treated him as a normal man, knowing that it was unlikely ever to happen? Well, now he had the chance to find out for himself.

The gods had blessed him with looks and brains, as well as the honour and burden of his birthright—so let him see whether they alone were enough to achieve what he so achingly wanted.

'Maybe you should,' he agreed, his voice silky with consideration.

Ella bit her lip. Hadn't part of her been hoping—praying—that he would arrogantly override her doubts and fears by taking her in his arms and kissing them all away?

'Would…would you like some?' To her horror and her consternation she began to tremble violently, and Nico watched her from narrowed eyes before lifting his hand to trace a thoughtful finger around the edge of her lips. 'Do you know what I think?' he whispered.

She shook her head.

'I think that you have made your entirely feminine stand. Honour has been maintained. But now you want me to kiss you again.' For a second his eyes widened, like a predatory jungle cat. 'Am I right, *cara mia*?'

She stared up at him. Yes, she thought. Yes, you're right. *Kiss me.* Kiss me now. *Right now.*

He met the silent demand in her eyes and bent forwards, his mouth tracing a slow, exploratory path across her lips with the lightest of touches—barely touching her at all—which set her already racing pulse scrambling into a rapid, thready beat. The soft no-kiss kiss went on and on, until she felt that the frustration of it might kill her, but finally the tip of his tongue flicked against her, moistening her lips, and she licked at them greedily, wanting to taste him. It was more than before, but it was still not enough, and she moaned.

He raised his head then, a look of mild bemusement momentarily softening the hunger that had hardened the angles of his face as he read her expression. 'More?'

She nodded.

'Say it.'

'Yes. Yes. More. More!'

'Nice girls say please,' he said, a sudden roughness entering his voice, and this time the kiss was urgent and seeking.

Ella felt her knees grow weak, as if her bones were dissolving, and maybe he sensed it, for he caught her up and carried her into the sitting-room. He lay down on the sofa and pulled her on top of him, so that she straddled him, warm thighs clasped against his hips.

Ella closed her eyes and gave in to it. She could feel all the sinews and angles of his hard body, the hard evidence of how much he wanted her as he ground his hips against her.

'Can you feel me?' he murmured.

'Y-yes.'

He pulled her closer still. 'And now?'

Oh, God—it felt almost indecently intimate the way he was pressing himself into her, despite the barrier of their clothes. She nodded frantically as he ran his fingertip up and down the cleft of her buttocks. She felt weak and faint—disturbed by the fact that she was letting him do this to her with such apparent ease. It was as if he had cast some kind of spell on her. It was wrong, she *knew* it was wrong, and yet she didn't want to stop him. She *couldn't* stop him.

'Nico.' Her hands fluttered helplessly, her fingers briefly coiling their way through the ebony tendrils of his hair, then drifting their way down to his shoulders. Through his cool linen shirt she could feel the muscular power sheathed by silken skin, and she kneaded the flesh with rhythmical, greedy fingers. 'Nico!' she gasped.

'Nico, what?'

'Kiss me again.'

He kissed her until there were no doubts left—until she was boneless and compliant—and only then did he move his mouth away. He began to undo the buttons of her dress, one by one, and she felt the cool washing of air on her heated skin as he peeled it down over her shoulders.

His eyes darkened as he saw the peep of her breasts edging over the delicate satin and lace of her bra. 'I want to see your breasts,' he murmured possessively, stroking thoughtfully at the nipple that was peaking through the silk. 'May I?'

A dart of pleasure so fierce that it was very close to pain racked through her body. 'Y-yes.'

His hand moved to her back, to flick the hook open with almost indolent ease, and her breasts spilled out, rose-tipped and pale and magnificent. Nico felt himself grow harder still.

'And panties?' he questioned unsteadily. 'Are you wearing matching panties?'

Hadn't she put them on specially. As though she had been expecting just this? 'Yes.'

'May I see them?'

She knew what he wanted her to do. She was like a puppet, being worked by a consummate master, and she crossed her arms over her chest and pulled the dress over her head, letting it tumble unnoticed onto the floor. She heard his breathing change as his eyes drank in the indentation of her waist, the way the silk skimmed her hips and the bare thighs that straddled him, then looked at her in a way that made her feel suddenly shy. But her shyness changed into feminine pride when she saw the look of fierce and possessive hunger on his face.

He leant back a little, like a man appraising a painting, and he noted the curves and shadows of her body. The skin that had been burned by the sun had now softened to a pale golden glow, providing a creamy backdrop for the underwear. He wanted both to rip it from her and yet to make love to her while she was still wearing it. But of course it was entirely possible to indulge in both fantasies...

He moved his hand down to the camiknickers, watching the pleasured darkening of her eyes as he touched her most secret place, feeling the warm, honeyed moistness through the scrap of silk and watching the way she instinctively squirmed against his fingers.

'Nico!' she cried out.

He wanted to tell her to unzip him, was filled with a desperate longing to have her undress him as though he was any other man. But he was not, nor ever would be, and his body was his own and always would be.

He lifted her effortlessly while he rasped the zip down and impatiently kicked off his trousers and his shoes, seeing that she was now totally in his thrall as slowly and deliberately he ripped her panties, then tossed them away. He lowered her back down towards him and Ella's eyes snapped open. She looked down at him in alarm and confusion, prepared and yet unprepared as she felt the first naked nudge of him against her.

It had all happened so quickly—too quickly. Should it be this way? To make love on her sofa for the very first time, when they were still partially clothed? The blood was pounding in her ears and she quivered as she felt him pushing against her. 'Don't...don't you want to take me to bed, Nico?' she breathed.

There was something unworldly and innocent about the question, something that nagged and tugged at his conscience, as if he had broken some fundamental rule he had not been aware of.

God forgive him for plundering—for taking just what he wanted as if it was his due! And—dear God!—for forgetting to take any precautions! He bit back a groan of frustration and forced the overwhelming heat of desire to still for an instant as he lifted a hand to smooth back a sunset-coloured strand of hair.

'But I do not know where the bed is!' he bit out, in a voice made tight with tension. 'Will you show me the way, Gabriella?'

She meant to. Which was why she tried to wriggle away from him. But the movement had entirely the wrong effect, since it positioned them so that the tip of him was now inside her, and she knew that she could not move from that spot. A delicious and unstoppable warmth began to well up within her.

His eyes narrowed. 'Too late?' he guessed silkily.

Oh, much too late. 'Later,' she breathed. 'I'll show you later.'

Maybe it was just the offer of propriety she required, for now she was urging him on like there was no tomorrow. Nico could barely think straight as he reached blindly for his trousers and slid on the necessary protection. His eyes transfixed by the swaying of her breasts, he drove into her with a groan, holding onto her hips so that he could go deeper still.

'Nico!' The cry of delight was torn from her lips.

Sweet heaven! She was like a wildcat! She began to scrabble at his shirt, tearing at the buttons and whispering his name as he moved inside her, then moaning it, over and over, as if she couldn't say it enough times. He attempted to subdue her with deep, drugging kisses, but all they did was send his hunger spiralling out of control. And he was free to indulge it. Free as a lion. He had never felt this free before. Unknown and free. Just Nico.

Still lost in the rhythm, he touched her breast, feeling the nipple pucker and harden beneath his fingers and a fierce dart of pleasure threatened to take him under.

'Gabriella.'

He said her name on a shudder of broken wonder that was almost a plea, and Ella opened her eyes to stare deep into his, to see straight into his soul, into the very essence of the man himself—and that was when the pleasure engulfed her.

'Oh,' she cried softly. 'Oh. Oh. *Oh!*'

He felt himself follow her, drowning in wave upon wave of sensation, rocked and silenced by it, holding her closely, almost reverentially, until after the storm had subsided.

The muffled beat of his heart pounded a primitive rhythm and Ella lay, dazed and satiated, as she felt the steady rise and fall of his chest. It took her a few minutes to realise that he had fallen asleep, and she was glad of the moment of respite, shocked by the depth of her response to him.

She had never been so uninhibited—never, ever, ever. Absently, she dropped a kiss on the warm silken skin of his shoulder, and as he stirred lazily she turned her head slightly. The last of the setting sun's rays spilled in through the French doors, spotlighting them like two dancers as they lay sprawled and still intimately locked together on her sofa.

With an inbreath of horror she bit down on her lip, realising that she hadn't given a thought to privacy—not a thought—and that it didn't get dark until gone ten!

Why, anyone might have seen them! She might discourage casual callers, but that didn't mean they didn't come visiting. Oh, Lord. Ella felt the flush of guilt creep up to tinge her already rosy cheeks and shook Nico gently. But she couldn't resist running her fingertips over the smooth surface of his skin. He felt like silk to touch.

'Nico!' she urged softly. 'Nico! Wake up!'

Nico stirred. It was warm here, and...peaceful... yes...utterly peaceful. And that beautiful featherlight stroking. Total relaxation was such a rare and precious state for him, and he sighed and drifted back towards sleep. He didn't want to leave this place. He shook his head. 'Non!'

'Nico! Wake up! You *must*!'

The female voice drifted in and disturbed him, bringing him back to life in her arms. It was the word *must* that jarred the most. An unfamiliar word.

Nico opened his eyes to her soft pink face bent over him, her russet hair all mussed, her mouth dark from kissing, her breasts naked and soft, digging into him.

Che cosa stava accendendo?

It took a second or two for him to realise.

The girl from the boat! He had come to her house and then made love to her. He raised his wrist and shot a narrowed glance at his watch. Pretty fast, too.

He flicked his gaze back to her. *'Ciao, bella,'* he said softly.

Ella tensed as some indefinable quality changed him from the man who had said her name on that broken note at the height of passion. Suddenly he looked forbidding—no, maybe it was more than that. Unknown. A darkly erotic stranger she had just made love to.

'We ought to move,' she said awkwardly.

'Move?'

How stupid to feel shy after what had just happened. 'Upstairs,' she elaborated. 'To bed. Just in case…' She shrugged as she pointed towards the windows. 'Well, I would hate it if someone saw us! You know…'

Nico froze.

Oh, yes, he knew all right. He knew people who would pay countless amounts for information about just such a damaging scenario. His mouth tightened. What had he been *thinking* of? Carefully he moved her away from him and sat up, shaking his head in disbelief and anger at himself as he became fully aware of their disarranged clothing.

'Do you have a bathroom?' he asked tersely.

The bubble burst into a myriad of rainbow droplets. How dared he use that tone of voice to her? 'What do you think?' she snapped.

He saw the look of anger on her face and wanted to applaud her for not bothering to mask it behind a smile. But why should she? he asked himself. She *doesn't know who you are*!

Without warning, Ella moved off him and got to her feet, automatically reaching for her camiknickers until she remembered that he'd ripped them apart. 'I'll show you where it is,' she said furiously, 'and then you can go.'

But he was on his feet in an instant, mesmerised by the sexy thrust of her bottom, and even more by the peremptory way she was dealing with him.

He caught her by the waist and lifted her hair to nuzzle the back of her neck with the rasp of his chin. 'Do not be angry with me, Gabriella, *cara mia*.'

'Then don't *make* me angry.'

He nuzzled at her neck again. 'Am I making you angry now?' he murmured.

She shut her eyes. 'You're scratching me, actually,' she said weakly, as his chin scraped against her.

'But you like it?'

Oh, yes, she liked it all right—but then she liked just about everything he had done since he had first rung on her doorbell. And yet if she stopped to analyse it they had behaved like two...two...

She spun round to face him. 'Do you make a habit of this kind of behaviour?'

'Do you?' he countered.

'Of course I don't!'

'Well, you should,' he mused thoughtfully. 'You

really should. You are exceptionally talented at getting the very best out of a man—'

She lifted her hand to slap him, but with lightning speed he captured her wrist before it could make contact and levered her towards him.

'You dare to strike *me*?' he questioned, outraged.

She realised what she had almost done and her face crumpled. 'Oh, God, Nico—I'm sorry! I've never tried to hit a man before! Never!'

He stared at her. 'So what is it about me that makes you behave so differently?'

She shook her head distractedly. 'Maybe I'm really angry with myself—for behaving in such an outrageous manner. For letting you…. For wanting you…' she finished, in a voice that was shaking.

'For wanting me?' he echoed, and pulled her back into his arms, burying his face in her hair to hide his smile of sheer delight. 'Is that it? Is that all?'

And that really told him everything he needed to know. She liked sex; well, so did he. They had clicked in a way that was little short of dynamite, and they could click again. A beautiful, captivating woman whose appetite matched his. Two bodies in total harmony, with the added spice of distance between them that would keep hunger alive and boredom at bay. Yes, she would make a perfect lover.

Sooner or later he was going to have to reveal his identity, but he didn't anticipate a problem with that—for when had it ever been anything but the ultimate turn-on? And he would not tell her yet. For this freedom he should surely cherish while he was able to.

He reached down to pick up the crumpled and discarded dress and handed it to her, splaying the other hand proprietorially just below her belly. The tips of his fingers tangled in the damp cluster of tawny hair, and his eyes glittered with anticipation as she sucked in a shuddering and helpless breath.

'Weren't you going to show me where the bedroom is?' he drawled.

CHAPTER SIX

THE telephone began to jangle and Ella jumped.

Let it ring, she told herself. Because if it is Nico—if *it* is—then nothing is sadder than someone who is just sitting around waiting for it to ring.

'I will call you, *cara mia*,' he had murmured, after a protracted kiss that had taken her breath away.

And then he had left, with half the buttons of his shirt missing. He had paused at the door and looked down at them, a mocking expression curving the sensual mouth. 'Good thing I'm not going straight to an appointment,' he'd murmured.

'Just where are you going?'

'To London. I have an early start.' And then, because he had needed to work out exactly how he wanted to play this, he had kissed her again. 'I'll call you.'

Up until now he hadn't. He was probably busy—at least, that was what Ella kept telling herself, trying to be cool about it, still believing that he really *would* call. Because the alternative was just too much to contemplate. That it was just a line he'd spun in order to leave without having to endure a scene. She had fallen into his arms with almost shameful ease, and maybe

64

he'd done that typically masculine thing of wanting her and then despising what came too easily.

But it wasn't just pride that made her hope he had been telling the truth—it was the fact that she was aching to speak to him. She had believed him when they had lain there, with Nico stroking her skin, telling her that she was the most fantastic lover ever, because she had wanted to believe him—*needed* to believe him. As if that in some way justified the rampant way in which she had behaved. And the words had almost made up for the fact that he had left before midnight, with the mocking murmur of, *'Ciao, Cinderella',* ringing in her ears.

She snatched the phone up. 'Hello?'

'Ella?'

She very nearly wept and slammed it down again, for the voice was not deep and sexily foreign and she recognised it instantly, although she pretended that she hadn't.

'Speaking,' she said guardedly.

'Ella, it's Mark.'

'Oh, hello.' The frost crept into her voice quite naturally. She had hoped she'd heard the last of him, after that disastrous boat trip. 'What can I do for *you*?'

'How come you managed to avoid getting put into jail along with rest of us?' he demanded.

'I was the only one who was sober, if you remember! And I was sick.'

'So I gather.'

'Look, Mark, I'm a bit busy—'

'Not too busy to hear what I have to say.'

Ella frowned at the phone, something in his tone alerting her to trouble. 'What?'

There was a pause full of undisguised excitement.

'You know the guy who called the police?'

She couldn't let this one pass. 'You mean the man who rescued us?'

'Yeah, whatever. Well, you'll never guess what his name is?'

She didn't need to guess. She knew his name, just as she knew that his kiss had taken her to heaven and his tongue had guaranteed her a permanent place there. Ella shivered, pleasure mingling with the nagging feeling that she might never hear from him again. 'Nico,' she said. 'His name is Nico.'

'That's not his real name!'

The first feelings of foreboding began to prickle at her skin. 'What are you talking about?'

'His real name is Nicolo!'

'So he abbreviates it,' said Ella coldly. 'Lots of people do. I do. So what?'

'Nicolo of Mardivino,' he emphasised carefully.

She still didn't get it. 'Yes, that's where he lives.'

'*Prince* Nicolo!' he declared triumphantly.

'Mark, have you been drinking again?' But even as she asked the question the import of his words finally struck home, and Ella very nearly dropped the phone. '*What* did you say?' she hissed.

'He's a prince!'

'Of course he isn't! He's… He's…' But her words

tailed off, instinct telling her she had to believe the unbelievable. But sometimes you fought instinct when it told you something you didn't want to hear. 'I don't believe it.'

'Check it up, then! He's the youngest Prince—there's three of them! Bit of a playboy, as you'd expect.' He gave a crude laugh. 'A daredevil and a ladies' man!'

Ella's fingers bit into the receiver. 'Was there anything else, Mark?'

A sly note was injected into his voice. 'So just what happened after we'd gone? Did you sleep with him?'

Ella slammed the phone down with a shaking hand.

Of course he wasn't a prince! Princes didn't rescue you and nurse you and then turn up at your front door and…

And make love to you.

Scarcely aware of what she was doing, she went straight back to her computer and tapped the words 'Mardivino + Prince Nicolo' into a search engine, licking her dry lips in horror as she saw that there were 36,700 entries. She clicked onto the first one and waited for what seemed like an eternity, until suddenly there it was—a picture of Nico who, it seemed, was not just Nico at all, but His Serene Highness Prince Nicolo Louis Fantone Cacciatore.

There were details about his schooling, in Mardivino and France and Italy, and pictures of him with his family—except that this particular family happened to be sitting in a throne room decked with ornate gold and precious jewels.

Ella honestly thought she was going to be sick.

The powerful car nosed its way like a silver predator along the narrow lanes and once again Nico glanced into his driving mirror, but the road behind him was still empty.

Should he have rung her?

No, better this way. Face to face and person to person.

He was clever with words and good with women. He would explain why he hadn't told her and make her understand. And then he would kiss her again, in a way guaranteed to have her forgive him anything.

He felt the deep ache of desire, tempered only marginally by his awareness that their lovemaking had been too…

The dark brows knitted. Too what? Too intimate? Intimacy was dangerous and misleading and to be avoided. It weakened you and it gave women expectations. Expectations that could never be met—particularly for someone like Ella.

But she had been everything. Tender. Passionate. Warm. Provocative. And maybe the most potent of all those had been the tenderness, because for Nico it was an unknown quantity. He never allowed people close enough for tenderness, and he hadn't been expecting it. It had crept up on him unawares—like the feeling of gentle torpor after just a mouthful of especially good wine.

Maybe it was because he hadn't felt the need—or *had* the need—to put up the usual barriers to protect himself. For once he had been able to pretend that he was just anyone, and she had responded to him with a passion that had taken him unawares.

And he wanted more of that passion.

He parked in the lane leading up to her cottage and slowly locked the car, pocketing the keys thoughtfully, aware of the lush green froth of the leaves on the trees and the sunshine that dappled the dusty ground. He could hear the sweet, soaring sound of birdsong and that surprised him, too—had his senses suddenly come alive?

It's just the power of new and different sex, he told himself. His appetite had been jaded and she had simply been something fresh on his tastebuds. And, oh, how he wanted to taste her again...

He rang the doorbell.

Standing out of view in the kitchen, Ella heard the bell above her thundering heart and thought about ignoring it. Surely that would be best? Presumably he would go away and that would be that. She couldn't see him standing waiting patiently all day—because that wasn't the kind of thing that princes did, was it?

But if she let him walk away then there would be no sense of closure. Realistically, she knew their paths would never cross again and she would never get the opportunity to say what she wanted to say. Or rather, to tell him what he *needed* to hear. The conniving, deceiving *snake*!

How would he be expecting her to react?

It nearly killed her, but Ella fixed a look of delighted surprise on her face as she pulled open the door. Well, even that wasn't completely false. He might have deceived her, but that didn't stop her responding to him on a purely physical level.

And as a man, he was utterly magnificent. The endlessly long, muscular legs were encased in dark faded denim, and he wore a black T-shirt that clung to every sinew of his impressive torso. His black hair was ruffled, as if he had been driving with the roof down, and his dark eyes were set like precious jewels in his olive skin.

But the thought of jewels made her remember, and she only just stopped herself from slamming the door shut again.

'Nico!' she breathed, in what she hoped was the manner of a smitten woman talking to her new lover. 'I wasn't expecting you!'

'I should have rung.'

She let the mildest reproach enter her voice. 'Well, you *did* say you would.'

He unconsciously relaxed, the tension leaving his body as he acknowledged the undramatic greeting. So she didn't know! Which meant, of course, that he was going to have to tell her.

But not yet.

Later…

First let him have one more heart-stopping afternoon of unburdened lovemaking in her arms. 'May I
come in?'

For a moment Ella's nerve almost left her. It would
be easier and less distracting if she told him here,
now. And then she steeled herself. Surely she wasn't
so weak and wimpish that she would let his overpow-
ering presence influence her in the light of what she
had discovered?

She set her mouth into a glassy smile. Such a practised master of deceit! Let Prince Nicolo of Mardivino
have a taste of his own medicine!

'Of course,' she said lightly, and whirled off towards the kitchen, leaving him to follow her. 'Come
through.'

Nico frowned, because now he really *was* surprised. Surely this time she *should* have melted into
his arms? Was she regretting what had happened?
Deciding that maybe it had been too easy last time?
The frown became a smile as he acknowledged yet
another facet of this unknown world. He could
wait…it would do him good to wait…and the waiting
would fuel his already sharpened appetite.

She was standing beside the fridge, looking as if
she was starring in an old-fashioned commercial, with
a bright smile on her face.

'What can I get you, Nico? Champagne?'

He began to grow uneasy. They had been to bed,
yes, and it had been pretty damned wonderful—but it
was hardly a cause for celebration, was it? He racked

back through his memory, trying to recall what he had said to her in those incredible few hours in bed. No, nothing to give her the idea that this wasn't anything other than a brief affair.

'Do *you* want champagne?' he questioned.

And Ella knew then that she could not maintain this façade a moment longer. 'Actually, I think it would choke me.'

His eyes narrowed. 'Then why did you—'

'But that's probably because it's fairly ordinary champagne.' She cut right through his words, noting his fleeting look of surprise. He probably wasn't used to *that*, she surmised. People *interrupting* him. 'And I expect you're used to drinking only the finest stuff, aren't you? *Nicolo*.'

His heart beat with the dull, heavy thud of something that felt a little like disappointment—if only he was sure how that felt. But one thing he was sure of was his own stupidity. He had been living in a fantasy all of his own making. 'You know?' he said dully.

'Yes.'

Of course she knew. His thoughts whirled round like a child's spinning wheel. When? When she had opened her eyes after her fever? Or even before that? Maybe she had known all along. Maybe he had completely misjudged her and she was an avid reader of those tacky tabloid newspapers that delighted in printing snatched photographs of him.

Maybe she hadn't been able to believe her luck

when she had opened her eyes to discover just who it was who had rescued her.

Had all this been planned and his first instinct the right one? That she was nothing more than a beautiful decoy, groomed to capture a prince? His body tensed. 'When did you find out?'

With a mounting sensation of disbelief she stared at him, hearing the cold shot of accusation in his voice. 'When do you *think*?'

Now he began to wonder whether their innocent and frantic coupling on the sofa had not been so innocent, after all. What if there *had* been photographers lurking in the undergrowth? Photographs now in existence that might now find their way onto some sick home-movie site on the Internet? The realisation of just how foolhardy he had been made his blood run cold.

'I don't know,' he said icily. 'That's why I'm asking.'

She had gone in on the attack and now she felt stung to defence. How dared he? How *dare* he? 'You think I knew all along, don't you?'

He hid his turbulent thoughts behind the icy mask that was second nature to him. 'Did you?'

Her eyes opened very wide. 'And you think that's why I went to bed with you?'

'Was it?'

If she had thought that she felt sick before, then nausea had just entered a whole new dimension. He could think *that* of her?

But why shouldn't he? She had behaved like a tramp! She had nearly slapped him before, but she could not and would not attempt to do so again. Why, in the light of what she now knew, he might have her arrested for some kind of treason!

The truth came babbling out of her mouth like a hotspring. 'I didn't have a clue who you were, if you must know! I thought you were just some guy who worked for a rich man.' Her eyes shot emerald fire at him. 'Why wouldn't I? Princes aren't exactly thick on the ground.'

He realised that he had wounded her with his stubborn, arrogant pride. He wished he could take the words back, but he couldn't, and so instead he moved towards her, his hands outstretched in a gesture of peace. 'Gabriella—'

'The name I use,' she said furiously, 'is Ella—just as yours is Nicolo. That's the reality. And the two people who made the mistake of getting close were not real. You were playing out some sort of fantasy, so let's just leave it at that, shall we?'

Her perception rocked him almost as much as the certain knowledge that this was something his easy charm could not fix. Not if the raging look on her face was anything to go by.

'What if I told you that I didn't want to leave it?' he questioned softly.

Her answering look was contemptuous. 'Presumably you've spent your whole life getting exactly what you want?'

He had the grace to shrug.

'Well, this time you're not! I want you to go now, and I don't want ever to see you again.' She sucked in a hot, dry breath, afraid that she might do something regrettable—like burst into noisy tears of humiliation. Far worse than the crushing realisation that he had led her on—fooled her with some game of make-believe—was the hurt she felt inside. She had been blown away by him, she had given him something of her heart as well as her body, and now there must be painful surgery to reclaim that little piece of her heart. 'Because I don't enjoy being made a fool of.'

Damn her for her insolence! For daring to talk to him in this way! He should turn on his heel, walk away and forget all about her. 'That is what you want?' he asked in a low voice.

'Shall I say it in French?' she mocked. 'Or Italian? Or Spanish? Will that help you understand a little better?'

Her anger had loosened her up enough so that he was able to take her off guard, whispering the tips of his fingers down over the silken surface of her cheek and noting the immediate tremble of her lips, the darkening of her eyes, with a strange and heady triumph.

For it was second nature to him to fight for what he wanted—to prove to himself that he was capable of getting it on his own merits, and not by relying on the entitlements that accompanied a mere accident of birth.

'*Muy bien,*' he murmured, lapsing instinctively into the tongue spoken by his ancestors—Spanish Conquistadors who had fought so long and so hard for Mardivino. 'I will leave you now, Gabriella, and you can reflect on your folly at leisure. For folly it is.' His eyes glittered with the light of battle. 'You are fighting a battle with yourself for no reason, because you still want me as much as I want you.'

'You really *are* living in fantasy land!' she declared witheringly.

The heat of desire beat through him. 'You will be mine again,' he promised silkily, crushing her fingers to his lips before turning on his heel and slamming his way out of the house.

CHAPTER SEVEN

ELLA stared at the letter as if it was contaminated.

'You don't seem very *excited*,' observed Rachel, her own eyes shining. 'I mean, most people would be jumping up and down to get a Royal request!' She picked up the letter again and read it as reverentially as if it had been a Dead Sea Scroll. 'I just can't believe it! A letter from the Mardivinian Bureau of Tourism,' she repeated wonderingly. 'Asking us for our professional advice!'

Ella sighed and she gave her assistant a weak smile. Rachel was young and enthusiastic, but those very qualities—which had led Ella to employ her in the first place—were also those that would make it difficult for her to understand why she had no intention of accepting this job. Though when she stopped to think about it what could she say to *anyone* that would make the facts believable?

How about if she just blurted it out? She could just imagine how the conversation would go.

Actually, it's just a ruse to get me to go to Mardivino, Rachel.

And why is that, Ella?

Well, the Prince rescued me from a stricken boat, only I didn't know he was a prince at the time. He

77

subsequently came here for dinner and I slept with him, and when I discovered that he had deceived me I told him I never wanted to see him again.

She chose her words carefully. Perhaps professional concern might be more advisable. 'To be honest, Rachel, I'm not sure if I can spare the time to go,' she prevaricated.

Rachel stared at her as if she had gone stark, raving mad. 'But I can handle the office here—you know I can!' A hurt expression came over her face. 'Unless, of course, you don't think I'm capable of running the office—though you've let me do it before!'

'Of course I don't think that!'

Rachel was shaking her head. 'I mean—this is like something out of a fairy tale!'

Maybe it was, thought Ella—but not in the way that Rachel meant. It was certainly like the part in the stories where the apple you bit sent you into a century-long sleep, or where your glass carriage became a pumpkin. The dark side of the fairy story…

'It could turn out to be a bigger project than a small firm like ours can handle.'

Rachel lifted her hands in a gesture that said, *So what?* 'If it's too big, then we just take on more staff!'

Ella stared at her assistant as an idea slowly began to take shape. A solution that would not just save her skin, but thrill Rachel into the bargain. And one that Prince Nicolo Louis Fantone Cacciatore couldn't possibly object to…

'Do you want to go down to the village and buy some bread for our lunch?' she said innocently.

As soon as Rachel had gone, Ella picked up the thick sheet of cream paper with the heavily embossed crest at the top and dialled a number with a shaking finger, hardly able to believe that it would get her straight through to the palace at Mardivino.

But it did, and she very nearly dropped the receiver when she heard the rich, silky voice. *'Si? Nicolo.'*

So how did she address him now? As Nico, or Nicolo, or Prince, or—perhaps most appropriate of all—as *rat*!

'Nico?' she said coolly, without any kind of formality.

Within the quiet, opulent splendour of his palace office, Nico could feel the deep, dark throb of his pulse as he heard her voice. As he had known he would. *'Ciao*, Gabriella,' he said silkily. 'Did you get my letter?'

'How else do you think I knew your number?' she questioned coldly.

His pulse quickened further. He was a man who constantly sought new adventures, and he had never before realised what a turn-on insolence could be. 'So when will you be arriving?' he enquired pleasantly.

Oh, but her reply was going to give her such great delight! A tiny revenge, it was true—but an empowering one, which would go a little way towards healing some of the hurt and humiliation she felt. 'I won't be. I'll be sending my assistant instead.'

There was a pause. 'Oh, no, you won't,' he said softly.

She ignored the silken threat in his voice. 'She's very capable—and this will be a wonderful opportunity for her!'

'But it is not your assistant that I want, *cara*—it is you.'

Despot! Well, he had better learn that she was *not* one of his subjects, and he couldn't just dictate to her as if she was. 'I think it's time I enlightened you, *Prince* Nicolo. Point one—it is pretty pathetic to invent a job just because you want to see someone again, especially when she has no desire to see you— ever! And, point two—either my assistant comes or you can kiss the "job" goodbye.'

He gave a low laugh, curling his long fingers around the phone in an instinctive movement of delicious anticipation. She was just crying out to be conquered, as he had conquered mountains and oceans ever since he could remember.

'Point one, Gabriella—your ego may be vast enough to regard this as simply a ploy, but my need for your services is genuine.'

'Oh, really?' she questioned disbelievingly.

'Yes, really.' He stared reflectively out at the sapphire sweep of the sea. 'Mardivino is a small island which needs to overhaul its tourist industry selectively. Its popularity is growing, and we have all seen the dangers of that elsewhere. When too many people come there is a risk that the original charm of a place will be destroyed. It is happening here, and it is happening now.'

'That isn't really my end of the market at all,' she said coolly.

'Then perhaps it should be,' he returned. 'I have had your company thoroughly investigated and I like what you do. I like it very much.'

'Actually, I'm not looking for your approval, Nico.' But she might as well not have spoken for all the notice he took.

'Sometimes a relatively untutored eye can see what all the so-called "experts" cannot—you have both vision and imagination, Gabriella, and that is what I am looking for.'

'Oh, hoist the flag! Declare a national holiday! Am I supposed to be pleased? Because I'm not! I never sought your approval and—'

'And point two,' he said, his words cutting through her protestation like steel lancing through soft flesh. 'Please understand that I mean what I say. I do not want your assistant. I want you.'

'Well, that's tough! I'm not coming!'

The fight and her resistance was tantalising him to an unbearable pitch, but the tone of his voice remained clipped and emphatic. 'I think that you will. Or rather, that you should. I am not used to having my requests turned down, and if you refuse then I am afraid that your business might.... How shall I put this?' There was another pause. 'You might discover that there has been a sudden downturn in your fortunes.'

Quiet menace underpinned his words, and with a chilling certainty Ella knew that he spoke the truth. She didn't know how he could damage her business, she just knew that he *could*. 'Are you...are you *threatening* me?' she demanded incredulously.

'It is all a matter of perception, surely?' he answered softly. 'I am merely offering you a wonderful opportunity, one that it would be exceedingly foolish of you to turn down. It would be professional suicide,' he finished.

He was a clever and perceptive man—damn him! For someone whose position must mean that he was largely protected from the world and all its problems, he knew about the value of a job like this. Or had he grown up knowing that he could have everything he wanted—just so long as the price was right?

Ella injected frost into her voice. At least that way she could stop it from trembling with rage. 'And if I accept? If I do the job which you say you have for me—do I have your word that you will leave me alone?'

'But I deal with tourism on the island,' he said innocently. 'It would make no sense at all for me to make a promise that I cannot keep, *cara*. You will, of course, have to *liaise* with me.'

He managed to make the word sound indecently sexual—which, presumably, had been his intention. And her impotent rage did not protect her from the sudden shimmering of sensation over her skin as she remembered with erotic clarity just how accomplished a lover he was.

'I think we're talking at cross-purposes here, Nico,' she said softly. 'And as for promises—I can make one that I have every intention of keeping, and that is that you will not get what it is you want.'

'But you do not know what that is, do you, Gabriella?' he mocked.

No, but she had a pretty good idea. She wasn't stupid, nor was she completely inexperienced. She hadn't been a virgin. There had been a couple of lovers in her past, but none of them had come even close to matching Nico. It was about so much more than technique—it had been as though she had never really made love properly before. With him it had been an experience that transcended anything she had ever felt in the arms of another man.

He had made it seem as if her body was boneless, weightless, melding with his as if it had been born to do only that. She had felt her heart beating beneath him and the hard heat of his body within hers. In his arms she had been helpless and yet powerful—and she had seen his face soften with a pleasure and a joy that had only added to her own. And they had tasted those pleasures for only one fleeting night—of course he would want to experience it all over again. Heaven only knew, just thinking about it now was enough to set her own body aching.

But things had changed. Even if he hadn't deceived

her—*which he had*—the relative innocence of what had happened between them could never be recreated. He was not who she had thought he was. He had kept his identity secret—and as secrets went it was a pretty big one.

Was his persistence due to the fact that she had sent him packing and that had never happened before in his privileged life? What other reason would he have for twisting her arm to fly to his island?

Well, he was in for a big surprise. Ella's family had often accused her of stubbornness, and she knew that it could sometimes be a fault, but at a time like now it was going to prove very useful indeed—although she would prefer to define it as resolve.

'So you are agreed, Gabriella?' the soft, mocking voice prompted her.

She briefly thought about appealing to his better nature—but she could hear his steely determination. She thought about calling his bluff. Would he really go through with something as hostile as ruining her tiny company simply because she would not accede to his will? Might he not just shrug those broad, hard shoulders and accept what she wanted with something approaching good grace? There must, after all, be literally hundreds of other women who would leap to be his lover.

No.

Instinct told her that he was used to getting what he wanted—and he wanted her. Well, he could have her—but only on her terms.

'Very well. I accept.'

'Excellent.'

She could hear the triumph in his voice and clenched her free hand into a little fist. Oh, why hadn't she slapped him properly when she had had the opportunity? She breathed in deeply, forcing herself to sound cool. 'But first I need a little more information about precisely what it is I am expected to do.'

'I think that will be a little easier when you are here. You shall have all the information you need.'

She ignored that. 'That's not good enough, Nico,' she said sweetly. 'I'd like you to fax me some statistics about numbers of tourists, their accommodation requirements and so on—can you please arrange that for me as soon as possible?'

Even at school he hadn't been spoken to in such a stern and bossy way! He should feel righteous indignation at her insubordination, and yet he had never heard anything quite so tantalising in his life. How great the pleasure would be of subduing her with the skilful touch of his lips! And if statistics were what it took to fly her out to Mardivino, then she could have all the damned statistics she wanted! Staring out of the palace window at the intense blue of the sea, Nico gave a slow and predatory smile. 'Very well.'

'I will fly out at the beginning of next week.'

'Tell me when and I will arrange a plane. In fact,' he added, on a low note of delight, 'I will fly you to Mardivino myself.'

Now there was triumph in *her* voice. 'Oh, no, you won't, Nico,' she said softly. 'Once was enough!'

'You are criticising my flying ability?'

'No, I am resisting your efforts to control me. You want my expertise and you'll get it, but you will be treated in exactly the same way as any other client. There will be no preferential treatment—not for you, and certainly not for me. I will take a scheduled airline flight, thank you very much, and I will add the cost to my bill.'

For a moment he was speechless, scarcely able to believe what he was hearing. She was refusing his offer! To be flown openly to Mardivino by the youngest Prince of that principality!

'Oh, and one more thing, Nico?'

She was making *more* requests? Through the haze of disbelief and thwarted desire he felt a glimmer of reluctant admiration for her tenacity and guts. 'Go on.'

'I trust that my accommodation requirements will be totally above board? I will require a room for me, and for me alone, and if you renege on that I will take the first available flight home and you really will have to find someone else.'

'Very well,' he said coldly. 'And now I will give you the number of my mobile.'

'Go on, then.'

He had never felt so frustrated. Did she not realise the honour he was according her—giving her access to him whenever she wanted? He had been about to tell her not to abuse the privilege, but now his lips snapped closed. Clearly she didn't even see it as a privilege!

'*Jusque là, cherie,*' he murmured.

Momentarily she was confused by the sudden switch in language. 'I thought you usually used Italian?'

He watched a speedboat sweeping across the bay. 'It depends. Italian is the language of love—although my French and Spanish cousins would disagree—and I am not feeling particularly *loving* towards you at the moment, Gabriella.'

She couldn't let this one pass. Oh, no. 'I think you're in danger of confusing love with sex, Nico,' she said quietly, and put the phone down.

CHAPTER EIGHT

'AND just *where* are you proposing she stay, Nicolo?'

'At the palace, of course.'

'No.' Gianferro's voice was flat and unequivocal. 'I will not tolerate one of your mistresses staying here in the Palace.'

Nico didn't react. Not straight away. Over the years he had learnt that considered argument was better than a hot-headed blaze of outrage—especially with his eldest brother. Biting back his words went against his nature but he had learned to school himself in diplomacy when dealing with Gianferro. For Gianferro was the heir. The glittering eldest son over whom the double-edged sword of leadership hung by only a whisper, since their father, the King, had lain sick in his palace suite for many months now.

In a way, Gianferro had both the best and the worst of the Royal world—the heady aphrodisiac of power, coupled with the stultifying burden of responsibility. The eldest son was seen as the most privileged, but Nico knew that despite how the outside world perceived it, there was no such thing as the perfect position in a Royal family of three brothers.

Guido, the middle brother, was currently living abroad—and middle brothers were notoriously touchy about being looked over and ignored. Even in so-called *normal* families they had difficulty establishing a legitimate role. It explained why he had left Mardivino as quickly as he could, making for himself the comfortable life of international playboy.

Nico, as the youngest, should by rights have been the spoilt baby of the family—except things had not turned out that way.

His very birth had heralded the illness that had killed his mother—and ever after his father's pride in him had always been tempered by sadness and melancholy.

Gianferro had almost stepped into the role of father—if such a thing was possible when the age gap was only seven years. He had always looked out for and fiercely protected Nico, and as the years had passed had been reluctant to lose that role of mentor. Nico had had to fight every bit of the way for independence.

'Gabriella is not my mistress,' he stated flatly.

'Oh, really?' Gianferro raised dark, disbelieving brows. 'Is this not the same flame-haired woman whom you took to the beach house? The consort of the drunks who spent the night in Solajoya jail?'

Nico stared at him. 'You knew about that?'

'But of course I knew. The Chief of Police rang to inform me of what was happening.'

'He gossips like an old woman,' said Nico darkly.

Gianferro laughed. 'He simply does his job. I know everything that happens on Mardivino, and it is my duty to do so—particularly when it concerns my brothers. And a mistress staying here at the palace would wreck your reputation—in the same way that one of those crazy sports you indulge in will soon wreck your life.'

Nico sighed. It was as pointless as whistling in the wind to attempt to defend his lifestyle. He had tried often enough over the years.

Just as it would be pointless to try to explain that nothing had happened between him and Gabriella at the beach. Given Nico's past catalogue of lovers, Gianferro simply would not believe him. And even if the truth *were* known—would that not offend his innate masculine pride and reputation?

'Are you *forbidding* it, Gianferro?' Nico questioned, in a voice that was only half joking.

'No.' Gianferro gave an answering glimmer of a smile which briefly softened his hard mouth. 'I am simply appealing to your sense of what is proper and what is not, Nico.'

'You know she is here on a legitimate assignment?' Nicolo said casually. 'She works in the travel industry.'

'How very convenient for you both.' There was a pause. 'And what precisely is she proposing to do here on the island?'

There was a brief pause, and Nico saw the dark light of challenge in his brother's eyes. He kept his counsel. 'I'll keep you posted,' he said lightly.

Gianferro gave a low laugh. 'Give her an office

here at the palace, then, but put her up in L'Etoile. That should be luxurious enough to impress her.'

'You think that is what I am trying to do?'

The brothers' eyes met.

'I do not know what it is that you are trying to do, but I know you well enough to guess,' said Gianferro softly. 'I understand that she is beautiful, and that speaks for itself—but never forget that for a man in your position she can never be anything more than a sensual diversion, Nico.'

Nicolo's lips curved in a cynical smile. 'I need no warnings from you, Gianferro,' he retorted softly. 'And to me she has never been anything *but* a sensual diversion.'

Ella's journey to Mardivino might have been on a scheduled flight for a national airline, but there all similarity to other air travel ended.

She had taken the earliest possible flight, and was fussed over and waited on like a heavily pregnant woman about to give birth. She doubted whether the other first-class passengers were being treated with quite so much regard. Was that because Nico—*Prince Nicolo*—had arranged for her to come?

She got a sudden disturbing glimpse of what it must be like to be him—with everyone always on their best behaviour and pandering to your every need. Was he ever able to have 'normal' interaction with people? she wondered. Probably not. And that couldn't be good for you.

Her lips tightened. It definitely wasn't. It could make you into a control freak—as he had just demonstrated. He had got her here by sheer and arrogant force of will. Had his whole life been spent doing exactly that?

His deception still hurt, but her inner sense of unease came from more than that. She had fallen into his arms and made love to him in a way that had been new and exciting and precious. But he had trampled on all those feelings with his duplicity. And if he had done it to her once, then he could do it again. A man in Nico's position would not care about a woman's feelings—why should he? Willing sexual partners were probably lining up halfway round the block for him.

She must keep her head and dampen down any dangerous see-sawing emotions every time they threatened to appear. Try to keep things in perspective. It had been great sex, that was all. She must not learn to care for him because nothing would come of it—nothing *could* come of it.

And you *are* a strong woman, she reminded herself. You know you are. Of course you can resist him.

Landing at Solajoya Airport was a dream—with no Customs or queues to get through. She was first off the flight and met on the tarmac by Nico himself, and despite everything she had vowed her heart began to race as he made his way towards her.

'Hello, Gabriella,' he said softly.

'I…I wasn't expecting you to come and meet me

in person,' she stumbled, because the impact of seeing him here unexpectedly had blown away most of her good intentions. Where was the strong woman now?

He gave a half smile. 'You thought I would send a servant, perhaps?'

'Something like that.'

'Well, I have put myself in that role.' His black eyes glittered. 'And I am at your service, *cara*.'

She thought that he'd managed to make it sound like an erotic declaration. 'Does that mean you will docilely agree to all my orders?' she asked, as he opened the boot of the car.

He turned to look at her, a mocking yet serious light playing at the back of his eyes. 'But you must treat your servants with respect,' he said softly. 'Or they will not respect you.'

And what about your lovers? she wanted to ask. How much do you respect them?

Yet as he took her bag from her and slung it into the boot of a low black limousine Ella couldn't resist the forbidden luxury of running her eyes over him.

She had seen him looking like a beachcomber, and as a coolly elegant European, but today he was unmistakably a prince. There was something about the way his suit was cut that, even to Ella's untutored eye, made it look about as costly as it was possible to be. His shirt was of palest blue and finest silk, unbuttoned at the neck to show a sprinkling of dark hair.

And I have seen him naked, Ella thought, with a

sudden debilitating rush of pride and longing. *I have held him in my arms while he thrust long and hard and deep within me.*

Yeah, you and a million others, mocked the cynical voice of reason. But reason did nothing to prevent an aching heart.

Nico turned round and frowned. 'Your cheeks are flushed, *cara*,' he said quietly. 'And your eyes are troubled—why is that?'

She buried the desire and regret, and lifted her chin in an attitude of pride. 'Why do you think, Nico? Could it have anything to do with the fact that I have been forced to accept this assignment against my better judgement? Blackmailed and threatened to do your bidding?'

Not quite, he thought wryly. Or she would be sending him a message of eager anticipation, not this outrageous defiance. 'And you are going to sulk about it for the duration of your stay?'

'Absolutely not. I intend to do the job I am being paid for to the very best of my ability. You asked me a question and I answered it. But if my "troubled" expression offends the Prince, then I shall replace it with a smile!' She fixed him with a bright and mocking curve of her lips. 'Is that better, Nico? Is that what you're used to?'

Nico's eyes narrowed. He had been expecting—what? That she would be secretly happy to be whisked back here to the island? That her protests were the kind that women sometimes made when they wanted something but knew that it was perhaps political not to show it? Now he was not so sure. And uncertainty was a feeling he was not familiar with.

'Let's go,' he said tightly, and held the door of the car open for her.

With Nico behind the wheel they sped out of the tiny airport, waved through and bowed to by guards. A group of people who were milling around by the exit, waiting at a taxi-rank, spotted their car and began pointing at it. One or two even started waving and shooting cameras in their direction!

Ella blinked in bemusement. 'Is it always like this?'

Nico gave a rather brittle smile. 'You ain't seen nothing yet.'

'That's rather a good American accent,' she observed.

'So it should be—I went to college there.'

'Whereabouts?'

'Stanford.'

Had she somehow thought that he had spent all his life on the island? An American education would go a long way towards explaining his easy, cosmopolitan attitude. 'And did you like it?' she questioned curiously.

He smiled. 'Loved it. But I was young then,' he said mockingly.

How little she really knew of him. She had thought that it was the big things that were important—his Royal status for starters—but in a crystal-clear moment of perception she realised that it was all the tiny things that provided the building blocks for understanding a person. People were complex, and none more than this dark, handsome figure beside her.

She remembered him telling her that he dealt with tourism on the island, and this was something she needed to know about. 'So, do you actually have a *job*?'

His smile was cynical. 'Did you imagine I'd sit around on a throne all day and be waited on?'

'Something like that,' she admitted, with a shrug. 'Sorry. Tell me a bit about it—I'd like to know.'

Genuine interest was pretty hard to resist, he was discovering—but wasn't there more to it than that? Didn't he want in some way to redeem himself in her eyes? To show her that he wasn't just some lazy dilettante with no real function, commitment, or purpose?

'I've been concentrating on hauling the city of Solajoya out of the past and trying to regenerate it,' he said slowly. 'Its size and location are pretty much perfect for the media and software industries.'

'So it would rely on more than banks and tax exiles?'

'You've done your homework,' he remarked.

'Please don't patronise me, Nico!'

'I wasn't,' he said, in a voice that was almost gentle. 'I was applauding your work ethic, if you must know.'

She didn't want to bask in his praise, like a cat sitting in front of a glowing fire, she wanted to remain immune to him—all of him. But she could see it wasn't going to be easy.

She settled back in her seat and stared out of the window. The sky was as blue as a swimming pool, and the sun beat down on the magenta blooms of the trees that lined the roads. She was filled with the sudden sense of exhilaration that a new and beautiful place always gave her—until she reminded herself of the reason why she was here. *Pretend he isn't twenty-eight and devastatingly gorgeous and virile. He's an old man. A grandfather.* 'So which is the *official* language of Mardivino?' she asked politely, because her reference books hadn't made this very clear.

He increased the speed of the car, a slight smile playing at the corners of his mouth. More homework, he guessed. 'The four languages of Italian, Spanish, French and English are interchangable,' he said.

'But isn't that very confusing?'

'Not for me,' he said softly. 'For a linguist it is extremely useful. It means that you are rarely at the disadvantage of not being able to understand what is being said.' His eyes gleamed. 'It also means that you can switch language so that people do not always understand *you.*'

Ella snorted. 'Well, if I were you I would brush up on your interpretation skills, Nico! Because I distinctly remember telling you that I didn't want to take this job, and yet you still twisted my arm to get me here!'

He laughed softly. 'Ah, Gabriella—do you not

know that a man finds it unbearably exciting when a woman spars with him the way that you do?'

'Particularly when he's not used to it?' she queried perceptively.

'Especially that,' he agreed. Why, meeting such defiance and insubordination head-on was almost like learning a new language in itself!

'That isn't why I'm doing it,' she objected.

'I know it isn't. Now, let's call a truce for the moment. You are here, and you might as well enjoy it, so why don't you look out of the window again and you can see how beautiful my island is?'

'Where are we going?' she asked suddenly.

'You will be staying at L'Etoile Hotel,' he replied. 'You have heard of it, perhaps?'

Of course she had—she had spent the past few days learning as much as she could about the principality— and for a small island it had a hell of a lot of history. L'Etoile was the kind of hotel that vied with the world's finest for style and luxury and elegance. The kind of place whose prices were beyond the reach of ordinary mortals.

With mounting dismay Ella stared down at her rather rumpled skirt. Wasn't she going to stand out like a very sore thumb?

You're in the travel business, she reminded herself. No one will be expecting you to compete with the jet-set.

'That should be fun,' she said evenly.

'And you will work from a small office within the palace,' he said casually.

Ella swallowed. If she had thought her clothes too ordinary for a luxury hotel, then how the hell was she going to compete in a *palace*? You won't, she told herself. You'll just be yourself.

'Could you drive me through as much of the main town as possible on the way there?' she asked coolly.

'Any particular reason why?'

'I just want to get the lie of the land. The more I know, the better prepared I will be.' *And the sooner I can get home again.* But her attention was caught by a cluster of gleaming white buildings that suddenly made home seem a very long way away.

'We're just coming into Solajoya now. I'll take you by the backstreets.'

And it was beautiful, thought Ella as she looked down. Utterly beautiful. The roads were narrow and winding, with tall shuttered houses decked with pots of brightly coloured flowers.

He negotiated steep curves towards what was obviously the centre, where the main streets were thronged with people—some clearly heading back from the beach, while others were clustered outside a large, white building, creating a kind of human bottleneck. There were long-haired students in jeans sitting on the steps to the building, writing postcards, and earnest-looking older groups, all studying guidebooks with rapt preoccupation.

Ella leaned forward. 'What's going on in there?'

'It is the gallery of Juan Lopez,' explained Nico. 'You know him?'

Ella frowned. 'He's an artist?' she remembered.

'Was. He died over fifty years ago—an early and tragic death—but for an artist that is always a good selling point.'

'How cynical!' observed Ella.

'How true,' he retorted softly.

'Tell me about him.'

He smiled, realising that their relationship had been forged in relative equality, and that she had no intention of tempering her attitude towards him now, in the light of what she had since discovered.

'He was what they call "an artist's artist"—a student of Picasso, and he lived most of his life here. Those who know him love him, and come from all over the world to see his work. He bequeathed it all to Mardivino, on condition that it stay here. He loved this island, you see.'

And, looking out at the distant harbour, Ella could see exactly why. It was like a toy town—the buildings all pure white, the main street lined with palm trees that swayed gently in the breeze.

The car approached the sea and suddenly there was L'Etoile—white against the sapphire backdrop, and glittering as starrily as its name implied.

Nico stopped the car outside and turned to look at her, and Ella's breath caught in her throat. It was okay in theory to tell yourself that you were going to be immune to a man's charisma, but quite another when

you were confronted with it in such close proximity—
so close that you could almost feel the warmth of his
breath, almost touch the silken texture of his olive
skin, see for yourself the black, glittering eyes that
both mocked and enticed.

'You have a choice, *cara*,' he said softly. 'I can
accompany you inside, if you prefer, but if I do there
will be something of a…a *fuss*,' he concluded, after
a moment.

She remembered the people pointing at him at the
airport, how he must live his life with a sense of being
continually on show. 'Do you go to that beach hut to
escape all the *fuss*?' she questioned, momentarily forgetting that she was supposed to be keeping this trip
on a purely professional footing.

'But of course. It is peaceful and isolated there.'
The corners of his mouth lifted in a lazy smile. 'Bar
the odd mermaid washed up on my shore, of course.'

'Then please don't come inside,' she said quickly,
but it was less to do with the projected 'fuss' than the
dangers of that achingly soft smile.

He nodded and glanced at his watch. 'Okay, I'll
leave you to unpack your stuff.'

'I haven't brought very much. I don't intend to stay
here longer than a week, Nico.'

His eyes glittered. She would stay here for as long
as *he* deemed it necessary—no more and no less. 'I'll
pick you up in an hour,' he said steadily. 'Show you
your office at the palace.'

'Make it two. I want to wander round on my own

for a bit first. Get a feel for the place before I enter the hallowed portals of the palace.'

'I will have someone accompany you.'

'You will not! I want to be free to explore on my own.'

Free, he thought, with a sudden sense of yearning. 'You are a very stubborn woman, Gabriella,' he said softly.

'I don't deny it.'

He opened his mouth to object, and then shut it again—for what could he do? Carry her off by force? Tell her that she was there to do his bidding?

Furiously recognising that at the moment she seemed to have the upper hand, he got out of the car, pulled her bag from the boot and handed it to her. She hadn't been joking—he had never seen a woman travel with such a small suitcase.

His eyes travelled to the pretty little shoes she wore—delicate, sexy little kitten heels, which showed the delectable curves of her tiny ankles. 'If you're planning to explore the city, then I suggest you wear something more sensible than those to walk in,' he said tightly. *'Fino ad allora, cara.'*

CHAPTER NINE

ELLA glanced around her hotel accommodation with a combination of excitement and disbelief—because the 'room' she had imagined staying in was actually a suite—and nearly as big as the ground floor of her home in England!

She let her eyes drift over to the floor-to-ceiling windows, which commanded a breathtaking view of the sapphire sweep of the sea beyond. Tiny cotton wool clouds batted playfully at one another in the vast blue arena of the sky, and sunlight glinted off the sleek lines of distant yachts.

On the other side of the bay she could see hills clothed in dark green, with ice-white villas set like jewels within them. It was a combination of natural beauty and vast wealth—a world accessible only to the very few—and in any other circumstances she would be pinching herself and enjoying every second of it.

She ran her fingertips over the petal of a waxy orchid, telling herself that she would be crazy not to enjoy at least *some* of this once-in-a-lifetime experience.

She dressed for sightseeing, putting on a pair of flat strappy sandals that matched her ice-blue sun-dress, and tying her hair back in a blue ribbon. She finished off with a wide-brimmed straw hat, and as she checked herself in one of the mirrors she could see the image she presented was cool and contained. Good. Long may it last.

The day was bakingly hot, but a light breeze stopped it from being oppressive and the hat had been a good idea. Nico had been right about the walking bit, for the hilly streets around the harbour were all cobbled—picturesque, but hardgoing. She peered in all the shop windows, where stores selling luxury goods and clothes jostled next to those selling boat accessories. So far, all pretty predictable.

There were pavement cafés galore, and she found an empty seat and sat outside one, ordering an extremely expensive cup of coffee. She sat sipping cappuccino and watching the people come and go. The main cause of congestion really did seem to be centred around the art gallery dedicated to Juan Lopez. At one point two coaches disgorged their contents at the top of one of the quaint streets, and as they surged forward it felt a bit like being outside a football ground before the match started.

Ella got out her notebook and wrote for a little while, and then went off and found a bookshop.

Inside, it was dark and deliciously cool. There was a whole section about Juan Lopez, but Ella's attention was distracted by a part of the shop given over entirely to books about the ruling family of Mardivino.

Here there were biographies and picture books,

family portraits and single portraits. In a sweet little tome entitled *Just Like Us*, she found a photo of Nico as a baby—a chubby-faced little cherub, wearing a cascading lace christening robe, being cradled in the arms of his nurse. Maybe that was normal for Royal princes, but she happened to know that his mother had died when Nico was just a baby.

There was a whole muted and solemn chapter about the death of the young Queen, and a heartbreaking shot of the three boys—the two older boys clad in matching dark grey coats and a crying Nico being held by another nurse—as they watched the flower-decked coffin file past.

She had read about the death of his mother during her research, of course, but seeing it here—in black and white and in Mardivino itself—somehow made it more real and more poignant.

It made her see him as flesh and blood—someone who really *would* bleed if you cut him. It made him seem lovable and in need of love—but surely that was just wishful thinking on her part?

Her fingers twitched irresistibly onto a chapter devoted entirely to Nico, entitled 'The Daredevil Prince'. Here were snatched shots of Nico the action man among the formal poses—Nico sailing a yacht, giving a thumbs up at the top of a snowy mountain, and astride a monstrously large-looking motorbike.

Ella read on, engrossed, until she glanced at her watch and saw to her horror that she should have been back at L'Etoile ten minutes ago. But she couldn't get the image of the motherless baby out of her mind. Did his love for all things fast and dangerous stem from a childhood without the grounding of a mother, with palace servants forbidden by protocol to show him real love? Or was that too simplistic an explanation?

She sped towards the hotel to find him waiting for her, leaning against the door of his car and her heart turned over.

His posture was outwardly relaxed, but as she grew closer she could see the tell-tale look of irritation that hardened his autocratic features and made his black eyes glitter. Her tender concern vanished under that cold look of censure.

'Sorry I'm late,' she said automatically.

'Not very *professional* of you,' he bit out—because he had felt strangely out of place, hanging around the car like a chauffeur. 'Perhaps it pleases you to make me wait?' he mused. 'Did you do so deliberately?'

'Oh, for goodness' sake! Of course I didn't—I just lost track of the time.'

She was completely unapologetic! Quite the opposite, in fact! Nico was consumed by a simmering rage overpowered by a bubbling frustration. He looked down into her flushed face, at her parted lips, and felt the urge to kiss her as a kind of punishment— to tell her that no one *ever* kept him waiting.

He held the door of the car open, shaking his head slightly. A kiss? As a kind *punishment*? Who the hell did he think he was kidding?

As she moved towards the door he had opened for her, her bare arm brushed against his. It was the briefest and most fleeting contact, but it was like the sizzle of electricity, tingling fire over her skin, and she stepped back as if she had been stung.

'Don't,' she whispered.

Their eyes met.

'Don't what?' He could feel the tiny hairs standing up at the back of his neck and he stared back at her, angry and slightly appalled at himself for being so affected by such an innocent touch. 'What did I do, *cara*?' he mocked. 'Don't blame me for your own feelings. You want me. You still want me—you're just too hypocritical to admit it.'

He walked round to the driver's seat and slammed the door behind him, leaving Ella to shakily take her place beside him.

Ignore it, she told herself. Because if you don't you'll only have to admit he's right.

The car screeched away and Ella stole a glance at Nico's stony profile.

'Who's sulking now?' she questioned.

With an effort he roused himself out of his reverie. 'Not me.'

'Just don't want to talk?'

He smiled. 'Talk away.'

'Will you tell me a little bit about Mardivino, then?'

It was, he admitted grudgingly, exactly the right thing to say. It took his mind off the ache in his groin and the idea—almost unthinkable—that bedding Ella Scott once more was by no means certain.

'What do you wish to know?'

'Everything.'

'"Everything" is a tall order, *cara*,' he mused. But his eyes on the mountain road ahead of him, he started to tell her of Mardivino's history in a voice that grew unexpectedly dreamy, and then sometimes fiery as he recounted crusades and battles for the prized land. He talked of Spanish Conquistadors and Italian aristocrats and French counts, who had all fought for ownership over the centuries, until at last agreeing to share the spoils of the exquisite island, set like a jewel in the sea.

His passion was infectious, and Ella found herself listening with the rapt attention of a child being told a wonderful story—but it wasn't just the story that captured her imagination—it was him. You could watch a man closely when you were listening to him—could remind yourself of his passion and his strength and then wish you hadn't.

But if she pushed that kind of thought away then even more troubling memories hurtled in to replace them—with graphic recall. She could almost see the moist flick of his tongue against his lips, almost feel it on her belly, against her thighs…

But her whirling thoughts were stilled by the sight of what lay before her. She had been so caught up in them that she had taken little notice of the view whizzing by outside the limousine window. But now high, gilded gates were parting and Ella stared ahead, her breath catching in the back of her throat as they opened onto the Rainbow Palace.

Her first impression was that it looked like a stage-set. Something that was real and yet not quite real. She wondered if behind its glittering walls she would find an empty stage and pieces of wood propping it up? Just as she wondered what really lay beneath all the different masks that Nico wore. Was nothing real in his world?

From a distance the palace really *did* look like a rainbow, with the whole spectrum of vibrant, dazzling colours from violet right through to a rich and royal red. It was only as the car grew closer that Ella could make out the tiny mosaic pieces of stone. It was all an illusion, not substance. Not a rainbow at all.

But as she got out of the car Ella began to get some idea of the perspective of the place, and it was vast. Emerald squares of perfectly manicured grass were edged with velvety dark red roses. There was a formal fountain playing the music of scattering water, and a wonderful statue of a woman that looked so real that Ella felt like reaching out to test whether it was marble-cold or whether real blood coursed through the stone veins.

'Come,' said Nico, looking down at her.

'I'm slightly overwhelmed,' she said truthfully.

His hard mouth softened by a fraction. When she stopped fighting him, she was really very sweet. 'Well, don't be. It's just the place where I live.'

But how many people in the world lived in places like this one? It would always mark him out as different, because Nico *was* different. And it would be worthwhile to remember that.

He led her through seemingly endless corridors that were hung with enormous oil-paintings of men and women wearing lavish silk and lace gowns. Dark-haired, autocratic portraits, whose mesmeric and glittering black eyes marked them out as his ancestors.

It was a different world.

Eventually he pushed open a door and Ella found herself in an office—or at least a room that was doing a passable imitation of masquerading as an office—because offices did not usually contain antique desks, nor have drapes that glimmered to the floor in costly folds.

'You can work from here,' he said.

Work. Yes, of course.

It was difficult not to be dazzled. He looked so at home in these lavish surroundings—but of course he would—it was his home, for heaven's sake! But it had the effect of making Nico of the beach hut and Nico the lover seem like mere figments of her imagination.

'Okay,' she said, and gave a brisk smile. 'Can you organise a map of the island for me?'

'There's one here.' He leaned over the desk and Ella caught the faint drift of a musky lemon fragrance. She briefly closed her eyes in despair. Scent was so evocative—it took you to places you would rather not go—and she had headily breathed in that scent when her face had been nuzzled into the warmth of his sleeping neck.

'Will this do?' He opened a large book showing a brightly coloured map of Mardivino.

She moved beside him and looked over his shoulder, and he turned his head and their eyes held. She found herself yielding, helpless in the soft, dark light that blazed over her.

'Gabriella,' he murmured caressingly.

She shook her head desperately, like a woman who was trying to convince herself. 'No.'

'Your lips tell me one thing while your eyes are saying something very different,' he observed quietly.

He lifted the tips of her fingers and touched them to his lips, feeling them tremble at that one brief contact. He increased the pressure of his mouth and saw her eyelids flutter to a close.

'Nico,' she whispered.

They fluttered open again and her eyes were like pure gleaming emeralds amid the tangle of dark lashes. He gave a small groan, briefly tangling his hands into the tawny splendour of her hair before pulling her into his arms, the dark light of conquest firing his eyes as he stared down at her.

'Nico, what?' he demanded huskily.

'This is...*wrong*,' she breathed.

But she made no move to stop him, to push him away or to detach herself from his embrace, and all he could do was drink in these lips and this face, which had haunted his dreams since that all-too-brief encounter of such tender and sensual beauty. And then he could wait no longer—could think no further than the need to taste and to kiss her once more.

Her hands caught and gripped his broad shoulders as if they were magnetised, her breath escaping in a gasp that mingled with his breath as she felt the hard, seeking warmth of his mouth.

'Oh,' she moaned weakly against him, as his hands splayed down to cup her buttocks, bringing her closer into the hard cradle of his desire. 'Oh!'

Urgently, he moved his hand downwards and drifted his fingers up her bare thigh, scraping the tips in soft, enticing circles. He felt her legs part in invitation.

He felt as if he was going to explode. As if he wanted to rip the cheap little dress from her and take her right there. He moved her panties aside and delved into her hot, sticky heat, and she gasped with pleasure.

'I want you, Gabriella,' he ground out. 'I want you so much.'

And she wanted him, too. So badly. Boldly she touched him back, drifting her hand over his hardness to feel it increase, and he tore his mouth away from hers.

'Come with me to my apartment,' he said urgently. 'Let me make love to you all the rest of the day and all through the night, until you have emptied me of all my seed.'

It was a curiously powerful and unexpected thing to say, and it shook Ella even more than the light, expert caress of his fingers and the memory of his passionate kiss. Quite what she would have done next, she didn't know—and she never had the chance to find out because there was a loud peremptory rap on the door and Nico froze.

She looked at him in horror. 'The door!' she whispered.

He acted instinctively, tugging her dress down into place and moving away from her, raking his hand back through his ruffled dark hair, aware that her musky perfume was still lingering on his fingers. He let out a brief, shuddering sigh.

'Yes?' he shot out.

The door opened and a man stood there, and even if she hadn't studied photos of him earlier that day Ella would have known instantly that it was Nico's eldest brother Gianferro.

She tried to picture the scene through his eyes. Outwardly, they were both decent—no clothing in disarray—but it must be obvious just what had been about to happen. Their heightened colour and hectic eyes held a sexual tension so taut that it felt as if it might snap, as if a mere breath could shatter it—and Gianferro just had. She wished that the floor would open up and swallow her as the Crown Prince stared at her.

Gianferro's dark, unreadable eyes moved from her

to Nico. 'Forgive me,' he said icily. 'This is obviously an inopportune moment.'

His expression was one that Nico could read perfectly, but he met the disapproving accusation head-on, brazening it out. And why the hell shouldn't he? He was not a child, and his brother was not his keeper! If he barged in on two consenting adults, then he just might not like what he would find.

'Gianferro,' he said, as coolly as if he had been taking tea with a woman on some sun-dappled terrace. 'I would like you to meet Ella Scott, who will be using her travel expertise to advise us. Ella, this is my brother, the Crown Prince Gianferro.'

Briefly and autocratically Gianferro inclined his head, and Ella sent Nico an agonised glance. Was she supposed to curtsey, or what? In silent understanding he sent her a barely perceptible shake of the head.

'And what is your *particular* area of expertise, Miss Scott?' drawled the heir.

She knew what he was implying, and if only she had been a sheet of paper she would have crumpled into a ball of shame. But adaptability was the name of the game. She couldn't pretend that what had just happened *hadn't* happened, but she could deal with it. She had committed no crime and she was not his cringeing subject.

'Actually, I specialise in the small-is-beautiful market, Your Royal Highness,' she said smoothly. 'Which sort of sums Mardivino up, don't you think?'

Nico sent her a silent look of admiration. Most

women of his acquaintance would have blushed and stammered their way out of *that* one. He had been about to leap in to protect Ella from Gianferro's barely veiled hostility, but now he could see that she was perfectly capable of looking after herself.

'Nico hasn't told me how long you intend staying,' said the Crown Prince.

'That's because I haven't yet decided how long I need to. I haven't signed any kind of contract.' She couldn't miss the unmistakable look of surprise on his face. And on Nico's. Presumably they were used to making the decisions, not employing people who made their own! 'But you can rest assured that my work will be accomplished in as short a time as possible,' she continued sweetly, seeing Nico's eyes narrow into dark, glittering shards. He wants to call all the shots, she recognised. And I am not going to let him.

'I am very pleased to hear it,' said Gianferro. He shot Nico another unfathomable look. 'Perhaps I could see you alone for a moment, Nicolo?'

Nico raised his eyebrows. 'As you can see, I'm a little busy.'

Ella felt her cheeks flaming. Was Gianferro trying to get Nico out of the office to warn him not to make love to her? Well, he could save his breath!

She closed the open book on the desk and picked it up, somehow managing a cool and professional smile. 'I was actually just about to leave,' she said. 'My trip here today was only intended to be an introductory one, and in future I will be working on my own.' Her green eyes flashed Nico a warning. 'I certainly won't need to waste any more of Nico's time.'

Nico's mouth tightened. She was playing him like a virtuoso, knowing that he would be unable to object in his brother's presence. How dared she? 'Will there be anything else, Gianferro?'

'I'll see you at dinner.'

Nico shook his head. 'I don't think you will.'

There was a pause while the brothers' eyes met and engaged in a silent ebony duel. 'Then perhaps you could make me an appointment in your diary some time this year?' returned Gianferro sardonically, and left the room with a curt nod.

Once he had gone, and the door was closed behind him, Ella rounded on Nico, her voice beginning to tremble with rage. 'How *dare* you expose me to that kind of humiliation?' she accused.

'I certainly wasn't expecting my brother to walk in,' he said drily.

'No?'

'Of course not. I would have gone to the precaution of locking the door had that been the case.'

Ella could have screamed! He didn't look in the least bit repentant—on the contrary, he simply looked irritated, as if he had had his fun cut short. Which, when she stopped to think about it, he had. 'Did you think you could just come up here and have your wicked way with me? Is that what you thought?' she demanded. 'Your *droit de seigneur*?'

'I wasn't doing much thinking,' he drawled. 'And I hadn't planned it, no, if that's what you want to know.' His eyes glittered. 'You are just too damned irresistible, *cara*.'

'What kind of a tramp must I have looked to your brother?'

'Tramp?' He raised his brows in surprise. 'That's fairly emotive language, Ella. My brother is no innocent—he won't judge you, or me, for doing what comes so naturally to a man and a woman. I really should have locked the door…' he said, half to himself.

That just about did it. 'I don't care about him judging me!' declared Ella, wildly contradicting herself in the heat of the moment. 'I'm judging myself, if you must know—and I'm pretty appalled at my own behaviour!'

'Why?'

'Because it was wrong—you know it was wrong!'

'I disagree.' He regarded her steadily, wondering if she had any idea just how magnificent she looked when she was angry. 'You want me, Gabriella,' he observed coolly. 'Don't deny it. You know you do.'

She stared at him, at the hot, glittering eyes and the autocratic curve of his sensual lips, and her heart flipped and there was nothing she could do to stop it. 'Oh, I don't deny that on some fundamental level I do—sure I do. But that's not how I operate, Nico— women rarely do. There has to be more than pure physical attraction.'

'That didn't seem to bother you last time,' he commented insultingly.

'That's because—' She bit her lip, terrified of showing her vulnerability, of letting him know that she had been beginning to build all kinds of dreams about him. She had seen him for what she had believed him to be—her strong, powerful rescuer and an intelligent, provocative man. But that had been an illusion that had crumbled into dust.

'Because?' he prompted arrogantly.

'Maybe I did behave hot-headedly,' she admitted. 'But I thought that you…' She cleared her throat. 'At the time I didn't realise that you…'

'Were a prince?' he supplied drily. 'Well, now you do, and I must say it's the first time that it's ever worked against me.'

Her eyes flashed fire. 'It's more than that, and you know it!'

'What is it?' he grated. 'Explain it to me! Why are you so hung up on my title, Gabriella?'

'It's not the *title*—'

'Isn't it?' he challenged.

'No! It's the fact that you didn't tell me! I don't like dishonesty in a man.'

'There is rarely total truth between new lovers,' he bit out frustratedly.

Maybe he was right. But it was suddenly about more than that. He's never failed before, Ella realised. This is possibly the first time in his life he hasn't got what he wanted—at least with a woman.

For a moment she felt filled with a heady sense of

power, but that soon fled and was replaced by something much more satisfactory. Because right then, despite everything, Ella felt his *equal*.

She gave him a thin smile. 'And now, if you don't mind, I really do want to go back to the hotel and make some notes.'

He could see that he was going to make no further headway. At least, not right now. But there would be plenty more opportunities. 'Okay,' he agreed easily. 'Let's go. We can continue this fascinating discussion later, over dinner.'

'No, we can not,' she refuted, revelling even more in his look of surprise. But she needed to safeguard herself—not just against his sexual charisma but against her own helpless reaction to it—and to do that she needed to put distance between them. 'I am going to spend the evening in my beautiful and lavish suite, and I shall order something up from Room Service.'

She saw his lips part in amazement as she walked past him, her head held high, and flung the door open—though more as a protective device than anything else. The room was now on view to the whole corridor, and with servants and brothers potentially lingering in the background surely he wouldn't dare try anything else?

By now he was laughing softly at her extravagant behaviour. 'Oh, but your surrender will be sweetness itself, *cara*.'

'It isn't going to happen, Nico,' she replied tartly, and hoped that her words carried more conviction than she felt.

CHAPTER TEN

AFTER a long and luxurious bath, and a delicious supper that she ate on her terrace overlooking the harbour, Ella began to pore over the map Nico had given her. By the time she fell into bed she was exhausted.

But fatigue did nothing to block out the images of his black mocking eyes, and when eventually she fell asleep it was to dream of Nico.

A car picked her up the following morning, and drove her to the palace, and a servant took her to the office that Nico had shown her the day before. There was a small cut-glass bowl of scented white roses sitting on the desk, with an envelope beside it, which she ripped open.

Inside was a note from Nico. It was the first time she had seen his handwriting and it was rather like the man himself—uncompromising and bold.

It said: *Today I have taken my bike up into the mountains. Will you have dinner with me tonight?* And it was signed simply, *Nico*.

She sat back in her chair and looked out of the window onto the palace courtyard. Should she?

Well, what else was she going to do? Sit in her suite night after night, ordering up Room Service? She picked up her pen and began to make notes.

It didn't take her long to discover that an office was an office wherever it was—palace or not. The only real difference about this one was that it was so *quiet*. She hadn't always worked from home, she had done her share in other places, where there had always been a buzz, with people stopping by for coffee, or the sound of telephones ringing and fax machines disgorging their pages. But here the silence was uncanny. Did the servants move around on noiseless feet? Probably. It hit her in a sudden rush of understanding just how *lonely* it would be, to be a Royal.

She worked hard, marking out places she wanted to visit, and she was just wondering what to do about lunch—she didn't imagine that there was a vending machine sitting outside the throne room!—when there was a rap at the door.

'Come in,' she called, and the door opened to reveal the tall, imposing figure of Prince Gianferro.

Somehow she wasn't a bit surprised.

She rose to her feet. 'I honestly don't know whether or not I'm supposed to curtsey,' she admitted.

He nodded. 'I think you can be excused,' he observed drily. 'This is, after all, a rather informal meeting. I wondered—since I believe you have been working all morning—whether you would care to see the palace gardens? After that, I could arrange to have some lunch sent here.'

So he wasn't actually inviting her for lunch! *He*

wants to suss me out, she thought suddenly. She nodded. 'I should like that very much.'

'Come.'

It was a quiet and silky command, but she thought it came to him as naturally as breathing—which, when she came to think about it, it probably did. He would have been obeyed without question since he was barely out of the cradle—how must that affect a man's character development? she wondered. How had it affected Nico's?

As they emerged from the cool marble corridor into the bright sunlit gardens, she felt a ripple of sensation whispering over her skin at the thought of Gianferro's youngest brother. She wished he were with her. He would protect her from his brother, she realised, from the searching questions she was certain would follow. Or maybe Gianferro was too subtle to interrogate her outright? Would not a man of his birthright establish and direct matters in a far more understated way?

He paused beside a circular bed of the most heavenly roses Ella had ever seen—great rumpled globes of saffron, the petal-tips edged in apricot-pink—and the sweet scent of the massed flowers wafted up to her. She breathed it in.

'Your work is going well?' Gianferro asked casually.

Ella nodded. 'I can see a lot that could be done.'

'Really?' Dark eyebrows were raised in imperious question.

It was Nico who was in charge of touristic development on the island, and Nico who had brought her here. She was not going to brief his curious brother before she had even decided herself just what plans could be implemented.

'Yes, really,' she echoed softly, and saw his mouth harden. She had not intended to be rude. She drew in a deep breath and looked around. 'These really are the most exquisite flowers I have ever seen,' she said quietly. 'And such an unusual planting.'

There was a pause while she saw his eyes narrow, and then he nodded, as if he had just learned something, but she couldn't miss the sudden bleakness that flared at the back of the black eyes that were so like Nico's.

'They are roses named after my mother. My father had them planted after her death,' he said flatly. 'If you look closely you will see that the bushes form the initials of her name.'

'I'm sorry. I didn't mean—'

'No.' He shook his head. 'It was a thoughtful and intelligent observation.'

Ella was too flustered to feel patronized—and besides, she did not think that had been his intention.

'Perhaps,' he continued thoughtfully, 'since you wield much influence over my brother, you could persuade him to stop tearing around and putting his life at risk? And while you are about it a word or two about mountain climbing might prove useful.'

Ella stared at him. She had no experience of this kind of life, and yet instinct told her that this was not a commonplace conversation for the heir to the throne to be having.

'I have no influence over Nico,' she said.

'Oh, I disagree. You have enough for him to bring you—an outsider—here to work for him.'

'That doesn't happen often?'

'No,' he said emphatically.

'Why don't you tell him your concerns yourself?'

'You think I have not done so?' He gave an odd kind of smile. 'Life may move on, but relationships with siblings stay firmly rooted in the past—and so it is with my brothers. Our battles mimic those of our palace nursery! But a man who courts danger will achieve no lasting happiness. In any sphere of his life. Danger is both seductive and addictive, but Nicolo's life is mapped out in a way that other men's are not. His destiny is written, his path clearly defined. In all directions.'

He was warning her, Ella realised. *Warning her off!* Suddenly she felt an overwhelming urge to kick against this rigidity and restraint. No wonder Nico courted danger—if his life was to be a straitjacket!

She stared up at Gianferro with clear green eyes. 'I really ought to be getting back to work,' she said apologetically. 'I have a lot to get through, and Nico is taking me out for dinner.'

She hid a small, determined smile. Suddenly she found she was looking forward to it!

*   *   *

Nico was just about to ring her when his mobile thrilled into life. His eyes widened fractionally when he saw the number flash up, and his lips curved into a smile.

'Nico?'

'Gabriella,' he murmured. 'I can't quite believe it. The woman who behaved in such a cavalier fashion when I gave her my number is actually using it! What kind of day have you had?'

'Productive.' And interesting. 'Are you still free tonight?'

He felt the automatic quickening of his pulse. 'What time did you have in mind?' he said softly.

'I meant for dinner,' she said immediately.

'Why, so did I,' he returned, his voice mocking her with innocent reprimand. 'What did you think I meant?'

'Nothing.'

He smiled. He rather liked her chastened. 'I'll pick you up.'

'Okay. About eight? Oh, and Nico?'

'Mmm?'

'Do you drive your motorbike very fast?'

He frowned. 'That's the whole point of having one, Gabriella. I'll see you later.' And he hung up.

She opened up the wardrobe, trying to be enthusiastic, but it wasn't easy. It was all very well, defiantly bringing only the barest minimum of clothes here, but she was going to have to wear some things twice if she stayed beyond a week. And he had already seen her in the black dress!

She stood beneath the jets of the power shower. Not that she would need to stay beyond that, she told herself firmly. She had conceived a simple idea to put to Nico, which she was certain would work—and then she could go. Before she did something really stupid, like starting to care for him.

But you *do* care for him, mocked an inner voice.

She switched the shower off with a flourish, and wrapped herself in a fluffy white robe.

She did *not* care for him. She was attracted to him sexually, that was all.

But you don't *do* sex on its own, Ella, taunted that infuriating voice again. You know you don't. And you've never done sex like *that* before.

She had a white broderie anglaise dress that she had been saving—though she wasn't quite sure what she had been saving it for. So after much deliberation, she put it on. It was sweet and feminine, with tiny cap sleeves that she could just about get away with. She was tempted to plait her hair, but in the end she decided against it and wore it loose—she didn't want to look as though she was auditioning for a part in *The Sound of Music*!

She was ten minutes late, and he was waiting for her downstairs, seated casually on a plush leather sofa. A man with a suspiciously bulky jacket was positioned conspicuously close by. As the lift doors opened the normal chatter of the foyer died to a hush and Nico rose to his feet.

People were watching him—either openly or not

quite so openly. Women, some standing with their husbands, positioned themselves so that they could be seen at their most flattering angle—pushing their breasts out and sucking in their already concave stomachs. But he was not looking at the women.

He was looking at her.

She saw him give a brief, barely discernible nod to the man, and was vaguely aware that faces were now turning in *her* direction, their expressions slightly incredulous. And she realised how cheap her dress must look in comparison to their designer finery.

What happened next was like some smooth, well-practised machine whirring into action. Subtle signals must have been given, for a pathway was magically formed, leaving their exit clear just as a long, low car purred to the front of the building, with a chauffeur behind the wheel.

She realised that she had never met him anywhere quite so public before—*that* would explain the high-profile security.

'Is it always like this?' Ella asked, as she wriggled onto the back seat and the door was slammed shut on them.

He turned to her, thinking how shining and fresh she looked in her simple white dress. 'Like what?'

She shrugged her shoulders. 'So choreographed. As if everything has been planned right down to the last second.'

'Not quite the last second,' he commented wryly. 'Since you were late.'

'Sorry.'

'It's okay.' He smiled.

'Do you like it—all the fuss?'

'It's just the way it is. What I cannot change I have to accept—or my life would be intolerable. I escape it whenever I can.'

'Like on the motorbike?'

'The motorbike, yes—you seem to be obsessed with my damned motorbike! And, yes, before you ask—the jet-ski, too! You know what they say—big toys for big boys.' His eyes glittered as he saw the faint rush of colour to her cheeks. 'Now, stop asking me so many questions and tell me how you got on today.'

'Not bad. I've got a few ideas.'

'Such as?'

She gave him a rather prim smile. 'I'm not going to talk about it until I've worked it out properly. But I've made a list of all the places on the island I'd like to visit.'

Which sounded a little like a refusal to tell him!

'Right,' he said, in a rather dazed voice. 'We're here.'

The restaurant had clearly been chosen as much for its discreet setting as its breathtaking view of the sea, but it only reinforced Ella's sensation of inhabiting a different world. There were women wearing a fortune in gems glittering around their necks, and she spotted a famous actress getting very cosy with a man who was definitely not her husband.

But all eyes were on them, watching as they weaved their way to a table in a candlelit alcove.

He ordered red wine, and then a steaming dish that arrived in a covered and distinctively patterned deep blue earthenware pot.

'What a beautiful dish,' observed Ella.

'You like it? It is produced only in Islaroca, on the north west corner of the island.'

'I've never seen anything like it before.'

'You soon will—there's a big export drive going on at the moment.'

It had been Nico's baby—his attempt to change something of the island's reputation for being just a tax haven for people with too much money. On an island with few natural resources, it seemed madness not to capitalise on the pottery industry—though Gianferro had initially opposed the expansion. His damned brother and his need to control!

When the waitress took the lid off the casserole, Ella stilled for a moment and turned her eyes towards Nico. 'I recognise this,' she said, sniffing.

He held her gaze. 'That's because I cooked it for you at the beach,' he said softly. 'Our national dish.' The corners of his mouth lifted in a sardonic smile. 'But this one probably won't be quite as good as mine.'

He was right, it wasn't—but Ella suspected that was because her hunger was not so honed as it had been back then.

And senses were both evocative and nostalgic—

taste no less so than sight or sound. One mouthful was enough to transport her back to that time and place, to recall his kindness and his gentleness towards her. Her memory froze and then galloped forward, to rekindle even more evocative memories…

She gazed across the table towards him and felt the tiptoe of longing take slow, skittering steps up her spine.

He saw the tip of her tongue flick out to moisten her lips and felt the dry, hard ache of need as he watched her.

'Gabriella—' he whispered.

But his words were interrupted by a small flurry of activity at the door. Heads were raised and turned in its direction, and Nico's eyes narrowed as a flamboyant-looking man with a shock of yellow hair beamed and began to walk towards their table.

He gave a small sigh, but Ella heard it. It was tinged with resignation and irritation, but his dark, handsome face did not make a flicker of reaction.

'Who is it?'

'It's the owner and sometimes chef,' he answered. 'He's a bit of a star on the island, as modern-day chefs so often are.' He gave a cynical smile. 'I thought he was in Paris.'

Ella stared at him as realisation began to dawn. 'Has he…?' She hesitated, because her supposition sounded so bizarre. 'He hasn't flown back all the way from Paris especially because you happen to be having dinner in his restaurant?'

His eyes mocked her. 'Well, what do you think?'

She thought it was completely crazy, that was what she thought.

Ella watched while the owner bowed to Nico, his eyes barely giving her a second glance. As though she didn't count. But, oh, Nico counted—that much was plain to see from the fawning bonhomie, the implication that Nico could demand a fresh strawberry flown from the Highlands of Scotland and a minion would immediately be dispatched to secure it.

After he had left, Nico studied her. 'Do you understand a little now, Gabriella—why I did not tell you who I was?'

And Ella nodded, feeling…feeling as if she had somehow been too hard on him. Had she been guilty of looking at it from just *her* viewpoint, without thinking of his?

'It must have been quite something…to be anonymous,' she said slowly.

'It was a taste of freedom which I found exhilarating.' He shrugged. 'And one which was heady enough to allow me to repress the knowledge that I was keeping something back.'

The same sense of freedom that made people such fans of dangerous sports, she realised. It all made sense now. 'I wouldn't have reacted quite so angrily,' she said, 'if I'd known.'

A faint smile touched his lips. 'No, I'm sure you wouldn't. But in one way I'm glad you didn't know. For once it was good to have someone behave…' He shrugged his shoulders and gave a faint smile. 'Well, *normally*, I guess.' And that had not changed. He could never remember having such a candid conversation with a woman.

Her heart was thudding, her palms grown clammy with this new turn of developments. And he was doing it again—appealing to some soft inner core of her. But surely that would only complicate things.

Because what he said didn't actually *change* anything. It made his actions more understandable, but his motivation remained the same. He had wanted sex with her, and that was what had happened. It might have been the most wonderful thing in her life so far, but she imagined that it was like that all the time for a man like Nico.

And the most fundamental fact of all could not be changed.

That he was a prince and she was just an ordinary young woman from the countryside. And unless she kept that to the forefront of her mind she was heading straight for heartbreak.

Nico drifted his eyes over her. She had drunk, he noted, very little—was that deliberate?—but she seemed less defensive than before. Nonetheless, instinct still told him that he must tread very carefully. He sensed that she was close to surrender, but one false move and he could blow it.

Later, when they were seated in the intimate interior of the luxury car, Ella waited breathlessly for a move that did not come. She was aware that her overriding feeling was one of disappointment. Stop it, she thought. Stop wishing for something that could only ever be bittersweet.

The car pulled up outside L'Etoile and he turned to her, his dark eyes glittering. 'Shall we drive to some of the towns and villages on your list tomorrow?' he suggested.

Ella nodded, her heart beating so hard that she was surprised he couldn't hear it. 'Okay.'

'We'll make a day of it,' he said casually. 'And I'll bring a picnic.'

CHAPTER ELEVEN

'You know that Gianferro spoke to me yesterday?'

'Did he?' Nico didn't take his eyes off the road. They were heading towards one of Mardivino's least pretty villages because Gabriella wanted to have a look at it, but she hadn't told him why.

'I'm thinking,' she had said, and would not be swayed.

It was, he thought wryly, an oddly erotic experience to tussle with a woman who would not be swayed.

'So what did he say?' he questioned, as he negotiated a narrow road that was a dream on the bike but not quite so amenable to the four-wheel drive he had considered necessary for this journey.

'He worries about you.'

Nico gave a short laugh. 'Don't tell me—he gave you the "dangerous sports" lecture?'

'You know about that?'

'Of course.' He changed down a gear. 'It wouldn't matter if I was strolling sedately along the beach at Solajoya—if Gianferro didn't approve, he would attempt to talk me out of it. It's less a fear of the consequences, in his case, and more the fact that he likes to control—it's in his blood. He takes his heir-to-the-

134

throne responsibilities a touch too seriously sometimes. That's why Guido doesn't live here any more.
Why he got out just as soon as he could.'

'You don't mind?'

'Oh, I've just learned to ignore him,' he said softly.

'Sounds like a bit of a communication problem to
me.'

'Skip the amateur psychology, Gabriella. If I want
advice about how to deal with my brother, then I'll
ask for it.'

There was silence in the car, the kind of claustro-
phobic, in-car silence that grew like a heavy, oppressive cloud.

'That was harsh of me,' said Nico eventually.

'No, you're right.' She shrugged. 'Your relationship with your brother is none of my business.'

No, it wasn't. Her personal opinion wasn't the reason he had brought her here—her professional opinion, maybe. But that wasn't strictly true, either, was
it? The job had simply been a manoeuvre to get her
here; her seduction had been uppermost in his mind.
But she had embraced the project with an enthusiasm
that impressed him, and yet he still remained a
stranger to her bed.

His brow creased into a frown. Nothing was turning
out as he had planned. Why was she continuing to
hold him at arm's length when he knew damned well
that she wanted him?

'We're here,' he bit out, as the car bumped its way
over the dusty road that led to the village.

It was an unprepossessing place—high and barren, the sea so far away that it looked like a sapphire strip of ribbon in the distance. Nico looked around him; he hadn't been here for years.

The local people still harvested their olive crop, but these days they had to compete with the mass-farming methods of larger countries, such as Greece, and it showed. The place looked run-down, the small restaurant on the main street tired. They walked through the village and back, struck by its emptiness and its silence. No one was on the streets bar a couple of children scratching symbols in the dust, who stared at them with wide, curious eyes. Certainly no one recognised him. It was like a ghost town, thought Nico dazedly.

'No one ever comes here,' he said slowly, as their footsteps drew them back to the car. Not even him. He might tear around the island on his motorbike, but he never really stopped long enough to look. To stand and stare. He shook his head, like a man waking from a long sleep. What could he do to help these people? he wondered.

You didn't have to be the heir to care, he realized, and part of him resented the fact that it had taken this stranger, this *Englishwoman*, to show him this. But who else would have dared? Who would have looked him straight in the eyes and said the things to him that Gabriella had done?

And didn't her complete lack of connection with

his island give him the rare opportunity to express himself? What would it matter to her?

'I have neglected places such as this.'

She heard the guilt in his voice. 'You can't do everything, Nico,' she said softly.

'I could do more,' he said suddenly.

'I agree. In fact, I think I have a solution for places like this—well, certainly this place in particular.'

She was good at her job, he recognised suddenly. Very good. His instinct that fresh eyes would provide a fresh perspective had been a sound one. Just so long as she understood her limitations…

Her hair looked like spun gold as the sun beat down on them, warming his skin, inexorably filling him with a languid feeling of contentment. She had sensibly worn a hat to shade her face, and it had the effect of making her look very pure and innocent.

Innocent?

With breathtaking clarity he recalled her skill as a lover, and the deep aching that he had been doing his best to suppress suddenly burst into life and dominated everything.

'Do you…do you want to hear it?' asked Ella, suddenly breathless—because when he looked at her like that it made her feel… She swallowed, suddenly aware of the sound of a distant bird, of the strong, heavy beat of her heart.

'Do I want to hear…what?' he questioned evenly, deliberately misunderstanding, deliberately sending her a silent, sensual message with his eyes.

She wanted him to stop that—and yet she wanted him to go on looking at her like that for ever. 'My…idea, of course.'

He gave a slow smile. 'Want to tell me about it over lunch?'

Her heart was now crashing a symphony beneath her breast. 'It's a little early for lunch.'

'We can look at the scenery for a while.'

Ella shrugged—as if it didn't matter, as if she didn't care. 'Okay,' she agreed, and wondered where the brisk, cool businesswoman had disappeared to. Lost in the soft ebony promise of his eyes, that was where.

He drove towards the interior, stopping the car near a small copse of trees she didn't recognise—tall, graceful trees, with broad leaves providing a canopy and tiny blue flowers intertwined. It was beautiful but it was secluded, Ella realised, her heart beating even faster. *So ask him to take you somewhere else,* mocked the inner voice of sense.

'Do you want to spread the rug out?' he asked carelessly. 'And I'll bring the picnic.'

Shutting the door on sense, she did as he asked, spreading the cashmere rug out on the grass with fingers that were trembling. As he put the basket down and sat beside her she knew what was about to happen. She wondered not would she be able to resist—but whether she really *wanted* to resist.

Nico leaned back on his elbows and studied her. Her body looked taut, expectant—oh, God, yes. It was shady beneath the trees and the dappled sunlight rippled over them in a kaleidoscope of gold.

'Why don't you take your hat off?' he suggested softly. 'I can't see your eyes.'

She wasn't sure she wanted him to. Wouldn't he be able to read in them her doubts, her fears? And, most of all, her longing. They were supposed to be working, yet working was the furthest thing on her mind right now.

But she removed it anyway, feeling as shy as if he had asked her to strip for him, and her hair tumbled down over her shoulders like heavy silk.

'Your beautiful eyes,' he murmured. 'So very green.'

His voice had dipped and softened, but his own eyes were bright—and hard. Her mouth felt dry and the tip of her tongue snaked out to moisten it. Say something, she thought. But words suddenly seemed as foreign as the place in which she found herself.

'Are you thirsty, *cara mia*?' he questioned, and his voice sounded husky and slumberous.

Italian, he had said, was the language of love. But this isn't love, she tried to tell herself. It's sex, pure and simple—for him.

'Stop it,' she whispered.

'Stop what?' he questioned, as he began to open the hamper. 'What kind of a host would I be if I didn't look after my guest?'

He had thought of bringing champagne, but champagne was too clichéd—and it held bitter memories.

She had offered him champagne as an empty gesture once before, but she had been angry with him then. She didn't look in the least bit angry now. She looked soft, and vulnerable, but ready and waiting—like a delicious cake just waiting to be cut. He took a silver flask from the hamper, filled a cup to the brim with iced lemon and handed it to her.

But Ella was shaking as she took it from him, her fingers trembling in a way over which she seemed to have no control. Some of the cool, delicious drink reached her mouth, but more of it splattered down the front of her dress, leaving damp splotches over the hectic rise and fall of her breasts like giant tears.

He took the cup from her with a hand so steady it could have performed brain surgery, and drank some himself. Then he put the cup down and leaned his face close to hers.

It swam in and out of focus—the dazzle of his eyes, the silken olive skin, the lush, sensual lines of his lips. She seemed to be able to breathe in his virile scent, and she was aware of the silence that surrounded them. The slow, heavy pounding of her heart was the only sound she could hear.

Yet *he* seemed so utterly in control—while inside she felt as fluttery as a captured butterfly. The balance is all wrong, she told herself, and yet deep down she knew that this was what she had wanted all the time.

'Gabriella,' he whispered. 'You have made me wait, and I can wait no longer.'

His breathtaking honesty made her melt—or maybe

it was the warmth of his breath on her skin that did that. Sometimes you could block out a need and a desire so much that when you gave it a peep of life it erupted and became unstoppable.

'We shouldn't be doing this,' she said helplessly, as he ran the flat of his hand down over her hair.

'Oh, yes, we should,' he murmured. 'It has been too long—much, much too long.'

'Nico—'

He stilled her words with the touch of his mouth, brushing his lips against hers with a light, experimental touch, feeling her shiver in response and then make a little moan of protest when he moved away again. He bit back a small smile of triumph as he kissed her again—only this time his hands slid up her back and captured her, moving her body hard against his.

Ella was lost in the piercing sweetness of him as he kissed her over and over again, until she was helpless with wanting. Deep, hard kisses, that sent her senses reeling as she moved restlessly beneath him, forgetting everything. Forgetting the deceit and the differences and all that had gone before, just kissing him, and touching him, the man whose own desire was like touch-paper to her senses.

He felt as if he was drowning, sucked deep and then deeper still into a dark swirling vortex of desire as he pulled her to the ground, overwhelmed by the need to take her. Swiftly.

'Nico!' His hand was on her leg, rucking her skirt up.

'Touch me,' he urged, hot fingertips finding the cool skin of her thigh. She gasped against his neck. 'Touch me.'

She moved her hand down, laying her palm over him to cup his hardness, and he moaned softly, almost helplessly. She felt a heady power because he was as much at her mercy as she was at his. She put her mouth close to his ear. 'You've…you've got me so I can't think straight…'

'Then don't think. Just enjoy it.' *Like I do.* He shuddered as her fingertips touched him so intimately. 'Oh, *Dio*, yes!' The words were torn from his lips in a warm torrent. All restraint had vanished. He had never felt so out of control—and it terrified him nearly as much as he exulted in the feeling. It was like standing on the edge of a cliff, knowing that you were going to jump even though to do so would be madness.

Aware that this was something he had to do, if it wasn't going to be over before it started, he pulled her hand away, taking it to his mouth and gently biting her fingers. '*Lentamente*. Take…it…slow…' he urged.

But he wasn't following his own advice, thought Ella, her head falling back against the rug as he began to slide her panties down over her knees. She felt the cool rush of air on her heated flesh and opened her mouth to protest that maybe they should move from here. That he was a prince…that this was all happening too quickly. But she opened her thighs, too…

And then his lips were on hers once more, and his fingers were delving into her honeyed warmth, and she was lost in the rhythm of a dance more ancient than either crown or privilege. And then she stopped thinking about that, and thought of Nico instead—this dazzling-eyed man who had haunted her thoughts and her dreams since the moment she had first laid eyes on him—touching her with such sweet accuracy so that she cried in ecstatic wonder against his skin.

Her mouth moved against the graze of his shadowed jaw, and she burrowed beneath his silk shirt to find skin even more silken where it stretched over hard muscle and sinew. She began to tug impatiently at his belt, and heard him give a low laugh of delight.

He stilled her hand as he lifted his head, and his ebony eyes were glazed with a desire that made them smoulder down at her like burning coal. He shook his head. 'No, let me,' he said roughly, his gaze never leaving her face as he unzipped his jeans.

He pushed her dress right up and moaned softly to discover that she was bra-less. He dipped his head to suck tightly on her nipple as he wriggled his jeans off, not wanting—not able—to wait to undress her completely. The little cries she was making were inciting him even more as he scrambled like a schoolboy to protect himself, and then there was no more waiting, and he plunged deep, deep inside her slick heat.

'Nico!' she gasped as he began to move, because last time it had not felt so full, or so tight, or so unutterably right. She threaded her fingers into his thick dark hair and pulled his head towards her, opening her mouth beneath his as if she couldn't get enough of him.

And Nico was lost…lost in something that was like new territory to him. He had always been a master of self-control, and usually he had the ability to take himself outside the act. To observe the woman and to lead—taking them both at the pace he wished them to follow, almost like a conductor of an orchestra.

But this time it was different. Was that because she had kept him on tenterhooks for what seemed like an eternity? Because he had never been quite sure whether this would actually happen, and, now that it was, its potent sweetness surpassed all his hot and wildest fantasies?

He found himself lost in a deep, dark pleasure where self was obliterated by sensation. His body no longer felt like his, but hers did. All his. His hands moved from her breasts to her hips, holding her tighter as he moved inside her over and over again. He felt that he might die if it did not end soon, yet he wanted it to last for ever.

Her cry split the air, her limbs tensed and then flailed, her eyes closing, her lips whispering his name like a prayer. And Nico followed her, dissolving into something so sweet that it felt sinful.

For a moment he felt the same heady sense of triumph he always experienced when he broke in a new and difficult stallion, or when he sailed hard against the wind.

And then the feeling was gone, and he was left with the more familiar feeling of emptiness.

He must have slept, for when he came to he was tangled in her arms, and the heart that beat beneath his was slow and heavy. He raised his head just as her eyes fluttered open, all smokily green with satiation.

'Oh, Nico,' she sighed.

He traced the line of her lip with a lazy finger, and desire returned with a potent power that shook him. His mouth hardened. Keep it in perspective, he told himself.

'So, tell me all about this idea of yours,' he drawled.

Ella stared up at him, blinking her eyes in a long moment of confusion. 'Idea?' she questioned dazedly. What the hell was he talking about?

He shifted away from her fractionally. Distance gave perspective, and right now he needed it. She could weave an extraordinary kind of magic in his arms, but that was all. That was *all*.

He turned onto his side and propped himself up on his elbow, his eyes drifting over hers with a lazy look of amusement. 'You have forgotten your idea already, *cara*?' he teased. 'If it cannot last beyond the hour then it cannot be an idea of any substance!'

His words brought Ella crashing back to reality

with a painful jolt as she heard the mocking truth in them.

No substance.

No *substance*.

She had wanted to lie there murmuring sweet nothings, but he wanted to talk ideas! At least he had reminded her of her place in the scheme of things.

She composed her face and tried to rid it of the look of dreamy soppiness. Sweet heaven, Ella, you gave him your very soul itself just now, so make sure you claw back every last little bit of pride.

'Well.' She drew in a deep breath and the oxygen cleared her head. 'I will, of course, be making a full list of my proposed recommendations, but there is one thing which I think would have immediate impact—and that's to do something about the crowds around the Juan Lopez gallery. They're a real eyesore, and they make a very real congestion problem.'

Had he been expecting her to pout? To tell him prettily that she didn't want to talk about work at a time like this? Nico's eyes narrowed. The very unexpectedness of her remark and her cool thinking caught him on the back foot, so that—perversely—he found *himself* struggling to concentrate on her damned idea, and not on the pure, soft curves of her body.

He stared at her suspiciously. 'And what do you propose we do about that? Mardivino is rightly proud of her strong links with Lopez.'

'Move it,' she said simply.

His suspicious look intensified. 'Explain yourself.'

Oh, but now he sounded like an autocratic Royal! Yet, oddly enough, Ella's strength of mind and resolve was returning by the second. Was she going to suddenly become one of those wet-blanket kinds of women just because she had cried out in ecstasy in his arms? No, she was not! Whatever she was feeling inside, she would hide it, and he would not know because she would not let him.

Blocking the yearning desire to brush her fingertips over the dark curve of his jaw, she smiled. 'Solajoya is buzzing and thriving and it always will be—because it's a port *and* the capital. People travel here especially to see the works of Juan Lopez, so they don't *need* to be housed in Solajoya. So you move the gallery somewhere else. Somewhere the tourists don't bother to visit. Somewhere which could do with the extra revenue those tourists would bring. Somewhere like the village we just visited. Why not?'

There was a pause. 'Why not?' he echoed thoughtfully, and then the black eyes glittered. 'It sounds too simple.'

'The best ideas often are.' But so were the worst ones. Agreeing to a picnic with him had been simple, and making love simpler still. And yet no matter how much her calm, professional expression tried to hide it she was left with a deep, dark aching in her heart. Because it was never going to be more than this, and if she couldn't accept that she was going to get badly hurt. *Stick with what you know, Ella.*

'That village is badly in need of rejuvenating. Think what this could bring. A brand-new gallery, which would make the most of the paintings, and all the stuff which would go with it. Postcards, and prints, and a restaurant or two. Of course...' her ideas began to gallop away with her, 'You would have to be very careful not to destroy the character of the village, but I can't see you letting that happen.'

'Why, thank you, Gabriella,' he said mockingly.

She licked her lips, which were suddenly parched. 'So, will you think about it?'

'I will.'

'Good.' She had saved the day. She had done what she had set out to do, taken the heat out of the situation, but now she needed to get out of here and get her head together. She sat up and began to pull her dress down, but he reached out his hand to halt her.

'What are you doing?'

'What does it look like? I'm...' Her words dried in her mouth as his fingertips began to touch her bare breasts, skating enchanting little pathways across the already sensitised skin. She closed her eyes. 'I'm getting dressed.'

He felt the hot, hard jerk of desire as he pulled her against him, smoothing the palms of his hands over the silken globes of her buttocks and feeling her shudder. It was about time he showed her who was boss.

'Oh, no, you aren't,' he negated quietly.

She wanted to stop him.

No, she didn't.

She *tried* to stop him.

No, she didn't.

Trying to stop someone should amount to more than a distracted little shake of the head. If she had really been trying to stop him then she would not now be squirming with delight as he stroked and touched her, nor be touching him back and hearing him moan so softly.

Nor would her heart be leaping with a wild and delirious kind of joy as he entered her once more. Her last sane thought was that this perfect act was going to achieve the impossible. Leaving her feeling complete.

Yet achingly incomplete.

CHAPTER TWELVE

THEY drove down the mountain road in silence, and for Ella it was a silence fraught with unanswered questions. There was none of the companionable ease she might have expected or hoped for after such a successful morning—which had culminated in that heartstoppingly erotic encounter.

For Nico had retreated.

She had seen it in his eyes once passion had faded. As if someone had suddenly changed the temperature of the tap while you were washing your hands, so that it had gone straight from warm to icy-cold, making you flinch. Even his features, which she had seen look so animated and alive during the act of love, were now simply cool and indifferent.

Oh, he had been sweet enough—he had buttoned up her dress and teased her, and drifted his lips over her skin in a teasing way—but it had felt as though he was simply going through the motions of how a lover *should* behave afterwards. There had been no sense of real closeness—no conviction that if she had asked him what was going on in that head of his he would have told her.

The intimacy that had been there both before and after they had made love had vanished. And something within her had been sapped. As if by pleasing her physically he had taken away her ability to talk to him as if he was just any man.

So, was this the end of her 'assignment'? Even if he did take up her suggestion about moving the gallery—did that entitle her to stay? Would she actually want to—was she just going to allow herself to be picked up and put down at will? A plaything for a prince...

She bit her lip and stared out of the window as the white rooftops of Solajoya began to appear.

Nico flicked her a glance.

Now what did he do?

He had a choice, of course. He could treat it as a one-off. Something he had badly wanted and that he had now been given, satisfying his hunger sufficiently enough to drive that hunger away. But it had not been. Even with that stiff, slightly defensive set of her shoulders, he found that he was still turned on. He still wanted to caress her, to run his fingertips over her until she opened up again, like a glorious flower—spreading her petals just for him, so that he could lose himself in their heady perfume.

He swore softly as he crashed a gear, and she turned her head, her eyebrows raised in question.

Nico glowered at the road ahead. He was a superb driver—good enough to grace the circuit of any international motor-race, dammit! So why was he acting like a nervous pupil out taking his test?

The car slid to a halt in front of L'Etoile, and, sucking in a deep breath to give her courage, Ella turned to him. She wasn't dealing with a normal man, she reminded herself, and she must not expect him to behave like one. No long lingering kiss, or promise to ring her. After all, they were in public now.

Keep it together, Ella, she told herself. Act like a sophisticated career-woman. If it was a one-off, then remember it as something very beautiful and take your heartache back to England with you, to nurse it in private.

She smiled. Take control. Give him a let-out. Give *yourself* a let-out. A plaything for a prince? *Never in a million years!* 'I guess I'd better think about booking my flight home.'

Her words took him by surprise. 'Home?' he demanded, his brow deepening into a frown.

'Of course.' The smile became easier—encouraged by the almost insulting look of astonishment on his face! Did his women usually cling with all the tenacity of a rock-climber hanging on for dear life? 'What is there to stay for now? I've made my recommendations to improve some of Mardivino's problems, and you've managed to have sex with me.'

'*Managed?*' he shot out, affronted. 'You make it sound as though you had nothing to do with it!'

'Do I?' Ella was enjoying herself now—how wonderful to see that look of indifference replaced by a genuine emotion, even if it *was* anger! 'Well, obviously that's not true. I—'

'How very good of you to concede that!' His

mocking words sliced right through hers, his eyes glittering at her in challenge.

'I was part of what happened.'

'Thank God for that,' he said drily.

'But there is no need for me to stay now. Not really.'

Nico's mouth hardened. She was right; there wasn't. The bottom line was that her job here *had* been a ruse. A threat. A demonstration of his power and privilege—and yet she had taken him at his word. He had presented her with a problem and she had coolly solved it. She had, in fact, exceeded all his expectations—both in and out of the bedroom. *But you haven't even taken her to the bedroom!* The voice in his head was taunting him, and his body began to ache even more as he realised just how much unfulfilled potential there was with Gabriella.

'I don't want you to go,' he said stubbornly.

She nearly said, *And Nico gets everything he wants.* Except that he didn't. No person did—not even princes—especially not princes. She thought of his lonely childhood, spent on show—brought out on high-days and holidays like a little mannequin. She had seen that for herself in all the photographs. Why on earth should she be surprised if he did not display 'normal' emotions?

She arched her eyebrows at him. 'Don't you?'

'No.'

She waited. She didn't want to go, either—but there was a difference between being honest enough to admit that and being a complete walk-over. Would he come even close to admitting that the feeling between them was powerful enough to make the obstacles of his birth seem momentarily insignificant? Or was that just her own interpretation?

He leaned towards her fractionally, so that she could breathe in the raw, feral scent of him, and his proximity weakened her, as he must have known it would. Say something that means something, she begged him silently. Tell me that even if you know it can't last, you care for me, even if it's just the tinest little bit.

'And surely you want to stay around to see your idea come to fruition?' he murmured.

She felt the sharp pain of a rejection he wasn't even aware of, but her face didn't give a flicker of reaction. It was time to start dealing with reality, not hopeless dreams. Unless she was prepared to do that she was onto a loser.

'I have a business to run back in England, Nico,' she reminded him gently. 'I can't stay around indefinitely.' But as soon as the words were out of her mouth she wished she could reach out and grab them back. Because it gave voice to a timespan. They asked for a time limit. She was asking the question she didn't have the guts to voice directly.

His eyes glittered, and he knew then that he must be up front with her. He wanted her—*Ah, si*—but on his terms—for there was no other way.

'I'd like you to stay on for a while, Ella. To put

your idea to Gianferro and to the planners, yes—but something more than that.' He shrugged, as if it didn't matter—*Dio*, it *didn't* matter! He would live if she said no. His eyes gleamed with dark intent. He had no intention of letting her say no. 'I want you as my lover, Gabriella,' he admitted softly. 'Just that.'

Just that.

As a declaration it was insulting.

Or just honest?

He was making up the rules, as he had probably done in relationships all his adult life, and Ella realised she could accept that—or not. It all came down to one thing…whether she was prepared to accept him unconditionally, or whether she was going to allow those unrealistic dreams to send her home.

He saw her silent tussle—the yearning in her eyes that she was doing her best to disguise—but he saw, too, the proud way she held her head, and suddenly it was the most irresistible of combinations.

'I want to kiss you,' he ground out, the blood heating like molten lava in his veins. He could feel the fire spreading over his skin. 'But I cannot do that. Not now and not here. Indeed, I cannot come to your suite here, for the same reason that you cannot visit me in my rooms at the palace—the gossips will learn of it and your life will be made hell.'

'And yours, too, of course, Nico,' she observed drily. 'Let's not forget that.'

'We must be discreet,' he said, as if she had not spoken.

Discreet. As Royal mistresses had been since the beginning of dynastic rule.

'I have a house just outside Solajoya,' he continued. 'We can use that whenever we please. It is very beautiful and very isolated.'

Just as he was. Ella stared at the ebony smoulder of his eyes, the soft curve of anticipation that made his lush lips so sensual. His strong, lean body was tensed and expectant. She could almost feel the pulsing of his desire as it shimmered through the air towards her, and it was a feeling that was met and matched by her own.

Shouldn't she just take away what she had experienced in his arms? Take it away to remember it with pleasure? Like a golden treasure to be pulled out on rainy days, to remind her of a time that had been both precious and matchless? There could be no future in a relationship with this man; the only outcome that lay ahead was certain heartbreak. And not, she suspected, simply because of his Royal position.

She remembered the way he had switched from warm and giving to cool and indifferent after they had made love. Surely an ability to compartmentalise like that was a much bigger obstacle than his lofty status? Was she hoping that he would change? That everything would change and that they would walk off towards the sunset, hand in hand?

Deep in her heart, she knew what she *should* do.

So what was stopping her?

He was. Just him. Just by being Nico. The very

essence of the man himself. She had wanted him from the first moment she had set eyes on him, and the wanting had only increased. She had wanted him when she had thought he had nothing, and she wanted him still.

'I don't know,' she said truthfully, but the doubt in her voice sounded like an invitation to be convinced.

'We could go there later, *cara mia*.' The velvet voice brushed deliberately over her senses. 'Spend the night in each other's arms. One night. Tonight. Why would you say no to that?'

With a mixture of excitement and dread, Ella knew that she could not resist. One night—what harm could it do? She nodded slowly, as if she was giving the matter consideration, but in reality it was to prevent him from seeing the vulnerability in her eyes, which was making her feel as raw and as naïve as a teenager.

She lifted her head, and now her gaze was proud and fearless. She had made her decision and she was going to enjoy every minute of it.

'Why not?' she said lightly, and pushed open the car door. 'Will you pick me up? Or shall I put on a dark cloak and wait on a shadowed corner?'

He laughed, suddenly filled with a reckless excitement. 'I will pick you up at eight,' he said. 'And I will cook for you again.'

But food was the last thing on Ella's mind as she soaked away the picnic dust from her body in a long bath.

No doubts, she told herself sternly as she brushed her damp hair. That's not the point of the exercise.

And the point of the exercise was…?

She slammed her hairbrush down on the dresser. Pleasure. Enjoyment. Simple, normal stuff—and she was *not* going to get heavy.

She slipped out of the side-door of L'Etoile to find his car waiting, and she slid into the seat beside him.

He smiled as he turned the ignition key. 'You smell like flowers, *cara*. A meadow of flowers.'

She was glad that the dim light concealed her blush of pleasure. But it's just the continental way, she reminded herself as the powerful car purred its way out of the capital. The men were schooled in elegant compliments in a way that Englishmen simply were not. She had found that out at the very beginning.

But sweet words could turn a woman's head, even if that was the last thing in the world she needed, and Ella felt an unbearable sense of expectation as he negotiated the bends. In a way, this tryst was nothing but a cold—or hot!—blooded sensual arrangement between two consenting adults, and yet not even that knowledge could still her mounting excitement. Soon she would be in his arms again, and suddenly that was the only thing that mattered.

The house was in darkness as he unlocked it, but he clicked a switch and light immediately flooded from a huge chandelier. Yet Ella barely noticed the grand and elegant proportions, the pieces of antique

French furniture that were dotted around the hallway, for he pulled her into his arms with a hungry groan, burying his face in her hair and breathing deeply, like a man who had been underwater for a long time.

He moved away and cupped her face between his palms, his black eyes glittering with an intensity that was brighter than the light overhead.

'Bed,' he whispered, and, taking her hand in his, led her up a wide and curving staircase.

Her mouth was too dry for words—but what use were words at a time like this? She was long past the stage of pretty protests that maybe they should eat supper first, or perhaps they should have a drink, because she wanted neither.

This felt grown-up—almost too grown-up—yet nothing could stop the heated longing that was clamouring its way through her veins, the longing to feel his skin next to her once again. Nico as Nico—stripped of everything—just a man of flesh against her flesh.

He pushed open a door to reveal a beautiful bed, hung with richly lavish embroidered drapes, and he turned her towards him, his eyes holding hers for one long, impenetrable second.

'Now kiss me,' he instructed quietly. 'Kiss me, *cara mia.*'

It was a command that she could not have resisted even if the building had been tumbling down around them. She looped her arms around his neck, stood up on tiptoe and pressed her mouth to his, and his soft moan filled her with delight and with daring.

As his lips opened beneath hers, and their tongues laced in languid exploration, she pressed her body closer to his and felt his breath mingling with hers as he gave another moan.

It was as if they had each been schooled in what was to come next for they moved in synchrony, in a silent wordless dance towards the bed, as if they had practised the steps over and over again, and yet Ella knew she had never moved like that before. Had he?

With hungry, conspiratorial smiles, they slid onto the bed.

'Gabriella—'

But she touched her finger to his lips to silence him and began to unbutton his shirt. Words would destroy the fantasy that he was hers—at least with her body she could pretend.

She had never taken the lead quite like this before, and there was a vague corner of her mind that wondered whether such a dominant man would allow her to. But her disquiet was only fleeting, for she could see from the look of rapture on his face that he was loving it.

She trickled her fingertips down over the tiny hard nipples, tracing butterfly circles around the sensitised flesh, and his hard, lean body writhed with pleasure.

'*Che cosa state facendo a me?*' he groaned softly.

Her hands moved to the hard, flat planes of his hips. 'In English, please!' she teased.

But he shook his head, the words forgotten and already redundant.

She undressed him as slowly as she could, until the tension between them was so fraught that it was almost unbearable. Her hands were shaking as she skated the silken camiknickers down over her hips, and then she climbed on top of him. Their eyes met in a silence broken only by their rapid breathing as she slowly lowered herself onto him, encasing him in her tight, exquisite heat.

And that was when it became too much. A little cry escaped from her lips, and suddenly she was trembling and out of control.

He was watching her, and he understood perfectly, pulling her face down to his to kiss her and tangling his hand in the satin hair before turning her onto her side and beginning to move inside her.

Ella gasped, and it was much more than the feeling of him filling her, deep and hard and true—it was the way that their gazes were locked, watching each other's reaction in a way that was almost scarily intimate.

She thrilled to see the pleasure that rippled up from his body to make his face relax in helpless rapture, and his delight fed hers until she could watch him no more. Until the waves that had been building and building rocked over her with a power that obliterated everything except the shuddering man within her arms.

He watched her orgasm, holding back his own, almost resenting it, because he didn't want this to stop. The urge to give in was unbearably strong now. *Signore dolce*, but he was having to battle with his body not to go under with each deep thrust. It was that feeling all over again. Like reaching the top of the mountain. Or falling from the stars.

He began to cry out then, his release bittersweet as he was caught up in spasms of pleasure so sharp that he felt he might die right at that moment. And then he let go, while the warm waves drifted over him, his eyes closing as he breathed in the soft, feminine fragrance of her.

For a while he held her tightly, but then suddenly and abruptly he rolled away and lay staring up at the ceiling, where the moon was making flickering silent movies in monochrome.

And Ella felt the sensation of loneliness creep in, where there had been only pleasure and fulfillment. He had done it again, she realised. Shut down. Shut her out. The closeness, the sense of complete unity— that was purely physical. Maybe he didn't realise he was doing it…

'Hey,' she whispered. 'Don't do that!'

She reached her hand out to him and ran her fingertip from shoulder to elbow. He turned his head to look at her, but he was not smiling.

'Don't do what?' he questioned coldly.

The tone of his voice should have warned her, but Ella was in such a state of helpless rapture that she chose not to heed it. She shrugged. How could he learn if she didn't teach him? 'You go all distant after we've made love. It can still be intimate, you know,' she added softly. 'Once it's over.'

Her flame-red hair looked like quietly gleaming fire in the light of the moon, but her eyes were in shadow and he knew that he could not continue to take from her—not when she gave so generously. For that had not been just mind-blowing sex—that had been making love. That was why it had felt so different. So wild. So free. So dangerous.

Nico knew what she was offering, and that if he continued to accept it without any return—or even with the unspoken promise of some return—then he would be nothing more than an emotional thief. However much it might hurt, he had to tell her. Though wasn't there a part of him that hoped that she might forgive him anything in the face of honesty?

His eyes were bleak as they searched her face. 'I don't love you, Gabriella,' he said quietly.

CHAPTER THIRTEEN

ELLA let Nico's words sink in, like a heavy rock disappearing without trace into the murky water, but her initial feeling was one of an almost euphoric relief. It was like going to the doctor and demanding to know the truth about a prognosis, because only then would you be able to tackle the problem head-on.

And cure it.

But the euphoria was almost immediately replaced by a feeling of real fear, and she wanted to say to him, *I know! I'm not stupid, Nico! I've known all along, and I would have been able to come to terms with it in my own time and in my own way if only you could have pretended.*

Just for one night.

One beautiful make-believe night.

Cure it?

How the hell was she going to do that? By playing dumb? By feigning ignorance? By saying in a cool, collected way, *What the hell are you talking about?*

No. He had had a lifetime of people telling him what they did not mean. Skating over the surface. Hours of conversation that was not real conversation, merely superficial small talk. If she was going to take anything away from her brief fling with him, it was going to be honesty.

And pride.

'I know that, Nico,' she said, and her voice was almost gentle. Funny, that. How softness should appear from nowhere, utterly concealing the shattering knowledge that this would be the last time. But it wasn't his fault. Not really. He was the man he was, not the one she wanted him to be.

He frowned, as if this was not the reaction he had been expecting. 'I'm twenty-eight,' he grated. 'And I don't want to settle down. With anyone. I don't *need* to settle down. And when I do it's going to be with someone—'

'Someone suitable,' she cut in wryly, seeing his narrow-eyed look of irritation. But hell, hadn't he interrupted *her* enough times in the past? 'I know that, too, Nico. Why the hell are you bothering to tell me all this?'

And why now? Couldn't he have waited until the morning and left her with the memory beautiful and intact? Not tarnished with the bitterness of truth.

She sat up, the turmoil of her thoughts almost making her forget that she was naked until she saw the smoky response of his eyes. He reached for her, as if conditioned to do so, but she shook him off. 'Don't,' she said steadily. 'Please don't touch me.'

There had never been a situation in his life that he could not charm his way out of, but he could see that she meant it. Stubborn, obstinate woman. He stifled a sigh. 'Come on, let's go and eat something.'

But Gabriella shook her head. How easy it would be to gloss over it. To go downstairs to his kitchen and let him seduce her with his cooking and conversation, to sip wine and become lulled, so that eventually the stark reality would fade into the background. And then they would kiss again and make love—only it would not be the same—how could it be? Because, despite the odds being stacked against them having any kind of future together, that hadn't prevented a stupid side of her hoping that maybe they could.

But his words had destroyed all hope, and without hope what was left?

Pride, she reminded herself. She still had that.

'No,' she said, shaking her head, trying to keep the sadness from her voice. 'There is no point. I want to go back to L'Etoile right now, and tomorrow morning I'm catching a flight back to England.'

He swore softly. 'Damn you, Gabriella,' he responded, and his words were equally quiet, but tinged with acid. 'I've been honest with you,' he said bitterly, wishing that he had said nothing until the morning. 'Why can't you just accept that?'

'Accept your terms without question, you mean?' she asked stiffly. 'Terms which don't give a stuff about my feelings? Sorry, Nico, but you can't have it all ways. You can't play the poor little misunderstood Prince who needs to keep his identity secret because of all the baggage that goes with his title and then turn round and arrogantly demand the unquestioning obedience which is part and parcel of that title!'

'How dare you say that to me?' he demanded.

'How dare I?' Her green eyes flashed fire at him. 'I'll tell you how I dare! Doesn't the fact that we've just made love give me any rights at all? Or do you treat all your women as though they are commodities? To be used until they begin to threaten you, or make demands on you which aren't part of your Royal game plan?'

'That is enough!' he rapped out.

'No, it is not enough!' she retorted. 'Maybe it's time someone started responding to you as a normal human being—but you can't take it when they do, can you? You profess to hate the restriction of Royal life, but you can't wait to hide behind it when it suits you!'

'Hide?' he echoed furiously. 'Me? *Hide?*'

Ella gave a cynical laugh as she realised she really *had* struck home. 'So I've offended your macho image, have I, Nico?' she questioned, and her eyes were sparking a challenge at him. 'Don't you know there's more to being a real man than jumping on motorbikes and endangering your life into the bargain?'

'Enough!' he snapped.

But she was driven on by a need so relentless that she could not have stopped even if she had wanted to.

'You say that you have a problem with Gianferro?

Well, I'm not surprised—he's worried sick about you! Just how long do you intend to carry on being "The Daredevil Prince", with your crazy stunts? Until you're an old man of fifty—tearing up the mountain roads on a motorbike? How sad it that?'

'I am not listening to another word of this!' he raged. 'I'll wait for you downstairs!'

'Yes—run away, why don't you? You'll probably spend the rest of your life running away from the truth!'

For a moment there was an incredulous silence. 'Running away?' he echoed.

'I think so. Subconsciously.' She stared at him, poised on this moment of revelation like a diver about to plunge into the water, and she dived in fearlessly. 'But you'll never be happy until you work out what it is you're running *from*.' She stared at him, waiting breathlessly for his response, like a condemned woman praying for leniency from the judge. But he simply gave a bitter and sarcastic laugh as he reached for his shirt.

'You'd better get dressed,' he said, barely flicking her a glance.

In a way it was the worst possible reaction. At least when he had been furious she had felt they were still connected in some way—as if a row was validation that there had been more between them than simply sex. But this new, barely feigned boredom was humiliating. As if he couldn't wait to be rid of her.

Had her words wounded him? She had spoken in

anger, yes—but she had felt justified in doing so. Her intention had been to enlighten and help him, not to hurt him.

Tentatively she reached towards the ruffled dark hair, but he moved away and slid his legs over the bed. He pulled on his jeans with a dismissive gesture that broke her heart into tiny pieces and she realised she had blown it for ever—detonated it with her harsh words.

No. He had blown it, too—by enforcing rigid rules that put paid to any growing closeness between them.

She reached for her crumpled camiknickers and shook them, seeing him watching her, the way the movement made her unfettered breasts swing freely. She saw his mouth tighten.

'Hurry up,' he snapped, and walked out and left her, his face an icy mask of haughty *froideur*.

With trembling hands she dressed in that moonlit room, her skin still flushed and rosy with the aftermath of their incredible lovemaking. And as she straightened up from fastening her sandals she caught a glimpse of herself in the Venetian mirror that hung over the ornate fireplace.

There she was, in her chainstore dress, her hair all mussed. The strange half-light cast by the moon only added to the surreal image in the mirror. She had no place here, nor ever would.

Slowly she began to descend the wide, curving staircase. Nico waited at the bottom, his dark, glittering eyes watching her as if she was some new species he had encountered and he was unsure of just what she was going to do next.

And she watched him, with eyes that were equally uncertain.

Wasn't there a part of her that regretted her words? A part of her that would now be responsive to having her mind changed? If Nico took her into his arms and kissed her and tried to cajole her into staying, would she honestly be able to resist him?

With an effort he tore his eyes away from the silken thrust of her thighs as she came down the stairs towards him.

'Let's go,' he said shortly, and gave an insulting glance at his watch. 'You might not be hungry, *cara*, but I am. I'll drop you off at the hotel and then I'm going out to dinner.'

Who with? she wondered. But the painful lurch of her heart was caused not by vague imagined jealousies, but by the realisation that already she was swiftly moving into Nico's past.

Soon she would be little more than a hazy memory.

CHAPTER FOURTEEN

THE trouble was that there was no one Ella could tell—not really—because even to herself it sounded completely unbelievable. What would her parents say—or Rachel, or her best friend Celia—if she suddenly blurted out the reason for her sudden mood swings and the tears in her eyes that swam up without warning?

Well, it's like this. I've fallen in love with a prince, but he doesn't love me. We've had an affair and now it's over, and I have to move on and get on with my normal life.

In the end she had to come up with some explanation, so she came up with one that said it all.

It's a man.

Then they all understood, and there was no need for any more explanation at all. No one particularly cared where he was or who he was—although Celia had a pretty good try—because the bottom line was that he was out of the picture and Ella was left nursing a broken heart.

And when she stopped to think about it that really was the fundamental issue. It didn't matter that Nico was a prince. If he had been a banker or a restaurant owner or a truck driver would her pain have been any less?

Of course not. Love hurt. It sliced through your heart with its particular and specific pain and you just had to wait for time to heal it. That boring prediction that everyone made. Time heals. On an intellectual level you knew it was true, but on an emotional one— well, you just couldn't imagine not living in this state of misery for the rest of your life.

Her departure from Mardivino had been hurried and inglorious. Oh, an elegant car had arrived to take her to the airport, but it had been driven by a chauffeur, not by Nico.

Her only contact with him after that night, when he had driven her home in a simmering silence, had been a terse and factual telephone call when he had informed her of flight times.

The only unexpected touch had come at the end of the conversation, when Nico had added, or perhaps *growled* might be a more accurate description of his tone, 'Gianferro thinks that your idea is an inspired one.'

And because she had been hanging onto her composure only by a thread, her response had come out as cool and sardonic. 'Please tell him that I am delighted to have been of service.'

So there you had it, thought Ella as she stared out of the window into her garden. Even the weather was reflecting her mood. It was one of those grey, depressing days when the clouds seemed so low they could touch your head, spilling out relentless sheets of rain.

It had been raining ever since she'd arrived home, and now the lawn was like a quagmire, with great boggy puddles splashed by the falling stair-rods.

Even by mid-morning the day did not seem to have lifted at all, and Ella had to light a lamp. She switched the radio on to find that a faded television personality was enjoying a renewed lease of fame by trekking to remote places all over the globe.

Maybe I should do something like that? Ella thought. Change of scenery.

She found that she missed Mardivino—but who wouldn't? She couldn't think of a single person who would not have ached for those clear blue skies and sapphire waters, and the green-clothed mountains and white-capped houses of the capital.

She fiddled with the radio, swapping the explorer for the more soothing sounds of classical music, and had just made herself a large pot of coffee when there was a ring at the doorbell. She sighed.

Please don't be Rachel, she thought. Or Celia. Or any other well-meaning friend who had decided that she needed 'taking out of herself'. For a second she thought about not answering it, but only for a second.

No.

The world wasn't going to go away, and nor should it.

When she pulled the door open, it was with a smile. Funny, that. Inside, your heart could be breaking into a thousand little pieces, but somehow you managed to disguise it with a bright smile.

But the smile froze into a burning slash on her lips, for it was not Rachel, or Celia, but Nico who stood there, with raindrops sparkling on his black hair, his face shadowed and his big, strong body so alive and virile.

He looked…

Ella swallowed.

He looked both man and prince. Despite the soaking flying jacket and the faded jeans, there was something indefinably regal about his proud and autocratic bearing.

Never had he looked more desirable, nor quite so unobtainable.

He stared down at her upturned face, pale and heart-shaped, with eyes like two enormous emeralds, and saw there the swift look of pain and regret. For a moment he almost turned away. Perhaps the feelings they aroused in each other were too intense—too incompatible with life itself—especially *his* life. Perhaps she had come to that conclusion herself. But he knew that he had to find out.

'*Ciao, bella,*' he said softly, and then, even more softly, 'Gabriella.'

He was the only person who had ever called her that. As if by using her true name he had awoken the true woman who had always lain beneath the surface. A woman who could love and live and feel and hurt—

a woman with the same passions as him, only he sub-limated those passions using damned *machines*!

Ella stared at him, wanting to pinch herself, trying to get used to the fact that he was not a figment of her imagination but standing here, on her doorstep.

She thought that he looked different. Harder, and leaner. Edgy. His jaw was dark-shadowed—taunting her with its potent symbol of virility. Seeing him again made the grey day suddenly seem bright, and Ella felt her heart melt. Oh, God—would she ever be able to look at him without curling up inside for love of him?

'Nico!' she exclaimed. 'What are you doing here?'

'Getting wet,' he said wryly.

'Oh, God—you'd better come in!'

His lips were curved in a rueful smile. When in his life had he ever been left standing in the pouring rain on someone's doorstep?

'Give me your jacket,' she said hurriedly, because it was easier to compose herself when she was doing something, and he *was* very wet. But her hands were shaking as she hung the dripping jacket up. *Compose herself?* Who did she think she was kidding?

She ran her eyes over his face, not daring to nurture the tiny flicker of hope she felt. Just because he was here, it didn't mean anything. 'Why are you here?' she whispered.

His very presence here was a statement that nor-mally would have been enough. But it was not enough. She had accused him of many things, but the one that had struck home had been *running away*. And using circumstances and privilege and things— yes, things—as a substitute for reality. Stark reality. Which was sometimes painful but which you could not hide from for ever if you wanted to live in any degree of peace.

But Nico was a man who had never explained his feelings before—never had to—and, as with learning all new skills, he found himself in the long-forgotten position of being a novice.

'I've got rid of my bike,' he said.

Ella blinked as her foolish little fantasies crumbled into dust. Whatever she might have been secretly hoping for, it had not been to talk about his damned motorbike! Her face was expressionless. 'Have you?' she questioned woodenly.

He realised that this was not what she wanted to hear. Like a child learning to swim, he attempted a second, tentative stroke. 'I don't want to be a "sad old man of fifty careering around the hills."'

He was throwing her words back at her. Ella bit her lip. 'I shouldn't have said that—'

'On the contrary, *cara mia*—you said exactly the right thing.'

'I did?'

He heard the disbelief in her voice and knew it was justified. 'How else could I learn?' he questioned simply, and he smiled as he saw her lips part in sheer astonishment. 'I didn't want to hear it at the time, but then no one had ever spoken quite like that to me before. I don't want those thrills and spills any more. They mean nothing. They count for nothing because they are not real.' Now his black gaze was very steady. 'But you thrill me, Ella, and you are real. Very real.'

She could scarcely breathe, but she knew that she wanted more than she suspected he was offering. And more than that she needed him to say it again, as if only repetition could convince her that he meant it, that it wasn't just a whim because the physical thing between them was such dynamite.

'You'll get good sex with another woman, Nico, you know you will.'

His face darkened. Stubborn, obtuse woman! 'I'm not talking about sex!'

'You're not?'

In the background he could hear the rippling notes of a piano being played, and the music drifted the most poignant sensation of contentment over his skin. 'No.'

'Then...what are you talking about?'

Nico scowled. 'I don't know. It feels like love.' This was an unimaginable admission, but it was not quite the truth. Hadn't she peeled back all the layers of his life, forcing him to look deep into the true and sometimes painful core of it? Did he now dare? For a man who had spent his life taking risks, there had never been one that seemed quite as daunting as this one. He shrugged his shoulders like a little boy. 'It is love,' he admitted. 'I am in love with you. I love you, Gabriella.'

'Oh, God,' she breathed. 'Oh, Nico.'

Her eyes were dazzling him—blinding him with a fervent emerald gaze that was more vivid than the shades found in any ocean. And in them he saw what she felt for him, a wordless declaration of how much he meant to her.

But was it enough? Would she be prepared to relinquish her freedom for a Royal life, aspects of which she professed to despise?

'Do you think we can have a future together?' he questioned softly.

Ella shook her head. 'I can't think beyond the next second,' she declared, her voice breaking. 'And if you don't come here and hold me then I think I might just die.'

Taking her in his arms was the easiest thing he had ever had to do, and to feel her arms wrapping tightly around his neck as though she was never going to let him go felt like coming home. Nico closed his eyes against the scented silk of her hair.

It defied all logic and sense, this feeling—more precious and more rare than any of the priceless jewels contained in his family's palaces. And he had only ever experienced it with her. Only her. In her arms. Like this. For this feeling men relinquished kingdoms, and he could understand exactly why.

'Shh,' he soothed as he felt her begin to tremble against him. 'I know. Believe me, *cara mia*, I know.'

He tipped her chin up and their eyes sizzled frantic seeking messages, questions answered without a single word being spoken. And then his mouth moved to blot out all the pain and the heartache, touching down on her lips with a tenderness she had never thought he would show, and she cupped his face in her hands and tenderly kissed him back.

And when eventually they drew back from it their eyes were dazed.

'*Cielo dolce*,' murmured Nico, shaken by the power and beauty of the embrace, for he had never known that a kiss could be anything other than foreplay. How little he knew! How much to learn. He stroked her face, like a blind man seeking to see by touch alone.

Ella stared up at him. Could this really be happening? And even if it was, what happened now? When two people were in love, of course they talked about a future—but this was not as it was for other people. How could it be? She pressed her finger to his cheek, which was still cool and faintly damp. 'We can't talk here. You're frozen—come and let's sit by the fire.'

The sweet, sane normality of her words made him smile. 'You've lit a fire? But it's only September.'

'And freezing! Come through. I'm going to pour us a brandy.'

He held his hands out to the blaze and sank down. It pleased her to see him sprawling on her rug, his long legs stretched out in front of him. She sploshed a measure of brandy into two glasses and went and sat down beside him. Only when they had sipped and put the drinks down in the hearth did she turn to him.

'So what has changed you from the icy man who stormed away to this…' She traced his lips with her finger, as if to confirm that he was real and not some dream that would evaporate in a second.

He opened his mouth and trapped the finger, sucking on it until it was quite wet. Seeing her eyes darken, he took it out again and absently wrapped it in a fold of his cashmere sweater, and left it there.

'You did. You changed me,' he said softly. 'You forced me to look at things I did not wish to. You made me see that, yes, I *was* running away—all the time—running from feelings, because feelings can hurt.' He shrugged. 'But, more than that, you made me see my life for what it was, and without you it is empty. I want to be with you, Gabriella.'

She forced herself to be practical, because if she started slipping into her greatest wish and then circumstances snatched it away again… 'But Gianferro will never allow it!'

'Because?'

'Because I'm a commoner and you're a prince! He will never approve of me!'

'He certainly *does* approve of you,' he contradicted drily. 'He was storming round the throne room yesterday morning, asking what it was that you had which could make me see sense, when he had been trying to drum it into me for years!'

'Approval is one thing,' she said slowly, 'but us

having a life together is quite something else. And how can we? I live here and you live in Mardivino. You can't live here, for practical reasons, and if I came out to join you in Mardivino then we'd have to conduct our affair in secret.'

'Not if we were married.'

Ella stared at him. 'I'm sorry?'

'Sudden onset of defective hearing, Gabriella?' he teased.

'Did you just mention marriage?'

'I did.'

'You want to marry me?'

'Of course I do! Don't you want to marry me?' He shot her a look of affectionate reprimand. 'Though you still have not told me you love me!'

'Of…' She drew a deep breath. 'Oh, my God—of course I love you, my darling, darling Nico—you know that I do.'

'*Si,*' he agreed, with arrogant contentment. 'I do.'

'But we can't get *married*!'

'Why not?'

'It's too soon!'

He shook his dark head and placed his hand on his heart in the most romantic gesture that Ella could ever have imagined. 'No, it isn't,' he contradicted softly. 'In fact, in this we are following tradition, for Royal courtships are never long drawn out.'

'But won't you need Gianferro's permission?'

'I would marry you without it, *cara mia*.' His eyes

glittered. 'But my resistance is academic, since he has already given it.'

Ella blinked. 'S-seriously?'

He nodded. *'Oui, c'est vrai.'*

She narrowed her eyes suspiciously. 'You told me that *Italian* was the language of love!'

He smiled. 'And so it is,' he agreed softly. 'But French is the language of the law—and marriage is both—a combination of love and obligation.' There was a pause, a silence broken only by the loud drumming of a heart. Was that his, or hers? 'Will you marry me, Gabriella?'

She didn't blurt her answer out. She gave it the consideration that she knew she must, for a Royal marriage *was* different. She loved him, yes, but obligation and duty were paramount if they were to be happy together, and she must only accept his offer if she could be certain that she would make him a good wife.

'Oh, yes, Nico,' she said softly, fervently. 'I would be proud and honoured to be your wife.'

EPILOGUE

EVERYONE loved a Royal wedding, and Mardivino was no exception. The world's press went crazy about the story of the youngest of the three darkly handsome princes falling in love with an 'ordinary' girl from England.

It was all a bit overwhelming.

In the end, Ella decided to confound all the pundits who were wildly predicting which of the world's most exclusive designers would be lucky enough to create her wedding gown. She opted instead for a beautifully simple dress of finest white lawn, lovingly crafted by her mother's dressmaker. In her arms she carried a bouquet of that most English of flowers—pure white roses.

'Understated is the new black!' screamed the pundits.

But for Ella it did not matter that they were marrying in Solajoya's exquisite medieval cathedral, with world leaders and Royalty among the congregation. She was marrying the man she loved, who loved her, and that was the only thing that counted.

When she looked into his eyes at the altar everything else retreated, for all she could see was Nico, and only Nico—her love and her life.

Nico had given her a free hand to refurnish his house outside the city, but they had also been given a suite of rooms in the palace itself. It could all have been a bit daunting, but Ella's love outshone everything else, and she took on her new role with both zeal and pleasure.

They would work together, too.

Although they would not live together until after the marriage, Nico had introduced her to all areas of his life, and she had discovered just how many different schemes he was involved with. Little wonder he hadn't had time to visit every single village on the island—but part of his new regeneration programme was to explore the under-funded towns, with Ella by his side.

He had ordered the relocation of Solajoya's main museum, and he wanted her to help plan a worldwide tour of Juan Lopez's work—to bring the 'artist's artist' to a much wider arena.

The new gallery was to be opened in the village by the new Princess before a wildly enthusiastic local population, grateful that a share of the island's tourism was now putting them firmly on the map. Architects and town planners had been flown in to oversee the gentle expansion, which was designed to blend into the scenery, not bleed it of all its natural simplicity.

Gianferro had asked for an audience with her soon after their engagement had been announced and she had flown out to the island to prepare for the wedding.

Her stomach had been churning as she had walked along the gilded corridor towards his suite of offices. He had given them his approval, yes, but what if secretly he had doubts about her ability to make a good wife and princess?

But Ella needn't have had any fears. His hard face had softened on seeing the look of anxiety in hers, and he had patted a space on the brocade sofa beside him.

'Come, Gabriella,' he had murmured. 'And tell me what magic you have worked on Nico.'

'No magic,' she had responded shyly. 'Just love.'

The black eyes, so like his brother's, had gleamed. 'I had intended to ask whether you really do love him,' he said. 'But I can see now that the question is superfluous—for it shines like the sun at noon from your eyes.'

'Ooh, Gianferro is *my* kind of man,' Celia had whispered adoringly on the morning of the ceremony, as she'd tugged at the pale pink lawn of her bridesmaid dress. 'Any chance you could do a bit of matchmaking?'

But Ella had shaken her head. 'I don't think so. He's a loner,' she'd said. Gianferro would soon be King, for their father's health was ailing fast—and to be King was a lonely destiny. Princes abounded, but Kings were few. Nico had been able to dispense with a certain amount of expectation by marrying her, a commoner, simply because he was the youngest son—with a lessened burden of responsibility riding on his shoulders.

But Gianferro's destiny was mapped out. When he took a bride she would *have* to be suitable. And when Ella looked at his sensual yet restless face, she wondered just how he would cope with the reality of having to marry a virgin bride.

Prince Guido had flown in at the very last moment, and Ella had witnessed an extraordinary phenomenon, as every female in his vicinity had taken on a look of longing that bordered on the incandescent. He was a remarkably good-looking man, she acknowledged, but his black eyes were bored, almost jaded.

'So you have beaten me to the altar, Nico,' he had drawled at the pre-nuptial ball.

'No surprise there!' his brother had responded drily. 'You have a wish to be married, Guido?' he'd added curiously.

'No wish at all,' had come the mocking response. 'I'm happy as I am.'

'Are you?' Ella had asked suddenly, and both brothers had turned to her. Nico had not mirrored Guido's surprise—but then he was growing used to her candid way of saying what she really thought!

Guido's eyes had narrowed. 'Of course,' he'd said lightly. 'I enjoy my life of self-imposed exile, for there is none of the expectation which surrounds me here. No damned matrons clucking and introducing me to their darling daughters.' And he'd given a rather bitter laugh as one of the said matrons had begun bearing down on him, her diamonds almost blinding them, a look of grim determination on her face. 'Forgive me,' he'd murmured. 'But it's time I wasn't here.'

'I'm afraid that Guido is a bit of a cynic where women are concerned,' Nico had confided to her later. Their guests had gone and they were standing side by side on the terrace, gazing up at the stars and a crescent moon.

She had turned to him with an expression of mock surprise. 'Never!'

Nico had laughed.

They did a lot of laughing. They held each other tight at night and thanked God they had found one another.

Ella had left an old life behind, but so had Nico, and the one they had found together was better than their wildest dreams.

THE PRINCE'S
LOVE-CHILD

by

Sharon Kendrick

With thanks for such wonderful help to:
Neale Hunt – Advertising Maestro.
Paul McLaughlin –
Editor of Kroll Inc's Report on Fraud.
The Prince of Spin – Olly Wicken.
And to Guy Black, who is a never-ending
source of inspiration!

CHAPTER ONE

Guido glanced at his watch and a flicker of displeasure briefly spoiled the sensual perfection of his lips.

She was late!

But his irritation gave way to a soft smile as he anticipated the heady delights to come. Lucy could not be blamed for the lateness of her plane—indeed, she did not even know he was going to be there.

Guido found himself wondering what her reaction would be when she discovered that he was, for she was that rare species among women—someone who constantly surprised him.

His eyes flickered to the arrivals board. The plane had landed and soon the flight attendants would be making their way through to the lounge…

Guido was aware of being watched, and his brilliant eyes widened slightly as he saw a woman looking as if she would like to leap on him and devour him. Predictability was so tedious, he decided, turning his head to see the faintest flash of red-brown as a woman with glorious Titian hair sashayed towards the gate. Most of it was hidden beneath a chic little hat, worn at a jaunty angle, but the colour was enough to mark her out, as was the unconscious grace with which she moved.

She was dressed in a sleek navy uniform, her long
legs encased in pale silk that he knew would be stockings, not pantyhose. Was it stockings which made a
woman walk differently? Guido wondered. Did the
feel of cool air on her thighs make her aware of her
sexuality? Or was that just something inherent in
Lucy's nature?

No. She was a contrast—a maddening and exciting
contrast of looks and attitude. Her hair was lit with
fire, but her expression was cool, and she seemed
oblivious to the men who stood to let her pass and
then just carried on standing there, following the sexy
sway of her hips with hungry eyes.

He felt the leaping of desire tensing his body but
he didn't move. She couldn't yet see him, and he
wanted to watch her reaction when she did…

Ahead of her, Lucy could see the jostle of crowds,
and the air-conditioning was as cool as ice-water on
her skin as she walked through the busy airport. This
city held all kinds of associations for her—some
good, and some just dangerously good. Hello, New
York, she thought.

'Are you coming straight back to the hotel?' Kitty
asked.

Lucy turned. Her fellow stewardess was applying
a coat of lipstick without the use of a mirror, and
Lucy made a silent gesture to indicate that she had
smudged it. 'Yes. Why wouldn't I be?'

'Well, I wasn't sure…' Kitty gave a mischievous

grin as she wiped away the errant trace of pink gloss. 'Whether or not you'd be seeing your *Prince*.'

This emphasis on the word was commonplace, and Lucy had grown used to the teasing by now, even though at first she hadn't quite known how to react. It had been a peculiar situation—not just for the rest of the cabin crew, but for her, too. Ordinary girls didn't date princes! And yet it seemed that they did. In fact, they—

But her thoughts were frozen and her steps very nearly followed. Some governing sense of instinct kept her moving forward, forward…because for a minute there she had almost thought she'd seen Guido.

'Isn't that him?' asked Kitty curiously, following the direction of Lucy's stare.

Thank God they were far enough away for him not to be able to see that her face had grown pale. Or at least Lucy was imagining that it *had* grown pale—for surely there would have to be some physical manifestation of the dizzy sensation she was experiencing. As if all the blood had left her veins, leaving her limbs dry and ready to crumple. Keep walking, she told herself. Just keep walking.

'It *is*!' breathed Kitty. 'Oh, my God—it's *him*! He's come to meet you! How romantic is *that*?'

Lucy let her brows slide up beneath the russet curtain of her fringe. 'I don't hear you sounding so surprised when other people's boyfriends come to meet them,' she observed drily.

'That's because other people don't go out with princes,' chided Kitty.

Lucy shook her head. 'He's just a man,' she contradicted faintly, but she knew that her words lacked conviction.

Because he wasn't.

She let her gaze drift over him as she walked towards the brilliant black eyes which had her spotlighted in their sight. Prince or no prince, he was the kind of man most women didn't happen across—not even once in a lifetime.

There was something about the way he carried himself which drew the eye, something about an air of arrogant assurance coupled with a lazy kind of supremacy. Had royal blood and upbringing given him those qualities which seemed to make him stand head and shoulders above the crowd, or would he have had them anyway?

He was standing beside a pillar, half in the shadows, for she knew that he would have sought shelter from prying eyes. Guido had rejected princely life, but its legacy meant that he could never quite shake it off. People were fascinated by the title, but more usually they were fascinated by him—and who could blame them?

Over and over again Lucy had watched as they fawned over him and hung on his every word—men *and* women, but especially women. They drank in the dark, imposing looks, and the sexy, accented drawl, and the careless sensuality which came as naturally to him as breathing.

He was a man in a million—and Lucy still wasn't quite sure what he saw in her. Sometimes she felt as though she was living in a bubble, and that one of these days it was going to burst and she would be left with the dull and rather stark reality of life without Guido.

Don't make it into more than it is, she reminded herself savagely. A casual love affair—nothing more and nothing less. And if, by nature of who he is, he provides a fairytale aspect to the affair—then just enjoy it and don't build it up.

Her half-smile staying in place as though it had been painted on, she waved a quick goodbye to Kitty and walked over to where he waited, a dark and brooding image in cool, expensive linen. The ecstatic clamour of her heart was deafening her, but she gave him a look as steady as any she would give to one of her passengers in First Class who was asking for a glass of champagne.

'Hello, Guido,' she said, in a low, clear voice. 'I wasn't expecting to see you here.'

He might have felt admiration if he hadn't been overwhelmed by frustration. Did nothing affect her bar sex itself? For it was then—and only then—that she let go completely. Looking at the serene smile which seemed to make a mockery of her schoolgirl freckles, he found it hard to imagine her whispering his name, or screaming it, or shuddering with helpless, racking moans against his shoulder.

Guido felt the quickening of his heart, knowing that

his instincts were fighting a battle with his reason. Had it not been her ice-coolness which had set her apart and made him determined to possess her? Had he somehow imagined that he would melt it away completely, leaving her in his thrall—like all the others—so that he could happily walk away?

'Perhaps I would not have bothered if I had known you would give me such a lukewarm welcome,' he parried silkily.

She saw the glitter from his black eyes—recognising now, as she had recognised from the very start, that here was a man who was used to lavish displays of affection and would be bored by them. So she had not given them. From an early age Lucy had learnt to do what people wanted—some might call it people-pleasing; she would define it as making sure she got on with folks.

'So, what would you like me to do?' she murmured. 'Fling my arms around your neck and scream with delight?'

'You can save that for later. In bed,' he returned mockingly, and was rewarded with a faint flush of colour which crept over her pale, freckle-splattered skin.

A blush might be beyond her control, but the flashing light of challenge which sparked from her eyes was not. She lifted her chin and mocked him back. 'Maybe I'm tired and need my sleep.'

'And maybe you don't.' He lifted his hand to her face and slowly drifted a fingertip down over her flushed face, finishing with a deliberately erotic tracing of her lips, which made them tremble slightly and open. He wanted to bend his head to kiss them, but of course he didn't.

He could just imagine the headlines. An erotic and public kiss in newspaper-speak meant only one thing—impending wedding bells.

But if he was cool, then Lucy was cooler still— and his eyes glittered as their gazes mingled.

'Give me your bag,' he said steadily. 'I have the car waiting.'

She had played her part. The necessary part. Not thrown herself into his arms. Hardly even a shiver of pleasure when he had touched her—but enough was enough and Lucy wanted him. Badly. She let him take her small case and allowed herself the luxury of a smile.

'Lovely. Are you driving?'

Lovely? Suddenly he was filled with the need to shatter her icy composure. 'No,' he said softly, as they made their way through the hall, oblivious to the curious glances they attracted. 'I have a chauffeur hidden behind dark glass, so he will be unable to see when I begin to kiss you. The glass is soundproof, too—so that when your breathing begins to quicken as I put my hand up your skirt he will not hear it.'

Her mouth had dried unbearably. 'Oh, Guido, don't,' she whispered.

He felt the exquisite hardness and knew that he must stop this. But not quite yet.

'Nor will he notice when I slide your panties down and pull you onto my lap...'

'Guido—'

'*Hard* down onto my lap.'

'G-Guido—'

He moved his lips to her ear, speaking in a silken whisper as he inhaled her fragrance. 'And I will move you up and down, up and down—filling you completely, until you gasp—'

'Guido!' She was gasping now, her head light, her pulse-rate frantic.

He saw the way her steps had begun to falter, and he caught her by the arm just as a black limousine purred to a halt beside them. In French, he bit out some terse instructions to the driver, and then he propelled her onto the back seat, sliding in beside her and slamming the door shut behind them, imprisoning them in a luxurious, dimly-lit world of their own as he imprisoned her in the warm circle of his arms.

She was so hot with wanting that she could barely speak his name as he pushed her down onto the seat and her hat fell from her head. 'Guido—'

But there was no reply other than the sweet pressure of his mouth as he began to kiss her, transporting her to that place where nothing mattered other than the feel and taste and smell and touch of him. She threaded her fingers luxuriously in the rich ebony satin of his hair and moved her body restlessly against his. And froze in excited horror as she felt his hand on her knee and remembered his words.

Surely he didn't mean to—?

But he was moving his hand, and she was writhing

in response to the direction it was taking, her hips belying the words which she forced herself to say.

'No, we can't,' she protested, her voice slurred with wanting. 'We mustn't. Not here.'

'Why not? The thought of it turned you on. You know it did.' He touched her above the stocking-top, where the bare flesh was a tantalising contrast of cool silk with warm blood pulsing beneath. 'I could read it in your eyes.'

'It may... Oh, God...' Her eyes closed and her head fell back against the soft leather upholstery as his fingertips skated tantalisingly close to where heat seared at her so frustratingly. 'It...it may have turned me on. It doesn't mean it's right.'

The hand stilled. 'Shall I stop, then, *cara mia*?'

Frustration ripped through her. She shook her head helplessly.

He put his lips right up to her ear. He loved her like this. Compliant. His. Her coolness exploding into hot and urgent need. 'I can't hear you, Lucy.'

'No,' she whispered. 'Don't stop. Please don't stop.'

Triumph coursed through him and possessively he pushed aside the panel of her panties to feel the acutely sensitised flesh. But it was over almost before he had started. He could feel her body begin to tense as he pressed his fingertip against her, and she caught him by the neck and dragged his mouth back down on hers, just as her legs splayed and she made soft, moaning noises of pleasure, like a cat.

They stayed like that for a while, their mouths

glued together, his finger still touching her intimately while she continued to spasm against him. When it was over, she drew away, her face sweat-sheened, still shuddering as she shook her head.

'What did you do that for?' She gulped breath into her lungs like a drowning woman.

He smiled as he tugged her uniform skirt back down. 'Because you wanted me to.'

'We should have waited.'

'But you didn't want to.'

No, she hadn't. It had been a long time—too long—and she had missed him. Had he missed her? she wondered. Even a tiny bit? She turned her eyes up to his, but as usual their glittering ebony depths were impenetrable. She wanted to kiss him again, but kissing seemed almost too intimate. How crazy was that after what had just happened?

'And what about you?' she questioned huskily, cupping him quite suddenly. She saw him briefly close his eyes and groan, before snatching her hand away to hold it close to his mouth, letting his breathing grow steady before he spoke.

She could feel his warm breath on her fingertips.

'But I can…wait, *cara*,' he said huskily. 'That is the difference between us.'

He was always so controlled—always—and in demonstrating his own self-discipline he had drawn attention to her own lack of it! But Lucy knew that there was more than his steely resolve at stake here. Physically, she might be able to change his mind, but mentally she didn't stand a chance.

He might have shrugged off all the trappings which came with being a prince, but he never ignored the responsibility which came with the title. His mind would have raced and overtaken the demands of his body. He would have imagined all the worst-case scenarios—them being disturbed by the driver, or police, or photographers, and one of the Princes of Mardivino being discovered with an air-hostess bent busily over his lap.

Lucy flushed and moved away, suddenly feeling cheap as she imagined how it would look to an outsider. *Woman gets off plane and lets man ravish her in car.* A man, moreover, who had never made any promises of commitment to her and never would. Was she valuing herself too low—and, if so, for just how long was she going to let it continue?

'Cara?'

His voice was soft, and in anyone else you might almost be fooled into thinking that it was tender—but tenderness was an alien concept to Guido.

He saw the way that her eyes clouded and some stubborn inner resistance suddenly melted away. He leaned forward so that their foreheads were touching and began to stroke her hair.

'Forgive me, Lucy,' he said softly.

Lucy closed her eyes. For what? For taking her to heaven in an indecently short space of time? Or for drumming home the fact that where sex was concerned he was very definitely the master and she the puppet?

She opened her eyes again. 'You make me feel helpless,' she admitted.

He shrugged. 'Sometimes a woman should be help-less.'

'But not a man?' she questioned provocatively.

'Of course not.' His eyes sparked back in answering challenge. 'It is why we were born the stronger sex—did you not know that? We're conditioned to fight wars and to hunt—not to roll over on our backs like tame little pussycats.'

'Like I've just done, you mean?'

He brushed his lips against hers. 'Mmm. You were quite perfect. I like to see you like that.'

'Oh, you're just a power-freak,' she said, half crossly.

A smile curved his mouth. 'But you like that, too.'

'Sometimes.' Not always. Sometimes she would give a hundred erotic highs just to see him show even the briefest flicker of vulnerability—but that would be like wishing for the sky to suddenly start raining diamonds instead of hailstones. 'Sometimes I wish you'd just relax a bit more.'

'I'll relax later,' he promised silkily, and pulled her into the cradle of his arms. 'I promise you.'

'I don't just mean in bed,' said Lucy primly. 'It may be an alien concept to you, Guido, but you are allowed to let your hair down at other times.'

'Shh. Enough. That is enough, *cara*.'

Lucy rested her head against his shoulder and lapsed into a silence that was just the wrong side of contentment as she registered his unspoken reprimand. Was she nagging him? She stared out of the window just as the expensive car purred its way up Park Avenue and came to a halt in front of a rather beautiful old building.

She turned back to find his eyes watching her intently. 'Why are we stopping here?'

'Because we've arrived.'

Behind the Titian swing of her fringe, Lucy knitted her eyebrows together. 'This doesn't look like a hotel!'

'That's because it isn't.' He smiled, as if nothing was at stake. But something was, and they both knew it. 'I thought you might like to see my apartment.'

CHAPTER TWO

LUCY could read nothing in the ebony glitter of Guido's eyes, and somehow she kept her own expression casual—even though, deep down, she felt slightly shell-shocked. Guido wanted to take her home! Well, to *one* of his homes, that would be more accurate. At last. Now, why would that be?

'Your apartment?' she questioned slowly.

Not the kind of rapturous excitement he might have expected—which just went to show that in life you should expect nothing. 'Wouldn't you like to see it?'

She smiled at him. 'Of course I would.'

Up until now they'd always stayed in hotels—a city-central room was one of the perks of her flying job and, as a fabulously successful property developer, Guido rented luxury suites all over the world. In New York and in Paris he did actually own an apartment, but Lucy had seen neither.

To be allowed to set foot inside her boyfriend's home shouldn't have felt like a major achievement, but somehow it did. Was that what happened when you went out with a man like Guido? she wondered. You began to normalise abnormal behaviour?

He bent to retrieve her hat from the floor of the limousine. 'Want me to put it on for you?'

She felt her cheeks growing pink as she shook her

head. 'I hate that hat,' she said, more fervently than her opinion on a hat really warranted, but she could read the expression in his eyes perfectly well. He was remembering how she had come to lose the hat, and what had happened subsequently, and despite her reservations already she could feel the renewed rush of desire.

'It looks *très chic* on you,' he whispered. And then, because he wanted her very badly, he took her hand and kissed it. 'Come. Let us go inside. The driver will bring your bags.'

'Are you quite sure about this?' she murmured, as they rode up in the elevator towards the penthouse.

Actually, Guido had suffered a couple of reservations—until he'd told himself that he was in danger of becoming some fabled recluse. And he knew instinctively that he could trust Lucy not to gossip about his home.

Idly, he stroked his finger along the indentation of her waist. 'I want someone to sample my cooking.'

This time Lucy couldn't hide her surprise as she tried and failed spectacularly to imagine him in the kitchen. 'You mean you *cook*?'

'Actually, no, I don't.' His black eyes gleamed. 'Do you?'

Lucy nodded solemnly. 'Oh, yes. I adore cooking. In fact, I adore waiting on men in general. So I do hope you'll let me run round after you just as soon as we get there. You will, won't you, Guido?'

It took about three seconds for him to register the sarcastic note in her voice, and he pulled her into his arms. 'You are a wicked witch of a woman, Lucy Maguire,' he growled, and began to trail his lips over her cheek.

She closed her eyes, the raw and lemony feral scent of him invading her senses like a potent drug. The teasing comment pleased her, for in his voice she had heard the faintest note of puzzlement.

He couldn't work her out; she knew that—and she had actively encouraged it—but it was much more than a game to her. He closed himself off from her, so why should it fall on her shoulders to provide a one-way emotional show?

At the moment she had an air of mystery which he found alluring. If she allowed him to twitch that curtain of mystery aside, to let daylight come flooding in, then who knew what would happen?

She turned her head so that her lips brushed warm and soft and provocatively against his, and his eyes widened, surprising her with their hectic glitter.

'I want you,' he ground out.

'I should hope so, too,' she answered demurely.

'I want you so badly I could do it—'

'Here?' she pre-empted, brazenly cupping him once more. Only this time he didn't push her away. This time he groaned. She continued to trickle her fingers against his rock-hard shaft, pressing her lips close to his ear, as he had done to her at the airport. 'Do you want me to unzip you, Guido?' she questioned softly. 'To free you and then to slowly take you into my mouth? To lick my tongue up and down until you can hold back no longer and—'

He gave a roar like an angry lion as the lift pinged to a halt, buckling back the doors as if they were the enemy and unlocking his apartment, thanking God that he had had the foresight to dismiss all his staff for the rest of the day.

He slammed the door shut behind them, and Lucy—for all her carefully suppressed curiosity—didn't get a chance to notice any princely artefacts, for Guido was taking her by the hand in a way which broached no argument. But there again, who wanted to argue? Certainly not her.

He stopped short of actually kicking the bedroom door open, but his punch to it was so forceful that he might as well have done. Only when it was shut behind them did they stand facing one another, like two protagonists squaring up for a fight.

His breathing was laboured, and Lucy's heart was beating so rapidly that she felt faint. She was blind to the beauty of the New York skyline captured outside the enormous window—blind to anything other than the beauty of his face. She drank in the stark hunger which momentarily made his features look almost cruel, and the knowledge that she had him on a knife-edge of desire filled her with a sense of daring.

He had awoken in her a sense of passion and experimentation which not one of her other—laughably few—lovers had come even close to.

Or was it, mocked a small voice in her head, simply because he was such an accomplished and experienced lover that she felt she had to keep pushing back the boundaries in order to match him?

She put her hands on her hips and surveyed him from between slitted eyelids, her provocative pose at odds with the starchy, almost prim appearance of her navy blue uniform.

'Would you like me to strip for you…sir?' she questioned, in a tone of husky subservience.

Guido groaned. Could he bear to wait? And yet could he bear not to? For a man whose hunger had become jaded over years of having exactly what he wanted, this new and acutely keen appetite was something he wanted to savour.

For did not the sensation of hunger make you feel more alive than when you satisfied it? Had the blood ever sung in his veins quite as much as it was doing at the moment? Or the hard ache in his groin threatened to make him fall to the ground in front of her in complete surrender?

He nodded, not trusting himself to speak for a moment as he walked towards the giant bed and lay back against the pillows.

'Yes, strip,' he ordered curtly. 'Strip for me now.'

Lucy let out a sigh as her thumb and finger rubbed at the lapel of her jacket, caressing the material as sensuously as if it was skin. In a way, it was almost a relief to be able to play this game—for the game detracted from reality, and the reality was that Lucy suspected she was falling in love. Dangerous. Oh, so dangerous.

At least while she was acting the sultry siren she was able to stop herself from running over to him and cupping his hard, handsome face between her hands with a sense of wonder, then smothering it with tiny heartfelt kisses, telling him over and over that he made her heart sing and her senses come to vibrant and stinging life.

But that was not what he wanted from her. A man didn't have to spell it out for you that he was happy with just a casual affair, and Lucy was perceptive enough to have worked it out for herself in any case. And because she wanted to stay in the game she followed the rules that he had set. Did that make her weak? Or simply responsive?

Guido saw her hesitation and groaned, fighting back the urge to have her join him on the bed.

'Strip.' His voice rang out, the word a single, clipped command.

His voice was hard, she thought, but his eyes were as she had never seen them before—on fire with need and desire, and she had to steel herself against that look, to stop herself from melting. She slipped the jacket from her shoulders and hung it neatly over the back of a chair.

'Oh, Lucy,' he murmured.

She surveyed him steadily. 'Am I going too slowly for you, Guido?'

He heard the challenge in her voice. Say yes and she would take even longer! He shook his head, not daring—not able—to speak.

She began to undo the buttons of her crisp white shirt and saw him run his tongue over his lips as the garment joined her jacket. Slowly she unzipped the slim navy skirt and let it fall to the ground, so that it pooled by her feet. She stepped out of it. She heard his sharp inrush of breath as she stood before him, wearing just her bra and panties, stockings, suspender-belt and high navy shoes.

She undid the lace brassière and as it fell to the floor she began to touch her breasts, capturing his eyes with hers.

'Come here,' he whispered.

She shook her head. 'Not yet. Take your shirt off.'

His throat was dry as he peeled off the layer of ice-blue silk and threw it at her feet.

'Now your trousers,' she instructed softly. 'Take them off.'

His heart was crashing against his ribcage. 'Why don't *you* do it?' he murmured.

'Because I want you to.'

'Oh, do you?' he drawled.

He was aware that she was treating him as no woman had ever treated him before—and, rather more disturbingly, that he was *allowing her to*. But the sexual tension which was escalating second by frantic second was just too good and too powerful to resist.

In his highly aroused state he carefully slid off his trousers and briefs, watching with a certain mocking triumph as her eyes widened, her lips forming a pouting and moist little circle when she saw just how turned on he was.

'Oh, Guido,' she whispered, on a thready note of wonder.

Her fingertips moved from where they had been circling over her nipple to press between the juncture of her legs and her head fell back. She closed her eyes, and for a moment Guido wondered if she was just going to pleasure herself in front of him. And—in spite of his aching desire for her—wouldn't that be unbearably erotic to watch?

Driven on by an overwhelming need, he stroked his hand over himself as greedily as a schoolboy, and looked up to find her staring at him. Their eyes met in a moment of complete and silent understanding.

'Okay, Lucy,' he said unsteadily. 'You've played your little stripper game. That's enough. I want you here. Right now.'

His command was raw enough to make her forget the harsh note in his voice as he had said *stripper*. Her hands were trembling as she pulled her panties down and tossed them aside, and half-ran across the room towards him. And then she straddled him, easing herself down onto his hardness, squealing with delight as he filled her.

She thrust forward with her hips, as if she was riding bareback. But he rolled her straight over onto her back, assuming the position of mastery.

'Now,' he groaned, as he drove into her, over and over, each sweet, savage thrust sending her careering close to the edge. *'Now!'*

He bent his head to kiss her. The touch of his lips seemed to set fire to the touch-paper embedded deep in her heart and unstoppable flames began to flicker through her veins. She gave a broken little cry, but she bit down on it. She wanted to tell him that only he could make her feel this way. But for Guido this was simply good sex, and everyone knew that men could get good sex from any number of women.

And then the release washed over her—great powerful waves of it which rocked her to the very core, obliterating everything except the sheer wonder of the moment. Lucy clung to him, burying her face in his shoulder as he began to tense inside her, and to feel him beginning to orgasm only magnified her own pleasure.

For Guido it went on and on, and even when it was over he lay back, gazing dazedly at the ceiling. He couldn't remember sex as good as that. Never. He yawned, aware that his defences were down, irrevocably slipping into the dark, cushioned tunnel of sleep.

Lucy lay quite still until she heard Guido's breathing steady, then slow and deepen, and only when she was certain that he was asleep did she risk turning onto her side to look at him.

In sleep he was beautiful and curiously accessible in a way he never was while awake—making it impossible not to weave hopeless fantasies about him. Only in sleep did his hard and handsome face relax. The cruel, sensual mouth softened and the piercing brilliance of the ebony eyes was shielded by the feathery arcs of his lashes, which curved with such childlike innocence against his cheek.

His dark head was pillowed against a recumbent hand, and the long, lean limbs were sprawled over the giant-sized bed.

Lucy wriggled up the bed a bit, resting against a

bank of drift-soft pillows, and looked properly around the room for the first time.

So this was the Prince's bedroom!

There was little to mark it out as a Royal residence—it just looked like home to a very wealthy man. The bed was bigger than any she had ever seen, and the view from the window was utterly spectacular. No cost had been spared in the restrained but elegant furnishings. It was minimalist and unashamedly masculine, without in any way being hard or cold.

Only a silver-framed photo beside the bed gave any indication of his identity, and unless you knew it could have been any snapshot of any rich and privileged family.

But it was not.

It was a picture of Guido, taken with his mother, his elder brother Gianferro, and their father the King. Guido, with his black hair and black eyes, looked to be about four or five. Lucy bit her lip, moving her eyes over the figure of the beautiful young Queen. There was no outward sign of her pregnancy with Nicolo—the youngest—and certainly no sign that within a year of that photo being taken she would be dead. Thank God humans could not see into the future, she thought, with a sudden stab of pain.

She stared at the young Guido. In the face of the child it was possible to see the man. His face was sweetly handsome, his expression almost grave, as if he was determined to be a grown-up boy for the mother whose hand he gripped so tightly.

But Lucy had only learnt all this subsequently. It was easy to find out things about someone when you were interested—and when they were in the public eye. Not that she had known that he was a prince when she'd met him. At least, not at first.

To Lucy, he had been just a heart-stoppingly gorgeous man who had struck up a conversation with her at a party.

CHAPTER THREE

IT HAD been one of those parties that Lucy hadn't particularly wanted to go to—she had been on a stop-over on her way back to London and desperate for some sleep—but the flight crew had overridden her objections. Apparently, parties didn't get much better or more highly connected than this one. One of the other stewardesses had said that a prince was going to be there, but quite honestly Lucy hadn't believed them.

Well, who would have?

When they had walked into the expensive Bohemian TriBeCa townhouse, Lucy had looked around her with interest. It had been like stepping into some lavishly appointed Bedouin tent—with embroidered cushions and rich brocade wall-hangings, and the heady scent of incense. The hypnotic drift of what had sounded like snake-charmer's music had only added to the illusion of being on a film set.

'When do the belly-dancers arrive?' she asked drily.

'Shh!' someone hissed. 'You know people tend to misunderstand your sense of humour!'

So Lucy decided to observe, rather than to participate, and went to stand in a darkened corner which nonetheless gave her a great view. She took a glass of punch with her and sipped it, then shuddered, hastily putting the glass down on a small inlaid table.

'Disgusting, isn't it?' came a rich, accented voice from a few feet away.

Lucy was just about to protest that he had startled her when her words somehow died on her lips. 'It's…a little heavy on the spices,' she agreed, blinking slightly, as if she couldn't quite believe what she was seeing.

'And the alcohol, of course.'

'Well, there is that, of course,' she echoed, and he smiled.

They stood looking at one another in the way that two people did at parties when there was a strong sexual chemistry between them.

Lucy was wearing a simple green velvet tunic dress—quite short, so that it came to mid-thigh and made her legs look endlessly long. But her baggy suede boots gave the outfit a quirky appearance. Her hair was loose, flooding down over her shoulders in a heavy Titian fall.

Guido thought that she looked like a very sexy bandit. Her face was pale and freckled—he liked the freckles—and her wide honey-coloured eyes were slightly wary—he liked that, too.

Lucy thought, quite honestly, that he was the most gorgeous man she had ever laid eyes on. But then, she had never seen a man who looked quite like this.

He was tall, and his body was both lean and powerful. His hair was as black as the night, and his eyes only a shade lighter, and he had an almost aristocratic bearing. She wondered if he was Italian, or maybe Spanish. He was certainly European.

And he almost certainly has a girlfriend, she told herself. If not one, then a legion of them.

Guido waited, but she said nothing, and he liked that even more. So, did she know? he wondered. And was she pretending not to? 'You're not from round here?' he questioned slowly.

'No.'

'You're on holiday?' he persisted.

'Not really. I work for Pervolo Airlines.'

'As a pilot?'

'You ask a lot of questions.'

His eyes glittered. 'One of us has to.'

Hers glittered back. 'I'm a flight attendant, actually—but thank you for not making the assumption.'

'Assumptions are such a bore, don't you think?' he questioned carelessly.

It was something about the way he spoke—some unknown quality underlying the velvet accent of his voice—which Lucy had difficulty recognising at first, because she had never heard it before. And then he gave her a silent clue in the proud way he was holding his head—in the dismissive little curve of his sensual mouth as a woman wearing so little that she might have been one of those belly-dancers started ogling him from the other side of the room.

It was privilege, Lucy realised. A sense of self-worth bordering on arrogance which radiated from him in a way which was almost tangible. Haughty, but with a devilish glitter to his eyes, he managed to be both gloriously touchable and yet impossibly remote at the same time.

'You're the Prince,' said Lucy slowly, and she felt the slightest pang of disappointment. Just her luck to find someone who could have whisked her off her feet and then discover he was out of bounds! 'Aren't you?'

His eyes narrowed. 'You knew?'

Lucy shook her head. 'No. I've just guessed. Someone said there was going to be a prince here, but I didn't believe them.' Her eyes were candid. 'What a bore for you—that everyone knows about you in advance.'

'The perfect catch for the ambitious society hostess,' he observed drily.

'Yes, quite.' So, was that arrogant? Or merely honest? Lucy expelled a sigh and gave him a small, regretful smile. She certainly wasn't going to fill the stereotypical role of hanging around and being starstruck. 'Well, it was nice meeting you—'

'But we haven't, have we?' he said suddenly. 'Met, that is. Perhaps we should remedy that?' His smile was irresistible, and so was his voice, and he took her hand in his without warning. 'I'm Guido.'

'Lucy,' she said breathlessly. His touch was sending her senses haywire. 'Lucy Maguire—but you'd better let me go—I don't want to monopolise you.'

'Liar,' he taunted softly, his fingers continuing to curl possessively around her narrow wrist. 'You know we both want to monopolise each other.'

'How outrageous!' she murmured, but she didn't move from the spot.

They talked all night. She was simultaneously lulled and stimulated by his quicksilver mind and sexy accent. He came from the Principality of Mardivino, but he had long ago rejected princely privilege. 'Perhaps you find that disappointing?' he mocked.

'I thought you weren't into making assumptions,' she returned crisply. 'Because that was an extremely arrogant one.'

'You sound like a prim schoolteacher,' he observed sultrily. 'Even if you do not look like one.'

Lucy raised her eyebrows but said nothing—certainly not anything that was going to lead into the tantalising land of sexual fantasy.

'So, what do princes do?' she questioned. 'When they're not being princes?'

'Oh, they wheel and deal,' he murmured, drifting his gaze over her freckle-spattered face. 'Just like other mortals.'

She didn't think so. Other mortals did not have the faces of dark fallen angels. 'A-anything in particular?' she stammered—because when he was looking at her like that it was difficult to breathe, let alone to speak.

'Property,' he said succinctly.

He offered to give her a lift back to her hotel, but Lucy refused—though she let him flag her down a cab. She wasn't sure she trusted his unique brand of sexy charisma enough to be alone in a car with him—

or maybe it was that she didn't trust herself not to respond to it.

He leaned into the cab and handed her his card.

'Why don't you ring me when you're next in town?' he suggested softly.

Lucy smiled politely and took the card, but the smile was edged in a frost he appeared not to notice. She got the distinct impression that he felt he was bestowing an enormous favour on her by giving her a contact number. Bloody cheek!

She didn't bother ringing. His arrogance had disappointed her, yes—but it was more than that. He was a prince, for heaven's sake—and thus completely out of her reach. Only someone with a streak of masochism would willingly subject themselves to such inevitable rejection.

But Guido, of course, had never before been ignored by a woman.

At first he simply couldn't believe that she wasn't going to bother to ring. But after several weeks he had no choice but to do so.

Why, he couldn't even remember her surname!

But that, of course, did not pose any real problem. Guido had left his life as a working prince behind a long time ago, but very occasionally he used his title. He still had to exist with all the drawbacks of having it, he reasoned—so why not enjoy some of the benefits?

And Pervolo Airlines seemed only too happy to release a few facts about one of their stewardesses to a prince!

He found out when she was next flying and settled back in his seat in First Class, anticipating her reaction with a certain degree of relish, feeling himself grow deliciously hard as he saw a pair of long, long legs slinking down the cabin towards him.

Lucy had noticed him, of course—it would have been difficult not to, even if they hadn't already been briefed by the Purser that there was a Royal prince on board.

But she had no intention of reacting to the look of appreciation which had softened the ebony eyes. She had no desire to be just another notch on a handsome, privileged man's bedpost, and she was perceptive enough to know that this man could be a real heartbreaker.

She reached him, her face set in an unflappable, official smile. 'Good afternoon, sir,' she said pleasantly. 'Can I get you a drink before take-off?'

He had been expecting…what? That she would blush and stumble over her words? Look regretful or uncomfortable? Suddenly he laughed, and his pulse began to race.

'No, you can have dinner with me tonight instead,' he murmured, and some of his arrogance dissolved as he stared up at her. 'Please.'

Lucy would have defied anyone to resist that look, or the one-word plea she guessed he hadn't had to make very often in his life. So she went for dinner with him, and then—after not much of a fight—to bed. She wanted him more than she had ever wanted anything in her life, and to hold him off any longer would have been hypocritical and self-defeating.

But, despite the passion of the night which followed, an instinctive feeling of self-protection made her noncommittal towards him the next morning. She was determined not to seem pushy, or to act as if it would be the end of the world if he didn't ask to see her again, and her very coolness seemed to fascinate him.

She guessed he'd never encountered it before, and to a man with an appetite jaded by exposure it was fresh and exciting fare. Soon it would no longer be fresh, nor exciting, and it would pale, but she was prepared for that—or at least that was what she told herself over and over again.

Apart from a minor blip at the very beginning, they now met up once every couple of months and it was perfect—for what it was. They had dinner, sometimes saw a film, and once or twice he had taken her to the theatre. But she had never met any of his friends, nor he hers. It was a complex game they played, with its own set of unspoken rules. As if she had been given her own separate compartment in his life—the one marked 'mistress'—and as long as she accepted that, then she was okay. The moment she started wanting more, then it would be over.

So why had he brought her to his apartment today? Why not the usual anonymity of a hotel?

She stared down at his sleeping face just as the dark lashes fluttered open and ebony eyes blazed sleepily up at her.

'*Ciao,*' he murmured, and reached for her breast. 'Come back here.'

'In a minute.' She let him stroke idly at her breast as warmth began to flood over her. If he had broken a rule of a lifetime, then why shouldn't she? Lucy trickled her fingertip down through the thick whorls of hair at his chest to dip it into his belly, and he groaned with pleasure. 'How flattering that you have allowed me onto your territory, Guido,' she commented softly.

'Why not?' His eyes were watchful black shards. 'Though you've never shown any particular desire to see where I live.'

'Ah.' She raised her eyebrows. And presumably if she had then his apartment would have been off-limits! 'Interesting.'

How her self-containment enthralled and exasperated him! Why, any other woman would have used his post-coital sleep as an opportunity to poke around the apartment! Yet here she was, naked and beautiful beside him, as though she visited his home every day of the week!

He narrowed his eyes as he felt the heavy throb of desire beating its way through his veins. As a lover, he could not have asked for better. She was responsive and beautiful and she made no demands on him. How unlike most women!

His mouth hardened as he thought about commitment and expectation. And, in particular, about the lavish christening of his nephew, soon to take place on Mardivino, and all that it would entail. He stared at the naked woman beside him and an idea began to form in his mind. Maybe her cool indifference could work to his advantage…

'Would you like to go away with me for the weekend, *cara mia*?' he suggested casually.

Lucy didn't answer immediately—it was never a good idea to appear *too* eager; every woman knew *that*! 'Did you have anywhere particular in mind?'

'But of course.' His eyes glittered as he wondered what her reaction would be. For if she read too much into it then it simply would not work. 'I thought that perhaps you might care to accompany me to Mardivino.'

There was silence as, for a minute, Lucy thought she was hearing things. 'To Mardivino?' she repeated blankly.

'Do try to contain your excitement,' he commented drily.

Oh, if only he knew! Lucy's heart was banging against her ribcage and she felt quite faint. He was taking her home—to meet his family!

A slow smile curved her lips. 'And to what do I owe this honour?'

Guido concentrated on whispering his fingertips over her tightening nipple. 'Maybe I'd like to show you the land of my birth,' he murmured.

Lucy closed her eyes, partly because the way he was touching her meant that she could barely think straight, but partly to hide her eyes. To conceal from him the breathless excitement she was feeling.

Don't frighten him away with emotion, she told

herself, sinking into his arms. Let's just take it one step at a time.

'Okay,' she said lightly, as if it didn't matter. *As if it didn't matter!* 'Why not?'

He smiled with satisfaction at her response. It was better than he could have anticipated! 'And maybe I would like a beautiful woman to accompany me to the christening of my nephew.'

There was a long pause as Lucy stared up at him. 'Say that again.'

'My brother's child is being baptised. Would you like to come?'

She blinked her eyes very quickly. A baptism was a private and very sacred thing, and he was asking her...*her*... 'Are you...are you sure?'

'I wouldn't ask you unless I was.' He ran a fingertip reflectively down over the bare silk of her shoulder. 'You will need something to wear, of course. We shall go shopping later, yes?'

It was as if someone had given her a gorgeous present and then snatched it away again, and Lucy froze. 'You're saying that you don't think I have anything suitable?'

There was not a flicker of reaction on his face. '*Cara*, you always look *meravigliosa*.'

'So what's the problem?'

'There is no problem.' He chose his words carefully. 'But it will be—of necessity—a very lavish affair,' he said slowly. 'And I would like to buy you an outfit.'

'You think I'm going to turn up in jeans and a sweatshirt?' she demanded.

'Of course I don't!'

'Well, then—I can buy my own outfits,' she said stubbornly.

'Yes, I know you can.' He moved his head away to look down at her, his black eyes like jet as he chose his words in a way calculated not to offend her sweet but misplaced pride. 'Let me put it another way,' he said softly. 'You are my lover, Lucy, and tradition dictates that as my lover I am allowed to spoil you. I *want* to spoil you,' he added huskily.

And this, too, was all part of the game, she realised. If she accompanied him then it was imperative that she look the part. It didn't matter if she dressed with style and panache—her budget was far too limited to allow her to be able to compete with other women at a Royal gathering.

And she wanted to go. Badly. If she allowed stubborn pride to rear its head then he might refuse to take her. And if she held out to wear one of her own outfits—then wasn't there a chance she might let him down?

Besides—if she was being one hundred per cent honest—then wasn't there a wistful Cinderella side to *every* woman—that wanted someone to wave a magic wand and transform them from an ordinary woman into a princess? Well, that was just what Guido was offering to do, and as long as she didn't expect the Cinderella ending then why not just go with the flow and enjoy it? What else was she going to do? Tell him no and have the relationship peter out?

The thought of that hurt far more than she wanted or had expected, and she shrugged her shoulders, as if the unwelcome stab of reality wasn't poking brittle fingers at her heart. 'Very well, Guido,' she said slowly. 'I accept.'

'You test me, I think, *cara*,' he observed evenly.

'Oh?'

'A man does not offer a gift to have it treated as though it is some kind of punishment to be endured.'

'A gift should be offered without ties or expectations,' she returned sweetly. 'Didn't you know that?'

'Do you always have a smart answer for everything, Lucy?'

'I certainly hope so.' She narrowed her eyes. 'If it is submissive gratitude you desire, Guido, then there must be any number of women who would be only too glad to provide it.'

And she was right, *maledizione*! He enjoyed much more than just her lovemaking because she challenged and intrigued him—he could not now dispense with those qualities when it suited him.

He put his hand between her thighs and heard her gasp. 'I am going to make love to you again,' he said, on a note of husky intent. 'And then I am going to take you out and dress you from head to foot.'

Lucy let him whisk her around Manhattan, unable to shake the slightly surreal sensation of feeling as though she was appearing in a film as Guido took her from shop to exclusive shop. Stuff like this didn't happen in real life, she told herself dazedly.

But it seemed that it did.

First came the lingerie—stuff like she had never seen before: drifts and drifts of delicate silk, trimmed with lace so fine that it seemed to have been spun from gossamer. A brisk, efficient Frenchwoman measured her, and it transpired that Lucy had been buying the wrong bra size off the peg for years!

'We'll take them both,' drawled Guido carelessly as she vascillated between a matching set in electric blue trimmed with cerise satin and a more conventional pure white outfit—which was, she thought with a fleeting wistfulness, exactly the kind of thing a bride might covet for her trousseau. 'And the black.'

'Guido, no!' protested Lucy as the saleswoman tactfully withdrew from the room.

'Guido, yes,' he argued, with a smile of satisfaction.

'I won't be wearing more than two sets of underwear in a weekend!'

'But after the weekend you will, and I want to see you in it all. And out of it,' he said, his voice dipping into a note of erotic promise.

Of course she couldn't possibly argue after that—because his words implied that their affair was going to run and run when they got back from Mardivino.

She silenced the cruel little voice in her head which asked her just how long she was prepared to dedicate her life to a relationship which was doomed to go nowhere.

In a succession of luxurious shops he bought her an outfit for the christening, plus the most gorgeous hat she had ever seen, two evening gowns, daywear, negligees, and a cashmere wrap.

'Sometimes the evening breeze which comes down from the mountains can chill the skin,' he murmured. 'Especially skin as fine and as fair as yours, Lucy.'

He ran his fingers lightly over her bare arm and Lucy began to tremble. Tersely he asked for the garments to be wrapped and delivered and then took her back to his apartment and made love to her all over again. He was wild for it, and so was she, and the sound of her ecstatic cries rang round his vast bedroom as she lay shuddering in his arms afterwards.

But once the storms of passion had abated Lucy felt different. Something had changed, or at least in her imagination it had, and she wondered if she had given away something of herself in her shamefully easy acceptance of his gifts. Her independence, maybe?

She snuggled into the crook of his arm, for he was sleeping, and her own eyelids began to drift down.

I will only wear the clothes on Mardivino, she vowed.

And after that I'll go back to being me.

CHAPTER FOUR

'Look down now,' said Guido, above the sound of the engines. 'And you will see the mountains of Mardivino.'

Lucy did as he said, though she was so distracted by his proximity that she might as well have been looking at the skyscrapers of a city for all the impact the breathtaking scenery made on her.

Was it the fact they were now most definitely moving into *his* exclusive territory that was making her feel very slightly disorientated—or just the rather daunting prospect of what might lie ahead? With an effort she forced herself not to think about the sexy and sophisticated Prince who sat beside her on the luxury jet, and to drink in the beauty of his homeland instead.

Beneath her lay a bewitching-looking island which sparkled like a jewel set in a blindingly blue sea. In the distance she could see the mighty peaks of the mountains he had mentioned, and as the plane circled she could see beaches and brilliant white buildings clustered together, like a handful of pearls.

'Wow!' she breathed. 'Is that a city there?'

He smiled. 'It's Solajoya—our capital. I don't know if it qualifies as a city, as it's pretty small— though it *does* have a cathedral.'

'Then it's a city,' said Lucy firmly.

Guido leaned over her to stare down. How long since he had been back? He had paid fleeting visits to see his father, of course, but he had not been back since his younger brother Nico had surprised them all and married the English girl.

At first it had been considered the most unsuitable of liaisons, and Guido had been expecting an explosive firework response from his elder brother Gianferro. But Ella seemed to have won him round, and Gianferro—against all the odds—had accepted her into the bosom of the family. And now she had secured her place there permanently, by giving Nico a son and heir.

His mouth hardened. Even Nico—the wild and devil-may-care Nico—had succumbed to the expectations which were his birthright!

He stared at Lucy's smooth cheek and the sweep of glossy Titian hair which contrasted so beautifully against it. Yes. She would make a very enjoyable deterrent against the subtle pressure of the Palace to settle down at last, with a suitable bride. Her presence at his side would shield him from the attentions of Mardivino's maritally ambitious women. His lips curved into a smile. And—best of all—he could relax and enjoy just about the best sex he'd ever had in his life.

'Excited?' he questioned softly.

Lucy nodded, because there seemed to be some kind of lump in her throat preventing normal speech. Excited? Well, yes—if excitement also incorporated sheer terror. She had always thought of herself as adaptable, and her job had taken her to all kinds of places to meet all kinds of people—but there was nothing in any rule book to tell her how to deal with a situation like this.

For a start, she didn't *feel* like herself—nor even look like herself, either. The pale linen trousers were cut low on the hip and were the most flattering pair of trousers she had ever worn. You got—as everyone always said—what you paid for, and Guido had paid a hell of a lot for these! They were teamed with a T-shirt which didn't really look like a T-shirt—its fit was so perfect that it seemed to take what should have been an everyday garment into a completely new dimension.

And beneath the expensive clothes were equally expensive undergarments—silk and satin which glided like honey over her curves and which managed to make her feel very sexy indeed.

Not that there was much point in feeling *that*, because Guido had been as untactile as it was possible to be ever since they had boarded the private jet.

She could understand it—but that didn't make it any easier. He was on show now—to the two pilots and the unbelievably beautiful stewardess, as well as to all the officials who had fussed them onto the plane. He might have rejected life as a prince, but that didn't mean he wouldn't conform to it when he needed to. That was simply good manners and aristocratic breeding.

Consequently, he hadn't touched her, nor kissed

her, nor even murmured provocatively in her ear, promising what he was going to do to her in bed later—not once, during the entire flight.

He had been cool almost to the point of being indifferent, and that had scared her—because it seemed to reinforce what she knew in her heart. He might like her enough to bring her here for the weekend, and he might like going to bed with her, but he certainly didn't love her—and therefore it was vital she didn't fall in any deeper than she already was.

So how did you stop yourself falling in love?

She looked out at the clouds which drifted like dry ice past the windows. What would she do if she knew that there was a bad case of flu going around? She would go out of her way to protect herself. She should do the same with her emotions. Enjoy the weekend for what it was.

The engine noise changed and the plane began to dip down towards the tiny airport. Lucy smoothed her hair back, hoping that the gesture didn't look nervous.

'Will anyone be there to meet us?' she questioned.

'Just a driver. I told my brother not to send a deputation.'

'Did he want to, then?'

Guido gave a hard smile. 'Gianferro likes pomp and ceremony—which is fortunate, since he's going to have a hell of a lot of it one of these days.'

Lucy hesitated. 'How is…your father?'

'He is slowly dying,' said Guido matter-of-factly, and he saw her flinch. But how could he explain that being pragmatic was his way of dealing with it? He had learnt early on about the finality and pain of death when his mother had been torn away from her family. Nico had been just a baby and Gianferro—as the oldest and the heir—had always been surrounded and protected by an extra layer of courtiers.

But Guido had been at the worst possible age for maternal deprivation, which was probably why they had flown him to stay with his mother's sister in America. He had loved his aunt very much, but she had not been his mother, and away from his brothers and Mardivino his sense of lonelieness and isolation had increased.

And when he had returned it had not felt like home any more.

No place had ever since.

A low black limousine was waiting on the runway, and it whisked them off to a palace which Lucy hadn't imagined could exist outside the pages of a fairy story.

'The Rainbow Palace,' said Guido, as the mosaic building glittered in the distance in a multicoloured dazzle.

'It's so beautiful,' breathed Lucy. 'Is this where you were born?'

'It is,' he said curtly.

'And where did you go to school?'

'I didn't. We had tutors at the Palace.'

So he would have been cut off from the outside world—in the same way that he now seemed to have cut himself off from the island itself.

Lucy sneaked a glance at him. His dark profile was

hard and noncommittal as the gates opened and the car swept through onto a vast forecourt which was studded with beautiful statues and bright with tropical flowers.

'Do your brothers mind me coming?' she asked him hesitantly.

There wasn't a flicker of reaction on his face. Nico had been interested—rather *too* interested, in Guido's opinion—and had quizzed him about actually bringing a woman with him to Mardivino until Guido had set him straight. He had told his younger brother that Lucy was his lover—nothing more and nothing less. 'Don't start writing hearts and flowers,' he had said wryly. 'Just because you've fallen in love yourself.'

Gianferro had been a different matter altogether—stating flatly that it was unthinkable for Guido to bring a woman to the Palace if she was merely a casual consort.

There had been a hot-headed exchange about this use of terminology, with Guido telling Gianferro that he was a modern, urban man who didn't go along with such a derogatory description of a woman.

Gianferro had gone to great pains to try to explain himself. 'I am not trying to insult this…Lucy,' he had said exasperatedly. 'But while you may consider yourself a "modern, urban man" you are still a prince. I am afraid that I cannot countenance the idea of you cohabiting with her on Mardivino.'

Knowing that he held all the cards, Guido had responded coolly. 'Then I shall not come.'

'That is unthinkable!'

'Precisely.'

It didn't matter how much Gianferro raged, on this Guido had been adamant—not only would he be bringing Lucy, but he wanted them to share a suite of rooms at the Palace.

'I am not going to behave like a seventeen-year-old schoolboy!' he had stormed. 'Sneaking into her room late at night.'

'Think of your birthright!' his brother had retorted.

'I do—constantly! I have chosen to live my life by my own rules, and I am asking you to respect that.'

He looked now into Lucy's honey-coloured eyes and gave a thin smile. 'No,' he said lightly. 'My brothers do not mind you coming.'

He supposed that some people might have called this a distortion of the truth, but in his world he would prefer to define it as diplomacy. Sometimes it was better all round if you told people what they wanted to hear.

The luxury car purred to a halt and various servants appeared from within the ornate doors of the Palace. As Lucy stepped out of the car, to feel the sun beating down on her bare head, the feeling of being in a dream was stronger than ever.

Guido was speaking to one of the servants in low and rapid French, while others were removing their baggage and taking it inside. He turned to her and his black eyes glittered.

'Shall we go to our rooms?' he suggested casually. 'You might wish to change.' His eyes glittered. 'And my brother Gianferro would like to meet you before we go down to dinner.'

It was not a question, Lucy realised, it was an order—subtly and charmingly couched, but an order nonetheless. As much as Guido might declare that he had left his Royal life behind, it was ingrained in his psyche, running as deep as an underground river. You couldn't escape your upbringing—leave it behind and forget it—simply because you wanted to.

On Mardivino he would inevitably be the Prince, and as his lover Lucy had her own part to play. So play the part, she told herself, but don't let the barriers slip—not by a fraction.

She remembered what Gary, her house-mate, had told her before she left: 'Everyone will love you! Just be yourself, darling!'. But what did that actually mean? That she should let rip with her feelings? Not in this case, no. She suspected that it was more a case of being natural and easy-going—in other words being the perfect guest. She would go along with everything and drink in the experience of a lifetime.

'Sounds wonderful,' she agreed equably.

Guido took her to their suite via a maze of wide marble corridors, hung with spectacular oil paintings, and then through an inner courtyard which was cool and scented, with a fountain sprinkling water which sounded like music.

He stood watching her for a moment as she sucked in a deep breath of wonder, for it was impossible not to be awed by such beauty.

'You like it,' he observed.

Lucy turned to face him, seeing the shuttered look in his black eyes. 'Don't you?'

He shrugged. 'I grew up here. You always look at things differently from the inside. And memories change how you view something.'

She heard the rawness in his voice. Had his bereaved and fractured childhood caused scars which could never be healed? But to ask him would be intrusive, even if he were the kind of man who invited such questions. And Lucy did not want to pry, or to add to his pain. There were other ways of telling someone that you understood.

'I know what you mean,' she said thoughtfully. 'It's like if you live by the sea—you get so used to seeing it that you take it for granted.' Her mouth twitched. 'And I guess that nothing can prepare you for growing up in the kind of place that most mortals pay ticket money to see!'

There was a pause, and then, unexpectedly, he began to laugh. His social status was so lofty that rarely did people tease him about it—though when he stopped to think about it rarely did he *let* anyone tease him.

His laughter broke some of the tension and replaced it with a new, much more acceptable kind. He stared at her. In the linen trousers and clinging T-shirt she looked like a sleeker and more expensive version of the usual Lucy. As if he had upgraded from a run-of-the-mill car to something top-of-the-range.

Had he tried to alter her? So that the woman he

admired and lusted after would now slip away, like sand between his fingers?

Suddenly he wanted to see her naked, stripped of all the finery that he had insisted on dressing her in.

'Let's go to our suite, *cara*,' he said unsteadily.

She knew exactly what he wanted to do from the look in his eyes, but she was hardly going to challenge him in the public arena of the Palace courtyard. Or rather she sensed that it was public—there was no one to be seen, but she could not shake off the idea that there were eyes watching them.

Maybe they have closed-circuit TV installed, she thought, with a slight touch of hysteria.

She barely had a chance to take in the sumptuous ice-blue and golden surroundings of their suite, for Guido pulled her into his arms, pressing his hard, lean body against hers. She felt the unmistakable evidence of his desire for her, and the melting response of her answering need.

'Guido,' she breathed against his ear as he began to tug at the waistband of her trousers and slide his hand inside them. 'We mustn't.'

'Mustn't what?' he questioned, his eyes gleaming like some dark, indefinable metal as he watched her pupils dilate, felt her syrupy moistness as he began to move his finger.

She closed her eyes, her knees growing weak. 'Your brother…' she gasped. 'He'll be waiting.'

The trousers pooled in a whisper by her ankles and he gave an unseen smile of triumph.

'And so, *cara*,' he said harshly, 'am I. And I can wait no longer!'

It all happened very quickly. He divested her of her costly garments, flinging them carelessly onto the floor as if they were of no consequence, and Lucy suddenly felt like a mannequin he could clothe and then unclothe whenever the fancy took him. As if she were his possession. And she was *not*!

Damn you, she thought. *Damn* you, Prince Guido Nero Maximus Cacciatore, with your cavalier attitude and your determination to get just what it is you want!

But didn't she want it, too? Oh, so badly…

She tugged viciously at his silk shirt, so that several buttons popped off, skittering and bouncing on the marble floor, and she heard him give a low laugh of delight as she scraped her fingernails against the dark hair which arrowed down over his torso.

'Lucy,' he moaned.

His sound of helpless pleasure fuelled her on, and somehow they made it to the bed, frantically pulling at their remaining clothes.

Lucy's breathing was frantic as she began to straddle him. 'Have you…have you locked the door?' she demanded, her voice shaking.

'*Si!*'

Sweet saints in heaven! His one word of assent was enough to have her lowering herself down on him, playing with him, easing the tip of him against her and then seeming to hesitate, as though she was about to change her mind.

'Lucy—' he begged, gasping with the exquisite

pleasure of it as she sank down onto him, taking in every bit of him, and he was so full, so tight, that he felt he might burst.

He buried his face in her breasts as she began to move, taunting and tormenting him as she changed the rhythm until he could bear it no longer. He caught her by the hips, increasing the speed, watching with pleasure as her eyes became slitted and her head fell back and she hissed out the word *yes* over and over and over again, until all his seed had pumped deep within her.

He shook his head slightly with disbelief and sank back against the rumpled pillows, pulling her sweat-sheened body against him. He wanted to sleep, but she was shaking him, her face all flushed and her silken hair falling about her pale freckled shoulders.

'Guido—wake up!'

He shook his head and wriggled his hips comfortably.

She touched the damp silken skin which covered the hard musculature of his shoulder. 'Didn't you say we had to see your brother?'

Reluctantly he opened his eyes, swearing quietly as he lifted his wrist to glance at his watch and then at her. With her tumble of tousled hair and the hectic glitter of her honey-coloured eyes she looked exactly what she was. A highly-sexed and wanton woman who had just been ravished. He felt himself harden, wishing himself far away from the constrictions of this old life again. What wouldn't he give to do it to her all over again?

'How soon can you be ready?' The question came out more tersely than he had intended, but he was trying desperately to detach himself—and for once it wasn't easy. Was that because she was the most equal lover he had ever had?

Lucy blushed, her already high colour deepening still further. 'I'll need to take a quick shower,' she said. 'And I'll have to get something from my suitcase. To wear,' she added.

'Some of your clothes will have already been hung up,' he said shortly. 'The rest are being pressed. Hurry up now, *cara mia*. The bathroom is through there.'

Still shaky, she moved away from the bed and stumbled towards the door he was indicating.

Lucy had been flying long enough to be able to get ready in fast time, but as she stood beneath the power jets of the shower it occurred to her that there had not really been time for what had just happened. He should have stopped. She had tried to stop him—not very hard, it was true—but she had done her level best.

Was it an act of defiance? Or some basic and territorial instinct that had made Guido want to make love to her so passionately and so immediately?

She was so busy selecting what on earth she should wear to go and meet the Crown Prince, and wondering why he had requested to meet her before dinner, that a vital fact completely slipped her mind.

CHAPTER FIVE

'His Serene Highness the Crown Prince Gianferro Miguel Laurens Cacciatore.'

Lucy rose to her feet as Guido's imposing brother entered the room, aware that her pulse was racing and her mouth dry.

It was strange—though understandable, she supposed—that she had always been remarkably unfazed by Guido's title and position, yet she felt positively nervous about meeting the heir to the throne for the first time. Maybe it was because she had met Guido socially, at a party, when he could have been just anyone—whilst here, in the Palace, she felt rather as she imagined a small child might feel if they had been chosen out of all their classmates to present a bouquet to the Queen.

Even though Guido had told her not to, she found herself making some kind of bobbing curtsey, and he nodded in response, a rather reluctant smile curving his lips.

'Please,' he said, and indicated a chair close to the rather more ornate one he had perched on. 'Sit.' He glanced at his brother. 'Guido, you will leave us?'

Guido gave an equable nod which belied the cold gleam of anger in his eyes. 'I'll stay. Lucy likes to have me around—do you not, *cara*?'

Lucy had a brother of her own, and she recognised sibling rivalry and unsettled scores when she came across them. The two men were glaring at each other across the Throne Room and she felt like piggy-in-the-middle. This was hardly going to bode well for the baptism—unless she could manage to turn it around so that neither man lost face.

'Yes, Guido,' she said softly, 'I do. But I'm happy to speak with your brother alone if you think I can manage it?'

Guido's eyes narrowed as they engaged in a silent, clashing duel with hers. Now she was making it sound as though he was watching over her to ensure that she did not make some monumental error of manners, leaving him no choice but to withdraw. He scowled. Why did women always play such complicated games?

'I will go and say hello to my new nephew,' he said abruptly, and shot his brother a mocking glance. 'Perhaps you would care to direct Lucy to the nursery, Gianferro, once you've finished your little…chat?'

Gianferro nodded. '*Si.*' But when Guido had left the room he turned to Lucy, a curious expression in the black eyes which were even harder than Guido's. 'How strange it is,' he observed, in a softly accented voice which seemed underpinned with a note of censure, 'that my brothers seem attracted to women who are light-years away from them in upbringing and experience.'

She didn't think he had meant to insult her, but an insult it undoubtedly was—though one couched in silken terms. *You are not Guido's equal.* That was what he really meant, and Lucy stared at him. Did he think she didn't already know that? That she hadn't been aware of the great and glaring differences right from the word go? Yet pride made her want to hang on to her dignity, not to state the obvious and pick over her humble background.

Her training as a stewardess had given her an invaluable lesson in the making of small-talk, and she seized on it now. 'Perhaps they enjoy variety,' she said lightly.

His eyes narrowed, as if he suspected that she had deliberately misunderstood him. He paused for a moment, and when he spoke the silken veneer of his words had been replaced with the harder ring of truth. 'I understand that you have been seeing him for almost a year.'

'Did Guido tell you that?' she asked in surprise.

'Not exactly.'

And Lucy recognised then that whatever Guido did his movements would be monitored and fed back to the Crown Prince. No doubt Gianferro would have said that he had Guido's best interests at heart, but wasn't it really a not-so-subtle method of spying?

Suddenly she felt protective of her lover. And defensive, too. 'We meet only infrequently,' she said quickly. 'Because of the nature of my job.'

'And *his* nature.'

Their eyes met. Now he was telling her that Guido was not the settling-down type, and once again his words were redundant. For she knew that, too. 'Perhaps,' she said slowly.

'So it is a modern relationship?' he continued softly. 'You are simply lovers?'

She would certainly never have described them as 'simple', yet couldn't help the smile which broke out briefly, like the sun through watery clouds. 'Indeed we are.'

There was another brief silence, and then he said, so casually that it might have been a careless throwaway remark had it not been for the questioning glitter of his dark eyes, 'And you do not hold out some hope that one day you will become a Princess of Mardivino?'

Lucy was stung by the slur, which implied that she was socially ambitious, that she had no feelings for Guido himself—and, God knows, she did. Even though a deep, self-protective streak had made her do her best to quash them. Yet her own feelings paled into insignificance beside the realisation of just how stifling Royal life could be. No wonder Guido had rejected it!

Her words came blurting out before she had time to think of the consequences. 'No, I do not, as it happens!' she retorted. 'But if I loved him, then nothing you could say would stop me from wanting him—no matter how ''unsuitable'' a partner you might deem me to be!'

A wry smile brushed the corners of his hard mouth, a combination of admiration and relief, and Lucy realised that she had given him exactly the answer he wanted. She had made it clear that they were indeed just lovers—and that Guido had no desire nor intention to make their relationship anything more than that. Gianferro could now see that she presented no danger. No threat. No wonder all the tension had left his hard, lean body.

'Good,' he said quietly. 'I am glad that we understand each other.'

He rose to his feet, gesturing for her to follow suit, and Lucy found herself wondering fleetingly what it must be like always to orchestrate each and every situation. To decide when to stand, to sit, to talk or not to talk. Did the burden of it all become too much sometimes, even for him? Was that why his almost cruel mouth so rarely smiled?

'Yes, your Serene Highness,' she said calmly.

He nodded, as if in acknowledgement of her curtsey. 'There is a member of staff waiting outside to conduct you to the infant Prince now.'

She bobbed him another curtsey and left the room, to follow a silent servant down one of the long, wide corridors, feeling like a tiny tadpole who had just been thrown into shark-infested waters. Was this what went on behind the Palace doors, then? Behind-the-scenes wheeling and dealing?

It is what it is, she told herself—and someone like you isn't going to be able to change it.

Her troubled thoughts flew straight out of her head when she was ushered into the Palace Nursery. The sight which greeted her made her heart turn over with a wistful kind of longing.

She barely noticed Guido's younger brother, nor the tawny-haired woman who was standing beside him. All she could see was Guido—her *casual* lover, she thought with an unwelcome pang—cradling the baby in his arms.

There was always something sweet about men who were unused to babies having to deal with them—although 'sweet' wasn't a word which would automatically sit comfortably with a man as overtly masculine as Guido.

But sweet he looked. Whatever she had seen him do, it had always looked utterly effortless and accomplished, but as he tentatively held the infant she surprised a bleak, almost anguished look in his eyes. Was that a need for reassurance, perhaps? Because he was unused to holding such a precious bundle and needed to know that he was doing it properly?

The tawny-haired woman beamed at him. 'Why, Guido, you're doing just fine!' she exclaimed, in an accent which surprised Lucy as being not unlike her own. But then, Prince Nicolo had defied convention and married an English girl.

Lucy saw Guido tense before she moved forward. They all looked up, but everything seemed to melt away into the background, for all she was aware of was the ebony eyes which were dazzling her with their dark fire.

'It's Lucy,' Guido said, in a tone she didn't quite understand. 'Back from her cosy little chat with Gianferro!'

Was he angry that she had insisted on facing

Gianferro on her own? And was that less from a sense of wanting to protect her and more from the fact that he liked to be in control?

Putting her troubled thoughts aside, she smiled as she approached him. 'What a beautiful baby,' she said softly, and tentatively touched the delicate silk of his little dark head.

The woman might be a princess, but first and foremost she was a mother, and she beamed at Lucy with fierce maternal pride.

'Isn't he?' she cooed, her mouth breaking into an infectious smile as she held her hand out. 'And you must be Lucy. I'm Ella, and this is my husband, Nico.'

Nico—or Prince Nicolo Louis Fantone Cacciatore, to be more precise—was younger than Guido, but with the same lean, muscular body, black hair and dark, golden good looks. Both men were heart-stoppingly handsome, but Nico's face was softer than his brother's—and you could see a certain air of serenity as he looked at his wife and his son, an inner glow which only added to his masculinity instead of detracting from it.

That's love, thought Lucy—not lust. And a cloud passed over her heart.

'*Enchanté,*' he murmured, and raised Lucy's hand to his lips in a gesture which managed to be both courteous and gloriously old-fashioned at the same time. Then he turned to his brother, with mischief in his black eyes. 'A woman who is both brave as well as beautiful, no doubt?'

LIMERICK
COUNTY LIBRARY

'Brave?' questioned Lucy, with a frown.

'You will have needed all the courage in the world to deal with my eldest brother,' teased Nico.

'How *was* Gianferro?' drawled Guido.

'Charming,' said Lucy diplomatically, and Ella shot her the briefest of sympathetic glances.

I bet she had to go through the same kind of interrogation with him, thought Lucy. But in her case it was warranted. She was in love with Nico, and he with her. Whereas in her case she was just here because…because…

Behind her fringe, her brow creased into a tiny frown. Just why *had* Guido brought her here? To keep his bed warm at night? Surely not. He had never seemed in need of close, intimate companionship in the past.

With an effort she pulled herself away from unanswerable thoughts and looked down at the sleeping bundle in Guido's arms, thinking what a contrast it made—the tiny baby cradled within his powerful grip.

'What's…what's his name?' she questioned.

'It's Leo,' answered Ella, and her wide mouth crinkled into a smile. 'Well, Leonardo Amadore Constantinus Cacciatore, actually—but Leo for short! Would you like to hold him?'

'Oh, I would! Can I?'

'Of course you can! That's if Guido can bear to let him go!' said Ella impishly.

'You like babies?' questioned Nico softly.

She looked up into a face which was so like Guido's yet a million miles away from his hard, handsome stare. 'I love them.' Lucy's voice was fervent, but then she had always been hands-on with her friends' children.

Guido's eyes narrowed. 'Here, Lucy.' His voice was a murmur. 'You'd better take him.'

It seemed almost too intimate as she took the child which Guido passed over to her with the care he might have employed if it had been handling a ticking time-bomb, and at first she held the child in a similarly over-exaggerated way. For a moment she was acutely aware that this was a Royal prince, perhaps the future King of Mardivino, since neither Guido nor Gianferro had shown any sign of producing an heir. All babies were precious, but this baby...

But those thoughts were forgotten the instant she smelt his particular baby smell and saw the easy warmth and trust of his innocent sleep. Instinctively she pulled him closer to her. With equal instinct the baby jerked his head, blindly searching for her breast, and Lucy blushed. Ella's peal of laughter quickly dispelled any embarrassment, but she looked up to meet the steely stare of Guido and her feeling of apprehension increased.

Was he wondering—as she was—what had happened to the independent sex-bomb of a girlfriend he had brought with him? It was true that she had played her sensual part back in the suite, but it seemed to displease him that she was now cradling his nephew and cooing and blushing like any normal woman.

But surely that was the whole point—that underneath it all she was just a normal woman with normal desires? It was all very well in principle to tell yourself that you were just going to have a wild and passionate affair, without letting any constricting emotion get in the way. But that was what women did. It was the way they were made—programmed to react in a certain way, especially when there were babies around.

'Here, Lucy. I'll take him,' said Ella, holding her arms out. 'I'd better feed him before we go down to dinner. Gianferro may be a total walk-over where his nephew is concerned, but I doubt he'd appreciate it if I started breastfeeding my son at a State Banquet!'

State Banquet! Guido hadn't mentioned *that*! Though when she stopped to think about it what had she expected—all of them having dinner on trays, clustered around a television set?

Lucy again looked at Guido, but this time he wasn't even glancing in her direction. Instead, his gaze was roving rather distractedly around the Nursery suite. As if he was seeing it for the first time.

As if he was wondering what the hell he was doing there.

When she went into dinner Lucy thanked her lucky stars that she *had* let Guido buy her some suitable clothes for this trip, because otherwise… Otherwise she would have been left *looking* like an outsider, instead of just feeling like one.

As it was, the sleek black sheath was perfect. Silk-satin and cut on the bias, it seemed to have the mag-ical properties of managing to emphasise all her good bits and completely disguise the bits she wasn't so fond of. Consequently, her breasts looked lush and her waist a mere handspan of a thing, while the curve of her hips seemed both shapely yet slim. Oh, how different the world would look if all the women in it could dress in couture!

She had pinned her hair up—the way she sometimes did for work—its Titian colour a lustrous red-brown gleam and its stark lines adding to the impact of the beautifully simple dress.

She had seen Guido's eyes darken as they watched her, but even as part of her had thrilled in the light of his silent and sensual appropation there had been something about his stern countenance which had made her wary.

For there was something so distant about him tonight. And not just physical distance—the fact that he was sitting far away from her at the long table, which was awash with beautiful flower arrangements and laid with ornate crystal and china.

It was as if he were a helium balloon and someone had cut the string which bound him to earth—sending him soaring ever higher into this lavish aristocratic stratosphere in which he moved so easily. While she was the little girl left staring at a fast-retreating, bobbing dot, knowing that she would never get it back again.

Oh, do stop it, Lucy, she urged herself, and pull yourself together. Just because he isn't smiling across the table at you!

For a woman who hadn't been going to read anything into anything she was doing a pretty good job of it!

So she fixed a smile to her lips and accepted a glass of champagne, and laughed obediently at the aged but rather amusing Count on her right side. After a while her laughter grew relaxed and natural, and she chatted to some visiting Lord on her other side, who was obviously out to flirt for Britain! And it was easy to ignore the women who were vying outrageously for Guido's attention—like a pack of fancy-plumaged vultures who were circling an especially delectable morsel.

Guido watched her, wondering why things which seemed so perfectly simple had a habit of complicating themselves.

What had prompted his strange sense of unease and the fleeting pang of some long-forgotten pain when he had been holding the baby? Thoughts of his mother and her death? Or was it merely that bringing a woman made everything seem so different? *He* was being treated differently, as if having a partner made him seem more human and approachable.

But it wasn't like that! Lucy was here as his lover and his distraction—and not just for him. As his partner she would send out a powerful message to the conniving matrons of Mardivino who were always so intent on manufacturing introductions to their precious daughters!

Hadn't he always longed for a relationship with a woman who thought as a man did? Who enjoyed the good things, like sex and laughter, and didn't produce the whole gamut of female emotions which made life so impossibly dreary and tortuous?

Was that what was troubling him? The fact that she had started coming over all gooey-eyed when she saw Leo? Or that she'd started looking a little too much at home? The trouble was that you got an image of a woman in your head, and when she started acting outside that image it made you feel you didn't know her.

He stared across the table at her. She was giggling at something the Englishman was whispering to her. His mouth hardened.

That was the whole point, surely? That he didn't *really* know her—and neither did he want to. That was what killed the excitement—once you started getting into that trap of caring and sharing and analysing every last damned thing. Or rather, when *they* did. Guido had never met a woman he could spend time with, day in and day out, in that parlous state they called commitment.

Lucy turned her head to look at him then, and very deliberately he ran the tip of his tongue over his lips. He saw her eyes darken and waited to see what she would do next, and he felt a hot jerk of sensual frustration to see her coolly turn her head and continue to talk to the man beside her.

After that the evening became an ordeal to be endured. He could barely wait to get her alone again, and yet he knew he had to—and matters were made even more exasperating by the fact that she seemed to be taking her time over everything.

It seemed to take for ever until he could get near

her, and when he did he dipped his head to her ear. 'Shall we slip away now?' he suggested silkily.

Lucy looked at him askance, though inside she was simmering. Ever since they had visited the Nursery he had virtually ignored her—apart from the occasional studied sexual stare. And now, at the very first opportunity, he wanted to whisk her away to bed. He hadn't even asked her to dance!

'Why, that would look terribly rude, Guido!' she reprimanded him softly. 'What *are* you thinking of? The band have only just started playing and I've had at least three offers to dance!'

He'd bet she had! He didn't like the tone of her voice, and neither did he like what she was saying. Had a few hours in the Palace been enough to make her forget her place in it? 'I don't need advice from you on how to behave in my own home!' he snapped.

'Well, I think you do!' she retorted sweetly. Let him stew! Let him… 'Oh—*oh*,' she gasped, as he pulled her into his arms without warning, his hard body pressing against the pliant softness of hers. 'What the hell do you think you're doing?'

'What does it look like?' he questioned as he slid his hand over her back, possessive against the bare skin, his fingertips tracing tiny unseen circles on her flesh which set her shivering. 'I'm claiming the first dance.'

Claiming. It sounded territorial—let's face it, it *was* territorial. So why was she letting him stroke her like that? Was she powerless to resist him, or simply unwilling? Close call.

Her head tipped back as if it was too heavy for her neck, and she could feel his warm breath close to her skin. 'Guido,' she said weakly, 'you must stop this.'

'But I'm not doing anything,' he said, as he pressed his hard heat against her.

'You know exactly what you're doing,' she gasped softly. 'You're using the dance to seduce me.'

God, yes. He could smell the desire on her skin, and he breathed it in like a man who had been drowning. 'And you don't like it?'

She opened her eyes very wide then, aware that her breath was coming in short, frantic bursts—like someone who had been running in a long, long race. How on earth was it possible to feel overwhelming passion at the same time as the heavy, stone-like ache of her heart at the realisation that *this* was what he wanted from her. Probably *all* he wanted from her.

But he had tortured *her*, so now let him have a taste of his own medicine. 'Oh, I love it,' she whispered. 'But it's making me wish that no one else was around. So that you could slide my expensive dress up…'

'And…and why would I want to do that?' he questioned shakily.

'To find out whether or not I was wearing any knickers, of course.'

'Aren't you?' he groaned.

'Well, yes—I am, actually. But we could soon dispose of those, couldn't we?' Fractionally, she pushed her breasts against him, and now it was his turn to moan. 'And then you could lift me up, wrap my legs

around your waist, and we could do it here...here...
right here and right now, Guido. Because that's what
you'd like, isn't it?'

He closed his eyes, because now the hot jerk of
desire was threatening to render him incapable of doing anything—except maybe acting out her outrageous fantasy. 'Can you feel what you've done to
me?' he bit out.

Could she? Lucy swallowed. 'Er, yes.'

'So how the hell am I going to get off this dance
floor.'

'You think of something so abhorrent that it completely freaks you out and makes you lose all that
desire in an instant.'

There was a long pause. Oh, that was easy! He
thought of marriage, and suddenly he was right back
where he wanted to be. In control.

Lucy stared at him, aware that the black eyes had
grown icy, and suddenly she was furious with herself.
Why had she played that stupid game with him?

'Guido?' she questioned, and uncharacteristically
her voice sounded weak and uncertain.

The smile he gave her was anticipatory, almost
cruel. He was enjoying the sensation now that the
situation was reversed and *she* was the one left doing
the wanting.

'I'll leave you to your dancing, Lucy,' he said
softly. 'Let me know when you want to go to bed.'

And something in his eyes made her feel
unaccountably scared.

CHAPTER SIX

THE following day, resplendent in a close-fitting jade-green suit, with a huge black picture hat trimmed with feathers, Lucy stood in Solajoya's small but majestic cathedral as Leo was baptised. The music of the organ and the accompanying choir soared celestially up to the high domed ceiling, and the church was filled with the great and the good of Mardivino as well as immediate family. Only the King was unable to attend—his health was too frail and these days, according to Guido, he rarely left his suite of rooms at the Palace.

Yet, despite the splendour and the grandeur, it was essentially a family occasion. Just as with every other family on the planet, there were small swapped smiles when Leo began to bawl as the water was sprinkled onto his forehead.

It was only when they stepped outside into blinding sunlight, where banks of fragrant flowers were massed, to the sound of cheers and the sight of what seemed to be the entire population of the island, that Lucy realised that it was a significant and very regal occasion, too.

Lunch was at the Palace—and far less formal than the State Banquet of the night before. This time Lucy was seated next to a woman named Sasha—a beauty not much older than herself, whose olive skin and dark eyes marked her out as a native of the island. She was sweet and charming, and incredibly interested to know all about Lucy.

'I can't believe that Guido has actually brought a woman home,' she confided softly.

Lucy smiled, though it felt brittle and unnatural.

When eventually they had gone back to their room last night, they had circled each other like two warring creatures. She had been wary of him, confused by him, and had wanted to distance herself from him—as he had done from her. To try to show him— and prove to herself—that he did not have an irresistible power over her.

How typical that her very reticence had seemed to entrance him and he had pulled out all the stops where charm was concerned. He had stroked her hair and told her that she was beautiful. Had undressed her slowly…oh, so slowly…as if he'd had all the time in the world.

Who could have resisted such advances, as he cajoled and soothed and incited her, all at the same time?

Even though a part of her had tried to fight it she had been unable to do so. He had made her molten and receptive and aching for him, as she always ached for him, and then they had fallen into bed and spent almost the whole night making love. Though maybe that was just her slant on what they had done.

The trouble was that there didn't seem to be any description which fell in between 'making love' and 'having sex'. It certainly hadn't been the former—

certainly not where Guido was concerned—and the latter sounded so…so clinical. And, whatever else it might have been, it had certainly not been clinical. It had been heavenly. Heartstopping. And once her turbulent emotions had melted under the onslaught of his caresses Lucy had had to bite back words of endearment.

Oh, why had she become involved with a man as unobtainable as Guido Cacciatore? And why had she not had the insight to realise that compartmentalising her feelings for him was as useless as whistling in the wind?

'So where did you two meet?' queried Sasha, with a smile.

'At a party.' Sasha's eyebrows were still raised in question. Lucy took another mouthful of champagne. 'In New York.'

'He loves New York,' said Sasha thoughtfully. 'But of course, it's where he went to live with his aunt, when his mother died.'

'I…I didn't know.'

Sasha shrugged. 'Well, you of all people know how closed-in he can be.'

She certainly did. 'Have you known him long?'

'Oh, all my life.' Sasha smiled again. 'Believe me, I've seen Guido in *all* his guises. We used to play together as children. He's a bit like…' She frowned, creasing up her nose. 'Not a brother, exactly—we're not close enough for that. More like a cousin—once or twice removed, I guess!'

Lucy hadn't thought he *was* particularly close to

his brothers, but she didn't say anything—and besides, she knew that the subtext to what Sasha was saying was that there was no romance—or longed-for romance—between her and Guido. Her reassurance was oddly comforting, and Lucy smiled.

'And you're a definite improvement on the last woman I saw him with!' said Sasha fervently.

It was one of those situations that you read about in women's magazines—where you knew you ought to completely ignore the statement and carry on talking about something else. But she couldn't help herself.

'Oh?' questioned Lucy casually. 'Who was that?'

'Oh, you know.' Sasha pulled a face. 'One of those sooty-eyed blondes who look like they're composed of plastic and silicone!'

In spite of herself, Lucy laughed. She wasn't naïve enough to think that Guido had come to her bed as a virgin! 'When was that?'

'Oh…ages ago. Last fall, I think. Yes. I'd flown to New England, and then called in to see Guido on the way back here.'

The sounds of chatter retreated and were replaced by a sudden roaring in her ears. Lucy's mouth dried and she quickly drank some more champagne, which made it even drier. She was aware that a pulse was slamming somewhere in her temple, as if someone was repeatedly knocking a hammer hard against it.

Last fall? Autumn?

So when would that have been?

September, maybe? Or even October?

But she had started her affair with him in June!

She felt the bitter taste of betrayal which made the champagne a distant memory. Had he been…oh, that horrible phrase…*two-timing* her?

How she kept her face from reacting she never knew. Maybe she had become an expert through hiding her real feelings from Guido. But whatever it was, she just managed a cool, grown-up smile. After all, there could be any kind of explanation…wasn't that what always happened in books? That the sooty-eyed blonde was really his sister?

But he didn't have a sister!

His cousin?

She kept the cool smile pinned to her lips. She would not jump to conclusions. Nor would she put Sasha in an uncomfortable position. She would ask him herself. Later.

And then, disturbing her thoughts with the rippling precision of a flat, round pebble thrown into an already turbulent pool, she heard his deep, dark accent.

'Are you having a good time, *cara mia*?' he murmured.

She turned her head to look up at him, grateful for the large hat which shaded her face and the troubled look in her eyes. He was wearing a suit and a snowy shirt, and a silken tie as sapphire as the blue waters of the sea which could be seen quite clearly through the Palace windows.

Last night he had been edgy, almost irritable, but it was amazing what a night of brilliant sex could do—for today he was as sunny as it was possible for a man like Guido to be. His black eyes were glittering with life and fire, and his olive skin gleamed with a kind of soft inner luminescence. He looked vibrant and vital and thoroughly irresistible, and her pulse began to scramble in a thin and thready way.

'It's lovely,' she said quietly, because in a way it was. If you had shown someone a photograph of the scene, they would have longed to be there themselves. The baby was now sleeping, and there was the smooth and easy flow of chatter which came at the end of a very agreeable gathering. 'Quite lovely,' she repeated, looking around as if she wanted to freeze-frame the scene, to lock it away in her mind so that she would never forget it.

Guido's eyes narrowed. There was something in her expression which he couldn't quite read, and he thought—not for the first time—what an enigmatic person she really was. She seemed to buck the modern trend of spilling her innermost feelings and thoughts within a nanosecond of knowing someone—and wasn't there something both intriguing and devastatingly appealing about a woman who always kept something back?

He bent his head even closer, so that his words were murmured enticements in her ear. 'Things will be breaking up here soon. What do you say to going back to our room—for a siesta? Mmm?'

Lucy swallowed. She would bet that his idea of a siesta didn't fit the traditional definition, but in a way wasn't that exactly what she needed? Not the physical part—which was doubtless his reason for asking her—but the opportunity to ask him about the blonde, and to ask him something else, too...

She smiled. 'Only if you're sure your brother and sister-in-law won't think we are rude to leave.'

'Are you crazy?' He raised his eyebrows. 'My brother would consider me lacking in any kind of sanity to do otherwise. Come.'

Quietly, they slipped away, and Lucy felt almost light-headed as they stole through the cool marble corridors. For this was all a farce—this pretence that no one knew where they were going, or guessed what their—his—intention was. The other guests would notice their absence, but it was more than that—there were servants along the way—always servants. Sometimes, like now, knowing they were not wanted, they would melt away—as if they were not composed of flesh and blood at all.

Yet Lucy knew that if Guido had the slightest wish or desire—for a drink, say, or a newspaper or book—then those self-same faceless servants would magically interpret what he wanted and would appear discreetly by his side to do his bidding.

Did that kind of attention all your life change you? It must do. When you became used to having a small world revolve around you then surely you could be forgiven for thinking that the normal rules of restraint and fidelity did not apply.

Did they?

Well, she was soon going to find out.

Once they were back in their suite, he carefully took her hat off and then, with equal care, unpinned her hair so that it spilled down over the green jacket of her suit. *The suit that he'd bought for her.* If you allowed a man to buy you clothes, then weren't you selling something of yourself into the bargain?

'Did I tell you how beautiful you looked today?' he murmured, stroking at the tip of her chin and then lifting it slightly with his fingertips, as if wanting to examine her face more closely.

She had planned not to let him touch her, but oh, how seductive a gentle, almost protective touch could be. Perhaps if he had gone all out for a blatant and hot-blooded seduction then she might not have been so responsive. As it was, all her nerve-endings seemed acutely sensitised, as if her skin was raw and new, craving the healing of his caress.

Should she let him continue? she thought wildly. Pretend that there were not questions bubbling away at the back of her mind and give herself up to his embrace and everything that would follow? Knowing deep down that it might be the last chance she could do so? One last taste of enchanted food before she went back to more normal fare?

But no. Passion was strong, but pride could be even more powerful. She pulled away from him and went to stare out of the window instead.

Outside, the soft breeze made the petals of the fragrant roses shimmer like a heat-haze. There were pink and gold and crimson flowers, and softest apricot, too. And a mass of white blooms surrounding a statue—looking as pure and as perfect as the clouds which scudded across the azure sky.

Who would have thought that an ordinary girl like her could end up somewhere like this? In a Palace. With a devastatingly handsome prince standing in the room behind her, desperate to take her clothes off and take her into his bed once more.

Sweet dreams are made of this, she thought—but inside, as relentless as the beating of her heart, was the awareness that the dream was in danger of turning sour.

She turned round and found his dark eyes narrowed, watchful—but then, Guido was a very perceptive man. He had sensed that something was not right but, like a consummate poker player, he was biding his time—waiting for her to play her hand before he came back with something to trump her. And could he? Were her misgivings and her unvoiced fears completely groundless? She prayed they were, conscious of the lack of conviction of her hopes.

But her question, when it came, was not the one she had been planning to ask. It was almost as if she was seeking background knowledge for the question which would follow. Like someone doing research into motive.

'Why did you bring me here with you, Guido?'

'You know why. I thought you would enjoy it.' He frowned. 'I thought you *were* enjoying it. Aren't you?'

She didn't answer that. 'Is it just because of that? I mean—there is no ulterior motive?'

There was a pause. She was not only an independent woman, but an intelligent one, too. Would it insult that intelligence if he tried to convince her that a dip into Royal life in the luxurious surroundings of Mardivino had been his only objective?

The question was whether she was grown-up enough to accept him as the man he really was—with all his faults as well as the qualities of any other man.

He shrugged his shoulders and accompanied the very Gallic gesture with a rueful smile. 'It is useful, having you here,' he murmured.

Of all the most insulting words he could have used, Lucy would have put *useful* in the top five. But what exactly did he mean? 'Useful?' she echoed, perplexed.

He began to loosen his tie. Could he make her understand? 'My presence here always invites a kind of feeding frenzy.'

'Feeding frenzy?' she echoed again, feeling like someone who was learning a new language by the simple repetition of a phrase. 'What do you mean?'

'I mean that the inhabitants of this island seem to feel it necessary to marry off their Princes; there is pressure on Gianferro to do so, but particularly on me. Gianferro's bride will be cherry-picked from a very small and exclusive orchard, but the field is rather wider in my case. Especially now that Nico, the youngest, has settled down and provided Mardivino with a new generation.'

He had the grace to look slightly abashed as he stared at her, looking almost little-boy-lost with those melting dark eyes. Did he think that such grace would absolve him from what he had revealed? Or that by being allowed to see a glimpse of vulnerability she would forgive him anything?

'Let me get this straight,' she said, and her voice didn't sound anything like her usual voice. 'My invitation—apart from giving you the obvious benefits of having a willing sexual partner who would place no demands on you—was a kind of talisman—or maybe woman—' she gave an ironic laugh '—who would ward off any prospective brides?'

'That's too simplistic a way of looking at it!' he protested.

'Is it?' She noticed that he didn't deny it—but how could he, when basically what she'd said was true? And would he answer the next question—the ramifications of which might really sound the death-knell to their relationship? But she reminded herself that the word *relationship* had a hollow ring about it in their case. What they had was not that at all—it was something merely masquerading as a partnership.

Her eyes were very clear, but her voice sounded strained as the words came tumbling out. 'Did you happen to go to bed with a blonde last September?'

He stilled in the process of pulling his tie off and his eyes narrowed into shards of smoky ebony. *'What?'* he questioned softly.

'You didn't hear me? Or you didn't understand?' she demanded, but pain had started to rip through her at the glaring omission of a denial. 'It's a simple enough question, Guido—all it requires is a simple yes or no answer. Did you or did you not sleep with a blonde woman last fall?'

'How dare you interrogate me in this way?'

'Is that a yes?' she asked steadily. 'Or a no?'

They stared at each other across a space which seemed to be enlarging by the second.

He nodded his head. 'Well, yes,' he said. 'But it meant—'

'Nothing?' she supplied sarcastically, and now the tear in her heart was widening, and someone was tipping into the space a substance with all the painful and abrasive qualities of grit. 'Isn't that what men always say? That it didn't mean anything? So not only do they damn the woman they betrayed, but also the woman they betrayed her with!'

'*Betrayed?*' he exploded. 'Do not use such emotive words with me, Lucy! I had met you on precisely two occasions up until that moment!'

'But you had slept with *me!*' she whimpered, like a dog whose master was raising the whip.

'So? For God's sake—don't you think you're over-reacting?'

She felt sick. 'How is that?' She trembled. 'How am I overreacting?'

'Because at the time what we had was casual. It was new. It was uncertain. It was all those things which are true at the beginning, and sometimes the beginning is the end.'

'Don't try to confuse me with your warped logic!' she raged.

'I am trying to tell it like it is,' he said, with a forced patience which was unfamiliar territory to him.

'We had made no arrangement to see one another again, had we? Remember?'

Through the mists of her pain she looked back through her memory, blindly searching for something which would make it all acceptable. The mists cleared. She had been back-to-back on a series of long-haul flights which had clashed with his trips around the globe in exactly the opposite direction. And, yes, in theory he was right—they had *not* made any arrangement to see one another again.

In fact, he had told her casually to ring him, but she had not bothered. She had been in that early stage of a relationship where she was uncertain of him— not sure whether he really wanted to see her again and not wanting to pursue *him* because that way lay heartbreak and the loss of respect.

Lucy had recognised that for a man like Guido the chase was everything, and that once a woman started reversing the traditional role she would be doomed.

She had almost been over him when his call had come, out of the blue.

'I thought you were going to call me!' he had accused softly.

'I've been busy,' she'd retorted.

'Oh, have you?' He had laughed, and his voice had dipped into a honeyed caress. He had been trying to forget her. She had touched him in a way he was not familiar with—a way which spelt some unknown danger and not the kind he wanted to embrace. But it had not worked. He had not forgotten her at all. 'I've missed you, Lucy,' he'd murmured, and she had been lost.

Intellectually, she could see now the logic behind his reasoning—but jealousy was a different plant altogether, and it flourished and grew like a weed.

'And how many more?' she demanded hotly. 'How many since?'

'None!' he exploded. 'After that it was only you— you know it was!'

On some level, yes, she did—for their lovemaking had been completely different when they had met up again. It was as if the break had allowed the barriers between them to fall—certainly the sexual ones. She had felt freer and more liberated—able to indulge his fantasies. And her own.

Perhaps she could have forgiven him then, had it not been for his motive for bringing her here. Her secret little dreams, that he'd wanted to introduce her to his family and to deepen their relationship, had been as nebulous as dreams always were.

'It still doesn't change your reasons for bringing me here.' She stared at him sadly. 'Have I reached such elevated heights in your regard for me that I should rejoice that you've brought me here to see off other women? To protect you from their advances like a human guard-dog?'

'You are making a....' For the first and only time since she had known him he seemed to struggle to find the right words in English. 'A mountain out of the molehill!' he declared passionately.

But then something snapped, and her own temper

exploded to match his. 'I don't think so!' she raged. 'I think that nothing very much has changed at all, if you must know! It was casual way back then, and it is still casual now!' Hadn't she said as much to Gianferro yesterday?

There was a fraught and odd kind of pause, which could never have been described as silence—for the sound of their breathing punctured the air with accusations and hurt.

'So what do you want to do about it?' he said eventually. 'Are you going to shout and rage a little more and then come over here and let me kiss it better?'

As if it was a tiny graze on her knee instead of a jagged, deep tear through her heart! She closed her eyes briefly to blink away the salty glimmer of tears, then shook her head. 'No. I want to go home,' she said shakily. 'And then I never want to see you again.'

He stared at her, scarcely able to believe what she was saying. 'Don't play games with me, Lucy,' he warned softly. 'For I have no appetite for them. If you threaten to leave then I will arrange it. But I shall not run after you, nor plead with you to stay. That is not my style.'

No, she couldn't imagine that it was. But she was not playing games—she was deadly serious.

'Then arrange it. Please.'

His narrowed eyes raked over her one last time. 'So be it,' he ground out, like a skater digging his blade repeatedly into the ice. He turned on his heel and slammed his way out of the suite, leaving Lucy looking after him, biting her lip to stop herself from crying.

Yet even while she was silently damning herself for ever having asked him anything the one subject she had not broached loomed up like a dark spectre in her mind.

But it was easy to flatten it down again.

Her philosophy on life had developed largely because her job involved a great deal of flying. Accidents *did* happen occasionally, but there was absolutely no point in worrying about them until they did.

CHAPTER SEVEN

HE COULD be a prince and you could be an air stewardess, but it made no difference—at the end of the day you were still both just a man and a woman, with all the problems that men and women had when they began relationships. Or—in her and Guido's case—ended them.

And what a problem it was.

Lucy stared at the blue line, as if looking at it long enough and hard enough might somehow change the end result. Her sense of disbelief was tempered by the hysteria which was growing by the moment.

She had gone through anger, concern, outright worry, denial, and now—now the most terrifying thing of all...

Confirmation.

She swallowed, putting the palm of her hand over her still-flat belly as if trying to convince herself that it wasn't true, that she couldn't be pregnant.

Could she?

She heard muffled moving around coming from the direction of the sitting room and her head jerked up. Gary was home! So what did she do? Did she tell him?

There was a loud banging on the bathroom door.

'You in there, Luce?'

She licked her lips nervously. 'Yes.'

'Well, are you going to be all day? I've got a hot date tonight and I need to beautify myself!'

Normally she would have giggled and vacated the bathroom while he had her in stitches about his love-life. Gary was a fellow steward, sweet and handsome and understanding and gay—and he seemed to spend ten times as long in the bathroom as Lucy did.

She had never felt less like giggling in her life. But she couldn't hide away in here for ever, and if she didn't tell someone soon she was going to be sick.

You already *have* been sick, she reminded herself. Long and retchingly this very morning, and yesterday morning, and for countless mornings before that.

She pulled open the door and was shocked to see the look of horror on Gary's good-looking face.

'What the hell is wrong?' he demanded.

How to tell him? How to tell anyone when she'd only just been able to bear accepting it for herself?

'I'm…I'm…'

His eyes raked around the floor of their usually immaculate bathroom. 'Oh, my God—you're pregnant!' he yelped.

'How…how could you tell?' Did that mean she actually *looked* pregnant?

He pursed his lips and his eyes flicked to the discarded cardboard box and the plastic strip which was lying in the sink. 'This may not be quite my scene—but you wouldn't need to be a detective to work it out. How long ago and who…?' The look of horror came over his face once again, and momentarily he clapped his hand over his mouth. 'Oh, God—don't tell me—it's the Prince!'

'Of course it's the Prince!' said Lucy tearfully. 'Who else do you think it could be? And his name is Guido.' Somehow that made it sound and seem more real. She couldn't possibly be pregnant by a prince, but she could be pregnant by a man with a real name—even if it was an exotically foreign one.

'Oh, love,' said Gary sympathetically, and gave her shoulder a squeeze. 'What on earth are you going to do?'

Tears welled up in her eyes and she scrubbed at them furiously with her fist. 'I'm going to have to tell him.'

Lucy.

The name flashed up on the screen of his mobile and Guido glanced at it with unflickering eyes, tempted to ignore it.

Why? Because that little ember of anger still smouldered away inside him? Anger that she—*she*—had had the temerity to leave him, when no woman had ever done so before? Or was it because she had made him feel bad about himself, and Guido didn't like to feel bad? He liked to float through life, taking only the good bits and discarding anything which looked as if it would even remotely lead to complications.

But even his anger could not quite extinguish his interest.

Why was she ringing him after having told him that

she never wanted to set eyes on him again? Was she maybe regretting her words and her actions? Remembering, perhaps, how good they were together...wanting a little more?

Even while desire leapt inside him, he half hoped that was not so. For Guido respected Lucy, and her adamant stance and her pride, and for him that kind of respect was rare—almost unheard of. Obviously she wanted more from a man than he was capable of giving—or wanted to give—and in a funny kind of way he respected that, too.

If she came back then surely his esteem for her would die. She would become like all the others, who would sacrifice their principles for a man who might never be King but would always be Prince...

Curiosity got the better of him, and he flicked the button with his thumb.

'*Si?*' he drawled.

'It's Lucy.'

'I know it is,' he said softly.

Then why the hell didn't you say, Hello, Lucy? She hesitated, because she couldn't think how to say it—and even if she could was it fair to blurt it out over the phone?

'How are you?' he questioned, because now he was perplexed. Had he been expecting one of those predictable conversations? The ones where the woman brightly asked how he was, and acted as if no harsh words had been spoken, and then casually mentioned that they just happened to be passing through...

It was a question she could not answer truthfully. 'I have to see you.'

Guido stared at the gleaming skyline and raised his dark eyebrows by a fraction. So she had come straight out with her desire to see him. Pretty up-front—if a little surprising. And yet there was no longing in her voice, no sultry undertone saying that she had missed him. The unpredictable was rare enough to excite him.

'Where are you?'

'In England.'

He frowned. 'And when are you coming to New York?'

'I'm not.'

'Then…?'

She drew a deep breath as she heard his faint puzzlement—as if to say, *Well, why are you ringing me, then?*

'I'm at home, in England.'

Pull yourself together, Lucy. But what could she say? *Come and visit me here because I can't face travelling?* He might refuse, and then where would that leave her? Which left her absolutely no choice at all but to tell him.

'Guido, I'm pregnant.'

He felt as he had never felt in his life—as if a dark whirlwind had swirled its way into his lungs, pushing all the natural breath away. For a moment he could not speak.

'What did you say?' he questioned at last, softly and dangerously.

She was not going to be cast in the role of the baddie, the guilty party. There were two people involved here, and they must both share the consequences—whatever they might be.

'You heard.'

'It's mine?'

She bit down on her lip. She was not going to cry. 'Yes.'

'You're sure?'

'Sure that I'm pregnant, you mean? Or sure that it's yours? Yes, on both counts.'

Guido's words were like bitter stones spitting from his mouth. 'What is your address?'

He didn't even know where she lived! With a feeling of hysteria she told him, aware of the almost laughable contrast between his penthouse apartment or his Rainbow Palace. 'Number five Western Road, Brentwood.'

'I'll be there tomorrow,' he said tightly, and terminated the connection.

Unable to concentrate, and fired up by the need to fill her waking moments with any kind of activity which might temporarily give her the comfort of allowing her to forget her precarious situation, Lucy cleaned the house from top to bottom.

Gary stood in the doorway, watching her scrub the floor on her hands and knees. 'What's this?' he questioned. 'Penance?'

'I want the place to look clean,' she said stubbornly. 'It might be an ordinary little suburban house, but it will gleam as brightly as any damned Rainbow Palace!'

'We do have a mop, you know,' he said mildly.

Lucy's mouth wobbled into a smile. 'I'm treating it as a mini-workout!'

Gary breathed a sigh of relief. 'Thank God you're smiling again!'

'Being miserable isn't going to change anything.'

'That's my gal! What time is he arriving?'

'He didn't say. This afternoon, probably.'

'Just my luck to be flying off to Singapore in a minute!' Gary put his hand on his hip in an overtly camp gesture which made her smile again. 'You know I'd always wanted to meet a real-live prince!'

By mid-afternoon the house was gleaming—and there were fresh flowers in vases and the smell of furniture polish wafting in the air. Why didn't she go the whole hog and bake a cake while she was at it? *Because you aren't selling your house, that's why. And neither are you selling yourself.*

She didn't know what she was going to say to him, but she knew that she was not going to allow him to talk her into anything she didn't want. And—

The doorbell rang and Lucy froze. She shut her eyes briefly. How many times in your life did you wish that something was just a bad dream?

Guido glanced down the road as he waited for her to answer. He had never been anywhere like this in his life—it was like a parallel universe. Neat little semi-detached houses, with sparkling windows and tidy gardens. He could hear the sound of birds, and walking down the road towards him was a woman with a pushchair, and a chubby toddler by her side, who kept stopping to peer at the pavement. He stared hard at them in a way he would never normally have done, and his mouth tightened as the door opened and there stood Lucy.

For a moment he was taken aback to see that she looked just the same—slim and strong and curvy. Had he somehow expected her to be already swollen? Perhaps wearing some floaty smock thing to disguise a growing bump? His eyes narrowed. No, not the same at all—there were faint shadows beneath her honey-coloured eyes and her face was pale. The world seemed suddenly silent—an immense, important silence—and yet his words, when they came, were ordinary words.

'Hello, Lucy.'

Just the sight of him made her heart turn over, as she had suspected it would anyway. But her feelings for Guido were deeper and more complex now—for this was the man who had sired the child which grew inside her. A strong and powerful man. How she yearned to just let him take over and protect her—an instinct which perhaps went hand-in-hand with pregnancy itself. But he was offering to do neither, and she did not have the right to ask—she had relinquished all such rights the day she had walked out on him...

Her heart was racing—could that be good for the baby?—and she nodded in acknowledgement. 'You'd better come in.'

It was a bit like stepping into a larger version of a dolls' house he had once seen as a child in a museum, when he had been staying with his aunt. He'd had no idea that proportions could be so scaled-down—that rooms could be so small!

She led the way into a yellow and white sitting room, and he was surprised by the sudden understanding of a word which was not usually in his vocabulary. *Cosy.*

'Would you like some coffee?'

He shook his head. 'No, I do not want coffee.' And then, because they both seemed in danger of ignoring something in the hope that it might just go away, he said, 'How many weeks?'

'I'm not sure—'

'How can you not be sure?' he demanded.

'We can work it out,' she said desperately.

'You haven't been to see the doctor?'

'Not yet.'

She saw the anger and the disbelief which sparked flames in the coal-dark eyes, and yet with a blinding blow of surprise she realised that not once had he interrogated her about who the father was. Which meant he believed her. A relief she hadn't been anticipating washed over her and she felt compelled to offer some kind of explanation. 'I was…in denial, I guess.'

'You did not plan it?' he questioned coldly.

A wave of dizziness swept over her. 'Plan it? You think I planned it? What? To try to trap you or something? Well, think again, Guido, that isn't my style—

and even if it were there were two of us. It isn't just the woman who is responsible for contraception—it's the man's responsibility, too!'

Something unfamiliar stole over him. A sense that here was something which he couldn't just have someone solve for him by snapping his fingers.

'Sit down,' he ordered quietly.

Maybe if she hadn't been feeling so woozy and so perilously close to tears she might have told him that she didn't need permission to sit down in her own home. As it was, she collapsed in one of the armchairs as if her knees had been turned into gelatine.

His eyes narrowed as he did a swift mental calculation. 'I remember when it was,' he said slowly.

He had been showing her round the Palace and she had made him laugh, made him feel...*normal* in those formal surroundings, and something primitive had ripped through him. Something so primitive that he had neglected to protect himself and her—and when before in his life had *that* happened?

There had been an overwhelming need to take her swiftly and without ceremony—a truly novel experience for a man whose upbringing had been swamped with ceremony. No, she was right. It *had* been his responsibility, too—and passion had made it fly straight out of his head. Damn the witch! He had recognised that for him she spelt danger, and it seemed that he had been right.

His eyes sparked with black fire, but what good would anger do him now? He needed his wits about him to achieve what he needed to achieve.

'Nearly three months, I make it,' he said.

Some of her strength began to return as she heard the clipped note in his voice, and her eyes flashed defiance at him. 'I'm having the baby!' she declared. 'No matter what you say!'

He registered this, his mind sifting through all the possibilities. He was left with the same and only one which had occupied his mind all during the flight. The question was how he should go about achieving it—for he knew that beneath today's rather shaky Lucy lay a woman with steely resolve. Who could walk out of his door without turning back.

'I agree,' he murmured.

She was in such turmoil that it didn't even occur to her to tell him that she didn't actually *need* his consent. Instead, she looked at him with suspicion. 'You want me to keep the baby?'

He flinched as if she had struck him. 'Did you imagine that I would contemplate any alternative?' he questioned, in a low, shocked voice.

For a moment she felt like a drowning woman who had been offered not just a lifeline but a warm change of clothes at the end of it. And then he snatched them all away with his next words.

'Have you not considered that you carry within you a child of noble blood?'

'Every baby—any baby—is noble in my view!' she declared.

A faint smile curved the cruel lips. 'I commend you for your passion, Lucy,' he said softly. 'But I am looking at this from a purely practical point of view.'

The black eyes bored into her, as coolly analytical as a lawyer's eyes might have been. 'You are carrying my child—a child in whose veins beats the Royal blood of Mardivino.'

Now who was being passionate? she thought tiredly.

'By birth, that child will have certain rights and privileges. He or she could one day become King or Queen if Gianferro does not produce an heir—which looks increasingly likely.'

No, Lucy had been wrong. It had *not* been passion she had heard in his voice—it had been practicality. Now he was discussing their child's position in Mardivinian society as a conquering army might discuss dividing up the spoils of a country.

She rubbed her fingers over her forehead. 'I don't know what you think we can do about it. If anything. We aren't a couple any more.' She gave a short laugh. 'If indeed we ever were.'

He stared at her. Was she mad? Did she think he was just going to accept her momentous piece of news and walk away from her? Allow her to bring up his child—a Mardivinian Prince or Princess—in this little house in the middle of suburban England?

Like a chess master edging towards a win, he considered his next move with care. The burning question was whether the baby was indeed his. He looked down into her pale and beautiful face. The faint tremble of her bare lips unexpectedly stabbed at his conscience and as he gazed into the honey-coloured eyes the burning pride and dignity he read there left him in no doubt. And doubt, he recognised with an overwhelming certainty, would be the one thing guaranteed to thwart his wishes. Her baby was his.

He felt the rapid acceleration of his heart, accompanied by an almost dizzy feeling and a strange, blunted pain where his heart should be—if every woman he'd ever known hadn't accused him of not having one. He shook his head, shaken by the unfamiliar physical sensations and the random process of his thoughts.

He was in shock!

But now was not the time to examine his reaction to impending fatherhood—there were matters far more urgent and pressing.

'The child must be born on Mardivino,' he said quietly.

'Must?' She stared at him.

'Do not fight me on this, Lucy,' he warned.

'But you don't live there!' she protested. 'You left your Royal life behind a long time ago—remember? You told me!'

'So I did.' His mouth hardened. 'But things are different now.'

How was it that he had slipped so quickly back into a traditional outlook? As if all those years of freedom had not happened. For a moment he felt dazed by the realisation of how indelibly his birthright had stamped its mark on him.

She tried one last attempt, knowing that she was fighting against something, but not quite sure what it was. 'It doesn't have to be difficult, Guido. Lots of women manage on their own—we can work something out.'

But he cut across her opposition as if it was of no consequence. 'Not only must the birth take place within the Principality,' he continued, 'it must also be legitimised.'

Her head was spinning now. 'What are you talking about?'

'Your Prince has come, *cara*,' he drawled sardonically. 'And he intends to marry you.'

Marry her? With a shotgun held to his back? 'No!'

'Oh, yes,' he said, and even though it was silky soft, there was no mistaking the undercurrent of steely purpose. 'You may wish to play the courageous single mother, but the reality will be an entirely different matter. It isn't going to happen. My baby will not be born illegitimately—he or she will inherit all that is their due, but that can only be achieved within wedlock.'

She stared at him, frozen into immobility by the iron edge of his words and the realisation that she had never seen Guido like this before. So cold and so powerful, and so…determined.

'Guido—'

'Don't even think of fighting me on this one, Lucy,' he said harshly. 'The odds are stacked highly enough in my favour to make it a laughably one-sided battle.' There was a pause to drive home his words, as if one was needed. 'Which I would win.'

She looked into his eyes and knew that he meant

it. Which meant that Lucy Maguire was going to marry a Prince.

It should have been a dream come true—but the reality was something different. It meant being shackled to a sexy but cold-blooded aristocrat. A man who didn't love her.

No, it was not a dream.

It was a living nightmare.

CHAPTER EIGHT

THEY were to be married quietly on Mardivino, on this blustery autumn day, with only their immediate families in attendance—including Lucy's rather bewildered parents, who kept looking around them as if expecting to wake up at any second. You and me both, she thought, rather grimly.

Her brother was a different matter, taking the whole bizarre situation in his stride and joking to her that she'd done 'better than I could ever have imagined, sis!' As if she'd won the Lottery!

But she knew that Benedict meant what he said. And that he actually liked Guido and thought he was a good man.

Well, of course he did! Hadn't Guido gone out of his way to win him round? Taking him sailing around the island and introducing him to glamorous women, and laying on bucketfuls of charm—which would have had even the most hardened cynic eating out of his hand?

Come to think of it he had been equally persuasive in winning Lucy over, getting her to agree to marry him—but in her case he had certainly not used charm. She wondered that he had not even bothered to try.

Perhaps he'd had no stomach for it, or perhaps he had instinctively realised that she would shrink away from it. For charm was nothing but a superficial and shallow veneer which people used as a front to hide their true feelings.

Instead, he had argued with cold and remorseless logic, citing historic precedent, making her dizzy with facts about the Mardivinian royal family and its progeny.

She supposed that if anything could be said in his favour it was that he hadn't bothered to dress up their proposed marriage to be something it wasn't.

And in the end she had been too tired to fight him, recognising that the full weight of a powerful regime would swing behind him if she dared to oppose his wishes. But perhaps pregnancy made you more vulnerable and susceptible—for she had found herself unable to let her own self-interest deny her baby its rights. What woman in her right mind would?

It would, he told her, be first and foremost a legal contract between them—and anything which went beyond that would have to be negotiated between them.

Their lawyers had thrashed out a long-prenuptial agreement. Lucy had engaged the best lawyer she could afford and she had taken his advice—though she had argued in vain about the clause which stated that should they divorce then the Cacciatore family would get custody of her child.

'Can they do that?' she had asked heatedly.

The lawyer had given a rather thin smile. 'Oh, yes. No contest—though you could try. Though can you see the courts letting you put a royal child with minders—while you carry on flying? These people will get whatever it is they want, make no mistake.'

So that was the deal. If she wanted to keep her child then she must stay married to its father.

And now here she was, on her way to the ceremony in all her bridal finery, with her stomach tied up in knots and feeling none of the joyful expectation of the normal bride.

'Good heavens,' breathed her father faintly as their horsedrawn carriage came to a halt in front of the cathedral steps. 'Just look at all those people!'

There were hordes of them—all waving flags and clutching flowers and cheering—their faces alight with what looked like genuine joy at their first glimpse of the bride.

'It'll be okay, Dad,' Lucy whispered, and squeezed his arm. 'Just pretend it's the village church.'

'I don't think my imagination is quite *that* good,' remarked her father wryly.

Lucy was wearing ivory—which flattered her Titian hair far more than pure white would have done. Anyway, she would have felt a hypocrite wearing white when both families knew she was pregnant— and soon the rest of the world would, too. There would be smug smiles all round, of that she was certain. Hadn't she scoured newspaper columns herself and done sums on her fingers to work out if a child had been conceived before or after marriage?

Her wedding gown was cut with flattering simplicity—a floor-length dress, its starkness relieved by a mere sprinkling of freshwater pearls sewn into the fabric. Over the top she wore a silk-chiffon overcoat which floated like a cloud in the breeze. Fragrant flowers were woven into her hair, and on her feet were a pair of exquisite high-heeled shoes which brought her almost up to Guido's nose.

The aisle seemed as long as a runway, yet all she could see were the groom's dark flashing eyes—a half-smile of what looked like encouragement as she made her way towards him.

'Are you okay?' he questioned softly as she joined him at the altar.

His heart was pounding. There had been a part of him which had wondered whether she would actually go through with it. Or just flounce off the island—since no one could have physically stopped her—and try to fight him through the courts for custody of the child. Had she been sensible enough to heed his words and realise that such a battle would have been lost before it had begun? Would that explain her fixed and determined smile? And was she also sensible enough to see that it was possible to make this work?

'I'm fine, thank you,' Lucy answered politely, discovering that it was easy to squash the haunting demons of bitter regret—if you practised long and hard enough.

She had decided that she was going to behave exactly as a bride should behave, and not let her parents—or herself—down. She was pregnant with Guido's child, and there were far-reaching repercussions which she had been forced to accept. She was certainly not going to start coming over like a petulant adolescent, sulking because her marriage was not the one she had sometimes dreamed of.

Oh, on the outside it was all those things—and more. Her friends had been in turn envious and disbelieving. For how many women with Lucy's background ended up marrying a devastatingly handsome prince from a picturesque Mediterranean island? How many would be made a princess the moment the ring was slid onto her finger?

Her schoolfriend, Davina, had voiced what most of the others were feeling. 'Huh—at least *you* aren't going to have to save up for ever for your reception— *or* your honeymoon!'

Lucy had allowed them all their envy—for pride had let her confide in no one that it was simply a marriage of coincidence. But it had been Lucy who had felt envious. Davina might have a few years of scrimping and saving ahead of her—of making do and pass-me-down baby equipment—but she had a fiancé who adored her, who would do anything in the world if it made her happy.

And that was the difference.

Lucy had Guido—royal and rich and powerful.

And utterly remote.

She stared into his black eyes and saw nothing there other than a look of quiet triumph and determination.

The ceremony was conducted in French as well as English—in order to satisfy Mardivinian law. And as Guido slipped the slim platinum band on her trembling finger Lucy was aware that her life was never

going to be the same again. She had left Lucy
Maguire behind at the altar and had become Princess
Lucy Jennifer Cacciatore instead.

They emerged from the cathedral to a storm of
swirling rose petals and the blinding light of flashbulbs, which set out in stark relief the banked flowers
lining the steps leading down to the waiting carriage.

Once the door had slammed shut on them Guido
turned to her. 'Have I told you how beautiful you
look?' he murmured.

She was feeling like a drooping flower, and not in
the least bit beautiful. 'We're alone now, Guido,' she
said tetchily. 'So you can drop the pretence.'

A pulse hammered at his temple. 'How you test
me, Lucy,' he observed steadily.

She smiled down at a small girl who had hurled a
rather battered home-grown posy into the carriage. 'I
don't see why. You've got what you wanted, haven't
you? Legally I'm your bride, but in reality I'm your
prisoner!'

'Don't be so melodramatic!' he said angrily. 'You
are free to move at liberty!'

'Oh, really? So if I took a flight back to England
tomorrow, then you'd be perfectly agreeable?'

'In theory, there would be no objection.'

'In theory?' She opened her eyes very wide, aware
that she was being prickly—but wasn't that a kind of
defence mechanism? She was trying to accept the situation for what it was, and not what she would like
it to be.

And she was trying to stop herself from loving a man who had used her right from the very start.

He gave a hard smile. 'But the doctor has advised you not to travel,' he said smoothly.

'Very conveniently for you!' she retorted. 'And I suppose that if the doctor had told me that I had to run round and round the Palace gardens every morning, no doubt you'd be behind it!'

'I think you can be assured that if I were using the doctor as my mouthpiece, then I could think of more satisfying commands to give than an early-morning run,' he murmured.

Lucy blushed, hot colour creeping all the way up her bare neck. 'That was unnecessary!'

'Really?' he questioned innocently. 'You don't know to what I was alluding.'

No, but she had a pretty good idea. Apart from Guido's one brief comment, during the run-up to the wedding they had not spoken of the physical side of their marriage. In the flurry of arrangements there had simply not been time nor the inclination—certainly not on Lucy's part. Besides, it was actually quite a difficult thing to discuss.

When you were a couple having sex you didn't discuss it—unless you were erotically describing your likes and dislikes. It was a subject which did not bear scrutiny or analysis. But they had stopped being a couple and stopped having sex a long time ago—it was only the baby which had prompted this bizarre wedding. Of *course* they were going to ignore it.

And when a subject was deliberately ignored and

not spoken about, then it became huge inside your head. Lucy found herself tortured with memories of just how good it had been...and how much had changed. It could never be the same, could it? Not now.

She turned to the squealing crowd with a wide smile which threatened to split her face in two.

'Are you intending to make this a proper marriage, Lucy?' he questioned quietly.

She moved her head back to face him. Wasn't there still some remnant of the schoolgirl idealist inside her, who did not want harsh words to mar what should have been the happiest day of her life? So that, no matter what happened in the future, she could one day say to her son—or daughter—that it *had* been a happy day.

What did he want? A submissive yes while they clip-clopped their way through the streets of Mardivino?

'Now is neither the time nor the place to discuss it, Guido!'

'As you wish, my Princess,' he mocked.

The Rainbow Palace was festooned with flowers, and a wedding breakfast was laid out in the formal Mirrored Dining Room—on which, legend had it, one of the rooms at the Palace of Versailles had been modelled. Lucy could see her bridal image reflected back from every angle. Was that pale and doe-eyed creature in a beautiful wedding dress really her?

The Crown Prince was talking to her and, with an effort, she flashed Gianferro a huge smile.

'You will eat something?' he was saying.

'I…'

Lately, her appetite had been sparrow-like, to say the least. About to refuse, she saw the look of concern on his face and nodded instead, obediently forking a sliver of some delicate, unknown fish into her mouth. She had actually lost weight. In the space of a fortnight, her wedding dress had been twice taken in by the Parisian couturier who had been flown over especially to make it for her.

'It's…it's delicious,' she said.

'You are happy, Lucy?'

Gianferro's unexpected question came out of the blue. How much had Guido told him? Did he believe it to be a love-match—and, if so, did she have the right to disillusion him?

Lucy knew then that no matter what was going on inside she had made a contract with Guido for the sake of the baby. And for all their sakes she must play the part of the blushingly contented bride.

She raised her glass of fruit juice. 'I am,' she said, feeling a pang of guilt as she looked across the table at her mother, who was giggling at something Guido was saying. She smiled, so proud of her. For a woman whose calendar highlight was the church Bring-and-Buy sale, she too seemed to be adapting remarkably well. Well, she must make her mother proud of her, too. 'It's a very exciting day,' she murmured.

'Indeed it is,' he said thoughtfully. 'And Guido is taking you to the mountains for your honeymoon?'

'Yes, he is,' she agreed steadily.

'You did not long for a more traditional destination? Paris or Rome, perhaps?'

'Oh, no. I want to get to know my new country,' she said staunchly. She couldn't tell Gianferro that those cities were for ever tainted with memories of how it *had* been between them.

Then it had been sex and laughter, and a determination on her part to play the independent role required of her—but it had all backfired on her. And nothing had changed in that regard. She was still playing a role—except that now it just happened to be a different one.

'And after the honeymoon?' Gianferro's voice cut into her thoughts. 'What then?'

'We haven't decided.' Or rather, they hadn't discussed it—like so much else. She bit her lip as she glanced across the table to find Guido's black eyes on her.

He had been watching her, and saw her easy and laughing interaction with his brother change into a frozen look of *froideur* as she met his eyes. As if she was wishing herself a million miles away...

Well, you and me too, *cara*, he thought bitterly. The last thing in the world he wanted was to be incarcerated here on Mardivino, back in the whole damned strait-jacket of formality and ritual.

But it had to be.

Or did it?

Were her surroundings only adding to her feeling of entrapment? Should he reassure her on that score— tell her that their stay here need only be temporary if that was what she desired?

But he felt the cold pulse of anger as she turned her head away from him, as if he were invisible. Well, if that was the way she wanted to play it—if she intended to be stubborn—then she would soon discover that he could be stubborn, too...

Unseen beneath the damask tablecloth, Lucy's hand crept to cover the faint swell of her belly, willing herself not to succumb to the tide of emotion which was washing over her. Was it the rushing of her hormones which was making her feel so vulnerable? If so, she must be sure not to show it. Because he would not care—and why should he?

It was pointless to look for a soft response in a man like Guido. He had never behaved in that way before, so why the hell should he change now?

She watched him rise to his feet, resplendent in dark morning suit, his black hair ruffled and his olive skin gleaming. He was coming towards her, and despite everything her heart turned over. Why were emotions so impervious to logic? Why the hell did love have to leap out and grab you so inappropriately? Make you want to care for someone even though instinct told you there would be nothing coming back?

He gave a short laugh as he saw her face grow pale, and his words were so silky-soft that they could be heard by no one else.

'At least try to maintain the charade of happiness

on your wedding day, *cara*. Your mother will be distressed if you do otherwise. Come, Lucy.' He held his hand out for hers, and as she looked up at him his eyes glittered like deadly black ice. 'It is time to leave for our honeymoon.'

CHAPTER NINE

'SO TELL me, Lucy.' The black eyes glittered with challenge. 'What do a couple do on honeymoon when they aren't engaged in the rather more traditional pastime?'

From beneath her sunhat Lucy looked at him, and despite her intention not to, a shiver of pure longing ran through her. How different he looked from the man with whom she had exchanged her vows. Transformed from a formal and dark-suited elegance to a totally laid-back look, like a man happily at home on the beach.

He wore a pair of faded cut-off denims, which showed hard, muscular legs, and a thin cotton shirt which was flapping open, giving her occasional and distracting glimpses of his hair-roughened chest.

His mocking eyes were still challenging her for an answer, and she knew then that she could not keep running from the truth. She answered like the old Lucy—that self-deluding idiot who had thought she could match this man in the emotional detachment department.

The old Lucy would have met that challenge head-on. 'Are you trying to tell me you're frustrated?' she questioned.

'Well, aren't you?' he shot back.

'I have other things on my mind.'

'Such as?'

She pointed to the book which was lying open on her lap. 'You should try reading some time.'

'So should you.' His mouth twisted into an odd kind of smile. 'That's been open at the same page for the last hour!'

'I've been admiring the scenery.'

'I know you have,' he mocked.

'And what's that supposed to mean?'

He shrugged, flopping down onto the sand beside her. 'If you find the sight of my body so irresistible that you can't bear to tear your eyes away, Lucy— then stare away! Who am I to stop you?'

'I was not staring!'

'Oh, yes, you were,' he contradicted softly. 'You can't stop looking at me...just as I can't stop looking at you.'

He let his eyes drift over her, in a pale-green swimsuit which so flattered her colouring. Shaded by a hat *and* an umbrella—that fair English skin of hers would burn very easily—she was sitting rather primly on the soft, fine sand, occasionally swigging from a large bottle of cool water. The thin, stretchy material was moulded to her like a second skin, emphasising the increased swelling of her breasts and the hint of rounded belly which would grow bigger by the day.

At least she seemed less on edge today—some of the tight tension which had come so close to snapping on their wedding day seemed to have dissolved. He had seen the sadness as she bade farewell to her parents—the slight crumpling of her face which she had been so desperately trying to hide.

In that moment he had wanted to reach out and comfort her, but then he had reminded himself that he would not be able to follow through. The stone around his heart was too deeply ingrained to ever be shattered. It was better to start as he meant to go on, and he knew he could never give her real love. And maybe in that sense at least Lucy was the perfect bride for him. Wasn't that one of the things which had always fascinated him about her—the fact that she wasn't emotionally needy?

After her parents had left for England she had busied herself with changing—obviously she hadn't wanted him to see her moment of wistfulness—and when she had emerged again it had been with a pale and set face.

They had travelled to their honeymoon destination—the Cacciatore mountain lodge—and that night she had resolutely dressed in cotton pyjamas and climbed into the low divan, turning her back on him in a silent gesture which spoke volumes.

His mouth had hardened as he had gazed upwards at the moonshadows which danced on the ceiling.

Did she imagine that he was going to beg her to make love? Or that he would wait for ever for her to change her mind?

Like hell he would!

Today he had driven her to the sea, in an attempt to fill up the day with something other than the unspoken frustrations and resentments between them.

But everything seemed to be having the wrong effect. She was wearing very little, and so was he. And the trouble was that the way he felt was becoming very difficult to disguise....

Nervously, she glanced at him, seeing for herself just how aroused he was, and feeling that wretched hot, moist ache once more, tempting her to give in. She wanted him. She had never really stopped wanting him. But what good was sex going to do them now? Wouldn't it only complicate a complicated situation still further? 'Don't look at me that way,' she begged.

'What way is that? You mean, the way that any new husband would look at his wife?'

'Oh, please, Guido!' she retorted. 'We're not like a new husband and wife at all!'

'In some ways we are,' he argued softly. 'Or rather, we could be.'

She shook her head. Not the way that counted, they couldn't. 'No.'

'Then that is your decision, *cara*, not mine,' he bit out. 'And you must live with the consequences.'

She stared at him. She could see the hot light of desire which lit his dark eyes. Once that alone would have filled her with a heady kind of pride at having him within her power. But now she could see that for what it really was—a shallow and insignificant pride. Just because a man desired you physically it didn't mean anything. He could desire all kinds of people— it just depended on who happened to be there at the time. He had already proved that to her.

'You think that us having sex is going to make everything better?' she said slowly.

'In a word, yes. It would certainly make things a little more…comfortable.' He shifted slightly, and he saw her look of horrified fascination as it was drawn once more towards his shorts.

'Sex as a physical exercise, you mean? A bodily function that needs to be fulfilled—like scratching an itch?'

'Don't knock it, Lucy,' he said softly. 'You certainly never used to knock it before.'

She bit her lip and picked up the bottle to drink thirstily from it, but it did little to relieve the dryness in her mouth and she put it back down, her eyes serious. 'Aren't there other things we should be discussing, Guido? More important things?'

'Oh?' He raised his dark brows.

'Well, for a start—we haven't even decided where we're going to be living.'

He sucked in a hot, dry breath. This was part of their deal. 'You get to choose, remember?'

Never in a million years could Lucy have imagined her home as a newly-wed being decided by something as businesslike as a pre-nuptial agreement. 'I don't want to live in New York.'

'Any reason why?'

'I don't think your apartment is suitable for a baby.'

'Then we'll move somewhere that is.'

She shook her head. New York was *his* city. She had tried to imagine his life going on, and hers at home with the baby, and the idea petrified her. He wasn't going to take her out and introduce her to all his friends and play cosy-cosy, was he? Not when it would be a façade he might have difficulty maintaining.

And besides, New York was jam-packed full of temptation...

'No,' she said quietly.

'So just where *do* you want to live?'

What would he say if she suggested England? But deep down, Lucy knew that was a non-starter—and it had nothing to do with the fact that England almost seemed too small to contain him. No. Her mother would take one look at her face and would guess at her daughter's unhappiness. She couldn't do that to her.

Which left only one place—the only place where she felt safe and grounded...

'I'd like to live on Mardivino.'

Guido nodded. He should have seen this coming. He had flexed his muscles over the marriage and now she was showing that she could do the same. She knew how he felt about Royal life. Was she perhaps hoping that by incarcerating him here he would yield to her? Grant her a divorce and custody and a settlement? He gave a tight smile. She would soon learn that he could not be manipulated.

'As you wish,' he said coolly.

Lucy frowned. She had expected more reaction than that. Her explanation had been rehearsed; she was just waiting for his terse interrogation. But it seemed he had no interest in hearing it. Just what did she have to do to get a reaction from him?

Talk about the things that counted, that was what. 'You know,' she said softly, 'there's something which we've avoided talking about altogether.'

'I can hardly wait,' he drawled sardonically. 'Do enlighten me.'

Was he being deliberately unperceptive? Or was he just in denial? 'The baby, of course!' The tiny creature which was growing in her belly even now. Growing, but almost unacknowledged—certainly up until now. But maybe they were all in denial.

Even her mother had only fleetingly referred to it. Was it delicacy which had prevented her—an old-fashioned idea that a shotgun marriage should not be seen as that? As if the honeymoon was going to wipe the slate clean so they could come back, the bad start would be forgotten and only then could they begin to discuss the forthcoming child?

'*Our* baby,' she added softly.

He stared hard and unseeingly at the sea. 'There is nothing to discuss.'

'Of course there is!' But she was unprepared for the look on his face when he turned it back to her. She had always thought of Guido as cold and remote, but now it was as if someone had chiselled his features from some dark, icy rock. She drew back from the look, startled. 'What is it?' she whispered.

He banished the nebulous fears which swirled like dark clouds around his mind and recovered himself. 'I thought that everything had been decided. You will be cared for by the finest obstetricians, and the baby will be born here on Mardivino.'

How cold-blooded he sounded! But he *is* cold-blooded, she reminded herself. 'And then?'

'Who knows what then? There are a million things which could happen between now and then. The most important thing,' he added savagely, 'is to ensure the baby's safety. And your own,' he finished, on a harsh note.

A forgotten memory flew into her mind. Was he thinking about his own mother and her confinement with Nico? For hadn't it been his birth which had heralded her death, resulting in the fracturing of the family? A Royal family, yes—with all the back-up and support that their wealth and position could provide—but no less vulnerable than any other young family.

She wanted to reach her hand out to touch him—not in a sexual way, more a comforting and reassuring one—to tell him that there was no reason that history should repeat itself. But his frozen and forbidden stance stopped her.

And, God forgive her, something terrible had occurred to her. If she died then she might briefly be grieved for by him as the baby's mother, but nothing else. She would be out of the way. No obstacle to his wishes or desires any more.

He felt rather than saw her shiver, and slowly turned his head to find a look of indescribable pain lurking in the back of her eyes. And this he found he could not ignore.

'What is wrong?' he questioned softly.

'How long have you got?' She shook her head, recognising that he had hit the nail on the head earlier—her thoughts really *could* be described as melodramatic. She forced them back to the real problems they faced and looked at him. 'How about the fact that we're both sitting on a beautiful beach and wishing we could be anywhere else on earth but here?'

'Is that what you wish?'

No. She wished for the impossible. That his face would soften with love and not just longing. That their baby had been conceived amid the flow of some emotion other than a wild and unstoppable desire. But that was like a child wishing for make-believe.

'I'm trying to imagine the future,' she said desperately. 'And I just can't.'

'But no one ever can, Lucy,' he said quietly. 'And you shouldn't even try. It rarely turns out as you imagine it to. It's the present you have to hang on to.'

Maybe that was even more difficult. This was the present, and she was all over the place, not knowing how to react or what to say. Unsure whether it would be right or wrong to succumb to him physically— whether that would improve their relationship or simply make her more aware of its glaring deficiencies.

'We don't even know one another!' she said desperately. 'Not really.'

He was silent for a moment. 'If you presented that problem to a third party, then they would say that the obvious solution is to try.'

'How?'

'You could start by not turning your back on me in bed. By not flinching when I come close to you.'

They were talking, she realised, at cross purposes. She was talking about peeling away all the layers that people protected themselves with—especially in his case—to find the real person who lay beneath.

Guido, on the other hand, was talking about something entirely different. 'It isn't just about sex!'

'But isn't sex a good place to start? To hold one another, to feel close to one another?'

It wasn't real closeness, but would it do? Wasn't it better to have something which masqueraded as intimacy rather than no intimacy at all?

Lucy nodded as she came to a decision, swallowing down the lump of apprehension which had stuck like an acrid rock in the back of her throat. She struggled to find the words which would allow her to keep her dignity—maybe even make him think that the Lucy who had enjoyed sex without involvement hadn't been real either. 'Very well,' she said quietly. 'I'll consent to having sex with you.'

A look of indescribable fury crossed over his face, making him look like the devil incarnate. 'You'll *consent*?' he questioned incredulously. 'You will *consent* to having sex with me?'

'I didn't mean it the way it came out!'

'Oh, on the contrary, Lucy,' he said icily. 'I think that's exactly what you meant.' He scrambled to his feet, the sun behind him making him into a forbidding silhouette which dominated her horizon. She couldn't see his face now, but she didn't need to—the bitter quality of his voice spoke volumes.

'Well, you must forgive me if I decline your delightful *offer*. I have never had a woman who has to endure sex with me, and I have no intention of starting now.'

'Guido, listen—'

'No, you *listen*!' He cut through her words, and for the first time she saw him as truly and ominously imperious. A distant and powerful prince with everyone in the world eager to do his bidding. 'I told you when you agreed to marry me—'

'Agreed?' She gave a bitter laugh. 'You mean when you forced my hand?'

'I told you,' he continued furiously, 'that the terms of the marriage itself would be up to you. So if you're planning to act like a Victorian wife and lie back and think of England—you can forget it! Either I have a warm and giving woman in my bed, or none at all!'

'And if none at all?' she questioned steadily. 'Are you planning to seek your comfort elsewhere?'

He bent down then, and now she *could* see his face. She could almost feel the fierce heat from the hot and angry fire in his eyes.

'What do you think, Lucy?' he hissed. 'That I'll settle for a life of celibacy?'

She stared at him unhappily. They had reached, she realised, a stalemate.

CHAPTER TEN

THEY cut the honeymoon short, of course. They had to—for the sake of their sanity.

After their bitter row on the beach, a state of silent and frozen warfare descended, which made their enforced proximity almost unbearable.

Guido went out of his way to avoid her whenever he could. He spent an inordinate amount of time sailing and running and swimming—coming back each day worn out by the sheer physical endurance with which he had tested himself to his limits.

And he had a dark look of simmering rage whenever he looked at her.

Lucy, meanwhile, carried on pretending to read her book—even going to the trouble of turning several handfuls of pages by the time he returned.

But he was not easily fooled.

'Want to tell me what the story's all about?' he challenged mockingly one evening, and her face flushed scarlet as she snapped it closed.

'We can't go on like this,' she said on their fourth evening, when he had just arrived back from a lone trip to the beach and she had been pacing around like a caged lion.

He was right—when a couple weren't doing what

they were traditionally supposed to do on honeymoon it left an awful lot of awkward hours to fill.

He was raking his fingers through the black tendrils of his hair, all sea-damp and knotted from his swim. On the broad bank of his shoulders was the faintest sprinkling of fine white sand, which contrasted alluringly against the deep olive skin. A pair of shorts which were moulded like rubber to the hard curve of his buttocks were the only brief barrier against his nakedness.

He turned his head to look at her, enjoying the discomfiture on her face. Deliberately he jutted his hips forward and saw her colour deepen.

'I agree,' he said smoothly. 'We can't. Shall we pack up and go back to Solajoya?'

Lucy blinked. Just like that? Had she hoped for another discussion—perhaps one with a different outcome this time? One which might see them ending up in bed and letting passion wash away much of the discord?

There's nothing to stop you going over to him now, mocked a voice in her head.

But there was—of course there was. The distance between them had grown so wide, she could imagine nothing which would bring them back together again. Instead, she was forced to endure the terrible hunger that gnawed away inside her.

And why did he not approach *her*? She had swallowed her pride once and offered to break the deadlock. Hadn't it been his arrogant dismissal of her fumbling offer which had caused all this bitterness to surface?

She shrugged. 'If you want.'

He gave a short laugh. As if she cared what he wanted!

'Guido?'

He met her eyes. 'What is it, my Princess?'

'Do you think that we can start being...?'

Being what? he wondered. Lovers? He raised his eyebrows imperiously. 'Well, what is it, Lucy?' he questioned softly. 'What do you want us to be?'

Friends seemed too much to ask for in the current circumstances, but surely there was a springboard from which things could move on—however slowly—and get better between them. 'Civil,' she said. 'To each other.'

Civil. He thought that she had a curious choice of words at times. It was an oddly mechanical description. Or maybe not. She was, after all, describing the workings of a marriage. Did she not realise how much she was asking of him?

'I think I can just about manage civility,' he murmured.

She nodded, breathless in that moment as peace briefly swam in the air around them.

'Do you want to wait outside?' he questioned softly, and looped his thumbs inside the waistband of his shorts. 'Because I'm just about to remove these.'

His calculated remark shattered that elusive calm, and Lucy left as swiftly as someone who had never seen a naked man before, banging the door behind her and hearing his mocking laughter ringing in her ears.

She drew in several deep and faltering breaths of the pure air as she stared at the picturesque mountains which dominated the skyline. The startling peaks were turning deepest blue and indigo against the flame of the setting sun, yet Lucy was immune to their beauty. She felt like someone in a spacecraft, viewing the earth from a long, long way away. Totally disconnected.

She placed a palm over her swelling belly and closed her eyes. Only her baby seemed real in this make-believe world she inhabited.

That morning there had been the merest butterfly fluttering—too fleeting and insubstantial to know whether it was movement or just indigestion. And she had felt an unbearable wave of sadness. If only things had been different she would have called him over, and he would have pressed his hand there and they would have held their breath, eyes meeting, smiling the complicit smiles of parents-to-be.

As it was, she had said nothing—just made a pot of herbal tea to distract herself.

Oddly enough, when they drove into Solajoya the Rainbow Palace seemed welcoming—who would ever have thought she would be so glad to see the grand and glittering building? Yet it felt like home.

Or maybe that was because Nico and Ella came running out to meet them.

'You're back early!' Ella exclaimed.

'Morning sickness,' said Lucy, not daring to meet Guido's eyes.

'But you're feeling much better now that you're back, aren't you, Lucy?' questioned Guido smoothly.

'But how was it?' asked Ella excitedly, linking her arm through Lucy's in a sisterly way. The physical contact was oddly moving and made Lucy want to start to cry. 'Aren't the mountains the most beautiful you've ever seen?'

Instinct made her nod, but then Nico made things a million times worse.

'Oh, Ella,' he purred, with a grin. 'I don't imagine that they will have done much sightseeing!'

And Lucy *did* look up then, straight into the mocking dark ice of Guido's eyes.

Gianferro's stern face softened when he saw Lucy.

'You are keeping well?' he questioned.

Lucy nodded. 'Oh, yes,' she said staunchly, as if her very life depended on it. 'Very well.'

And, of course, there was Leo—gorgeous, gurgling Leo—who Lucy couldn't resist.

Guido came to the Nursery bathroom one day, just as Lucy was towelling him dry. She had suds in her hair and her face was rosy, and she looked up from blowing raspberries on Leo's plump little stomach to find her husband standing in the doorway watching her, some indefinable emotion flitting across his face. But she reminded herself that Guido didn't do emotion.

'Nico and Ella have gone out for lunch,' she said, by way of an explanation he had not asked for.

He frowned. 'And there is no nursemaid?'

She pinned a nappy in place—there were no new-fangled disposables at the Palace—and looked up at him. 'It's her day off, and besides—I like doing it.'

The way she was kneeling made the size of her growing bump quite unmistakable, and he wondered how she managed to look so sexy when she was dripping with water and dealing with a squirming baby. He felt the jack-knifing of desire. God, if he had to endure a second longer of this hot-house of frustration then he would burst.

'You have to have something to fill your day, I guess.'

She nodded. It wasn't a very subtle barb, but she would ignore it. She certainly wasn't going to have a row when there was a little baby around. All the child care books—which she was currently devouring—said that babies were very susceptible to the atmosphere around them. Which did not bode very well for the future.

'I need as much practice as I can get, of course.'

'Of course,' he echoed. He stood there for a moment or two longer and then said, 'I have to fly to New York.'

Her fingers stilled in the act of buttoning the crisp lawn romper suit, and she looked up, feeling the blood drain from her face. 'To New York?' she questioned dully.

'That's right.'

'Oh?' Her voice trembled. 'Any reason why?'

He smiled. 'I have business to attend to—why else?'

A couple of reasons sprang to mind, and one of them was disturbing enough to make her tremble. But if she challenged him he would only deny them, and then it would look as if she didn't trust him.

But she *didn't* trust him!

He paused, still standing like a dark, carved statue by the door. 'You could always come with me.'

The suggestion was made from the other side of the bathroom—not a million miles away, though it might as well have been.

Lucy tried to imagine what it would be like—just the two of them on his territory, with Guido busying himself with work while she was trapped in that vast luxury apartment. At least here in Mardivino she felt comfortable—surrounded by family who seemed to like her.

She shook her head. 'I don't know if it would be a good idea to travel in my—'

'Condition?' he mocked softly. 'Oh, come, come, Lucy—you can't use the baby as an excuse for everything! I thought that the modern way was for women to climb mountains in the latter stages!'

'I'm happy here,' she said stubbornly.

'Yes.' He flicked her a thoughtful look. 'You seem to have taken to being a princess with a passion.'

Lucy sat back on her heels. 'What's that supposed to mean?'

He smiled, but it was a hard, cruel smile. 'Just that I guess the luxuries of Royal life must go some way towards compensating for other areas which are somewhat…lacking.'

Was he accusing her? Of taking to her role rather too well? When all the while she had wanted him to be proud of her…

She picked Leo up. 'And how long will you be away?'

The dark eyebrows were elevated. 'Why?'

'*Why?* Because you're my husband and I have a right to know!'

His mouth tightened. 'I wouldn't get into a conversation about "rights", if I were you,' he said acidly. 'And I don't know why you refer to me as your husband.' The black eyes burnt into her. 'We may be married, but in all the ways that matter I am certainly not your husband.'

CHAPTER ELEVEN

Guido had gone, and Lucy's world suddenly felt as though there was a large and vital chunk of it missing. But things became much clearer without his disturbing presence.

Lucy realised that she had placed far too much importance on distracting herself from what was happening within their marriage, and that in a way it had been all too easy. There was always something going on—other family to talk to, and servants who had a habit of appearing, putting paid to tense atmospheres. And there were lunches and dinners and receptions which filled enough of her life to keep her relatively contented.

Or so she had thought.

Yet without Guido around all these things became meaningless. Nico and Ella had their real life together, with their son, and Gianferro was busy ruling the Principality. Lucy was just an observer—a shadowy figure on the outside—trying to join in but having no real part to play. And she wanted her husband to come back.

She began to obsess about his real reasons for going. He had cited work, but he could work from anywhere—he had only to pick up the phone.

There had been no physical contact at all between

them—and no sign that the deadlock would ever be broken. So had he decided that enough was enough? That while she might accept this loveless marriage he certainly would not?

She stared out at the Palace gardens, where autumn was beginning to rob the landscape of the last of the flowers, and she bit back the sob which was forming in her throat. She might as well have given her written permission for him to go away and have an affair with someone!

Whose advice could she ask? No one's. That was the trouble. No one to tell, or to confide in. Oh, she liked Ella a lot, and they got along just fine. But Ella was her sister-in-law and she would be bound to tell Nico, and then everyone would know how bad things were between her and Guido.

And wouldn't that destabilise everyone—especially with the King lying there, so sick?

She turned away from the gardens to look at herself in the mirror. Her bump was really very noticeable now, though the rest of her was still very slim. In fact, it was only from the side that you could really tell she was pregnant at all. She was wearing jeans and a beautiful floaty shirt made of velvet and silk and bits of feather, which she had bought in one of Solajoya's more exclusive boutiques.

Her skin was the clearest it had ever been and her eyes were as shining as her hair. In some ways she had never looked better. Pregnancy suited her, as did the clean air of Mardivino and the wonderful fresh food which was served to her every day.

But all this meant nothing. She had allowed the distance between herself and Guido to flourish and grow, with each trying to outdo the other in terms of stubbornness. If a stalemate had been reached, then someone had to break it. And if Guido was too proud then it would have to be her. And wasn't it only fear which was stopping her? The fear that if she let him get close to her then it would open up the floodgates around her heart and let out all those feelings she had bottled up?

She bit her lip. He had been gone over a week now. Maybe it was too late. Maybe even now he was in bed with another sooty-eyed blonde—someone who didn't 'mean' anything, but who could provide him with the physical comfort his wife was steadfastedly refusing to give.

Pain and regret and jealousy lanced through her heart and she closed her eyes before coming to a decision.

She would fly to New York!

Obviously she'd need to clear it with Gianferro first, but what was the point of being a princess if you couldn't just fly to America on a whim? But she would beg Gianferro's silence, for she wanted it to be a surprise.

She just prayed it would be a pleasant one…

The sound of the doorbell punctured the sultry wail of the music, and Guido narrowed his eyes with irritation. Who the hell was that, and why the hell had they been allowed up? He had specifically told the porter that he did not want to be disturbed....

It pealed again. Unbelievable! He rose to his feet and pulled open the door, unable to make the connection for a moment. It was a bit like seeing an iceberg in the middle of the desert—completely unexpected. The very last thing he had expected was to see his wife standing on the doorstep.

'Hello, Guido,' she said quietly.

'Lucy!' He raised his eyebrows. 'This is certainly a surprise.'

It wasn't the greeting she had wanted or hoped for. He was standing there with a wary look on his face, yet his hard, lean body was tense and expectant.

'Maybe I should have phoned. Aren't you going to invite me in?' And then she stopped focussing on him and focussed on the sound of sultry saxophone drifting through the air from behind him. Her eyes opened wide in horror. 'Unless...unless—' Oh, God. 'Unless you're busy, of course?'

He heard the accusation in her voice and his mouth tightened. 'And what is it you think I might be busy with, Lucy?' he questioned, in a soft, dangerous voice. 'You think I have someone in here with me?'

The world stood still. She looked into his eyes, black and stormy as the night. 'Have you?'

'Why don't you take a look for yourself?'

She needed courage then as she had never needed it before, and she brushed past him, her head held high, two wings of colour burning across her cheeks.

The room looked set for seduction. Soft lights. Soft

music. There was even a bottle of wine opened. Her eyes scanned the table. One glass! She turned back to look at him again, only this time his eyes were taunting her.

'Seen enough?' he mocked.

She had come to a tentative decision on the plane, and the emotions which were rollercoastering around inside her now made it crystallise into certainty. She was through with treading carefully, as if she was negotiating some rocky and unknown path. From now on she was going to start walking proud and strong.

'Are you alone?' she demanded.

He gave an odd kind of laugh and walked over to the table. He poured himself a glass of wine, glancing over his shoulder at her. 'Will you join me?' he questioned, in a mocking voice.

He still hadn't answered her question! But surely his careless attitude must mean that there was no one else in the apartment? Not even Guido could demonstrate *sang-froid* like that if some female was hiding out in the bedroom. The thought of that made her wince.

'I'm pregnant!' she said, relief making her snap at him. 'Remember?'

'How am I likely to forget?' he lobbed back, and then sipped his wine. 'Sit down. Take the weight off your feet and tell me why you're here.'

Lucy sank onto one of the sofas, suddenly exhausted. Why *was* she here?

'Or let me guess,' he continued. 'You thought you would turn up unannounced to ''surprise'' me, but in reality you were expecting to catch me in bed with someone—isn't that right, Lucy?'

The strain had been building up for a long time, and now it had reached an unbearable pitch. His words were enough to make her snap. She stared at him, all pretence gone, for she did not have the appetite or the energy for it any more. 'Yes!' she cried. 'Yes, I did! Yes, yes, yes—I did!'

His face was a cruel, dark mask. 'And that would have played right into your hands, wouldn't it? For, no matter how watertight a prenuptial agreement, what court is going to look kindly on a man who is unfaithful to his young pregnant bride within the first month of marriage? Was that why you refused to have sex with me, Lucy? Hoping to drive me to just that response? Because, if so, I hate to disappoint you— but on this occasion I'm going to have to. Feel free to search every nook and cranny of the apartment, but you will find it empty.'

She had thought that she could not be hurt any more than she already had been, but she had been wrong, for his wounding words slashed right through what remained of her composure. Did he really think she was so scheming that she would concoct such a thing? That she would use their sex-life—or lack of it—as some strategy—a carefully devised plan? Did he think so little of her that he thought she was capable of such deviousness?

A long, shuddering cry escaped her, and, willing the tears not to fall, she buried her face in her hands. 'Lucy?'

She heard the concern in his voice but shook her head as if to deny it, her hair spilling untidily over her shoulders.

'*Lucy!*' he said urgently, and then he was by her side.

'Go away.'

'Look at me.'

'No!' Her words were muffled by her hands, and as she felt him draw them away she stared at him defiantly. 'I didn't scheme, if that's what you think, but, yes, I did think you might have someone here— or that you might in the future. And what's more…what is more…who could really blame you if you did?'

He stilled. '*What did you just say?* That sounded very like you giving me permission to stray, *cara*.' His voice took on a deadly tone. 'Is that what you would like? To free me so that another man can be your lover? Do you have someone in mind, then, Lucy?'

How wrong could he possibly be? 'No!' She stared at him as if he were completely mad. 'I haven't wanted anyone else! Not since I met you—not for a second.'

'Then perhaps you would explain what it is you're talking about?'

She shrugged her shoulders desperately. 'I know that you're a hot-blooded man—and I had no right to withhold sex from you.'

'Oh, for God's sake—there you go again!' he exploded. 'I don't want it to *be* like that. It isn't something that *I* want and *you* won't give me—it should be something we both want. And you don't, do you, Lucy?'

There was a long, long silence. Was she strong enough to do something to rectify a situation which was becoming daily more unbearable? Or was stupid, stubborn pride going to stand in her way?

'Yes, I do,' she whispered. 'I want you very much.'

Her words were soft and indistinct, but he heard them, and he smoothed back the mussed hair from her cheeks to see confusion in her eyes.

'Oh, Lucy,' he said softly.

'I don't know how it's come to this,' she admitted on a whisper.

And neither did he. He rippled his fingers down her neck and her eyelids fluttered to a close. 'You are worn out,' he said unsteadily.

'Yes.'

'Come. Come with me.'

Her eyes flew open as he bent to scoop her up into his arms—as if he carried pregnant women every day of the week. 'Are you taking me to...bed?'

His eyes were smoky with hunger and his blood was on fire with need. Expectation was racing over his skin and making it burn. 'Oh, I think I have to—don't you?'

She was trembling and excited and scared all at the same time as he carried her through to the vast and airy room, where he lay her down on the bed. His eyes narrowed as he took in her chalk-white complexion, the freckles standing out in bold relief on her skin, as if they had been painted on. Unexpectedly he began stroking her cheek, using rhythmical, soothing fingers, as if he were petting a pampered cat, and gradually the tension began to leave her. The hectic glitter left her eyes and she felt herself sinking into the comfort zone which her keyed-up body craved, her weighted eyelids sinking irrevocably downwards.

To her astonishment, she must have slept, for when she opened her eyes again the room was empty.

Had she dreamt it all? Blinking, she sat up and looked at the empty space on the bed beside her. It was smooth and unrumpled. There was a glass of water on the bedside table and she gulped it down thirstily. When she glanced up again it was to see his dark, silent form in the doorway, watching her from between narrowed eyes.

Carefully, she put the empty glass back down. 'How long have I been asleep?'

'Two hours.'

'Two *hours*?' She stared at him. So he had changed his mind—when the opportunity had presented itself he had not wanted to make love to her after all.

He saw the look on her face and began to unbutton his shirt.

Her hand flew to suddenly trembling lips. 'Guido?'

'Mmm?' His voice was husky and deep with desire. 'You want this, Lucy,' he murmured. 'In fact, I'd say that you need it. We both do.'

There was no affection in those words, but right then she didn't care. Her mouth bone-dry, she watched as the shirt fluttered to the floor and he began to tug at his belt. He rasped the zip down and stepped out of his trousers, kicking his shoes off until he was standing proudly and unselfconsciously naked before her.

Lucy began to tremble even more—and she was not a trembling kind of person. She had seen him aroused many times, but never like this. He was walking towards her now, his face full of purpose and desire, and some soft inner core of her wanted to cry out, to ask where the tenderness of earlier had disappeared to. But he was right. Her need was as deep as his. And no words came other than the breathy sound of his name on her lips.

'Guido.'

With a fierce look of concentration, he began to undress her with hands which were steady—until she too was naked, and then they began to shake as he saw the evidence of how lush she was with his child. Her once-flat belly was now a proud, hard swell, and he felt his throat tighten as he looked at it. Should they be doing this? After her long flight and such a stormy reunion? Was it…was it *safe*? Instinct fought with desire, but desire conquered him as she lifted her arms up to loop themselves around his neck and pull him down close to her.

He gasped, as her warm, expanded body pressed against his flesh. It was a new and profoundly shattering sensation, and blindly he reached for one of the cashmere blankets which lay at the end of the bed and pushed its soft folds against her skin.

'Cover yourself!' he commanded unsteadily.

She could feel him moving away from her, but she gripped his arm tight, forcing their eyes to meet.

'You don't want me?'

'Are you crazy? Of course I want you! But I didn't realise...' He swallowed. '*Signora Dolce*, but it is a long time since I saw you naked, Lucy.'

'Too long.' One barrier had fallen down to be replaced by another, but she was damned if she was going to allow him to put her on the untouchable pedestal of the Madonna. 'And too long since we have been together like this.'

'You want me?' he demanded unsteadily. 'You are sure?'

More than anything. But she was too choked with emotion to speak for a moment. She had never seen her Guido look so undecided. 'Yes,' she breathed eventually. 'Oh, yes, I'm sure. Very sure.' And she watched his doubts dissolve.

Like an explorer discovering uncharted land, he ran the flat of his hand over her hard, pregnant swell. After a while she put her hand between his legs, and he groaned.

It felt strange and wonderful. Both disconnected and real to rediscover his flesh and his firm, hard body, to let him work the magic he always worked, as she did on him. In bed they were still dynamite together, even when she was clumsier than usual with the baby. They locked their legs around each other with the delight of familiarity sharpened by the hunger of abstinence, and their kisses were breathless.

He pulled his head away and looked down into her

face, his expression sombre. 'I am afraid of hurting you, *cara*.'

She shook her head. 'Well, you won't.' In bed, he never hurt her.

'Will you show me?' he whispered.

She could hear the uncertainty in his voice and she reached down to guide him inside her, thinking that he had sounded almost *vulnerable*. Oh, please stay like that, my darling, she prayed silently. Please.

And afterwards they lay, sucking in greedy breaths of air, Lucy in that state of sleepy satisfaction she had almost forgotten. She turned to look at him, and yawned. 'Bet you've never made love to a pregnant woman before!'

He frowned as he ran his fingertips over her bump again, only this time it was like a doctor checking for broken bones. 'Do you feel okay?'

'Guido, I feel *fine*.' And then her heart sank in disbelief as he pulled away from her and got up off the bed. 'Where do you think you're going?'

He pulled on a towelling wrap and gave her a careless smile.

'To make you some food.'

'Guido, I don't want anything to eat!' I want *you*. I want us to make things right between us—and nothing else matters apart from that.

He was running—from what, he didn't know. And what was more, he didn't care. 'You ate...when?'

She sighed. 'There was food on the plane—'

'Which you never eat—you told me yourself you

hate airline food!' he declared softly. 'Now, no protests, please, Lucy—you must look after yourself.'

Pointless to argue, for she recognised the determination in his voice. Some women might just have lain back against the down pillows and rejoiced in being waited on, but all Lucy could feel was a great, aching gap. With that one distancing gesture he had reminded her that she wouldn't even be here if it weren't for the baby. Yet they had just come together in an act that had been as much about reconciliation as making love, and that was a start. Surely the food could have waited while they talked about it?

But Guido didn't want to talk about it—and certainly not straight after sex, when his defences were down.

In the distance, she could hear him clattering around in the kitchen, even singing to himself softly in Italian, like a man well pleased with himself. But of course he would be. One fundamental appetite had been satisfied; he was now simply addressing another one.

Or was she being a little hard on him? Perhaps he needed to collect his thoughts after what had happened.

He returned to the bedroom carrying a tray loaded with coffee and sandwiches.

'You're doing my old job!' she joked. 'You'll be wearing a stewardess's uniform next!'

He smiled, but it was nothing more than a distant and sexy smile.

'Eat something,' he murmured. 'You'll feel better.'

Better?

He put the tray down to plant a long and lingering kiss on her lips, and it had the desired effect of making her skin shiver with longing. But his next words killed it stone-dead.

'Just because we have a marriage which was born out of practicality,' he said softly, 'doesn't mean to say we can't make it work—does it, Lucy?'

Her blood ran cold, for it was such an analytical and businesslike assessment, and at that precise moment Lucy realised nothing had changed. He could have been a million miles away from her instead of in the same bedroom. They might have become close in the physical sense, but that was all.

Emotionally, the stalemate remained exactly the same—with her wanting more than her cool Prince of a husband was prepared to give.

CHAPTER TWELVE

THEY stayed put in New York.

'Don't you want to be away from my family for a while?' Guido whispered beguilingly. 'Just the two of us?'

'Y-yes,' she said uncertainly—but how could she even think straight with him dipping his head to run his lips with a butterfly brush down her neck like that?

'We can fix you up with an obstetrician here, if that's what you're worried about.'

Well, actually, it wasn't—but in a way it was easier to hide behind the natural anxieties of a mother-to-be than the concerns which still lay like a steel barrier between them.

What had happened to walking proud and strong? She had come up against a rock, that was what. The stony and unchangeable knowledge that you couldn't control someone. You couldn't *make* someone love you.

Lucy nodded her head, as if her doctor's appointment had been what was troubling her all along.

He introduced her to his life in the city. His friends. His business colleagues. They went to England for Christmas to visit her parents in their rambling cottage, where they had spent a Christmas which had not proved to be the endurance test she had been dread-ing. But then Guido had been charming and diplomatic—skills which had been drummed into him from the cradle—and her mother and father had not even begun to guess at the great emotional distance which lay between them like a canyon.

Back in New York, there were trips to the opera and weekends out of town. And he took her shopping—he liked taking her shopping—even though she tried to curb the amount of clothes and jewels he lavished on her.

'Guido, I don't *need* all this stuff!' she protested.

'Well, no one ever said you *needed* diamonds,' he remarked drily. 'But I thought they were what every woman wanted.'

Were they? Her fingers touched the icy splendour of the huge diamond pendant which dangled between her swollen breasts. A glittering trophy whose cost she didn't even dare to think about. Would it sound ungrateful to say that sometimes she felt like a little girl who was being given free access to the dressing-up box?

The maternity clothes she wore were cut to cleverly flatter the bump and were shockingly expensive. But as a princess she knew that she needed to look the part. She couldn't attend all the functions Guido took her to making do with a couple of well-worn and practical maternity outfits, as most of her school-friends seemed to have to.

She could have coped with Guido's extravagance—with almost anything—if only his behaviour towards her had evolved into something deeper, closer—but it hadn't. Oh, on one level, things were vastly improved—they did the things that most married couples did now, and regular sex seemed to have made some of his tension disappear. And hers too, if she was being honest. She had made a vow that first night that she was no longer going to use sex as a bartering tool. Apart from anything else, it was counter-productive in Guido's case.

Resolutely, she put aside her doubts and her fears, and the nagging insecurity that one day he might fall truly in love with another woman and then—contract of marriage or not—it would all be over.

It didn't matter how tenderly she held him during the night—the true closeness she yearned for somehow evaded them. She felt as though she was playing a part again—only this time the part of young, pregnant bride.

When they were out together she could see people looking at them, sighing wistfully—and part of her could see why. They made a textbook couple, and she was the textbook working woman who had ended up with a fairytale marriage. If only they knew that her husband had never once told her he loved her and that she did not dare to tell him how much—despite all the odds—she loved him.

For love was blind to reason. It wasn't a balance sheet on which you weighed up all the pros and cons of why you should or should not love someone. Either you did or you didn't, and Lucy did.

Sometimes she wanted to burrow deep into that cold, clever mind of his and ask him what he really *felt* about her—except that such a question would sound like the mark of a desperate woman. And what if he told her the truth? Could she face the rest of her life living with it?

She stared at him one morning when they were finishing breakfast. Guido was scanning the financial pages of the newspapers, though she sometimes wondered why he bothered. He had all the wealth a man could want and more—and yet it was never enough. He always seemed to have the burning need to prove himself. To keep climbing the slippery slope of success, even though he had already conquered it.

'Guido?'

'Mmm?' His eyes were watchful as he glanced up from his newspaper, but this morning she seemed composed enough. He was never quite sure what kind of a mood she was going to be in—but he put that down to her hormones. In a way, he would be glad when the pregnancy was over and they could address the matter of just how their life was going to be lived from then on.

'I want to go back to Mardivino.'

A small frown pleated his forehead. 'What is your hurry, *cara*?'

'I thought the baby had to be born there.'

'So it does…but—'

'Well, I'm not allowed to fly after thirty-six weeks, and can only fly then if I have a doctor's note,' she said crisply.

He felt the violent pounding of his heart as he stared into her eyes, realising with a start that the time was almost upon them. Had he been deliberately putting it out of his mind? And did all prospective fathers—even normal ones—feel this powerful and rather terrifying realisation that their lives were never going to be the same again?

'Well, that's no problem. If we can't take a scheduled flight I'll charter a plane, or we'll get Nico to fly out from Mardivino closer to the time. He is a fine pilot.'

The last thing she wanted to talk about was his brother's dexterity with a joystick! It was Guido's reluctance to fly home which disturbed her more than anything. Was he hoping to win her round so that she would adapt to motherhood in his adopted city?

'We can't, Guido,' she said practically. 'Airlines, even private jets, impose rules like this for a very good reason. They don't want to risk a woman giving birth early—which they can. Imagine if the baby was born thirty-five thousand feet up?'

His eyes narrowed. Over his dead body! 'Very well,' he said coolly. 'We will return to the Principality.'

It was the wrong time to ask it, but Lucy was fed up with always waiting for a right time which never seemed to come. 'And…afterwards? What are we going to do then?'

There was an uneasy silence. 'How would you feel about bringing the baby up here, Lucy?'

'In New York?'

'Why not? They do have babies here, you know.'

So her suspicions had been right all along. Well,

she couldn't. She just couldn't. New York was a wonderful place, but here she felt like an outsider in a
way she never had done on Mardivino.

She shook her head. 'This apartment isn't right for
a young child.'

'Then we'll move further out! Buy a big house with
a garden. Think about it, Lucy.'

She didn't need to; she already had. She wanted a
safe harbour for her and for the baby. A flare of stubbornness reared its head, for this was, after all, *her*
part of the pre-nuptial. That *she* got to choose where
they would live.

'No, Guido,' she said doggedly. 'I want to go back
to Mardivino.'

He slammed the newspaper down on the table. She
had made it unshakably clear where she stood. He
turned away and gave a wry, slightly bitter smile. She
certainly wasn't letting him think that she was one of
those women who followed her man to the ends of
the earth. But then, only women in love did that, and
she had never given him any indication of being that.
Not even before all this happened…

She had never been like other women, with their
wistful sighs and hints about the future. That had been
one of the things he had admired about her—her no-
nonsense independence.

And now?

He shook his head, trying to rid it of the mists of
damnable confusion.

'Very well,' he said curtly. 'We'll fly back to the

island at the end of the week. And who knows? You might feel differently once you've had the baby.'

She opened her mouth to say that she wouldn't, but then shut it again, rubbing her fingertips distractedly at her temples.

Spring had come early to Mardivino, and Lucy's breath caught in her throat as the plane descended towards Solajoya, for there were fields of yellow, purple and white flowers. It was like a miniature world all on its own, she thought—a place where you could see beaches and mountains at the same time.

Yet now, as she looked down at the island, which was growing larger as the plane descended, she realised that Mardivino had crept in and captured some of her heart. It was as much her home as anywhere now, for her child was to be born here. A sudden wave of emotion rocked her, as if she was one of those tiny, vulnerable little boats which were bobbing around in the harbour beneath.

'Oh, Guido,' she sighed. 'Just look at it.'

But he was not looking at the view, which he had seen countless times before. His associations with flying home had never been happy ones. He preferred to look at Lucy. At the way her lips had parted, and the way she seemed suddenly to have come to life, trembling with an excited kind of anticipation.

She really *had* taken to life as Princess, he thought wryly, but especially here. In New York it didn't mean much—it was only another title—but on Mardivino itself she had real power and real status.

Things which obviously meant more to her than the husband she had been forced to marry...

As soon as they arrived at the Rainbow Palace Guido turned to her. 'I'm going to see my father,' he said briefly. 'I'll see you at dinner.'

Lucy watched him go, feeling their closeness— however superficial it had been—evaporating into the warm spring air.

At least the others seemed overjoyed to see her. Ella was chattering with excitement, and Lucy saw Gianferro's hard face relax with relief when he saw her.

'Why, you are blooming, Lucy,' he observed with a smile. 'The pregnancy progresses well, I understand?'

'Very well.'

'And how was New York?'

'Oh, it was just like New York,' she said lightly. 'It's good to be...back.'

'Indeed,' he agreed, and although a look of curiosity flashed into his black eyes he said nothing.

Lucy was walking around the Palace gardens on a warm, bright afternoon when the first pains began, and she doubled over, trying like crazy to shallow breathe, as she'd been taught.

Stopping every few minutes, she managed to make her way back to their suite and Guido was brought to her. Concern and fear etched deep shadows on his hard face as he saw the doctor bending over her.

'*Come e?*' he demanded.

'Highness,' said the doctor, straightening up. 'For a first baby, this one is intent on arriving very quickly. We must get the Princess to hospital.'

'Then do it!' he said urgently.

It all became very blurred after that—the screeching of wheels and the flashing of lights, and the pain getting more and more intense. In the back of the ambulance Lucy's nails bit into Guido's palm.

'Don't leave me,' she gasped. 'Will you?'

He wanted to tell her that Royal husbands did not stay with their wives during labour, but he saw the stark terror in her eyes and sensed her isolation with a perception which he would have usually blunted.

'Of course I will stay,' he bit out. 'Don't worry, Lucy—it's going to be all right. Everything is going to be all right.'

But he was aware that his words were hollow—for who could utter them with any degree of certainty? Nature was in charge now—random and cruel nature—who could change lives at one capricious stroke. His mouth tightened and he smoothed a damp strand of hair back from Lucy's brow. He wasn't going to think about that now.

Lucy's preconceived ideas about how she'd wanted to have the baby, while floating in a tank of water, were immediately banished by the midwife, and soon she was on a hard bed with her legs in stirrups. She tried not to thrash around.

'Oh, what must you think of me, Guido?' she moaned.

He was having difficulty speaking. 'I think you're pretty damned wonderful, if you must know.'

Had the gas and air made her completely uninhibited? 'You'll never fancy me again now you've seen me like this!' she wailed.

This was more like the Lucy he knew! A wry smile curved his mouth as he saw the midwife's look of horror. 'Let us not concern ourselves with that right now, *cara*,' he murmured smoothly. But then he saw her face twist with pain once more, and an unfamiliar wave of helplessness washed over him.

'Can you not help her?' he demanded.

'We are doing everything we can, Highness!'

Lucy was in a hot, dark tunnel of torture. There were instructions not to push when she wanted to push, and then to push when she was so tired she could barely open her eyes. And the pain! She whimpered, and then drew in all her strength for one last, huge effort.

The midwife was encouraging her, and Guido was saying something disbelieving in Italian, and then their baby daughter was born—all black-haired, like her daddy, and covered in gunk.

They put her on Lucy's stomach, and she stared down at her with a kind of wonder.

'Hello,' she said tremulously, and a tear of relief began to slide from between her eyelids. She scrubbed it away with her fist before she looked over to see Guido's reaction.

But he had gone to the window and was standing

there, completely motionless, staring out at the fresh, pale light of the spring day.

'Guido?' she whispered tentatively.

He turned round, but his proud and beautiful face gave nothing away. As usual.

He bent to gently kiss her forehead, and then to brush his mouth against the cheek of his daughter.

It took a moment or two before he was able to speak with the composure which was expected of him.

'Well done, Lucy,' he said. 'She is very beautiful.' Then he turned to the midwife and the doctor with a formal smile. 'And may I thank you for all your hard work?'

Lucy sank back onto the pillows as they took her daughter away to clean her, and an overwhelming wave of sadness swelled up to hit her like a fist. She did not know what she had been expecting him to say, but it had not been enough.

Maybe she was chasing the impossible—for with Guido it was never enough.

CHAPTER THIRTEEN

THE books said that having any new baby was exhausting, but Lucy decided that it must be especially so if you had one as lively—and intelligent!—as Nicole Katerina Marguerite Cacciatore. The new Princess seemed to have an aversion to sleeping at times when babies should be sleeping. It was a good thing, thought Lucy, that she compensated for her active nature by being the most beautiful baby in the entire world. But then she would be, wouldn't she?

For she looked exactly like her father.

Guido glanced up one morning to find Lucy yawning, dark shadows having planted faint blue thumbprints beneath her eyes, and he frowned.

'*Cara*, this cannot go on.'

'What can't?' The fact that he hadn't come near her since the baby had been born, bar the odd brief, perfunctory hug? Or that he had gone back to being that restless and wary Guido, who walked around like a caged lion?

He seemed to have slipped away from her again, and she wondered if he would ever come back. A woman who had newly given birth didn't usually feel beguiling enough to play the temptress. Even in normal circumstances...

'You are exhausted,' he pointed out. Her tiredness

was almost palpable. He had taken to sleeping in an adjoining room, because the last thing she needed at a time like this was a husband who couldn't keep his hands off her. 'I have never seen anyone look so tired.'

'Well, new mothers generally are.'

'Then why not engage a nanny?' he questioned.

Lucy bit her lip and poured herself a cup of coffee. She could go on bottling up her fears for ever, but that meant that nothing would change and she would be destined to spend a life only half lived. Trying to be all things to a man who seemed content to operate on such a superficial level of existence that he didn't even want to share her bed now the baby had been born!

'Because I don't need a nanny,' she said stubbornly.

'Maybe you do. Look at you! A nanny would take over at night—at least let you get some proper sleep.'

'I want to do it all myself,' she emphasised. 'All my friends do.'

He wanted to point out that her friends were not princesses, except he suspected the argument would fall on deaf ears—for Lucy was weaving a strong bond with their baby which, as a father, he should commend. So what, exactly, was the problem? He drank a mouthful of inky coffee which was much too hot, but he didn't wince.

Sometimes he watched as she played with Nicole, thinking herself unobserved. From the shadows he saw the way she kissed the tiny baby head, listened to the crooning little sounds she made, and long-buried memories resurfaced. He remembered standing by the door while his mother cradled his new brother, experiencing a sense of being an outsider—which every older sibling must feel.

And then…

He drew a deep breath, pushing the pain to the back of his mind. Patience was not one of his virtues, but he was beginning to recognise that it was what new mothers needed more than anything else.

'Okay,' he agreed. 'But she could help you during the day. How about that?'

Lucy looked at him—casting him the bait and hoping that he would take it. 'But the baby gives me a *raison d'être*,' she said quietly. 'You've set up an office for yourself and you spend all day working in it. What else am I going to do if someone else is taking care of her?'

'Ella manages.'

But Ella had Nico, and they were a couple in the truest sense of the word. She drew a deep breath. 'Ella is settled.'

His eyes narrowed. 'And you're not?'

'Not really, no. How can I be? Everything feels so…so…*temporary*. You don't want to be here.'

'That is not true,' he said heavily.

'Guido, you know it is! If I said yes, you'd be out of this room booking tickets to New York this morning!'

'Then say yes,' he said softly.

She saw the appeal in his dark eyes. Was it pride

which was stopping her, or fear of the unknown? Didn't there have to be compromise for marriage to work? And if he wouldn't—then wasn't it down to her?

'If that's what you really want,' she said woodenly. 'Then I will.'

How plain she made her feelings for him! His voice was cold as he put his napkin down on the table and stood up. 'Oh, please, Lucy! Anyone would imagine that I was proposing rehousing you in some slum! There is no problem—we will stay here if that is what you prefer. That was, after all, the agreement.' He paused. 'My father would like you to take Nicole to visit him this morning.'

Lucy's eyes grew wider. The King had been very sick and unable to see his new granddaughter. His sons visited him daily, but he had been advised against all other callers.

'He's better?' she questioned hopefully.

'Well, he is better than before.' He shrugged. 'There is no magic cure—but it will bring him great joy to see his granddaughter.'

'You'll…you'll come with me?' Her voice was nervous. Her meetings with Mardivino's ruler had been infrequent. He had shown her nothing but kindness, but, despite his frailty, he was still a formidable man.

He shook his head. 'I have work to do.' He saw the hurt which clouded her eyes. 'And he wants to see you alone,' he finished softly.

She knew that it was pointless to ask him why. He

would shrug and give her that mocking look of his, tell her that she would find out soon enough, that it was not his place to tell her of his father's wishes—if indeed he knew them—or to second-guess them if he did not.

She took ages dressing Nicole in a pretty little Broderie Anglais dress—which she was promptly sick over. By the time she had changed her she had time only to throw on a floaty dress which she hoped disguised her post-pregnancy tummy. She brushed her hair until it shone, then shot a slightly despairing look at herself in the mirror. Hardly the image of the calm and composed Princess which no doubt the King would be expecting!

But for once Nicole behaved like a little angel—or maybe it was the quietness and calm of the King's apartments which quietened her, for she was fast asleep in Lucy's arms by the time they were summoned inside.

The King lay resting in a bed which had been turned to face the gardens outside, where the bright and beautiful flowers danced. He was very old now, but you could see that he had once been a strong and powerful man, and his face bore the hallmarks of pride and dignity. His faded eyes had once been black, like his sons', and for the first time Lucy realised that his mouth was very like Guido's.

She managed some sort of awful attempt at a curtsey, but he shook his head and patted the side of the bed.

'Sit,' he commanded.

As she sat, he leaned forward. An ever-present nurse sprang to attention but he waved her away.

'Leave us,' he commanded.

'But your Royal Highness—'

'Leave!'

The nurse left and the King examined Nicole's face carefully, then lifted his head and gave Lucy a tired smile.

'She is very beautiful,' he observed.

Lucy was trying to remember all the etiquette of not speaking until she was spoken to, but in the circumstances it was difficult—and when it all boiled down to it wasn't she just like any proud mother showing off her baby to his grandpop?

'Yes, she is, isn't she?' She beamed. 'She's got Guido's eyes, of course, and his colouring—'

'But your nose, I think,' he said unexpectedly.

'Well, yes,' answered Lucy, pleased. 'I think so.'

'And my late wife's name. Nicole.'

'Yes. Guido wanted it.'

'A medieval French name,' he observed rather dreamily. 'Although I believe it is popular again now.'

They sat for a few moments in companionable silence, watching and listening while Nicole nestled in Lucy's arms and made little sucking noises.

'Would you like to hold her?' she asked tentatively, but the King shook his head.

'My arms are too weak to cope with such vigorous life,' he said sadly, but then his faded eyes twinkled at her. 'And, if the truth were known, the Princes of

Mardivino were not raised to deal with infants! Nico has broken the mould of that, of course,' he observed thoughtfully.

'Yes.'

He looked at her properly then, and she could see the quiet gleam of perception in his dark eyes. 'And Guido? He is…what is that term they use for fathers nowadays?'

'Hands-on?'

He smiled. 'Yes. Is Guido…hands-on?'

Lucy chose her words carefully. 'Not really. He loves her, of course—but he's one of those men who's almost a bit too frightened to pick her up, in case he drops her.'

The King appeared to digest this. 'I should never have sent him to America,' he said suddenly.

It was such an astonishing thing for him to say that Lucy just stared at him. In the long silence which followed, the King seemed to be deciding whether or not to speak.

'When his mother died I think I went a little bit mad,' he admitted eventually, and then he gave a ragged little sigh. 'It was such a shock, you see.'

Lucy said nothing, for there was nothing in the etiquette books to prepare you for a disclosure like this one.

'Nico was just a baby, of course—and oblivious to what was going on.'

'But he would have missed his mother,' Lucy pointed out.

He nodded. 'Of course he did. And for a while he

was a lost little baby. But his physical needs were such that his nurse was able to fulfil them. Gianferro was different—he was almost eight, and my heir, and as such he had always been treated in isolation from the other two. His whole life has been a role of preparation,' he said. 'He has always been taught to adapt to the changes that time brings.'

Lucy thought that little had changed—that Gianferro still lived his life in isolation. She held the baby closer and carried on looking at the King. Some instinct told her that he was leading up to something, but she didn't know what it was.

'But Guido was shattered,' he said quietly. 'He was especially close to his mother. For a while it seemed that the Palace was in uproar. Indeed, the whole island was—my people grieved for her so—and when my wife's sister offered to take him for the summer in Connecticut—I…well, I seized the opportunity.'

'You did what you thought was best,' said Lucy staunchly. But people's thinking was often muddled when they were grieving. And no one could predict the effect that their actions would have on the future.

'How do you think he felt?' asked the King.

She didn't question him on why he had asked her, or begin to wonder whether he had heard rumours that she and Guido were not happy. The important thing was that he *had* asked, and she must answer. Truthfully.

'He must have felt very…alone,' she said slowly, and a wave of guilt rocked her. How blinkered she had been. She had been so busy thinking about what *she* wanted—about what was best for *her*—that she had never stopped to think about why Guido was the way he was, why he acted the way he did.

She tried to imagine his confusion and his anger and his hurt at the time. Close to the mother who had been so cruelly taken from him, and then sent away from the only home he knew. He must have felt as if he wasn't wanted. No wonder he found it difficult to adapt to life on Mardivino. And she had selfishly refused to understand why.

But he never talked about it—he never talked about anything close to him.

And can you really blame him?

He had been too young to articulate his feelings at the time—he must have just blocked them out to make them bearable. And perhaps the habit had become one which had followed him into adulthood, impossible to break.

The King was looking at her, but he made no comment on the way she had bitten her lip in sorrow and self-recrimination.

'He never cried, you know,' he said suddenly. 'Not once.'

Feeling that if she heard any more then her heart would break, Lucy stared down at Nicole. A fierce need to make things right filled her with a new kind of determination. She didn't need the fairytale love-story—for how many people ever got that?—but if she could make her daughter happy, then surely she could make Guido happy, too. But how? Well, she could start by agreeing to move to New York! That was no hardship, really, was it?

She stared at the King, seeing him begin to wilt a little, and as if summoned by an invisible command the nurse reappeared. Lucy got to her feet. 'Thank you for seeing me today, your Serene Highness,' she said quietly.

'It has been my pleasure.' He pointed to his forehead, and, immensely moved, she bent to kiss it, then held the baby forward for him to do the same to her.

She was about to move away when his next words halted her.

'Do you ever sing to her?' he asked.

Lucy blinked. 'Occasionally. Why?'

'There is a lullaby, a French lullaby—*"Bonne Nuit Cher Enfant"*—do you know it?'

Lucy shook her head.

'Then learn it, and sing it to her some time.' He smiled conspiratorially. 'Our little secret.'

Their eyes met and Lucy realised that he did not have long to live. For why else would have said such an extraordinary thing? Abandoning Court formality to suggest she learnt a lullaby!

But she had learned so much else during her unconventional conversation with the King, and she was lost in thought as she made her way back from his apartments.

When she arrived in her own suite of rooms it was to find a message from Guido, telling her that he had unexpectedly had to go to the other side of the island, and he would be back the following day.

Her heart sank. She had been bursting to tell him her news, and now he wasn't around to hear it! And it wasn't the kind of thing that she wanted to tell him over the phone…she wanted to see his face.

Well, she had waited this long to come to her senses. A little longer wouldn't hurt her.

After lunch, she took Nicole for a walk, and happened to see Nico in the Palace gardens. He was wearing shorts and a singlet and was dripping with sweat. He had obviously been out running. Lucy smiled. It was times like this that really emphasised the fact that this was a family home as well as a Palace.

Well, maybe not for her. Not any more.

Yet, strangely enough, the idea now gave her no disquiet. She could live here for as long as she wanted to—but what was the point if Guido was unhappy? Inevitably, he would do what he had done once before—start taking more and more frequent trips to New York. Only with a baby she would not find it so easy to follow him…

'Hello, Nico,' she said.

'Hi!' he panted, and stopped to peer into the pram. 'How is she?'

'Gorgeous.' She looked at him. 'Nico?'

'Mmm?' His dark eyes crinkled at the corners.

'Do you know a lullaby called *"Bonne Nuit…"* something?'

'*"Bonne Nuit Cher Enfant"?*'

'That's the one!'

'Yeah, I know it.' He raised his eyebrows. 'Why?'

'Well, I wondered if you…' This was very important—she didn't know how, or why—she just knew that it was. 'Nico, will you teach it to me?'

CHAPTER FOURTEEN

DUSK was falling on the Palace by the time Guido returned, and he stretched and yawned as he walked along the long marble corridor leading to their apartments.

It had been years since he had visited the western side of the island, and he had been impressed to see the result of his brother's hard work. Nico was slowly helping to build up the infrastructure on Mardivino— to improve the roads and access to more remote parts of the island—but without destroying any of the natural and stunningly beautiful habitat. Indeed, the small fishing village of Lejana was as picturesque as any place he had visited. But maybe he had been viewing it with new eyes...

For Guido had found himself appreciating the landscape in a way that he had always seemed too busy to do before. That thing about making the most of the little things—taking time to stand and stare. Maybe having Nicole had changed him more than he'd realised. His heart gave a little leap at the thought that he would soon see her again. He glanced at his watch. If Lucy hadn't already put her to bed.

Briefly, his eyes closed as he thought of Lucy, and the longing and frustration gnawed away at him. Sometimes discoveries took an awful long time to make, and he knew now that he had not been fair to her—in so many ways.

Quietly, he opened the door to their suite, and then a sound stopped him in his tracks. He froze as he heard a voice singing a tune so familiar that it twisted his heart around.

Lucy's voice.

The words wafted through the still, early-evening air.

'Bonne nuit cher enfant...'

Guido closed his eyes.

'Quand tu dors dans mes bras...'

He stood motionless as a statue until the final lilting strains.

'Comme un ange dans mes bras.'

He did not feel the tears which lay damp on his face. He moved like a man in a dream—maybe he was—until he opened the door to the nursery and saw them. Mother with child. Rocking gently in the big old chair which had seen generations of Royal babies nursed.

And there it was—his past, his present and his future, all merged into the tableau silhouetted by the window.

Lucy looked up and her lips parted in disbelief. 'Guido?' she whispered, as if she had seen a ghost— and maybe she had—for this was her husband as she had never seen him before.

'I didn't know you knew that song,' he said unsteadily.

'Do you?' It was one of those unnecessary questions, but it needed to be asked. It was a floodgate question.

He nodded. 'Of course I do. My mother used to sing it.'

So! With swift care she deposited Nicole in her crib and went to him, brushing away his tears with gentle fingertips. Then she wrapped her arms tightly around him with not a thought other than to comfort him, not caring if he wanted this from her or not—because right then he *needed* it. They sometimes said that it took a weak man to cry, but Lucy knew that was wrong.

For strong men could cry, too.

'Oh, my darling,' she said softly. 'My darling, darling Guido—what is wrong? Tell me.'

But a lifetime of not talking about things didn't just vanish in an instant, and Lucy knew that she had to help him—show him the way forward—let him know that a life lived to the full in *all* the ways that mattered was a better life for them all.

She drew a deep breath for courage, praying that in his pain he wouldn't push her away. 'You never grieved for your mother,' she said slowly, and saw him flinch. 'You never even cried. Your father sent you away and you felt you weren't wanted any more. You were a lost soul in America, and when you came back it didn't feel like home. Nowhere did, nor ever has.'

'Who told you this?'

'Your father gave me the bare outline—the rest of it I filled in myself. Some of it I had already guessed.

That's why he told me to learn the lullaby and sing it to Nicole—'

'My father told you to do *that*?' he demanded incredulously.

Lucy nodded. 'He must have known that sooner or later you would hear me singing it.'

He was dazed, like a man who had been knocked out and was slowly coming round again. 'That is a remarkably perceptive thing for him to have done,' he said, still on a disbelieving note.

'I think he *is* a perceptive man,' she said. 'But as King he rarely shows it quite so openly. Or maybe his position doesn't allow him to.' And then she realised that perhaps there were other reasons why the King had enlightened her. That she had her own part to play in the healing process.

'Don't be hard on him for what happened, Guido,' she said softly. 'He acted with the best possible motives. He was missing your mother and having to help the people of Mardivino to adjust. Maybe he knew that there was no time to give to a five-year-old boy who was grieving. But he loves you,' she finished. 'He loves you very much.'

She prayed again, for the courage and the strength to say what she knew she had to without prejudice. Not because she wanted anything back from him— well, she did—but because Guido needed to hear this.

'As I do,' she said softly, and she looked up at him, her voice and her eyes very clear and very steady. 'As I do.'

Guido heard the deep love in her voice, unvarnished by any kind of vanity, and he gave a small cry, as if he had been wounded. A sweet, answering emotion began to lick warmth into his cold heart. He tightened his arms to enfold her closer and thought what a fool he had been. He buried his face in the sweet nectar of her hair, and for the first time in his life allowed his feelings to wash over him.

They bathed him with a bitter pain and regret until he thought he could bear it no longer, and then, inexorably, the tide turned and they gave way to a blessed kind of peace and hope. He raised his head and looked down at her.

'Will you forgive me, *cara*?' he said shakily.

'Why?' Her eyes widened. 'What have you done?'

Now he could read her own fears. *Dio*, but he had never stopped to think about how she might really be feeling herself, deep down. Was that because he had not cared? Or had not dared?

He touched her lips with his own. 'Not enough,' he said gently. 'Not nearly enough.'

'Guido, you're talking in riddles.'

'Then that does not bode well for the future, *cara mia*,' he responded. 'Since I have just come to my senses!'

'Guido! Please! What is it?'

'I want you to listen to me now, and hear me out. Do you think you can do that?'

She closed her eyes, praying that he hadn't decided he couldn't go on…not before she had had a chance to tell him that she was prepared to change. If he didn't want love then she would deal with it—because she wanted to work at her marriage. To do anything in her power to make it better. Weren't some Royal marriages based on that kind of understanding anyway? All she knew was that she didn't want to lose him.

'I have been a selfish, stupid fool, Lucy,' he said bitterly. 'I have just taken and taken—without even considering what it is that you might want. Without bothering to give anything back.'

'Guido, I—'

'Weren't you going to hear me out?' he queried gravely.

She nodded, because now she doubted whether any words would come, for her throat was knotted by the terror which was beating hotly through her veins.

'It was insensitive and thoughtless of me to expect you to live in New York.'

She wanted to say *But...* Except that she had promised to listen...

'Yesterday I went to visit Lejana—do you know where it is?'

'Isn't it on the coast by the Western Isles?'

A smile of satisfaction curved his lips. 'You know your Mardivinian geography,' he approved.

'Well, our daughter will need to—it's her heritage!' she retorted, and his smile grew wider. 'What about it?'

'There is a big plot there that we could build a house on.' He saw her frown. 'But if you want to stay in Solajoya, then you can—any damned part you choose!' He then made what was, for him, the ultimate sacrifice. 'We can even carry on living at the Palace if that's what you want.'

'But I don't!'

He narrowed his eyes. 'Don't what?'

'I don't want to live on Mardivino—I want to live in New York!'

Now he was confused. 'You do?'

'Yes!'

He frowned. 'So what's changed your mind?'

'I want to make our marriage work, Guido. You won't be happy living here, and if you're not happy then I won't be either—and everyone knows that women are much better at adapting than men.' She drew a badly needed breath. 'So I will.'

He began to laugh, and once he had started he couldn't stop—but then he had never laughed with quite such uninhibited joy before. It was like balm to his soul, music to an ear starved of sound.

Lucy stared at him as if he had taken leave of his senses. 'Shh! You'll wake Nicci!'

He pressed his lips together like a schoolboy trying not to giggle in church. 'Let's get this straight, Lucy. You want to live in New York because I do—and I want to live on Mardivino because *you* do?'

'Um…well, yes, I suppose so. Oh, Guido—this is terrible—it's like Catch 22! What are we going to do?'

'I don't think we need to decide *right* this minute, do you? I think that there are rather more important things to do.' Like finding the right words to convince her that he didn't care where the hell he was, just as long as she would be by his side. He felt like a blind man who had just stumbled into the light. And that, he knew, was the restorative power of love.

'Guido…'

'Shh.' He raised her hand to his lips and kissed it, then wrapped his palm around it very firmly and led her over to the crib. In silence they stood there, looking down on their daughter. Her dark lashes were like crescent moons on her perfect skin, and her little rosebud of a mouth pursed itself and made tiny sucking noises. One miniature arm was raised above her head, and it ended in a tiny clenched fist.

'Do you think she'll be a fighter?' he whispered.

And Lucy recognised that she had so nearly thrown in the towel and given up on Guido.

'Oh, I hope so,' she answered fervently. 'I really hope so.'

EPILOGUE

IT WASN'T all plain sailing from there on in—of course it wasn't. No marriage ever was, and especially not one which had started out like Lucy and Guido's. Guido had much to learn, and so did Lucy—about living together, about being newly-weds and new parents—oh, the list went on and on!

Mainly they had to learn about each other, but the magical thing was that they both wanted to—with a passion which made the steep learning curve seem like a doddle, and all the little hiccups fade into insignificance.

What had started as a tiny thaw in the ice which surrounded Guido's heart melted under the onslaught of the love given to him by his wife and his daughter. It was crazy, but love really *did* change everything—the way he felt, the way he viewed the world, and his place in it.

His own love flourished, and he learned that to show it did not make him less of a man, but more—for it made him a complete man. And as Guido's love grew, so Lucy basked in it, growing more secure and more confident—certainly enough for the feisty streak in her nature to re-emerge.

The two of them were back to their magnificent combative best! In fact, as Gianferro remarked rather

180

drily to Guido, it was something of a relief for the rest of the family now the house he'd had built for them in Lejana was finished!

It was, Lucy decided, the most beautiful house she had ever seen. So airy and light and full of windows—all the better to see the commanding sapphire of the nearby sea, which beat and roared and filled the air with its siren music.

The grounds sloped down to their own private beach—where Nicole would learn to swim and sail, taught by her father, who these days had the time.

Because Lucy had been right all along, Guido realised. She had told him often enough that he was achieving for the sake of achievement's sake, and he didn't need to do it any more. If he wasn't careful then life would pass him by while he was tying up unnecessary deals. And now that he had a family of his own the lure of making money in his property business had begun to pale—especially if you looked at it with the cool logic he always liked to employ—except maybe where his wife was concerned.

Even if you discounted his inherited wealth—which he had put into a Trust Fund for Nicole and any future children—he had earned all the money he could want, and more.

So he'd stopped wheeling and dealing across the globe, and put his energies into Mardivino instead—and his expertise in property stood him in good stead to advise on issues of architecture and planning.

As a couple, they stayed away from a lot of Royal functions—unless, as Lucy joked, they needed to 'swell the numbers'. They were happy to help out when needed, but that was all. Guido hated the rigidity of Court life, and Lucy wanted to create for him as normal and as happy a nuclear family as she could. The kind he had grown up missing…

The two of them were sitting on their terrace one evening, watching the setting sun sink like a blazing lollipop into the vast sea. It was the end of a baking hot summer day—there had been a family picnic, and the last of their guests had gone. Nico and Ella and Leo had been there—Ella pregnant with their second child, being fussed over by her husband, while their son played happily on the sand with Nicole, watched by an ever-attentive nanny.

Gianferro had—surprisingly—agreed to make a place in his busy schedule to come, too. As the King's health declined, so Gianferro's workload increased. Lucy had thought how utterly exhausted he looked as she watched him build a sandcastle for Leo to demolish, and how rare it was to see him let his guard down.

Bathed in the red-gold light of the setting sun, Lucy turned to her husband, revelling in the fact that his lean, hard body could look so relaxed these days. When she had first known him he had been so fired-up—always restless—as if he had been constantly seeking something but hadn't quite known what it was. Had he found it?

'Didn't you think Gianferro looked tired today?' she questioned slowly.

Guido shrugged. 'No more than usual.'

'Well, I think he drives himself too hard.'

'But that, *cara mia*, is the natural consequence of his destiny.'

'Can't you and Nico help him a bit more?'

He surveyed her with a small sigh of satisfaction—for her heart was deep and generous. With each day that passed his regard for her as a woman increased, and sometimes he wondered what he had ever done to deserve such a woman as this.

'No, my love,' he answered simply. 'We cannot. For one day Gianferro will be King, and Kings must always reign alone.'

Lucy's heart melted. 'How lonely it must be.'

'Inevitably.'

'And he doesn't even have a wife—nor any sign of one!'

Guido's eyes narrowed. 'That, of course, is an entirely different concern—and one which it is within his power to change. For he needs to have children if he wants to continue his bloodline. If not, then our own children stand in line to rule Mardivino one day.'

Lucy had known this on some unacknowledged level, but hearing Guido say it made the prospect seem frighteningly real. Her eyes widened. 'You don't want that for them, do you?'

He tried to imagine his little Nicole as Queen and his mouth tightened. It was hard to think of any child of his having to endure the trappings and tribulations of Majesty, but he forced himself to let his misgivings go, as Lucy had taught him. For what was the point of worrying about something which might never happen?

'No, I do not,' he said softly. 'But I cannot fight what might come to pass—I must embrace it whole-heartedly. We will wait and see what transpires.'

'Perhaps we ought to try and find a wife for Gianferro!'

He raised his dark eyebrows by a fraction as he pictured quite clearly his eldest brother's reaction to such an attempt at matchmaking. He would be out-raged! 'Or perhaps not,' he said drily.

Lucy bit her lip. 'Do you think…do you think he'll ever marry for love?'

'Ahh…' He held his hand out to her and Lucy took it, going to sit on his knee, her hands holding on to his broad, strong shoulders as if he were her anchor in a choppy sea. He shook his head. 'No, I do not—he is not in a position to allow himself such a luxury.'

She affected indignation. 'So you think that love is a luxury, do you?'

He smiled. 'No, my darling,' he said softly, and lifted his fingertips to touch the silken surface of her cheek. 'I think it is a necessity.'

She saw the sudden fierceness of his expression, heard the intensity behind his words, and she waited, a little flicker of hope burning away in her heart as she looked at him expectantly. For while Guido had learned to show his love in every way that counted he was still slow to speak it. It was as though—even for a man who could already speak four fluently—the language of love was the hardest of all!

'You are my world, Lucy,' he said simply, and he could see her beautiful mouth begin to wobble. That fleeting trace of insecurity both wounded him and spurred him on to tell her how much she meant to him. How very much. 'As vital to me as the water I drink and the air that I breathe. You are the sun that rises in the morning and the moon that lights my evening sky.' There was a pause, heavy with emotion, as he lifted her chin and dazzled her with the ebony fire from his eyes. 'I love you, *cara* Lucy. And I lay down my life for you.'

'Oh…oh, Guido…Guido.' She was not aware that a tear had begun to trickle its way down her cheek—not until he gave a soft smile and traced its path with the tip of his finger, then solemnly lifted the finger to his mouth to suck the salt away.

'No tears,' he said. 'No tears. Why are you crying when I have just told you how much I love you?'

She nodded, gulping them back. 'Because… because that's the most wonderful thing anyone has ever said to me!'

'I should think so, too!' he said fervently. 'For I am your husband!'

'Yes.' Her husband. Her lover. Her friend. Father to her child and—oh, so much more than that. For he was her sun, too—and her moon and her stars. As vital and vibrant as the mighty sea which filled their house with such incomparable light. 'I love you so much, Guido,' she said shakily.

He took her into his arms and began to stroke her until she relaxed, as molten and as malleable as soft wax, and at some point the stroking stopped and the kissing began. Deep, searching kisses—silent declarations of feelings which were bigger than both of them.

And some time after that he pulled her down onto the wooden decking of the moonwashed terrace. He slipped off the bikini she wore, and slid off his shorts—and when he entered her it felt like the most elemental thing which had ever happened to her. And the most precious. As if all those acts of fulfilling love had merely been a rehearsal for this, the real thing.

There was just the sound of lips exploring and small sighs of wonder as their bodies moved in harmony—like the planets which danced in the heavens around them—until at last their cries of mutual pleasure rang out and were lost in the music of the waves.

'I love you, Lucy,' he murmured against her lips.

'I love you, too,' she murmured back.

He kissed her hair and yawned, and began to wriggle into sleep, and Lucy rested her face against the muffled pounding of his heart and sighed with pure happiness as his naked body enfolded hers.

It was a very good thing, she decided, just before her eyes closed, that theirs was such a *private* house...

THE FUTURE KING'S BRIDE

by

Sharon Kendrick

To Blackadder, with love

CHAPTER ONE

GIANFERRO had always chosen his mistresses well.

He looked for beauty and intelligence, but above all for discretion—for obvious reasons. Since the age of seventeen there had never been any shortage of willing candidates for this unofficial and unacknowledged place in his life, but that would have surprised no one. For even if you discounted the restless black eyes in the coldly handsome face, and his hard, lean body, there was not a woman alive who would not long to become a mistress to the Prince.

Especially a prince who would one day be King of Mardivino—the heavenly Mediterranean island over which his family had ruled since the thirteenth century. A prince who owned palaces and planes and fast cars, as well as a string of world-class racehorses. Untold wealth was at Gianferro's fingertips—and who could blame women if all they wished was for him to stroke those fingertips over their bodies?

But now his quest was different, and daunting— even for him. Before him lay possibly the most important decision he would ever make. He could put off the inevitable no longer. It was not a mistress he sought, but a bride.

And his choice must be the right choice.

His two brothers were now married and had produced children of their own—and therein lay the danger. There was one way and one way only to ensure that *his* bloodline inherited the crown of Mardivino.

He must marry.

His heart was heavy as he glanced around the bedroom he had been given when he'd arrived yesterday. It was very different from the architecture of his own Rainbow Palace, but it was still a very beautiful room indeed. He looked around him. Yes, a very English room.

The huge windows were composed of mullions and transoms and diamond panes which caught and reflected the light from many different angles, so that it resembled an interior as airy as a birdcage. But—his mouth twisted into an ironic smile—a cage from which he was unlikely to break free.

Caius Hall, an exquisite sixteenth-century house, was home to the de Vere sisters—the elder of whom he was intending to marry. Lady Lucinda de Vere—affectionately known as Lulu—was everything that he could want in a woman. Her blood was as pure as his, and she added blonde and beautiful into the bargain.

Their families had known each other for years—both fathers had studied together at university and had stayed in touch, though meetings had inevitably become fleeting and infrequent over time. Gianferro had even spent a holiday here once, but the two girls had been young then—indeed, one had been just a baby.

And then, late last year, he had met the older daughter at a polo match. It had not been by chance— but brokered by a mutual family friend who had thought it high time he meet someone 'suitable'. Almost without thinking, Gianferro had put his defences up, but he had been struck by Lulu's self-assurance and her outstanding beauty.

'I think I know you, don't I?' she had questioned cheekily as he bent to kiss her hand. 'Didn't you stay in my house once—years ago?'

'A long time ago.' He frowned. 'You were in pigtails and ribbons at the time, I believe,' he remembered.

'Oh. How very unflattering!'

But that long-ago meeting provided a certain kind of security, a bedrock which was vital to a man in his position. She was no stranger with hidden motives; he knew her background. The match would be approved by everyone concerned.

After that they had met several times—at parties which Gianferro knew had been laid on specifically for just that purpose. Sometimes he wondered: if he snapped his fingers and demanded the moon be brought to him on a plate, would a team of astronauts be dispatched from Mardivino to try and procure it for him?

Throughout their covertly watched conversations there had been an unspoken understanding of both their needs and wants. He wanted a wife who would provide him with an heir, and she wanted to be a princess. It was the dream of many an aristocratic English girl. As easy as that.

Today, after lunch, he was going to request that their courtship become formal. And if that invisible line was crossed there would be no going back. There would be subtle machinations behind the scenes in Mardivino and England as marriage plans were brokered, as he intended they would be.

In a few short hours he would no longer be free.

Gianferro allowed himself a brief, hard smile. No longer free? Since when had freedom ever been on the agenda of *his* life? Crown Princes could be blessed with looks and riches and power, but the liberties which most men took for granted could never be theirs.

He glanced at his watch. Lunch was not for another hour, and he was feeling restless. He had no desire to go downstairs and engage in the necessary small talk which was so much a part and parcel of his life as a prince.

He slipped out of the room and moved with silent stealth along one of the long, echoing corridors until at last he was outside, breathing in the glorious English spring air like a man who had been drowning.

The breeze was soft and scented, and yellow and cream daffodils waved their frilly crowns. The trees were daubed with the candy-floss pinks and whites of blossom, and beneath them were planted circles of bluebells, magically blue and, like the blossom, heart-breakingly brief in their flowering.

Taking the less obvious path, Gianferro moved away from the formal gardens, his long stride taking him towards the fields and hedgerows which formed part of the huge estate.

In the distance he could hear the muffled sound of a horse's hooves as it galloped towards him, and in that brief, yearning moment he wished himself astride his own mount—riding relentlessly along the empty Mardivinian shore until he had worn himself and his horse out.

He watched as a palomino horse streaked across the field, and his eyes narrowed in disbelief as he saw that the rider was about to make it jump the hedge.

He held his breath. Too high. Too fast. Too...

Instinct made him want to cry out for the horse to stop, but instinct also prevented him, for he knew that to startle it could be more dangerous still.

But then the rider urged the mount on, and it was one of those perfect moments that sometimes you witnessed in life, never to be recaptured. With a gravity-defying movement, the horse rose in a perfect, gleaming arc. For a split-second it seemed to hover in mid-air before clearing the obstacle with only a whisper to spare, and Gianferro slowly expelled the breath he had been holding, acknowledging with reluctant admiration the rider's bravery, and daring, and...

Stupidity!

Gianferro was himself talented enough a horseman to have considered taking it up as a career, had it not been for the accident of birth which had made him a prince, and he found himself tracing the deepened grooves of the hoof-marks towards the stables.

Perhaps he would advise the boy that there was a difference between courage and folly—and then perhaps afterwards he might ask him if he would like to ride out for him in Mardivino!

The scent of the stables was earthy, and he could hear nothing other than the snorts of a horse and the sound of a voice.

A woman's voice—soft and bell-like—as it murmured the kind of things that women always murmured to their horses.

'You darling thing! You clever thing!'

Gianferro froze.

Had a *woman* been riding the palomino?

With autocratic disregard, he strode into the tack-room and saw the slight but unmistakably feminine form of a girl—a *girl*!—feeding the horse a peppermint.

'Are you out of your mind?' he demanded.

Millie turned her head and her blood ran first hot, then cold, and then hot again.

She knew who he was, of course. Millie had often been accused of having her head in the clouds—but even *she* had realised that they had a prince staying with them. And that her sister Lulu was determined to marry him.

The place had been swarming with protection officers and armed guards, and she had heard her mother complaining mildly that the two girls who had been drafted in from the village to help had done very little in the way of work—the place was so filled with testosterone!

Millie had managed to get out of meeting the Prince at dinner last night, by pleading a headache—wanting to escape what she was sure would be a cringe-making occasion, while her sister paraded herself as though she was on a market stall and he the highest bidder—but now here he was, and this time there was no escaping him.

Yet he was not as she had thought he would be.

He did not look a bit like a prince, in his close-fitting trousers and a shirt which was undoubtedly silk, but casually unbuttoned at the neck to reveal a sprinkling of crisp dark hair. He was as strong and as muscular as any of the stableboys, with his hair as gleaming black as her riding boots. But blacker still were his eyes, and they were sparking out hot accusation at her.

'Did you hear me?' he grated. 'I asked whether you were crazy.'

'I heard you.'

Her voice was so low that he had to strain his ears to hear. He could see that she had been sweating—saw the way the thin shirt she wore clung to her small, high breasts—and unexpectedly a pulse leapt in his groin. There was no deference in her voice, either—didn't she know who he was?

'And are you? Crazy?'

Millie shrugged. She had spent a lifetime being told

that she rode too fearlessly. 'That rather depends on your point of view, I suppose.'

He saw that her eyes were large and as blue as the flowers which circled the trees, and that her skin was the clearest he had ever seen—untouched by make-up and yet lit with the natural glow of exercise and youth. He found himself wondering what colour was the hair which lay beneath the constricting hat she wore, and now his heart began to pound in a way which made his head spin.

'You ride very well,' he acceded, and without thinking he took another step closer.

Millie only just stopped herself from shrinking away, but his proximity was making her feel almost light-headed. Dizzy. He was as strong as the grooms, yes, but he was something more, too—something she had never before encountered. When Lulu had spoken about 'her' Prince she had made him sound like nothing more than a title…she certainly hadn't mentioned that he had such a dangerous swagger about him, nor such an unashamedly masculine air, which was now making her heart crash against her ribcage. She stared into his dark eyes and tried to concentrate.

'Thank you.'

'Though whoever taught you to take risks like that should be shot,' he added darkly.

Millie blinked. 'I beg your pardon?'

'You'll kill yourself if you carry on like that,' he said flatly. 'That jump was sheer folly.'

'But I did it! And with room to spare!'

'And one day you might just not.'

'Oh, you can't live your life thinking like that!' said Millie airily. 'Wrapped up in cotton wool and worrying about what might happen. Timidity isn't living—it's existing.'

Something about her unaffectedness made him feel almost wistful. As did the sentiment. How long since he had allowed himself the luxury of thinking that way? 'That's because you're young,' he said, almost sadly.

'While you're a grand old man, I suppose!' she teased.

He laughed, and then stilled, the laughter dying on his lips, and something crept into the enclosed space of the stable—something intangible, which crackled in the air like the sound of the fresh, hot flames of a new fire bursting into life.

And as they stared at each other, another debilitating wave of weakness passed over her. Millie was brave and fearless on horseback, but now she prickled with a feeling very like fear, and the sweat cooled on her skin, making her clammy and shivery. As if she had suddenly caught a fever.

'I'd better finish up here,' she said awkwardly.

'Who are you?' he questioned suddenly. 'One of the grooms?'

Some self-protective instinct made her unsure what to say. If he thought she was just one of the hands he would be out of here like a shot. And I will be safe, she thought. Safe from that dark, dangerous look and that unashamedly sexual aura which seemed to shimmer off his olive skin.

'Yes,' she said. 'I am.'

For a moment a cold, hard gleam entered his eyes—a sense of the condemned man being offered one final meal before his fate was sealed. Her lips were curved, slightly open, and he could see the moist pinkness of her mouth. He longed to kiss her as he had never kissed a woman before, nor ever would again.

And Millie saw it all played out in that one, lingering look. She was almost completely innocent of men, but she had observed enough of nature to know what passed between the sexes. She knew exactly what was going on in the mind of the Prince, and for a moment her heart went out to her sister. What if he turned out to be the kind of man who played away? Serially unfaithful—just as their own father had been?

But Lulu would handle it; she always did. She had had men eating out of her hand for years, and why should this man be any different? But this man *was* different—and not just because he was a prince. He was...

Millie swallowed.

He was fantasy come true—virile and strong and masculine—even she could sense that. And women would always gravitate towards him, in the way that a mare always went for the most robust of the stallions. Her feelings did a rapid turnaround, and for a moment Millie almost envied her sister.

She stared for a second at the arrogant thrust of his hips and found herself blushing—terrified that he might be able to guess what she had been thinking. 'I...I'd better go,' she stammered.

He laughed again, but this time the laugh was regretful, and tinged with something else which he couldn't identify. 'Yes, run along, little girl,' he said softly.

'But I'm nineteen!' she defended, stung.

'Better run along anyway,' came the silky response.

She stared into the dark glitter of his eyes and did exactly what he said—rushing from the stable as if he was chasing her, out into the spring day which had been transformed by the mercurial April weather. Where before there had been bright sunshine now the clouds had suddenly split open, and rain was cascading down. But at least the droplets cooled her hectic colour and flushed cheeks as she dazedly made her way back to the Hall.

Wet through, she leaned against the wall of the kitchen-garden as she steadied her breathing. But her mouth felt as dry as summer dust, and her heart was still pounding as if it wanted to burst out of her chest.

She felt as if she was a cauldron, and he had reached inside and stirred up all her feelings, so that she was left feeling not like Millie at all, but some trembling stranger to herself.

And she still had lunch to get through.

CHAPTER TWO

'MILLIE, you're late!'

Above the hubbub of chatter, Millie heard the irritation in her mother's voice. It was a voice which had been trained to rarely express emotion, but under circumstances such as these, with one daughter poised to marry into such an exalted family, it was easy to see her customary composure vanish when the other turned up unacceptably late.

Millie had tried to slip unnoticed into the Blue Room, where everyone had gathered before lunch, but the majority of the guests were thronged around the tall, imposing figure of the Prince. 'Sorry,' she said, her eyes looking down at the priceless Persian carpet because she did not dare to look anywhere else, terrified to look into those dangerous, dark eyes...because...

Because what? Because in the time it had taken her to wash the mud and grime and sweat from her body and to dress in something halfway suitable she had been able to think of nothing other than the shockingly handsome man who would one day become her brother-in-law? Trying not to imagine what it would have been like if he *had* kissed her.

'Millie, it's just not *done* to keep Royalty waiting,'

16

scolded her mother, and then added in an aside, 'And couldn't you have worn some lipstick or something, darling? You can look so pretty if you put your mind to it!'

The implication being that she didn't look at all pretty at the moment. Well, that was a good thing. She wanted to fade away into the background. She didn't want him looking at her that way. Making her feel those things. Making her ache. Making her wonder...

'But I'd have been even later if I'd stopped to do that,' Millie protested, and then a dark shadow fell over her, and she didn't need to look up into that hard and handsome face to know whose shadow it was. She found herself having to suppress a shiver of excitement as he came to stand beside them and hoped that her mother hadn't noticed.

'Prince Gianferro,' said Countess de Vere, with the biggest smile Millie had ever seen her give, 'I'd like you to meet my younger daughter, Millicent.'

Millie risked glancing up then—it would have been sheer rudeness to do otherwise—and she found herself staring up into his face, all aristocratic cheekbones and dark, mocking eyes. *Say you've met me,* she silently beseeched him. Say that and everything will be okay.

But he didn't. Just lifted the tips of her fingers to his lips and made the slightest pressure with his mouth, and Millie felt a whisper of longing trickle its way down her spine.

'Contentissimo,' he murmured. 'Millicent.'

'Millie,' she corrected immediately as she dragged her hand away from the temptation of his touch and met his eyes in silent rebuke, some of her fearlessness returning to rescue her. 'Should I curtsey?'

His mouth curved. 'Do you want to?'

Was she imagining things, or was that a loaded question and—oh, heavens—why was she even *thinking* this way? He was Lulu's, not hers—and by no stretch of the imagination could he ever be hers— even if Lulu *wasn't* in the picture.

She nodded her head as she dipped into a graceful and effortless bob, hoping that the formal greeting would put proper distance between them.

'Perfetto,' he murmured.

'Yes, it was an *excellent* curtsey, darling,' said her mother, with a glow of slightly bemused satisfaction. 'Now, please apologise to the Prince for your lateness!'

'I—'

His eyes were full of devilment. 'I expect you had something far more exciting to do?'

He was weaving her deeper into the deception, and she was wondering how he would react if she said something like, *You know perfectly well what I was doing*, when to her relief the lunch bell rang.

'Lunch,' she murmured politely.

'Saved by the bell,' came his mocking retort, and Millie saw her mother blink, looking even more bemused.

Probably wondering how her mouse of a daughter had managed to engage the Prince's interest for more than a nanosecond!

There were twenty for lunch, and—as Millie had fully expected—she was seated at the very end of the table, about as far away from him as it was possible to be. And I hope you're enjoying your lunch, she thought, because every mouthful I take is threatening to choke me!

But Gianferro was not enjoying his lunch, and course after course made an appearance. The food was sublime, the surroundings exquisite and the company exactly as it should be—except...

His eyes kept straying to the girl at the end of the table. How unlike her sister she was. Lulu was as pampered and as immaculate as a world-class model—while Millie wore a simple dress which emphasised her long-limbed and naturally slim body. Her pale blonde hair was tied back and her face was completely free of make-up, and yet she looked as fresh and as natural as a bunch of flowers.

From close at his side Lulu leaned over, and he caught a drift of her expensive French perfume. Inexplicably he found himself comparing it to the earthy scent of horses and saddlesoap.

'You haven't touched your wine, Gianferro!' Lulu scolded.

He shrugged. 'Did you not know that I never drink at lunchtime?'

'No, I didn't! How boring!' Lulu pulled a face. 'Why ever not?'

'I need to have a clear head.'

'Not always, surely? Isn't it nice sometimes to be… um…' She shot him a coquettish glance. '*Relaxed* in the afternoon?'

He knew exactly what she was suggesting, and found himself…*outraged*. Or maybe, he admitted with painful honesty, maybe he was just looking for an excuse to be outraged. But it was more than that. Gianferro was an expert where women were concerned, and today he had seen Lulu on her home territory—and instinct told him that she was not what he wanted.

She was beautiful, yes—and confident and alluring—but her manner had been predatory since he had first set foot in her house, and while it was a quality which was admirable in a mistress it was not what he wanted from a wife.

Now she was flicking her hair back and letting her fingertips play with her necklace—all signs of sexual attraction, which was well and good. But he had realised something else, and he knew deep down that his instinct was the right one.

She was not a virgin!

Whereas Millie…

His gaze flicked down the table and he found her eyes on him. Huge and blue, confused and troubled. And as their eyes met she bit her lip and turned away, as if she had been stung.

Once again he felt the unexpected throb of a desire so primitive that it felt like something deeper than desire.

'Gianferro?'

He gave his most bland and diplomatic smile as he turned to the woman by his side. '*Sì?*'

Lulu's eyes were shining with undisguised invitation. 'Would you like me to show you round the estate this afternoon? I mean, *properly*?' She smiled. 'There are all kinds of hidden treasures in Caius Hall.'

Gianferro steeled himself. All his life he had controlled—had chosen the correct path to take—and yet the route he had been following had suddenly become blurred. He knew that the unspoken understanding which had existed so precariously between himself and Lulu would now never be voiced. No offer had been made and therefore there could be no rejection.

She would know, of course, and be disappointed—yes, invariably—but far better a mild disappointment at this early stage than engaging in something which he knew would never work.

He knew what he should do. Walk away today without looking back—but now he found he had chanced upon an unexpectedly clear path to take. His route no longer seemed blurred at all.

'Shall we all move places for dessert?' questioned Millie's mother.

Gianferro nodded. 'Indeed. I should like the chance to talk to both your daughters.'

It was undeniably a command, and the very last

thing she wanted—*or was it?*—but Millie knew where her duty lay, and she took her place next to him with a fixed smile on her face, trying to ignore Lulu's mutinous expression and wondering what on earth she was going to say to him.

Or he to her!

His smile was mocking as he bent his head to talk in a low voice. 'So why did you lie to me, Millie? Why did you pretend to be one of the grooms?' he accused softly.

Millie bit her lip. There was no way she could come out and explain that he had made her feel all churned-up and confused. He would think she was *mad*!

'Just an impulse thing,' she said truthfully.

He raised his dark brows. 'And are you often given to impulse?' he queried.

'Sometimes,' she admitted. 'Are you?'

He gave the same kind of almost-wistful smile he had shown her earlier and shook his head. 'Alas, such an indulgence does not go with the job description.'

'Of Prince?' she teased.

'Crown Prince,' he teased back.

'But you're a person as well as a title!' she declared.

How beautifully passionate she was, he thought. And how hopelessly naïve. 'The two are inextricably linked,' he said softly.

'Oh.'

'Anyway,' he said firmly, 'it is boring to talk of such things. Tell me about you, Millie.'

'Me?' She blinked in astonishment.

'Is that such a surprising thing to want to know about?'

She didn't want to say yes. To tell him that when you had an especially beautiful older sister very few people were interested in *her*. But he began to ask her about her childhood, and seemed genuinely to want to hear about it, and Millie began to relax, to open up. That strange and rather fraught encounter of earlier melted away as she began to tell him about the strictures of her life at the all-girls boarding school she had attended and about the jokes they had played on the nuns. And when his dark eyes narrowed and he began to laugh Millie felt as though she had achieved something rather special.

Until she realised that the whole table had grown silent, and that everyone was looking at them—her mother in surprise and Lulu with undisguised irrita-tion.

'What would you like to do this afternoon, Gianferro?' questioned her mother.

He saw Lulu raise her eyebrows at him.

'I will tell you what I would like to do,' he said softly. 'I should like to go and look at your horses.'

Lulu grimaced. 'The *horses*?'

'But, yes,' he murmured. 'I have many fine mounts in Mardivino, and I should like to see if you have anything here to equal them.'

'Oh, I think you'll find that we do!' laughed one of the men.

From the centre of the table Lulu waved a perfectly manicured hand, first towards the window and then against her shell-pink couture gown. 'But it's *raining*!'

'I like the rain,' he said softly.

Lulu tapped her fingernail against the polished wood. 'Well, if you want to get soaking wet, that's fine by me—but don't expect me to join you!'

There was an infinitesimal silence. He could read in her eyes that she now fully expected him to capitulate, to say that he had changed his mind and would see the horses another time, but he would never do that. Never. Never would he bend his will to a woman!

'As you wish,' he said crisply.

His displeasure was almost tangible, and Millie saw her mother's stricken face as her lunch party threatened to deteriorate. She licked her lips nervously. 'I could show the Prince the horses, if you like?'

Her mother gave her a grateful smile, which only added to Millie's growing sense of discomfort. And guilt. 'Oh, darling—*would* you?'

Gianferro smiled. 'How very kind of you, Millie. Thank you.'

The easy atmosphere had evaporated and now the tension was back. Her heart beating hard against her ribs, Millie pushed her chair back, hating him for the way he was behaving and hating herself just as much, without quite knowing why.

'Come on, then,' she said ungraciously, and was rewarded with a slight narrowing of his eyes.

'But you'll need to change!' objected her mother.

'Oh, I'm okay—a little bit of rain never hurt anyone,' said Millie firmly.

Lulu gave an edgy laugh. 'Millie won't care if she gets soaked to the skin—she's such a *tomboy*!'

It was the kind of taunt which had haunted her down the years, but Millie didn't feel a bit like a tomboy as Gianferro followed her and the room fell silent. Inexplicably—and uncomfortably—she had never felt more of a woman in her life.

At the east entrance, she opened the door. Beyond the rain was an almost solid sheet of grey.

She turned to him. 'You can't honestly want to go out in that?'

'Yes. I do.'

She grabbed a waterproof from the hook and half threw it at him before pulling on one herself. 'Come on, then.'

Perversely, he liked the ungracious gesture, and the angry look she sparked at him as he pulled on the battered old coat, with its smell of horses and leather. He stepped outside and felt the rain in his hair and on his cheeks. It was coming down so fast that when he opened his mouth it rushed in—knocking all the breath out of him.

'We'll have to run!' said Millie, but suddenly she

felt a strange sense of excitement. The dull, formal lunch had become something else. He wanted to see her beloved horses, and this was where she felt at home. *But it is more than just that, Millie, and you know it is.* She shook her head, as if she could shake away the troublesome thoughts. 'Come on!'

Laughing with a sudden recklessness which was alien to him, he ran behind her, dodging puddles and watching as the mud splattered droplets up her pale silk-covered legs. Tights? he wondered. Probably. She was too gauche and unworldly to pull on a pair of stockings. What was he doing here, and why was he allowing this to happen? This was craziness. Madness. He should stop it right now.

Yet all the time a feeling was growing deep inside him, a sense of the irrevocable about to happen, as though his fate was about to be sealed in a way in which he had least expected.

By the time they reached the stables Millie's hair was plastered to her skull, and she turned to him, brushing cold droplets of rain away from her skin as if they were tears, not knowing and not caring what was the right thing to say any more.

'Why didn't you tell my mother we'd already met today?'

'You know why.'

'No, I don't.'

'Yes, you do. Just as you know what is going to happen next.'

She shook her head, trying to quell the glow of

excitement, trying to pretend it wasn't happening. 'You're talking in riddles!'

'Why did you agree to bring me here, Millie?' he questioned silkily.

'Because you…because you wanted to look at the horses, didn't you?'

In any other woman it would have been a coy question, but Gianferro knew she meant it. 'No. You know very well what I wanted. What I want. What you want, too—if you can dare to admit it to yourself.'

Her eyes were like saucers as she saw the expression on his face and read the sensual intent there, so dark and so powerfully irresistible that she shook her head, willing it to go away even while she prayed it never would. 'No,' she breathed. 'No. We mustn't!'

'But we have to—you know we do,' he whispered. 'For you will die unless we do.' And so will I.

'Gianferro!'

He pulled her into his arms and tumbled her down beneath him onto the spiky bed of a bale of hay, pushing back a strand of hair from her rain-wet face. For one long moment he stared down at her, ignoring the bewilderment in her eyes, before blotting out the world with the heady pressure of his kiss.

For Millie it was like jumping the highest jump in the world—she'd never felt such a heady blend of excitement and fear before. She could feel the muscular strength of his body, and his hands cupping her face, his lips grazing over hers.

'Oh!' It was a broken plea, a request for something

she wasn't aware she wanted, and as she made it he opened her lips with the seeking brush of his tongue. She gasped as it flicked inside her mouth. Fireworks exploded inside her head and she began to ache as she gripped onto him, drowning in the sweetness of it all, her body seeming to take on a life of its own as it pushed itself against the hard sinews of his. Dimly, she was aware of the heavy flowering of her breasts, and their sweet, prickling ache made her want him closer still.

With a terse exclamation he pulled himself away from her, his breathing ragged and unsteady as he stared into the sultry protest of her slick lips.

'Why did you stop?' she questioned, in a honeyed voice which sounded like a stranger's.

'Why?' He gave a short laugh. 'Why do you think?' And then he read the uncertainty and the hunger in her big blue eyes and relented, his dark brows knitting together. 'Have you ever kissed a man before, Millie?'

She stared at him. So he had guessed! 'Not…not like that.'

The dark brows were elevated in lazy question. 'And what way is that?'

She wanted to say *With your tongue*, but she couldn't. It made it sound so anatomical. As if what had just happened had been all about experimentation, and it had not been about that at all—more a great whooshing feeling which had swept her away and made her feel like…like…

She shook her head, as if that could make the mixed-up feelings go away. 'Nothing.'

A sense of triumph began to bubble up inside him as he acknowledged just how inexperienced she was, and he pulled her back into his arms. 'You kiss very beautifully,' he said softly. 'Very hard and very passionately.' He traced the outline of her lips with the tip of his finger and they trembled beneath his touch. 'But there are other ways to kiss a man too, and I shall show you them all. I shall teach you well, dear Millie.'

His words seemed to bring her to her senses, and she pulled herself away from him. He did not stop her. What the hell was he suggesting? What had he lured her into, and why had she *let* him? Distractedly, she tugged strands of hay from her hair and cast them down on the stable floor as she stared at him.

'You won't do anything of the sort!' she spat out, her voice shaking with emotion. 'What kind of man do you think you are?' *And what kind of woman was she?* 'You're going to marry my sister!'

He shook his head. 'No,' he said heavily. 'I am not.'

'You are! You are!' she cried desperately. 'You know you are!'

'I cannot marry her,' he said flatly, and he reached out and captured her chin, turning her face towards his to imprison her in the ebony spotlight of his gaze, melting her with its intensity. 'And we both know why that is.'

CHAPTER THREE

'I'M GOING to marry Gianferro.'

Lulu paused in the act of brushing her hair. 'Are you out of your tiny?'

Millie swallowed, but the words had to be said, no matter what the reaction. 'I'm sorry.'

The eyes which were reflected in the dressing-table mirror narrowed, and then Lulu whirled round. 'What the hell are you talking about?'

'Gianferro, and I...we are to be married.'

'Tell me you're joking.'

Millie shook her head. The right thing to say now would be, *I wish I was,* but that wouldn't have been true. And she had decided that she could not shirk the truth. Lulu was going to be hurt—through no fault of her own—and it was Millie's duty to stand there and take the flak. 'No. I'm not joking.'

For a second Lulu's mouth twisted, and then she said, in the same voice she used to use when she told Millie that men didn't like girls who smelt faintly of manure, 'Millie—you may have decided to develop a crush on that cold-hearted bastard, but it really isn't a good idea to start living in fantasy land. If you come out with bizarre statements like that then people are bound to get to hear. And people will laugh.'

'She means it, Lulu,' said a voice at the door, and both sisters turned round to see their mother standing there.

'You knew?' questioned Millie in bewilderment.

'Gianferro rang me this morning,' said her mother. 'Supposedly to ask my permission for your hand, since your father is no longer with us—though I got the distinct impression that my agreement was academic. That he intends to marry you whether I sanction it or not, and that he is not the type of man who will take no for an answer.'

Lulu was looking from one to the other, like a spectator at a tennis match, a look of puzzlement on her face. 'But she doesn't even *know* him!'

There was an uncomfortable silence.

'How can she be marrying him?' continued Lulu, in disbelief. 'If she hasn't seen him since that day he ruined our lunch party and broke my heart into the bargain?'

'He didn't break your heart, darling,' said her mother gently. 'You've been back with Ned Vaughn ever since!'

But Lulu wasn't listening. 'Are you going to give us some kind of explanation, Millie? You've only met him once!'

The Countess's eyes were shrewd. 'I think you'll find she's met him a great deal more than once— haven't you, Millie?'

Millie nodded, biting her lip, summoning up more courage than she had ever needed in her life.

'When?' snapped Lulu. 'And where?'

'At Chichester. And Cirencester. Once in Heathcote.'

Lulu's eyes narrowed. 'At *horse* fairs?'

'That's right. Well, where the horse fairs were being held. We didn't actually go to any.'

There was silence for a moment, and then Millie drew a deep breath as she met the question in her sister's eyes. Just tell it. Tell it the way it is—because that way you might be able to believe it yourself.

'He wanted to see me again and thought we should meet up at places that I actually had a legitimate reason to visit—that it would be the best way to avoid suspicion.'

'Why, you sneaky little cow!'

'Lulu!' said their mother warningly.

'No,' said Millie. 'She has every right to say it. And more.' Her voice was even lower than usual. 'I'm truly sorry, Lulu—I really am. I didn't mean for it to happen, and neither did he. It just did.'

Lulu gave a high, forced laugh. 'You little fool!' she spat. 'Don't you know he's just been spinning you a line to get you into bed? Your first lover! Don't you realise that for a man who has everything—and has *had* everything—a woman's virginity is something you can't put a price on?'

'We haven't…' Millie's words tailed off as she registered the incredulous look on Lulu's face. 'Nothing has happened between us, and nothing will—at least not until after the wedding. That's the way Gianferro wants it.'

'*"That's the way Gianferro wants it!"*' mimicked Lulu furiously.

'I wanted you to be the first to know, Lulu—'

'Well, thanks! Thanks for nothing!' Lulu's eyes narrowed again, and this time her rage reminded Millie of the time when she had been turned down for the starring role in the school pantomime. 'You must have told him!'

'Told him what?'

'That I'd been...' Her breathing quickened. 'Did you blab about me and Ned? Did you tell him that we'd been lovers?'

'Of course I didn't!' Millie cried, appalled.

'There's no "of course" about it! You were obviously determined to get your hooks into him, and it seems you've succeeded! Or are you really expecting me to believe that he came here with *me* in mind and changed his mind when he saw *you*?'

'I don't know how or why it happened,' said Millie miserably. 'It just did.'

'Well, may I offer you my congratulations, darling?' came a gentle voice, and Millie jerked her head up, looking at her mother with tear-filled eyes. 'We must be glad for your sister, Lulu,' she added firmly.

'You just want one of your daughters to marry into Royalty!' said Lulu crossly. 'You don't care which one!'

'Nonsense! You'll be perfectly happy as a wealthy

landowner's wife, ordering Ned here, there and everywhere—you know you will. Gianferro would never have suited *you*, my darling—you're much too independent of spirit.'

Lulu looked slightly mollified, but she wasn't finished with her sister yet. 'And do you really think—with your zero experience of men—that you can handle a man like Gianferro?'

Millie stared at her. 'I don't know,' she said honestly. 'All I know is that I've got to try.'

The Countess pushed her gently down onto a chair. 'Won't you tell us how it happened, darling?'

Millie knew that she owed her family some kind of explanation—but where to begin? And how much would Gianferro be happy for her to reveal?

Already she was aware of the great gulf between her and the rest of the world—one which was widening by the second. She was to be the future King's bride, and with that came responsibility—and distance. Gianferro was not a man like other men—she could not gossip about what he'd said to her. There could be no blushing disclosures of how he had asked her to marry him. But there again, thought Millie, with a touch of regret, it was not the kind of proposal which would go down in history as one of the most romantic. No, for Gianferro it was a purely practical arrangement. She understood that was the way it had to be.

There had been a series of meetings—carefully arranged and discreetly choreographed. Silent, purring cars had been dispatched to collect her from train stations, whisking her away to various houses—safe houses, she believed they were called—where Gianferro would be waiting for her. The armed guards and the protection officers had been kept very much in the background—like crumbs swept away before the guests arrived.

Their hosts had often been strangers to her, but she had known one of the couples fairly well. She remembered the hostess looking her up and down, unable to hide her expression of faint surprise. Yet Millie knew that those meetings would not be spoken of. Not even to her mother—not to anyone—because Gianferro would have demanded total confidentiality and because the stakes were too high. *What stakes?* she asked herself, but it was a question she did not dare answer, just in case she was hopelessly off the mark.

There had been small lunch parties, when she'd been gently quizzed on her attitude to politics and art—what she thought of the women's movement. Her responses had come over as quite lukewarm—even to her own ears—and it had made Millie realise how insular her life was, how little she really thought about—other than her horses.

I am being tested, she'd thought suddenly. *But for what?*

Yet she had known, deep down, just what was expected of her—and exactly how to behave—for in a way hadn't she been brought up to do exactly this?

One day she'd been chattering her way through a tour of some magnificent gardens—properly showing interest in all the trees and shrubs. She'd seen their host nodding, and Gianferro's look of satisfaction as she recognised the bud of a rare Persian rose. She'd felt as if she was jumping through hoops.

Afterwards, it should have been a treat to be shown the magnificent Andalusian horses which were stabled there, but for the first time in her life she had found she wanted to be elsewhere, not here—no matter how magnificent the breed. Alone with the tall, brooding man who was still such a stranger to her. The man who had occupied every second of her waking hours—and the dreaming ones, too—ever since he had blazed into her life with all the force of some dark and dazzling meteor. She had shot him a glance, but his intention had been focused firmly on the horses.

His manner was so formal towards her—there had been no repeat of that wild intimacy which had taken place in the stables that rainy afternoon. She found herself aching for him to take her into his arms again, but the longer it became, the more impossible seemed the very idea that the whole thing had ever happened. As if she had merely imagined it. Her increased exposure to him had only served to emphasise how gorgeous he was—yet he seemed more remote, and Millie's confusion grew at the same rate as her longing for him.

She had smoothed her hand over the gleaming roan

flesh of a horse. 'She's beautiful, isn't she?' she questioned tentatively.

'Not bad,' he murmured.

'Not bad?' laughed their host. 'This is the horse of Kings—and this particular mare will breed you future champions! She is yours, Gianferro!'

'You are too generous!' he protested.

'Yours,' emphasised the host softly.

'Thank you.' Gianferro inclined his head, acknowledging the honour, but knowing that no gift came without expectation. It had happened all his life, but now it was with increasing regularity, as the time for his accession to the throne grew ever closer. These gifts were the blocks which people used to build relationships with a future monarch, just as they were willing to make their houses over to his requirements. They wanted to feel that they were close to him, but he knew that no one could ever really be close to him. Not even his wife. For to be a king was essentially to be alone.

He glanced over at Millie and saw their host gave a small smile as he correctly interpreted Gianferro's wishes. 'Perhaps you would both care to see the library? Before lunch is served.'

To Millie's relief they were left alone—completely alone—and, frustrated with this no-man's land in which she found herself, she ran across the room into his arms, unable to stop herself.

She heard his breath quicken as he bent his head to kiss her, yet she sensed his restraint as she pressed her body closer to his. But she didn't care. Her senses had been awoken and she was greedy for his touch. For a moment she felt as though she had hit a button straight to paradise, as his mouth moved with such sweet intimacy over hers, but when she gave a little moan of delight he disentangled her—rather like someone restraining a sweet but rather over-eager puppy.

She turned bewildered blue eyes up to him. 'You don't want me any more?'

Gianferro frowned and quelled the desire deep inside him. How sweetly passionate she was! He was unused to such unfeigned enthusiasm, but he recognised that it was a double-edged sword. He must remember that there was a downside to her innocence, and he was going to have to teach her to school and to temper her desire. She must learn that he would always be the initiator of intimacy—unless in the privacy of the bedroom.

'You know I want you,' he murmured softly. 'But not here, and not now. Come and talk to me, Millie.'

'I *can't*,' she whispered. 'I feel out of my depth, and I don't know what is happening to me.'

'Don't you?' He took her by the shoulders and his eyes were fierce and black and burning. 'Have you not guessed why you are here?'

Millie shook her head. 'Not really.'

It was time. He drew a deep breath and his voice was both silken and yet commanding. 'You know that something was forged between us that day in the stable? Something I had not expected?'

'Nor wanted?' she guessed painfully.

The dark eyes became hooded. She must learn that introspection was an indulgence which brought with it only pain and no solution.

'What I want is an irrelevance—it is what I need which is at stake, and that was never in any doubt,' he said firmly. 'I have found what it is I am looking for.'

She felt as though she was poised on the edge of a precipice, staring down into a swirl of dark clouds, so that nothing before her was clear. But Millie's instincts were sound—and the most astonishing one was welling up inside her, even if she didn't quite dare to believe in it. She hesitated before she dared to voice it. 'Which is?'

'You,' he said quietly. 'I am going to marry you.'

She felt curiously flat. 'Aren't you suppose to ask me first?'

He gave a hard, almost brittle smile. Shouldn't he at least allow her the small fantasy of believing that she had some choice in the matter? That she had it in her to resist him when he had his heart set on something! 'Will you, Millie? Marry me?'

She didn't say anything.

'Your hesitation is good,' he observed softly. 'For it indicates that you understand the significance of what it is I am asking you.'

Millie put her fingers to her cheeks. She could feel

them flaming. 'But *m-marriage*?' she questioned shakily, her heart racing. 'Isn't a proposal supposed to follow—?'

'What?' His eyes were jet shards as he cut in, anticipating her next words. 'You imagine that I am able to offer you what other men would? A kiss goodnight on the doorstep? Trips to the theatre, perhaps? Or supper parties to meet mutual friends?' He took one hand from her face—her left hand—and turned it over in his, studying it thoughtfully. 'It can never be that way for me, Millie. When someone in my position chooses a bride, none of the normal rules of courtship apply.'

'You mean…you mean you're above the normal rules?'

'Yes,' he said simply, and it was not a boast— merely a statement of fact. 'If I meet you openly it will create a great media storm—not only here, but also in Europe—and it will compromise you. Public expectation will grow so intense that your every move will be monitored and recorded and the strain could become unbearable—I have seen it happen before. And for what purpose, Millie? When I know that you embody everything that I seek in a bride.'

'But why?' she questioned, still bewildered. 'Why me?'

'The truth?' She nodded, dimly aware that she might not like it. 'My requirements are simple. My bride must be pure, and she must be of aristocratic stock.'

Like one of the horses they had just seen, thought Millie, with a faint feeling of hysteria.

'You haven't taken lovers, and that is exactly how it should be.' His voice dropped to a sultry caress. 'And your first lover will surpass anything that any other man could ever offer you, that I can promise you.' Her blush pleased him, and excited him, too.

'But why not a Mardivinian woman?'

He shook his head. 'That would be too complicated, and I know all the possible candidates too well. There would be no sense of freshness among the women who would be suitable—and besides, my two sisters-in-law are English. They will provide you with the company you need to prevent you from becoming homesick. And your upbringing will have equipped you perfectly for the task which lies ahead.'

'Task?' she echoed.

He nodded. 'English women are brought up to be independent and resilient and resourceful—and your aristocratic background will enable you to mix with anyone, to understand how a future king will be brought up. For, as my Queen, you will bear my sons.'

Queen. The word hung in the air as if it had dropped into the conversation out of a fairytale. But this was definitely no fairytale—for if it had been then surely he would have mentioned the word that every bride-to-be the world over wanted to hear. Love. Millie stared into the proud, handsome face. She did not want words of love if he didn't mean them—and how could he possibly mean them when they barely knew one another, not really?

'Yet still you hesitate,' he observed softly, and he played his final winning card as he drifted her fingertips towards his lips and brushed them against the sensual lines with slow deliberation. He felt her shiver beneath his touch. 'Shall I tell you what is most important of all?' he questioned silkily.

'Y-yes,' she said breathlessly. 'Tell me.'

'This connection between us. It is strong. Powerful. It cannot be ignored. You feel it, too—you cannot deny it, can you, Millie?' His eyes were lit with triumph, but with something else, too. 'And so do I,' he finished on an afternote of bemusement.

'Yes,' she agreed boldly. 'I feel it, too.'

The blood drumming through her veins was threatening to deafen her and she nodded mutely, shivering with increased excitement as he lowered his head to tease her with the lightest and most provocative of kisses.

'See the way you make me feel…here.' And Millie nearly died when he guided her hand to his loins. She felt his hot, hard heat pressing against her, and some answering flame leapt up into life inside her, making her melt and making her ache. The sensation obliterated all others—including the one painful and fleeting thought that perhaps for Gianferro that was all there was. Chemistry. Sexual chemistry. And suitability.

'Yes,' he whispered exultantly as he saw her eyes

darken and her lips part, heard the breathless little whimper she made. 'Without this there can be nothing between a man and a woman. For all your innocence I desire you very much—perhaps more than I have ever desired a woman before, because never before have I had to wait. It shall be my body that you know, and mine alone. I shall tutor you in the ways of love and teach you how to please me as much as I will please you. You will be Queen of Mardivino and you shall have everything your heart desires. The finest racehorses will be yours for the asking. Jewels. Baubles. All the things that women crave are within your reach, Millie.'

She wanted to tell him that those things were not important, not in the grand scheme of things. That somehow he had ensnared her with a dark and silken certainty, capturing her heart to ensure that she would never be free of him—nor ever want to be free of him. 'Gianferro—'

'And I shall tell you something else,' he forged on relentlessly. 'If you do not accept me, then you will spend the rest of your life regretting it—for you will never meet another man of my equal. All men will be shadows in comparison, mocking you and taunting you with the thought of what might have been.'

If Millie had been older she might have damned him for his arrogance—but even with her almost laughable innocence she recognised the truth behind his words. Maybe she should have asked for more time, but time seemed as rare a commodity to him as privacy. She could do nothing but stare into the dark promise of his eyes, and as she did she felt her knees threaten to give way. She clutched onto him as if he was her anchor in a stormy sea. 'Gianferro!' she gasped. 'Please! Please! Won't you just kiss me?'

He hid his smile of satisfaction, for it was then that he knew she was his.

CHAPTER FOUR

UNSEEN, Millie put the tiny contraceptive Pill into her mouth and swallowed it—then walked into the bedroom, her face as white as the wedding gown which was hanging there. She shook her head from side to side. 'I don't know if I can go through with it, Lulu,' she said huskily.

'Stuff and nonsense!' said Lulu, giving the kind of brisk, no-nonsense smile which only big sisters could get away with. Especially big sisters who had only recently forgiven you for stealing their boyfriends. Her smile increased. 'As someone else once in pretty much my position quipped—your name's on the tea-towels now, it's much too late to back out.'

And Lulu was right—it was. Her name and Gianferro's. Not just on teatowels either, but on tea-sets too—and splashed all over breakfast trays, and some specially minted coins—all carrying the same formal and rather rigid pose of her and Gianferro, which had been taken on the day that their engagement was announced to the world.

Bizarrely, she found herself wondering if Gianferro had ever even *used* a teatowel. She doubted it. Or cooked a meal for himself. Equally doubtful. Her own upbringing had been privileged, yes—but at least she and her sister had been Brownies with the local pack. She knew how to clean and how to cook, and how to produce a plate of squashy-looking cupcakes which people would buy for charity.

But not Gianferro.

With every day that passed she became more and more aware of the rarefied and very isolated world he inhabited. Getting to see him was fraught with difficulty—like trying to make an emergency appointment at the dentist. He was surrounded by aides, and one in particular—Duca Alesso Bastistella, a devastingly handsome Italian nobleman whom Lulu had confessed she could 'fall in love with at the drop of a hat'.

Well, Millie couldn't. Alesso was like a gatekeeper—oh, he was always smoothly charming and diplomatic, but he seemed to have almost permanent access to Gianferro, whilst denying it to everyone else.

'We were at school together and he is my right-hand man,' said Gianferro one day, when she questioned him on it. 'I trust him,' he added simply.

He made trust sound like a precious and rare commodity, and Millie wondered if it would ever be possible to befriend the powerful Alesso. Well, if she wanted to get close to her husband, she was going to have to try.

She tried not to get too down about it, but she could have counted on one hand the number of times she had been alone together with Gianferro, when he had teased her with kisses which had made her melt inside, imprinting his lips upon hers with sensual promises of the pleasures to come. Of course she understood that his father was gravely ill, and that there had to be amendments made to the Constitution because of the forthcoming wedding, but even so...

'And anyway,' said Lulu softly, 'you're off to the Cathedral in little under an hour, to make your wedding vows—so you couldn't back out of it even if you wanted to!'

'I know I am,' said Millie faintly, and went to sit down. But Lulu held up her hand like a traffic policeman.

'Be careful, or you'll crumple your lingerie!'

'There doesn't seem enough of it to crumple.'

'That's the whole point!' Lulu gave a foxy smile. 'Anyway, I want to do your make-up now, so come over here and sit beside the mirror. Carefully.'

At least she had made it up with her sister. Thank heavens. But then Lulu—for all her fiery temper—had never been one to bear a grudge. Once she had accepted that the wedding was going to happen whether she liked it or not, she had accepted it with good grace. Especially when she realised that she had the chance to be a bridesmaid.

'The *only* bridesmaid, I hope?'

'Well, there will be Gianferro's tiny niece, but you'll be the only adult one, yes.'

Since then, Lulu had been over the moon.

'Just think of all the people I'm going to meet!' she had sighed.

'But what about Ned?' Millie had queried.

'Ned who?' Lulu had laughed.

For the past month, since the engagement, Millie had been living in a 'small' house within the Palace grounds, with Lulu and her mother on hand to chaperone her. Not that their services had been needed for *that*, she thought somewhat resentfully as she stared at her bare face in the mirror. Gianferro was taking restraint to the extreme—for they had barely spent a moment on their own.

But all that would change after the wedding, she thought, as Lulu began to slap some sticky moisturiser onto her cheeks. That was what honeymoons were for—proper old-fashioned honeymoons—when a couple got to know each other in all the ways that mattered.

Would she be a good wife to him? Would instinct and the books she had been poring over help guide her in the bedroom department? A nervous shiver ran down her spine, and Lulu's hand halted in its process of dipping a damp sponge into some foundation.

'*Now* what's the matter?'

Millie bit her lip. 'Nothing.'

'Not worried about the sex bit, are you?' questioned Lulu perceptively.

Millie shook her head. She couldn't voice her fears—she just couldn't—not to anyone, and especially not to Lulu. If she started talking about it, then she would end up feeling—not for the first time—as if her purity was the *only* reason Gianferro was marrying her. And besides, there were some things which should remain private.

'Not a bit,' she said staunchly.

Lulu smiled. 'Pity you did all that horse-riding,' she commented.

'What's that supposed to mean?'

'Well, isn't there some kind of ancient ritual which demands you hang the bloodied sheet from the Palace windows?'

'Oh, *do* shut up, Lulu!' Millie closed her eyes. 'Have you seen the papers?'

'I thought you weren't going to read them any more.'

'I know I wasn't—but there's a certain irresistibility about it—like being told not to touch a hot plate in a restaurant—you immediately want to.'

There was nothing in the latest batch of publications which hadn't been there from day one. She had been dubbed the 'unaffected' aristocrat, which she gathered was newspaper-speak for someone who didn't know her way round a make-up bag. Or a wardrobe.

Thank heavens she had Lulu on-side—for it had been Lulu who had taken her on a grand tour of Paris's top couturiers in a search for the Perfect Wedding Dress. The procession of garments which had been paraded in front of them had made her know what she *didn't* want.

In the end Millie had bought the dress in England—all soft layers of tulle that floated like a ballerina's petticoats, much to Lulu's disgust.

'It looks like a meringue!' she had exclaimed. 'You looked far sexier in that silk-satin sheath.'

But brides weren't supposed to look sexy—they were supposed to look virginal and, in her case, regal. Millie knew that there were high expectations about the gown, and that it was her duty to meet them. Little girls would pore over pictures of it. They wanted a fairytale princess, and she would make sure they got one.

'Surely that's enough mascara?' she ventured anxiously.

'Can't have enough,' said Lulu, with one final sweep of the wand. 'Your eyes will come out much better in the photos if you slap it on—you'll look gorgeous.'

'Especially to the world's panda population,' said Millie weakly, as she slid on the hand-made pearl-encrusted shoes and then, at last, slithered into the dress itself.

'Oh, wow!' said Lulu softly, as she adjusted the soft tulle veil. 'Wow!'

Millie just stood and stared at herself in disbelief.

Was that really her?

The high collar made the most of her long neck, and the beaded sash emphasised her tiny waist. Tight white sleeves ran down into a point on her hands, and the skirt shimmered to the floor in a soft haze of filmy white.

It was just her face which took some getting used to. With the unaccustomed make-up transforming her eyes into Bambi-like dimensions, and the pale blonde hair coiled into an elaborate chignon to accommodate the heavy diamond tiara she would don after the vows, she didn't look like Millie at all. She looked… she looked…

'Like a *princess*,' breathed Lulu.

Please let me be a good one, prayed Millie silently as a servant gave a light rap at the door. She picked up her bouquet, taking a deep breath to calm herself. The Princess bit was only part of the deal—far more important was that after today she would legally be Gianferro's wife, and they would be together, and they would learn to grow and share within their marriage. An image of his dark-eyed face swam before her and her nervousness became brushed with the golden glimmer of excitement. Oh, but she wanted to be alone with him!

Not for the first time Millie found herself wishing that Gianferro was just a normal man, and that they were making their vows in the tiny village church near her home, where her own parents had married. That they were going back to Caius Hall afterwards for the wedding breakfast, instead of the Rainbow Palace—so vast that she felt like Alice in Wonderland every time she set foot inside it.

Yet her two English sisters-in-law seemed to have

adapted well to life as princesses—and they had both been commoners, without a drop of aristocratic blood in their veins. But they had been older, she reminded herself. And experienced. And the Princes they had married had not been future Kings…

Millie could feel the palms of her hands growing clammy as the ride to Solajoya's Cathedral passed as if in a dream. There seemed to be thousands of people out on the streets, and the flashbulbs of the photographers were so blinding and ever-present that the day seemed bathed in a bright, artificial light.

Her wedding gown and flowers had been left to her, but Gianferro had masterminded the rest of the wedding plans, and Millie had been happy for him to do so. She understood that there were certain rituals to be followed, and she understood the weighty significance of the ceremony itself. The world and Mardivino were watching, and the Cathedral was packed with Royals and dignitaries and Presidents and Prime Ministers.

She knew that there was a small knot of her own relatives and family friends close to the altar, but she could not make out a single familiar face—they all swam into one curious and seeking blur. Never in her life had she known such a sense of lonely isolation as she began to walk towards him.

Because her father was dead, there was no one to give her away. A long-lost uncle had been half-heartedly suggested, but rejected by Gianferro.

'No,' he had said decisively. 'You will come to me alone.'

The aisle seemed to go on for miles, as music from massed choirs spilled out in some poignantly beautiful melody. Millie clutched her bouquet just below waist level, as she had been told to, and there, by the flower-decked altar, stood the tall, dark figure of Gianferro.

She could not see his face—all she was aware of as she grew closer was that he was in some kind of uniform, and that he looked formidably gorgeous. But a stranger to her, with his medals, and his hat with a plumed feather tucked beneath his arm.

Now she could see him, his proud and unsmiling face. She searched the dark glitter of his eyes for some sign that his bride-to-be pleased him, and a frisson of fear ran through her. For a moment her sure and steady pace faltered.

Was that…surely that was not *displeasure* she read in his eyes?

For a moment Gianferro could scarcely believe what he was seeing—but it was not the customary pride and elation of a man looking at the woman he was about to marry, transformed into an angel with her wedding finery.

Ah, *si*, she was transformed. But…

Where were the unadorned pure features which had so captivated him? Her eyes looked so sooty that their deep blue beauty was lost, and the lips he had kissed so uninhibitedly were now slicked with a dark pink shade of lipstick. She looked like a...a...

His eyes narrowed. He was going to have to speak to her about that. She must learn about his likes and dislikes, and he detested heavy make-up. Yet his face gave nothing away as she reached his side—only the tiny pulse hammering at the side of his temple gave any indication of his disquiet—and he could do nothing to control that.

The hand she gave him was cold, but then Mardivino's Cardinal began to intone the solemn words, and all was forgotten other than the import of what he was saying.

As they emerged from the darkness into the brightness of the perfect summer's day, he turned his head to look down at her. She must have sensed it, for her moist eyes turned up to him, like a swimmer who had spent too long under water.

'Happy?' he questioned, aware that cameras were upon them, that video tapes would be slowed down and analysed, his words lip-read. A world desperate to know what he was really thinking, to hear what he was really saying. Gianferro had never known real privacy, and it was a hard lesson that Millie was going to have to take on board.

She felt the squeeze of his hand, which felt like a warning, and managed a tremulous smile. 'Very,' she replied. But she felt light-headed—the way you did when you'd had medication just before an operation, as if she had temporarily flown out of her own body and was hovering above it, looking down.

She saw her painted doll mask of a face, and the little-girl trepidation in the heavily mascaraed eyes. And then Gianferro was guiding her towards the open carriage—her tulle veil billowing like a plume of white smoke behind her, diamonds glittering hard and bright in the tiara which crowned the elaborate confection of hair.

The Rainbow Palace looked like a flower festival, and every step of the way there was someone to meet or to greet. Another person offering their bowing congratulations. Millie could see ambition written on the faces of the men who spoke to Gianferro, and narrow-eyed assessment from the women. Who was this bride their Crown Prince had brought to Mardivino? their expressions seemed to say.

Good point, thought Millie—just who am I?

She was beginning to despair of ever getting a moment alone with him—this outrageously handsome man who was now her husband—but at last they were seated side-by-side in the Banqueting Hall, dazzled by the array of gold and crystal.

He turned to her. 'So, Millie,' he said softly. 'The first hurdle has been crossed.'

She laughed. 'I can think in terms other than horse-riding, you know!' she hesitated. 'You...you haven't said whether you like my dress,' she said shyly.

'The dress is everything it should be.'

And? *And? Say I look beautiful, even if you don't*

mean it… For wasn't every bride supposed to look beautiful on her wedding day—just from radiance and excitement alone?

He dipped his head towards hers; she could feel his breath drifting across her skin. 'Why did you cover your face with so much make-up?'

Millie blinked, remembering Lulu's words. 'For the cameras, of course!'

He had chosen an innocent country girl—not some Hollywood starlet, concerned about her image above all else! His mouth flattened.

'You don't like it?' ventured Millie painfully.

He shook his head, trying to dispel the tight band which was clamped around his head. The strain of the last few weeks had been intense, but after the wedding breakfast they would be alone at last, and then, in slow, pleasurable time, he could show her exactly what *did* please him.

'Your skin is too fine too clog it up like that, *cara mia*,' he observed softly. He saw her lips begin to tremble at the admonishment and he laid his hand firmly over hers, olive skin briefly obscuring the new, shiny gold of her wedding band. His voice was little more than a whispered caress. 'Later you will scrub it off—do you understand? You will come to me bare and unadorned, stripped of all finery and artifice.' He felt the deep throb of desire, which he had put on hold for so long that it seemed like an eternity. Carefully he took his hand away, for touch could tempt even the most steely resolution. 'And that, *cara* Millie—*that* is how I wish to see you.'

With a tremulous smile she nodded, then accepted a goblet of champagne from one of the footmen with a gratitude which was uncharacteristic. Never had she needed the softening effect of alcohol quite so much, and she drank deeply from the cup. Her very first test as the future Queen and she had failed him!

She longed to rush out to the bathroom and wash it all off, there and then—but she would not dare to take such a liberty; new princesses did not nip off to powder their noses. In fact, from now on, her behaviour would have to be choreographed right down to the last second. The simple things which other people took for granted would be out of her reach. Even her mother had remarked drily, 'You'd better cultivate a strong bladder, Millie.'

'Smile for me now, Millie,' he instructed silkily, wishing to see those dark shadows pass from her eyes. 'And think instead what it will be like on our honeymoon.'

This was a thought which had made her alternate between giddy excitement and stomach-churning nerves in the run-up to the wedding, but now the champagne had dissolved away her misgivings, and she felt her heart well up with the need to show him how good a wife she would be to him.

She began to pleat her napkin, until she remembered that all eyes were upon them and stopped. 'You haven't told me yet where we're going,' she observed quietly.

His eyes glittered with ebony fire. 'Traditionally, is not the honeymoon supposed to be a surprise—a gift from the groom to his bride?'

She wanted to say that, yes, of course it was—but suddenly it seemed to represent a whole lot more than that. Because of tradition Gianferro had taken charge of the wedding, and she understood that, but couldn't he have bent tradition in a way that would not have mattered to anyone other than the two of them? To have told her their destination—or, better still, to have allowed her to help choose. She felt disconnected. Out of control. As if her life had become a huge stage and she had been given the tiniest walk-on role.

But she didn't want to start their marriage on the wrong foot. If she wanted to change the unimportant things in the status quo then it had to be a gentle drip-drip—not like a child, instantly demanding a new toy. Gianferro was not used to living with a woman, just as she was not used to living with a man, and compromises must be made—she knew that, her mother had told her so. And he would not be familiar with compromise. Instinctively she recognised that negotiation was not part of his make-up, neither as a man or a prince. It would be up to her to lead the way. To show by example.

She wanted to say all the right things—as if her careful words could wash away that look of displeasure she had seen on his face in the Cathedral. To start together from now—a shiny new surface on which their future could be drawn. 'Yes, of course it is!' she said brightly. 'I love surprises!'

Gianferro smiled, pleased with her reaction, suddenly wishing that he could take her into his arms and kiss her. Properly. But there would be time enough for that later. 'Then I must hope that mine lives up to your expectation,' he murmured.

His words licked at her, with dark and erotic promise, and suddenly Millie was assailed with nerves. Please let me be worthy of him, she prayed. Let me be a good lover to him.

Gianferro's eyes narrowed. 'Why do you frown, *cara* Millie?'

She pulled herself together. Now was not the time to bring up her sexual inexperience! 'I wish my father could have been here,' she said truthfully. 'And yours.'

He nodded and gave her a soft smile, pushing away his untouched wine and reaching for a glass of water instead. His father had been frail for so long now that he could scarcely remember the vigorous man who had governed Mardivino with such energy—hiding well his heartbreak when his beloved wife had died. And lately he had grown more gravely ill. A dark shadow passed over his heart, but ruthlessly he banished it.

'Ah, but they were both here in spirit,' he answered quietly, remembering the look of relief which had spread over his father's careworn features when he had taken Millie to meet him. 'And my father is over-joyed that I have chosen a bride at last. This marriage has pleased him enormously.'

'And…it pleases you, too, Gianferro?' she questioned, emboldened by the wine.

He smiled. She was to step into the role demanded of her, and it seemed that his instincts were correct. She was the perfect choice. 'My destiny has been fulfilled,' he murmured.

It wasn't quite the answer she had been seeking, but Millie supposed that it would have to do. Quelling the butterflies in her stomach, she sat back as Gianferro's brother stood up to make a toast to the new Princess.

CHAPTER FIVE

'So, do you approve, Millie?'

Millie smiled, wishing she could rid herself of these stupid nerves. Calm down, she told herself—you're not the only virgin bride on the planet!

'It's…it's beautiful,' she said softly.

The white stuccoed house stood in its own beautifully landscaped gardens, which eventually ran down to the most beautiful beach she had ever seen—its powdery white sand was studded with pretty, pale shells which contrasted against a sea of blinding blueness.

As a honeymoon destination it was perfect.

Except…

Well, for a start they had been greeted at the door by a butler, a housekeeper, two maids and a chef.

'A skeleton staff,' Gianferro had remarked carelessly.

Millie had grown up having staff around, yet— naïvely, perhaps—she had thought that their honeymoon might be the exception. But apparently not.

Inside the house a small table had been laid up for tea in the sitting room, and she sipped at the scented brew gratefully, but had little appetite for the tiny sandwiches and feather-light cakes which accompanied it.

'You do not like to eat?' Gianferro frowned. He had wanted to do something to remind her of England, to make her feel at home.

Millie saw the look in his dark eyes and bit into a cucumber sandwich as if her life depended on it. 'I guess I'm just a little tired,' she explained carefully. 'All the excitement of the day.' And all the days leading up to it. And the restless nights...

Gianferro's eyes narrowed. 'Then let us go to our bedroom,' he instructed silkily.

So the moment had come at last.

Millie felt like a novice swimmer who had been put on the highest diving board as they made their way to a beautiful room containing a vast bed, and there was a valet, removing the last of their empty cases.

She smiled politely at the servant. When would they *ever* be left on their own?

There had been one brief moment when they had left the wedding breakfast to go and change, when it had been just the two of them, and Millie had stood shyly in Gianferro's suite of Palace rooms—hers, too now, of course—and looked at him.

He had read the plea in her eyes correctly, taken her veil off with care and then bent his head to kiss her, and the kiss had been like setting fire to a heap of dry twigs. She had eagerly wrapped her arms around his neck, opening her mouth beneath his seeking lips, and given a little yelp of pleasure until he had smiled and shaken his head slightly.

'*Cara,*' he had demurred, gently but firmly unwrapping the arms which clung to him. 'Not now. Not yet. And not here.'

'But…' Her blue eyes were wide with bewilderment. 'We're alone. We're married.' *And I want you.* 'Why not?'

He gave a little sigh, as much composed of regret as frustration at her lack of understanding. He glanced at his watch. 'Because our departure has been arranged right down to the last second. The car is timed to leave in half an hour—and after that all the journalists can go away and file their copy. The guests cannot leave until we do—and I cannot leave Premiers and Presidents cooling their heels while I make love to my new wife!'

Millie flushed. 'Of course not. How stupid of me!'

'Do not worry. You will learn.' With the tips of his fingers he tilted her face upwards. 'There will be time enough for the pleasures of the bedroom, Millie. And I do not intend our first time to be a quick…' His eyes glittered. 'How do they say? A "wham-bam", followed by a hurried dressing which would arouse the knowing smirks of Palace staff.'

Mille's colour deepened even further. She didn't want a quick 'wham-bam' either—whatever *that* was! She had hoped for passion and for spontaneity—but now she saw that those hopes were incompatible with her new status.

A great wave of panic began to swell up inside her, but with an effort she wished it away again. Stop fretting, she told herself. It will be all right.

But she was trembling as she turned her back on him, feeling so strange standing there in her pure white wedding gown. 'Would you mind...unzipping my dress?'

He opened his mouth to call for the new dresser he had appointed for her, but thought better of it, instead sliding the zip slowly all the way down to the small of her back. How tiny her waist! And just above where the zip ended was a peep of the transparent lace of her panties. He swallowed as temptation washed over him, and began to unbutton his uniform.

'There,' he said thickly. 'You can manage now.'

She buried herself in activity—scuttling into the bathroom in her bra and panties, feeling overwhelmingly shy as his dark and impenetrable gaze followed her. She took care to wipe most of the offending make-up from her face and, once she had removed the tiara, tugged all the constricting pins from her hair and brushed it free. Then she slipped on the dress and hat which had been chosen as her going-away outfit.

'How's that?' she asked as she reappeared.

He gave a slow and lazy smile. A pink voile dress, cream shoes and a large cream picture hat, trimmed with blowsy pink silk roses which looked almost real. Her blonde hair was a pale waterfall which gleamed over her shoulders and emphasised the youthful bloom of her skin. She looked like a picture from an old-fashioned book. *'Perfetto,'* he applauded softly. 'My beautiful and innocent English rose!'

And Millie smiled back with relief.

Gianferro's brothers had tied metallic balloons to the open-top car, and Princess Lucy had scrawled 'Just Married!' in deep vermilion lipstick on the bonnet of the expensive car!

But there were outriders, too, and shadowy figures in a car which sat on their tail as they moved away.

Millie had thought that they would all disappear once they had driven through the cheering crowds and out of the capital, but they were still there as the powerful vehicle began to ascend the mountain road.

She glanced behind her. 'They're not coming with us, are they?' she said, only half-joking, but she had her answer in the slight pause before he answered.

'Naturally.'

She opened her eyes very wide. 'They are?'

'They are my bodyguards, Millie,' he said quietly. 'Where I go, they go, too.'

All the conflicting emotions of the day made her feel light-headed enough to blurt out the first thing which came into her head.

'I presume they won't be joining us in the bedroom?'

Gianferro's mouth hardened. Well, what did she expect? Really? 'Of course not,' he answered coldly.

It was a variation of the look he had given her in the Cathedral—displeasure. Another person might have hidden it.

But another person would not have been Crown Prince! Who had spent all his life having his wishes acceded to, his moods catered for. Why should he bother hiding something? More importantly, how was she intending to handle it, as his wife? She with no experience of any man at all?

Maybe that was better. Her slate was clean and ready to be written on. There was no murky history to look back over, to compare with what was happening to her now, with him. They were starting over, and if she wanted an intimacy with him which she suspected had been completely lacking in his life, then she must let him show her how. It could not be done in a minute, or even a day—but slowly, bit by bit.

She would not be offended if he was cool with her! Instead she would ignore it, find a way to work round it. And if she encountered a rock in the path which led to their happiness, then she would simply step over it!

She smiled with delight now, as she looked round at their luxurious honeymoon bedroom, where roses and lilies were crammed into priceless vases, scenting the air with their incomparable perfume.

'That is better,' he murmured with approval as he saw her face. The door closed softly behind the valet and his gaze briefly flickered over to it, his lips curving into an answering smile. 'And what would you like to do now?' he questioned softly.

Millie blushed, not daring to tell him how much

she wanted him to take her in his arms again. For all she knew another servant would come bouncing into the room, or there might be something else they were supposed to be doing. 'I have no idea,' she said shyly.

He took her by the shoulders, his eyes now burning black fire and glittering with a certain kind of mischeviousness, too. 'You don't?' he teased. 'Millie, I'm disappointed in you!'

'Gianferro—'

'Shh!' He lowered his lips to tease them against hers in a light, brushing kiss and felt her breath escape in a low rush of pleasure. 'Ah! Yes! Yes, I know. It has been so long.'

Millie sank against him, her eyes fluttering to a close as she felt sensation begin to close her off from the world. 'Too long,' she sighed.

'Shall I close the shutters?'

Her eyes snapped open. 'But…but won't the bodyguards see? Won't they know what we're doing?'

He touched her long hair with an affectionate gesture. 'You think that we will only be permitted to make love once night has fallen and the guards have retired for the night?'

'I don't *know*.'

He continued to stroke the silken strands. 'My position dictates that I must be protected from threat— which means that my bodyguards must never be far away,' he explained slowly. 'But their position also dictates that they know their place, and now that place is to turn a blind eye to what happens. We shall not have the freedom of other honeymoon couples, Millie—I cannot, for example, make love to you on the edge of the shore, while the waves rock us with their own particular rhythm.' He smiled as he saw the startled look on her face. 'But we can create whatever fantasy we wish within this house. I think you will find that we do not need the stimulation of the outdoors or the lure of the forbidden—for us to travel to paradise.'

His words were a catalyst to the yearning which had been growing and growing inside her since the very first time he had kissed her and branded himself upon her heart and her body.

'Will you show me how?' she questioned shyly.

It was probably the most erotic thing that anyone had ever said to him—but he was aware that its allure lay in its innocent rarity.

He felt his blood thicken, quicken. 'Oh, yes,' he breathed, as he threaded his fingers luxuriantly in the golden silk. 'I shall show you everything. By the end of our honeymoon you will know as much as any courtesan, Millie.'

Sometimes his words frightened her—like now— for they hinted at his past and mocked her for her own innocence. And she realised that, while she might be the pupil, she had to assert some of her own authority. She would not wait—mute and malleable as a puppet—while he called all the shots. For surely he would bore with always being the one to crack the whip?

'Stop talking,' she said urgently. 'Kiss me. Properly.'

The contrast between her inexperience and her eagerness was like a starting pistol firing deep in his groin. All the pent-up desire he had buried for so long licked into life and he bent his head once more. Only this time it was not a light, grazing kiss, but deeper, drugging, soft and hard all at the same time, and filled with sensual purpose.

'Oh!' cried Millie, and this time he did not stop her when her arms reached up for him. She felt her lips begin to open and flower as mouth explored mouth with the excitement of a child being presented with a beautiful box and being told that, yes, she could open it.

He reached to cup her breast in his palm, could feel its small swell grow heavy, the nipple begin to point, and he circled his thumb round and round it, her soft moans of pleasure making him want to rip the dress from her body and bury his mouth there instead.

But he must take it slowly. Her initiation was important; it would affect how she viewed sex for the rest of her life. She had waited and he had waited, and their patience must be rewarded with a long and lavish feast.

He skated the flats of his hands down over her narrow hips, then changed direction, letting one lie with indolent possession over the barely perceptible curve of her stomach. He felt her move restlessly and he gave a low and predatory laugh as he moved, drifting his fingers between the fork of her legs and then drifting them away again.

'Oh!' she gasped automatically—the one word torn from her lips in a muffled protest.

'Oh, what?' he questioned lazily, still drifting his finger back and forth, back and forth.

But she couldn't speak, couldn't think—her heart was thumping so forcefully that all she could do was nod her head, terrified by the strength of the feelings which were scorching the nerve-endings of her body, and yet terrified that they might simply go away again.

'I think it is time that we took your dress off, don't you, Millie?'

With a practised, almost careless touch, he peeled the voile gown from her body and threw it aside, and then he stood back to look at her, appraising her scantily clad body as a connoisseur might appraise a painting.

Standing before him in just her underwear, Millie should have felt shy, but something in the increased darkening of his eyes filled her with a new and strange kind of power. For, yes, Gianferro was the expert, the seasoned lover, but she had something that he wanted as badly as she did.

Instinct, as well as skill, had made her a fearless and accomplished horsewoman, and instinct took over now to instruct her in the lessons of love. She raked her fingers up by her ears, lifting great handfuls of shiny gold hair, as if she were gathering sheaves of wheat, and the movement made her hips jut out slightly and emphasised the thrust of her breasts.

He sucked in a breath. 'Beautiful.' He slowly ran the tip of his finger down over his shirt. 'Come and unbutton this for me.'

It was the simplest task imaginable, but never had a task seemed so impossible. Gianferro smiled as she fumbled at the buttons.

'No need to ask whether you've done this before,' he teased.

'Don't make fun of me,' she begged.

'But I'm not. I never would.' His voice was serious because inexplicably he was moved. 'It's wonderful. Your innocence is all that a man could dream of.'

She pushed away the thought that it was what she represented, rather than the person she was, which made his black eyes gleam with such a soft, territorial pride, and concentrated instead on the newness and the excitement of the moment.

She'd never seen his chest before. It was olive-brown and silken satin in texture, crisp with dark hair, the faint line of rib barely visible. She touched a wondering finger to each nipple, then looked up at him to see his face a study of fierce concentration, as if he was holding himself back. His eyes opened again and he gave a little shake of his head, a smile which was almost rueful.

'Come,' he said huskily. 'For I cannot wait much longer.' And he scooped her up into his arms and carried her to the vast bed, which both taunted and tempted her as he laid her down on it and slid the shirt from his powerful shoulders.

He kicked off his shoes and, enraptured, Millie watched as he unbuckled his belt and slid the zip down. But she closed her eyes when the trousers came off, for she could see the proud, hard ridge through the silk of his boxer shorts.

'Open them, Millie,' he instructed quietly. 'Do not be afraid of what you see, for a man and a woman were made for each other. You know that.'

Yes, she did—and she had spent a lifetime of watching this most basic of acts in the stables, and in the farms surrounding her home in England. But animals were different from humans. Animals just got on and did it—you didn't get a mare standing there and hoping against hope that she would please her stallion!

'It will be fine,' he said sternly, but there was a mocking and teasing note to his next words. 'It *will* be fine—for I command it and you must obey all my commands!' She laughed then, and he pulled her against him. 'That is better. We will not rush. We have all the time in the world, *cara mia.*'

He had never known what it was to use restraint in the bedroom, for he had been spoiled by women all his life—women eager for his hard, beautiful body and for the cachet of having slept with a prince.

But Millie was different. His wife and his virgin. He must be gentle with her, but above all he must show her just how good it could be.

She had thought that it would be happening by
now. She had thought... But then he began to kiss
her again, and she just slipped into the beauty of that
kiss, all her doubts and questions dissolving away.

He touched her skin with fingertips which whispered over the surface, and where he touched he set
her on fire with need, like a painter, bringing to life
a blank canvas with the stroke of his brush. Yet he
touched her everywhere except where the books had
told her she could expect to be touched, and this had
the curious effect of both relaxing her and yet making
the tension grow and grow.

Tentatively she stroked him back, tiptoeing her way
over the landscape of his body, exploring and charting
all the lines and contours. But there was an area which
was out of bounds, for she didn't dare...

Against her lips she felt him smile, and he pulled
his head away. 'That's okay, Millie—I actually do not
want you to touch me there.'

The fact that he had guessed mortified her, but her
confusion increased. 'You don't?'

'If you play with me, I will not do you justice.'

'I'm not a meal, to be eaten!' she protested.

'Oh, but you are,' he demurred, tempted to show
her—but experience told him not to swamp her with
too much, too soon. The first time should be unadorned—the myriad of variation on that one simple
act should be revealed slowly, in time.

Soon she was aching, melting, longing—and when
she thought she might die with it he took her bra off

and peeled down her panties, touching the searing heat between her legs until she cried out.

Wild and hungry for him, her fears and doubts fell by the wayside and she boldly touched him back, feeling him start as she encountered the steely column.

He nodded, as if she had pressed some invisible button, and peeled off his boxer shorts. She felt the naked power of him butting against her, dimly aware that he was moving on top of her. She laid her hands on his buttocks and felt him shudder as he shifted position slightly and then…then…

'Millie!' he gasped, as he eased his way inside her. So tight! So perfect!

And Millie gasped, too. The newness of the sensation felt so strange and yet so right, as her body adjusted to accommodate him. Her skin felt flushed. All her senses felt as though they were newly sensitised. And her heart felt as though it wanted to burst from her chest as he sealed the union with a kiss which felt far more intimate than any previous kiss had done.

He began to move, slowly at first, dragging his mouth away to look down at her, his eyes narrowing—for he realised that just as this was new for her, in some ways it was the same for him. 'I am hurting you?'

She shook her head, and a laugh bubbled up from the back of her throat. It was so easy. 'No! Oh, no, not at all! It's…perfect…'

He shook his head. 'Not yet. Be patient, and you will see how perfect it can be.'

And then there were no more words or questions as their bodies melded and moulded and began to move in sweet harmony. Sometimes he teased her, and sometimes he thrust so deep that her heart felt as though it had been impaled by him, and all the time there was something tantalising, sweet and intangible, which was building and building inside. Over and over she felt that she was almost there, and her body reached for it greedily, but Gianferro did speak then, bending his mouth to whisper into her ear.

'Relax. Let go. Let it happen.'

When it did, she was unprepared for the power of it. And the beauty.

'G-Gianferro!' she gasped in astonishment as it took her up, lifted her in its nebulous arms like a whirlwind, and then rocked her, again and again, sucking all the air from her lungs until she fell at last, laughing and crying with the sheer wonder of it.

He stilled for a moment as he watched her—the genuine joy of her fulfilment touching him in a way he had not expected—and then he started to move again, and her eyes flew open. She read something in his eyes and she put her hands around his buttocks, pulling him in closer, deeper.

And when it happened for him she watched him too—drinking in his face greedily as she imprinted each reaction on her memory. She saw his eyes close, his head jerk back. A moment of rigidity, before he moaned, the sound of surrender being torn from the back of his throat. And when he opened them again, he seemed almost dazed, murmuring something softly in Italian.

Millie propped herself up on one elbow to look at him, her hair falling all over her shoulders as she studied his face. But the dazed look had disappeared, replaced by the harder, guarded and more familiar expression.

But Millie had seen it. For a moment or two he had been—yes, *vulnerable*—not something you would usually associate with him. She wondered if it was the same for all men—whether they opened up just a little and allowed you to see the softer side of them. And was it only after making love?

'What was that you said?' she questioned.

He shook his head. 'Nothing.'

Millie pulled a face. 'Oh, that's not fair, Gianferro! You can't use your fluency in other languages to exclude me.'

'Can't I?' he challenged softly, his words light and teasing, but she recognised that he meant them. 'Perhaps what I said was not suitable for a woman to hear.'

This was even worse. 'I may have been innocent,' she protested, 'but I'm not any more! I want to learn—and how better can I learn the secrets of the bedroom than from my husband?' Her mouth curved into a smile. 'I want to please you.'

'But you do.'

'And I want to enlarge my knowledge,' she added firmly.

He gave her a rueful look and pulled her into his arms. 'I was voicing my surprise and my pleasure because it is exactly as other men say it is.'

Millie frowned, not understanding at all.

'To make love without protection,' he elaborated. 'To ride bareback, as I believe the Americans call it.' He saw her colour heighten. 'You see!'

But Millie was shaking her head, trying to make sense of what he was saying. 'You mean…you mean you've never made love to a woman without…' She hesitated over the word—new to her, like so much else. '*Protection* before?'

He seemed astonished that she should have asked. 'But, no! Never!'

'Because…because of the risk of disease?' she ventured.

'Of course.' He nodded, picking up her fingers and kissing them, his breath warm and his smile full of satisfaction. 'And there are no such risks with you, *cara mia*. But it is far more than that…you see, my seed carries within it the bloodline of Mardivino, and it cannot be spilled carelessly!'

On the one hand it was a very old-fashioned and poetic way of putting it, and yet it was mechanical, too—as if she was nothing other than a very clean vessel. Millie bit her lip.

'I told you you would not like it,' he said softly as he observed her reaction.

But it wasn't that. It was the way his voice had

grown so stern when he had mentioned his bloodline. She realised that they still hadn't got around to discussing contraception. He must have just assumed that she would get herself sorted out before the wedding, as everyone had advised her to do.

She snuggled up against him. 'Don't you think that there are a few things we ought to talk about?'

'Before or after I make love to you again?' he questioned, his voice silky with erotic promise, and Millie shivered in anticipation as she felt the hardening and tensing of his body.

She closed her eyes as he began to touch her breasts. 'I guess…I guess it can wait,' she said shakily.

This time there was a sense of urgency, but there was a question burning inside her, too, as Millie wondered if it could possibly be as good again.

She was still a novice, but already she had learnt. Already she was comfortable with his body, and this time she was not afraid to touch him as freely as he did her. She saw his fleeting look of surprise, quickly followed by one of pleasure as their cries shuddered out in unison.

Oh, yes, she thought happily. Just as good. She stretched luxuriously. No. Better.

He turned to face her, a flush highlighting the aristocratic cheekbones and the hectic glitter of satisfaction in his black eyes giving no indication of the bombshell he was about to drop.

'So, *cara*,' he drawled softly, 'do you think we have made you pregnant?'

CHAPTER SIX

FOR a moment, Millie froze—her body as motionless as a stone—yet her mind raced with a speed which was frightening.

She played for time. 'Wh-what did you say?'

He smiled, but his voice was edged with a kind of territorial anticipation. 'I was thinking aloud, *cara*,' he murmured. 'Wondering whether even now my child begins to grow within your belly.'

She forced herself not to be swayed by the—again—poetic delivery of his words, but to concentrate instead on the implication which lay behind them.

She gave a strained smile. 'You...you wouldn't want me to be pregnant right now, would you?'

'But of course!' His eyes narrowed and he frowned. 'Marriage is for the procreation of children. That is its primary function, in fact.' He gave a glimmer of a smile which only partly defused the sudden sense of terror she felt. 'Particularly in my case, *cara* Millie.'

My case, she noted. Not our. But she must keep calm. She must. Obviously they weren't going to see eye to eye on every topic, not straight away. Marriage was also about compromise, she reminded herself. And negotiation.

'I was sort of…hoping that we might have some time together first…getting to know one another,' she ventured. 'Before children come along.'

He pulled her against him, loving the way that the silk of her hair clothed her chest like a mantle, beginning to stroke it almost absently. 'Perhaps we will,' he mused. 'But the decision is not ours to take.'

Millie opened her eyes very wide. 'It isn't?'

'Of course not! The conception of our child is outside our control! It lies in the domain of a power far greater than ourselves.'

This was the moment to tell him. The moment to announce the fact that her doctor had prescribed her six months worth of the contraceptive Pill to be going along with.

But something stopped her, and Millie wasn't quite sure what it was.

Fear that he seemed to have everything so mapped out? Or fear that she had taken a step which instinctively she knew he would disapprove of?

If she told him, she could imagine him—perhaps after again expressing his displeasure—tossing the Pills away in a macho kind of way before making love to her again. And then what would happen? Well, you wouldn't need to be a biologist to work that one out. She might fall pregnant. Immediately.

Millie tried to imagine what that would be like— and the thought of it filled her with horror. Everything else was so startlingly new—Mardivino, being married, getting used to being a princess. How on earth could she cope if she threw motherhood into the equation?

Perhaps she could slowly work round to it…make him see things from her point of view. That there was nothing wrong with waiting for a while…that was what most couples did.

Idly, she trickled her finger around one of the whorls of dark hair on his chest and saw him give a nod of satisfaction. 'It would be nice to have a little time on our own first,' she observed drowsily. 'Wouldn't it?'

She must learn lessons other than those of the bedroom, thought Gianferro. Did she think that they were to become one of those couples who shared *everything*, as was the modern trend? Who were together from dawn to dusk? He repressed a slight shudder. Even if his position had not ruled that out, it was an option he would have run a million miles from anyway. 'That is what honeymoons are for, *cara*,' he said lightly.

'But we're only on honeymoon for a fortnight!' Millie protested.

He wondered if she had any idea of just how privileged she was to have a whole two weeks of his uninterrupted company. Of the planning that had gone into absenting himself from his duties as Crown Prince. Perhaps she should learn *that*, too.

'My life is a very busy one, Millie.'

'And I want to share it with you!'

Again, he bit back the urge to tell her that what she wanted was a foolish desire which would never come true. Nor ever could. To soften the blow—this would be a lesson for *him*, too. He was used to dictating his terms, to doing exactly as he pleased and having people fall in and accede totally to his wishes. But he recognised that to make this marriage a comfortable one he must learn to use tact and diplomacy.

'But you *will* be sharing it,' he said firmly. 'As my wife and as the mother of my children.'

For a moment she was scared again. It was as if she had taken a leap back by half a century. If not yet barefoot then certainly pregnant as soon as possible—if Gianferro had his way.

'Just that?' she questioned quietly.

'Of course not,' he answered silkily. 'There will be so much more to your life than that, Millie.'

She couldn't quite stop the shaky breath of relief. 'There will?'

'Naturally. You will not be tied by children—because, just as in your own childhood, there will be plenty of staff to look after them.'

But Millie's heart did not leap for joy at the thought of handing the care of her children to other people. Quite the contrary when she remembered her own experience, and especially the brief period when she had gone to the local school before being sent off to boarding school. It was there that she had realised for the first time that her life was different from other people's.

How vividly she remembered the empty ache inside when her classmates had been met by their mothers at the school gates instead of an uncaring au pair or stony-faced nanny. And even more poignant had been the stories they used to relate—of mothers who bathed them and made cakes for them, and fathers who played with them, taught them how to swim and climb a tree. She had only ever seen her parents at bedtime, when she was all washed and in her pyjamas to say goodnight—and sometimes not even then. Did she really want that for her own children? And times had changed…even for Royal families. Wouldn't Gianferro long to have a closeness with his offspring which had never been there for him?

'It might be nice to be a little bit hands-on with them,' she suggested lightly.

Gianferro kissed the tip of her nose. 'That will not, I think, be either possible or desirable. Our children will be brought up the way of all Royal children. And besides, you will not have time.' His dark eyes crinkled. 'There will be many charitable institutions which will require your patronage. Do not worry, sweet Millie—there will be plenty to keep you busy.'

It was a horrible phrase. *Keep you busy*. It implied that she would be filling in time, instead of embracing it fully, and it was worrying, for it was not how she imagined her future to be.

'I see,' she said slowly.

Gianferro could hear her faint note of disapproval and he frowned. How demanding women could be! She might be young and unspoiled but, like all women, she required symbols of her position in his life. Not diamonds, in her case, but…

'And we must not forget your horse, of course,' he said softly, with the air of a man who had pulled a rabbit out of a hat.

Millie blinked. 'My horse?'

The corners of his mouth edged upwards into a small smile of satisfaction which accompanied the sudden anticipatory gleam of pleasure in his black eyes. 'I told you that you would have the finest mount money can buy, and so you shall, Millie. I had intended to keep it as a surprise, but since you are obviously dissatisfied—'

'But I'm not—'

He cut through her protest as if she hadn't spoken. 'Then I see no reason to keep you in suspense. During the second week of our honeymoon I intend to take you to my stables on the western side of the island—which are world-class, incidentally.'

'Yes, I've heard of them,' said Millie, in a small voice.

'And there you shall choose a horse to bring back to the Rainbow Palace with you.' He watched her carefully, for her reaction was not the one he had been expecting. He knew how much she loved horses—so why was she not flinging her arms about his neck and thanking him? Did she not realise the honour he was according her? Why, there were top breeders who would give up everything they possessed to own one of the horses he was offering her! 'You are not pleased with the idea, Millie?'

She heard the coolness in his voice and attempted to redress the balance. She couldn't expect him to understand her doubts and her fears, and to express them would sound like whining defeatism. If you took the Royal part out of their situation, it helped put things in perspective. Because when it boiled down to it they were just two adults starting out on married life together—and communication was vital if the journey was to be a rich and fulfilling one. 'No, I am pleased—I'm delighted, if you want the truth, Gianferro!'

She was going to have to tell him about the Pill. He wasn't a Neanderthal—he was a sophisticated man of the world. And, yes, he might have a perfectly understandable desire to give Mardivino an heir—but surely he was also reasonable enough to be prepared to wait…even for a few months?

'Gianferro—'

'I know.' He anticipated her next words. 'You are worried about riding while with child, and I share your fears. I think that as soon as you become pregnant the riding will have to be curtailed until after the birth—no matter what the current thinking is! But abstinence only increases the hunger—and when you finally get back in the saddle it will be with an even greater excitement, that I can guarantee.'

He smiled, recalling his own self-imposed abstinence. The sacrifices he had made! He had not taken
a lover for over a year—it had seemed morally wrong
when he was actively seeking a bride. And of course
once he had found one he had felt morally bound to
continue, enduring the test on his sensual appetite as
he waited until after the wedding. He stroked Millie's
breast and felt her shiver. The wait had been well
worth it!

Millie lay there, listening to his words with a
mounting feeling of disbelief and panic. He had it all
worked out. No compromise, no negotiation at all.
And it pained her to admit it, but she knew that it
was true…there was no *room* for negotiation in
Gianferro's mind. He knew what he wanted and he
intended to have it. And he expected her to be grateful
for a couple of months of riding before she faded even
more into the background of his life once he had
made her pregnant!

But she was in the situation now, and it was pointless to try to rail against him on a subject which was
clearly so important to him and on which he clearly
would not budge. He wanted an heir and she was
perfectly happy to give him one. Just not yet. What
harm could it do if she waited a while? Lots of couples had to wait before a baby came. Why, they would
get lots and lots of practice!

Millie felt her body respond as he continued to
stroke her, the clamour of her senses smoothing down
the sharp edges of panic in her mind. They would get

close this way, she told herself. Closer and closer, until all the barriers fell.

She closed her eyes, and Gianferro felt a brief moment of triumph as he bent his head to kiss her. Had he not chosen her as much for her malleability as for her true innocence? She would learn that he would make the decisions—indeed was compelled to. That he knew best—for how could it be any other way, given the disparity in their individual experiences of the world?

Millie gasped as his mouth moved from lips to breast, his tongue flicking out to tease the hardening bud, and she clasped his dark head against her as pure pleasure shafted through her body.

He raised his head with a wicked smile which made her forget that he was a prince. Made her forget everything.

'Do you like that, Millie?' he murmured softly.

'It's...' Millie swallowed, finding it overwhelming to cope with all these new feelings—both physical and emotional. Her response was forgotten as he moved his head down to her belly. And then beyond. 'Gianferro!' she gasped, as shock mingled with pure ecstasy.

He tasted her with pleasure, the squealing uninhibitedness of her response only adding to his own hunger, and as he felt her spasm and dissolve against his tongue he fleetingly thought how wonderful it was going to be. He would be the only man she would ever know—her skills would be honed for just him!

Afterwards, they lay silently for a while, and then Gianferro yawned. 'We'd better think about getting ready for dinner,' he murmured.

She snuggled against him. 'I'm not hungry.'

'Well, I am.'

'Oh!' She wriggled even closer to him, feeling as though she'd found paradise here in his arms and unwilling to relinquish it, even for a second. 'Can't we just have something in bed?'

Gently but firmly he disentangled her arms from where they lay, wrapped around his hips. 'Unfortunately, no, *cara*. The chef will have gone to some trouble to prepare something special for our first night here, and we are obliged to eat it.'

Obliged. The word jumped out at her, reminding her of what Royal life was all about. Millie sighed. 'Of course. How silly of me not to have thought of that.'

'Indeed.' He nodded with satisfaction. 'And the sooner we eat it, the sooner the staff can be dismissed.' His voice dipped into a provocative caress. 'And the sooner we can come back to bed!'

The anticipation of *that* made her misgivings seem inconsequential. For a moment she felt like the old Millie—even if the memory of her was becoming more hazy by the second. Or at least she felt a bit more comfortable in the skin of the *new* Millie... though she was even *more* of a stranger. But the other Millie had been a girl, and now she was most definitely initiated into the ranks of womanhood. 'But we've spent most of the afternoon in bed!' she teased.

He relaxed as he saw her eyes shine. 'I know,' he agreed softly, and for one rare and blessed moment he felt completely at ease. He bent his mouth to her ear. 'And I intend to spend many more afternoons in exactly the same place!'

As Millie dressed for dinner she deliberately squashed the thought that she was deceiving him. She was *not*. She was acting in their best interests, and for the future of their relationship. And hadn't her mother told her that it was wise to always keep something back? That mystery added to a woman's allure…

But dinner was another trial—and Millie was no stranger to lavish dinners. Opposite sat her brand-new husband—looking dark and unruffled and cool in an open-neck cream silk shirt which gave a glimpse of the tantalising arrowing of dark hair beneath. His skin was olive and gleaming and he looked completely sensual and irresistible. He had lain naked in her arms, he had been joined with her in the most intimate way that a man and woman could be—so why, looking at him now, did that seem almost impossible to imagine?

The staff who served the meal spoke very little, but when they did it was in French or Italian, and Millie had rather neglected languages at school. For a moment she thought of Lulu. Lulu was effortlessly fluent in French, and if it had been her sitting here—as originally intended—she would no doubt have had all the staff smiling sunnily at her.

'Merci beaucoup,' she said, when their coffee was brought, and saw her husband give a small smile as the butler left the room. 'Oh, Gianferro—my French is terrible!' she wailed.

'It will improve.'

'I shall take lessons.'

'Indeed.' He nodded. 'I will find you a tutor.'

Millie hesitated. 'I was hoping perhaps I could go to a class with other people?'

Imperious dark brows elevated. 'Other people?'

'You know…' Millie shrugged her shoulders awkwardly. 'Like a regular class, or something. You must have them in Solajoya.'

'Of course we do. Our education system is one of the finest in the world.' Thoughtfully he ran a long olive finger over a glass of pure crystal. 'Though in your case it may not be appropriate.'

Millie blinked. 'Oh?'

'I do not hold with the idea of Royalty being accessible,' he observed quietly.

She thought she heard a warning note in his voice. 'You mean you want me to be…remote?'

'That is not the word I would have chosen.' He dropped a lump of sugar into one of the tiny gold-lined cups and stirred. When he looked up again his dark eyes were serious. 'You will need to be one step removed from your people—a part of them and yet apart from them. As if you were standing in the next-door room. Knock down the wall which divides you, and you run the danger of the roof caving in.'

Millie nodded, her thoughts troubled once more. All these things lay ahead. Such big things. Babies who would be heirs and a crown which was destined to be hers. With this dark and intelligent man by her side, whom she yearned to know better. But would she—when he was a self-confessed champion of be-ing…not remote…but removed? She drank some cof-fee. She would persist. Whittling away at the barrier with which he surrounded himself. Some things could only be accomplished over time—and at least she had that on her side.

But the getting-to-know-him-properly bit had to start some time. She looked into his face—such a dark and forbidding face—except when he was making love, of course. She shook her head slightly, still filled with that slight sense of disbelief of what they had been doing together not so long ago.

A faint smile curved Gianferro's lips. 'Why do you blush so, Millie?' he questioned softly.

'I was just thinking…'

'Mmm?'

She heard the indulgent note in his voice—as if she was a child to be humoured. Would it sound unat-tractively naïve if she tried to tell him just how much of a woman he had made her feel in bed, but that now they were out of it all her glowing self-assurance seemed to have fled? Maybe it would be better to stick to basics. To start to get to know him in a way she had not previously been able to.

'What was it like,' she began, 'growing up on an island?'

He curved his finger around the warm coffee cup. 'In what respect?' he questioned carelessly.

Was she imagining the evasive note in his voice? Millie gave him a shy smile. Forget he's a prince, she told herself. Just ask him the kind of things you'd ask any man. But that was the trouble. She had no experience—not just of the bed bit, but all the other stuff which went to make up a relationship. In a way, the bed bit was easy—like learning to ride a horse. There were certain actions and movements you had to master—and after that it was up to you to modify and improve them.

But talking was harder. She had had none of the normal exposure to male/female interaction which most young women of her age had. No brothers, for a start, and then a single-sex school. There had been no nightclubs and precious few parties. Her life had been centred around the countryside and her horses—and that, of course, was one of the reasons he had made her his bride.

'Well, did you go to school?'

'My brothers and I were educated within the Palace.'

'That must have been quite…well, quite limiting, really.'

He raised his eyebrows. 'Not really. You went to

a boarding school, didn't you? That's a closed environment in itself.'

'But at least there were lots of other girls there.' Millie stared down at her cooling coffee and then looked up into his eyes once more. They were blacker than the inky coffee and they gave absolutely nothing away. Was that how he had been conditioned to look—as enigmatic as any Sphinx? Had he been trained to keep his feelings hidden—rigorously conditioned into not letting anyone have an inkling of his thoughts? Or was that just his own particular makeup? She smiled, sensing that she needed to soften her questioning. 'Didn't you sometimes long for the company of people other than your brothers?' she asked quietly.

How little she understood! Isolation had been part and parcel of his heritage—even *with* his brothers. Being born the Crown Prince had made his life different from Guido's and Nico's. Even as a boy he had been taken aside by his father—gradually introduced to the mighty task of what lay ahead of him.

'Oh, there was plenty of other company,' he said easily. 'We had friends who came to play with us when we were tiny, and then to learn to ride and swim with us.' But the friends had been cherry-picked—the offspring of Mardivino's aristocracy. The only times he had ever come into contact with the ordinary people of the island were when he had accompanied his father to hand out prizes, or to open a new school or library.

Millie hesitated. She wanted to know this man who was now her husband—to *really* know him. And she didn't just want the answers to her questions, she wanted him to learn to confide in her. She had gone to the trouble of reading a book about Mardivino during their engagement—but the facts were just words on a page, with no real root in reality. It had all happened years and years before she had been born. She wanted to ask Gianferro a very obvious question about his childhood. Almost to get it out of the way—in case it hovered, ever-present, like a great dark cloud in the background.

'It must have been…' She struggled for the right word, but no word could convey the proper sympathy she felt. 'Terrible. When your mother died.'

He hoped that the candlelight concealed the faint frown which creased his brow. Was she now going to probe? To dig at the wound caused by his mother's death? The scar was old now, but it was deep. He had buried his grief as a way of coping at the time, and he had never resurrected it.

'In that I was no different from any other child who loses their mother,' he said flatly. 'Being a prince does not protect you from pain.'

But being a prince meant that you could not show it. She suddenly understood that as clearly as if he had told her.

Millie reached her hand out to lay it on top of his. Her skin was very pale in comparison to the rich olive of his, and her wedding band was shiny bright as her fingers curved around his possessively.

But at that moment there was a knock on the door, and Gianferro couldn't help experiencing a brief moment of relief as he withdrew his hand, welcoming this interruption to her intrusive line of questioning. Then his brows creased together in a dark frown.

'Who is this, when I told them to leave us alone?' he said, almost in an undertone. His frown grew deeper. 'Come!' he ordered, his voice stern.

It was Alesso who stood there, and Millie's heart sank. Couldn't he even leave them in peace on their honeymoon? But on closer inspection she saw that the handsome Italian's face was tight with tension—an unbearable, weighty tension.

And there were no words of remonstrance from Gianferro, for he sprang immediately to his feet, his face growing pale beneath the olive skin.

'Qu'est-ce que c'est?' he demanded.

Something told her that this was uncharacteristic behaviour, and Millie stared at him in confusion.

But it was only when Alesso bit his lip and began to speak that the grim reality of what had happened began to dawn on her.

'The King is dead!'

Alesso's words were rocks that smote him like an iron fist, and Gianferro waited for a moment which seemed to go on for a lifetime. A moment for which he had spent a lifetime preparing.

'Long live the King!'

And then Alesso dropped deeply to his knees in front of Gianferro and kissed his hand, not raising his head again until Gianferro lightly touched him on the shoulder. It was in that one single instant that the new King realised how much had changed…a lifelong friend would not be—nor could ever be—the same towards him again.

In a heartbeat, everything was different.

CHAPTER SEVEN

MILLIE felt as if someone had just picked her up and thrown her into a wind tunnel which led to a place of mystery.

Alesso bowed before her, lifted her hand and pressed her fingers to his lips.

'My Queen,' he said brokenly, and Millie sat motionless, as if turned to stone, looking at Gianferro in desperation. How on earth did she respond? But she might as well have been the shadow cast by one of the candles for all the notice he took of her. It wasn't just that he didn't seem to see her—it was almost as though she wasn't there. She felt invisible.

But she pushed her feelings of bewilderment aside and tried to put herself in Gianferro's place. She must not expect guidance nor trouble him for it, certainly not right now. His father had just died, and he had inherited the Kingdom. The role for which he had been preparing all his life was finally his.

She looked into his face. It was hard and cold, and something about the new bleakness in his eyes almost frightened her. What on earth did she *do*?

She was no stranger to bereavement—her own father had died five years ago, and although they had not been close, Millie still remembered the sensation of having had something fundamental torn away from her. And Gianferro had lost his mother, too. To be an orphan was profoundly affecting, even if it happened when you were an adult yourself.

But Millie was now his wife, his help and his emotional support, and she must reach out to him.

She moved over to him and lifted her hand to touch the rigid mask of his face.

'Gianferro,' she whispered. 'I am so sorry. So very, very sorry.'

His eyes flickered towards her, her words startling him out of his sombre reverie. He hoped to God that she wasn't about to start crying. It was not her place to cry—she had barely known the King, and it was important for her to recognise that her role now was to lead. That the people would be looking to her for guidance and she must not crumble or fail.

'Thank you,' he clipped out. 'But the important thing is for the King's work to continue. He has had a long and productive life. There will be sorrow, yes, but we must also celebrate his achievements.' He nodded his head formally. 'You must be a figurehead of comfort to your people,' he said softly.

But not to you, thought Millie, as a great pang wrenched at her heart. Not to you.

'And now we must go back to Solajoya,' he said flatly, and Millie nodded like some obedient, mute servant.

After that everything seemed to happen with an alarming and blurred speed, and with the kind of efficiency which made her think it must have been planned. But of course it would have been. There were always provisions in place to deal with the death of a monarch, even if that monarch were young—and Gianferro's father had been very old indeed.

It was Alesso, not Gianferro, who instructed Millie to wear black, for the new King was busy talking on the phone. Normally, a bride would not have taken black clothes with her on honeymoon, but the instructions she had been given prior to the wedding all made sense now. Gianferro had told her that Royals always travelled with mourning clothes and so she had duly packed some, never thinking in a million years that she might actually need to wear them.

The car ride back to Solajoya was fast and urgent, only slowing down to an almost walking pace when they reached the outskirts of the capital. And Millie had to stifle a gasp—for it was like a city transformed from the one she remembered.

All the flowers and flags and the air of joy which had resonated in the air after their wedding had disappeared. Everything seemed so sombre…so *sad*. People were openly weeping and the buildings were draped in black.

A line of pale-faced dignitaries was awaiting them as they swept into the Palace forecourt, and Gianferro turned to her as the car came to a halt. He had been preoccupied and silent during the journey. She had longed to say something which would comfort him, but she had not been able to find the words—and something inside her had told her that he would not wish to hear them even if she could. She sensed that he was glad to have his position and authority to hide behind. Perhaps for Gianferro it was lucky that expressed emotions would be inappropriate right now.

She reached out a tentative hand towards his, but he didn't even seem to notice, and so she let it fall back onto her lap and stared out of the window instead, her mind muddled and troubled. Her future as Princess had been daunting enough, but as Queen? It didn't bear thinking about.

His voice was low and flat. 'After we have been greeted you will go to our suite,' he instructed. 'I will come to you as soon as I can.'

'When?' she whispered.

'Millie, I do not know. You must be patient.'

And that was that. In a daze, Millie followed behind him as dignitary after dignitary bowed—first to him and then to her.

Once in the suite, she pulled the black hat from her head and looked around the unfamiliar surroundings with a sense of panic.

Now what did she do? She felt as though she had been marooned on a luxurious but inaccessible island, with no one to talk to or confide in. No one to weep with—except that she felt bad about that, too, because there were no tears to shed. She felt sad, yes—but she had only met Gianferro's father once. She hadn't known him at all—and wouldn't it be hypocritical to try to conjure up tears simply because it was expected of her?

Her two sisters-in-law called on her, both dropping deep curtseys before her.

'Please don't feel you have to do that,' begged Millie.

'But we do,' said the taller of them, in a clipped, matter-of-fact voice which was distorted with grief. 'It is simply courtesy, Your Majesty.'

Millie heard the term of address with a sense of mounting disbelief. She had not yet had a chance to get used to it, and it seemed so strange to hear it coming from the lips of two women who were, in effect, her peers.

Ella and Lucy were both English, and both genuinely upset at the King's death. Millie felt like a fraud as she watched Lucy's face crumple with sorrow.

'I feel so bad for Guido!' Lucy wailed. 'He's beating himself up about having stayed away from Mardivino for so many years!'

'Nico's doing exactly the same,' said Ella gloomily. 'He says that if he hadn't given his father so much worry about his dangerous sports over the years, then he might still be alive.'

'But the King was an old man,' said Millie softly. 'And he had been sick for a long time.'

They both stared at her.

'But their mother died when they were little,' said Lucy, swallowing down a gulp. 'And the King was all they had.'

Millie could have kicked herself. She had been trying to offer comfort, that was all—and now she had probably come across as cold and uncaring. Or—even worse—perhaps they thought she was rejoicing in her new role.

She could see the curiosity in their eyes as they looked at her—and was aware that her lofty new status had put distance between them without her ever having had a chance to get to know them properly.

She drew a deep breath. She didn't want them to think her heartless. Or snooty.

'I'm so very sorry,' she said, though she wasn't sure what she was sorry about. Her inability to cry? The distance she was afraid she might have created between herself and the two women who were in the perfect position to be her friends? Or the fact that maybe she should accept that no one would be able to get close to her now that she was Queen?

The funeral took place in the Cathedral where she had been so recently married—but whereas that day had been Technicolored and jubilant, this day was mournful and monochrome.

Millie was exhausted by the time the last of the world leaders had left, and she could see the strain etched deeply on Gianferro's face—he looked as if he had aged by five years. She had sat next to him during the service, but since then she hadn't been able to get close to him. It seemed that everyone wanted a piece of him, and she was the last in line.

Eventually she went to their suite, stripped off her black suit and hat, and soaked for ages in a bath. But he didn't return. She surveyed the froth of exquisite handmade silk negligees which had made up her trousseau, and pushed the drawer shut on them. It seemed somehow wrong to dress in pale and provocative finery when the Palace was officially in mourning.

The honeymoon was over almost before it had begun.

She must have fallen asleep, for she was woken by the sound of a light footfall in the room. She blinked open her eyes and, once they were accustomed to the dim light, saw the silhouetted figure of her husband standing by the bed.

'Gianferro?'

'Who else?' His voice sounded raw, as if someone had been grating at it with a metal implement.

'What time is it?'

'Late. Go back to sleep, Millie.'

But she didn't want to go back to sleep. She had been pushed away by protocol, but there was no protocol here now—not in the dim, darkened privacy of their bedroom.

She lay there, not knowing what to do.

Gianferro wriggled his shoulders to try and remove some of the tension which was making his neck ache. He had been on some kind of autopilot all day. It had been crazy since he, like so many of the courtiers, had been expected to know exactly what to do. But how could he? Some of the older dignitaries remembered the death of his mother—but he had been only a child.

Yet the day had gone smoothly—even well. There had been no hitches or glitches, no assassination threats or attempts. The massed choirs had inspired people to say that it had been a beautiful service. And now his father was buried deep in the ground and he felt…what?

He didn't know.

Empty, he guessed. As if he had been scrubbed clean of all emotion. There had been no place for private grief—not today. Not with the eyes of the world's press trained like hawks upon him—greedy for a slip in composure which would be taken as a sign of weakness and an inability to rule.

'Gianferro?'

Her voice stirred over his shattered senses like a gentle breeze, but he needed to be alone with his thoughts. *Wanted* to be alone with them, as he had been all his life. To sort and sift them and then push them away. Of all the times to find himself with a wife there could not possibly have been a worse one. 'Go to sleep,' he said tightly.

But Millie had had days of being pushed away. No, she would not go to sleep! She sat bolt upright in bed and switched on the light. She heard him suck in a ragged breath. Was he shocked that she was naked? Was it also a sign of mourning for the Monarch that she should be swathed in some concealing night attire?

He had taken most of his uniform off, and was standing there in just a pair of dark tapered trousers and a crisp white shirt which he had undone at the collar. He looked as if he had stepped straight out of one of the many portraits which lined the corridors of the Palace. A man from another age. But maybe that wasn't so fanciful—for weren't Kings ageless and timeless?

The King is dead…long live the King.

'Gianferro?' she whispered, more timidly now.

How could it be that when his senses felt dead— his feelings as barren as some desert landscape—desire should leap up like some hot and pulsing and irresistible hidden well?

'Millie,' he said simply.

It was the most human and approachable she had ever heard him, and that one word stirred in her a response which was purely instinctive. She held her arms open to him. 'Come here.'

She looked so clean and fresh and pure. So wholesome—glowing like some luminescent candle in the soft light which bathed her.

So he went to her, allowed her to tightly enfold him in her arms, and she smoothed at his head with soothing and rhythmical fingers, and he felt some of the unbearable tension leave him.

Millie felt as though she was poised on a knifeedge—one wrong move and he would retreat from her once more. And yet it was not sex she sought, but comfort she wanted to *give* to him—for at this moment he was not King. Just a man who had lost his only surviving parent and who must now take up the heavy burden of leadership.

Time lost all meaning as she cradled him the way she supposed women had cradled their men since time began. And again, relying solely on an instinct which seemed to spring bone-deep from some hidden and unknown source, she began to massage the tight knot of his shoulders.

'That's…that's good,' he said thickly.

She carried on, working at the hard muscle as if her life depended on it. And when she moved her hands to unbutton the rest of his shirt he made no attempt to stop her, just remained exactly where he was—his head still resting on her shoulder as if it was too heavy for him to lift.

She slid the stiff, starched garment from his shoulders, exposing the silken olive skin which sheathed the hard musculature of his lean body. And then she bent her head and kissed him very softly on the cheek, and a pent-up sigh escaped him.

He did lift his head then, and he looked at her—at her eyes, which were innocent and troubled and yet hungry, too. And something inside him erupted into life—something strong and dark and powerful and unrecognisable. He moved his arms around her back, crushed her breasts against his bare chest and kissed her—a kiss which was fierce and all-consuming.

Beneath the heady, hard pressure of that kiss Millie went under as if she was drowning. She wanted to tell him that it was comfort she was offering him, that they didn't have to do this—but he did not seem to want her words. And wasn't she secretly glad that she did not have to say them?

He tore himself away and stripped off his trousers, and he was so aroused that for a moment she felt a tremor of fear as she looked at him. But he vanquished that fear with the expert touch of his hands and replaced it with desire, stroking her until she was molten and aching.

He moved above her, his big, hard body blotting out the light. His face was shadowed, but she didn't care. Nothing mattered other than the primitive longing to have him close to her again, to have him inside her, to feel the sense of triumph when he shuddered helplessly in her arms.

She moved distractedly and caught him by the shoulders.

'*Sì*,' he murmured, as if in answer to an unspoken question. When he thrust into her she cried out, and he stopped, frowning down at her. 'I am hurting you?'

Would it sound pathetic to tell him that the sensation had overwhelmed her—both mentally and physically? That he filled her so deeply that he seemed to have pierced her very heart? Or that making love at this time of loss seemed to take on such a poignant sense of significance?

But Gianferro did not like analysis at the best of

times, and right now would be the worst of times to try to tell him. She shook her head. 'N-no. No, you're not hurting me.'

But he held back a little as he began to move again, and never had he found it so difficult to contain himself. He was a most accomplished lover, and yet now he wanted to pump his seed into her without restraint. Yet he could not, for he was also a generous lover. Instead he switched off, and concentrated solely on her pleasure—using the vast wealth of experience he had learned from so many women over the years.

Millie felt torn in two. Her body couldn't help but respond to what he was doing to her, but his face was the dark and beautiful face of a stranger. He looked so intent…so focused. There was no love nor tenderness nor emotion on those carved features.

But you can't have everything, Millie, her greedy body seemed to cry out to her, and then feeling took over completely and she was lost. Lost…

He saw her face dissolve into passionate release and at last he let go. It seemed as if he had been waiting all his life for this to happen. He had always been a silent lover, but now he called out—a faltering, broken cry—for it was as if he had been locked in tight bands of iron and someone had suddenly snapped them open.

The power of his orgasm seized him like a mighty wave, caught him unawares, despite the fact that he had longed for its incomparable release. It threw him into a maelstrom of sensation so intense that he gasped aloud as wave upon wave of pleasure made him wonder if he could stay conscious. For a moment he felt weak with it—this alien and unwelcome realisation that he could be lured and weakened like any other man.

He shut his eyes for a second, and when he opened them again it was to stare up at dancing diamonds of light reflected from the waterfall of the chandelier. How elusively simple life could be at times. He expelled a long, sighing breath. If only...

Millie heard him and propped herself up on her elbow, with her hair falling all over the place, flushed with pleasure and aware of the first shimmerings of sexual confidence. He had wanted to sleep and she had persuaded him not to! In his time of grief and distress she had brought him solace in the only way she knew how.

'Gianferro?'

Her voice was like an intruder and his eyes became shuttered. When before had his steely will been bent? And why now—by her? Was it her unworldliness which had struck a chord in him—or the fact that death made you want to grab onto the life-force and embrace it, hang onto it as if you needed to be convinced in the most fundamental way of all that you were still so very much alive yourself?

But this would not do. There was much to be done and he must not be distracted. Furthermore, Millie must learn that he would *not* be distracted. She must bend to *his* will—not expect him to bend to *hers*. It was the only way.

'Gianferro?' she repeated, hating herself for the diffident note which had crept into her voice.

'Go to sleep, Millie,' he said, and shut his eyes again.

She had been hoping for kisses. She was not asking for words of love that he did not feel for her—just for the intimacy and closeness of being sleepy together. What had just taken place had shaken her to the core, and while she was still very new to all this, she was not stupid—it had shaken Gianferro, too, she knew it had. And yet despite the wonder and the strength of what had just happened he lay there now as if his body had been carved from stone—as distant as one of the rocks out at sea. When this moment—surely—was one when they could be as close as two people could be.

She turned onto her back and lay looking up at the ceiling, feeling suddenly very alone. Was this what her marriage was going to be like? And if so, could she bear it?

He had corrected her when she had asked if being Royal meant being remote, implying that she had misunderstood him—that he had meant to say removed.

But she didn't believe him. For at this precise moment he was as remote as it was possible for any man to be.

She listened to the deepening of his breathing and realised he had fallen asleep.

Millie bit her lip.

For sanity's sake—she wasn't going to think about it.

CHAPTER EIGHT

MILLIE drew a deep breath. 'Gianferro?'

The King looked up from his desk, his mind clearing as he saw his wife hovering in the doorway of his study. How beautiful she looked today—with her pale hair wound into some complicated confection which lay at the back of her long, slender neck. She wore a simple blue dress, which emphasised her lithe and athletic build and her long legs. Legs which had last night been bare and wrapped around his naked back. He smiled with satisfaction. 'What is it, *cara mia*?'

'Do you have a moment?' she questioned.

The faintest glimmer of a frown creased his brow. Millie, as much as anyone, knew just how tight his schedule was. 'What's on your mind?'

She wondered what he would say if she told him the truth—that she was feeling lonely and isolated, and that a night-time dose of passion did not compensate for those feelings. But she could not tell him. Gianferro was far too busy to be worrying about *her* problems—which to an outsider would probably not look like problems at all. And why would they?

To an observer, she had everything. A gorgeous husband who made love to her with such sweet abandon that sometimes she seriously thought that her body could not withstand such pleasure. She lived in a Palace and she could have whatever she pleased. The things which other women dreamed of were hers for the taking…even if, ironically, they were not what she coveted.

'I want you to cover your exquisite body in jewels,' Gianferro had murmured to her huskily in bed one night.

'But I'm not into jewels!' Millie had protested.

'No?' Lazily he had drifted a fingertip from neck to cleavage, and she had shivered with anticipation. 'Then I shall have to be ''into'' them for you, shan't I, Millie?' His black eyes had glittered. 'I shall buy you a sapphire as big as a pigeon's egg, and it will echo your eyes and hang just above your glorious breasts and remind me of how I bury my mouth in them and suckle on their sweetness.'

When the man you loved said something like that what woman *wouldn't* be putty in his hands? Suddenly the idea of a priceless necklace *did* appeal—but only because Gianferro would choose it. For her and only her. As if it meant something— *really* meant something—instead of just being a symbol of possession. An expensive bauble for his wife. A material reward for her devotion to duty as his Queen because he was unable to give her what she really craved—for him to love her. Properly. The way that she loved him.

And she did.

How could she fail to love the man who had awoken the woman in her in every way that counted and set her free? She had been living in a two-dimensional world before Gianferro had stormed in with such vibrant and pulsating life.

He had taken her and transformed her—moulded her into his Queen and his wife. At least externally he had. Inside she was aware of her own vulnerability—of a great, aching realisation that he would never return the love she felt for him.

Sometimes she looked at him in bed at night, when he was sleeping, and could scarcely believe that he was hers. Well, in so much as someone like Gianferro could be anyone's.

He was everything a man should and could be— strong and proud and intelligent, with a sensuality which seemed to shimmer off him. The leader of the pack—and weren't all women programmed to desire the undisputed leader? Especially as he treated her like…well, like a princess, she supposed. Except that she wasn't. Not any more. She was now the Queen.

The Coronation had been terrifying—the glittering crown which had been placed on her head at the solemn moment had seemed almost as heavy as she was. But at least she had been expecting it—had been warned about the weight of it—and Alesso had suggested she practise walking around the apartments with it on her head.

'It takes a little getting used to—the wearing of a crown, Your Serene Majesty.'

It had seemed more than a little bizarre to be wearing jeans and a T-shirt and a priceless heirloom on her head! Millie's eyes had widened. 'It weighs a *ton*!' she'd exclaimed, as she had lowered it onto her blonde hair.

'Do not tilt your head so. Yes, that is better. Now, practise sitting down on the throne, Your Majesty,' he had instructed, and Millie had falteringly obeyed, feeling like one of those women who had to carry their crops home on top of their heads!

At least she hadn't let anyone down on the big day—herself included. The newspapers had praised the 'refreshing innocence' of the new young Queen, and Millie had stared unblinkingly at the photographs.

Was that really her?

To Millie herself she seemed to resemble a startled young deer which had just heard a gunshot deep in the forest. Her eyes looked huge and her mouth unsmiling. But then she had been coached in that, too. It was a solemn occasion—heralded by the death of the old King—not a laughing matter.

Afterwards, of course, there had been celebrations in the Palace, and Millie had overheard Lulu exclaiming, 'I can't believe I'm sister to a *queen*!' and had seen Gianferro's brief and disapproving frown.

At least that had dissolved away the last of her residual doubts about Lulu. She could see now that her sister would not have made a good consort to Gianferro—she was far too independent.

And me? What about me? Millie had caught a reflection of herself in one of the silvered mirrors which lined the Throne Room. *I am directionless and without a past, and therefore I am the perfect wife for him.* The image thrown back at her was a sylph-like figure clad in pure and flowing white satin. In a way, she looked more of a bride on her Coronation day than when she had married—but she had learnt more than one lesson since then, and had toned down her make-up to barely anything.

Yes, her husband revered and respected her, and made love to her, but he was not given to words of love. Not once had he said *I love you*—not in any language. And Millie was beginning to suspect that was because he simply did not have the capacity for the fairytale kind of love that every woman secretly dreamed of. How could he?

He had been rigidly schooled for the isolating rigours of kingship, and his mother had been torn away from him at such a crucial stage in his development. A mother might have softened the steeliness which lay at the very core of his character—shown him that to love was not a sign of weakness.

Millie had tried from time to time to talk to him on a more intimate level, but she had seen his eyes narrow before he smoothly changed the subject. *Don't even go there,* his body language seemed to say. And so she didn't. Because what choice did she have?

Only in bed, when his appetite was sated—in that brief period of floating in sensation alone before reality snapped back in—did he ever let his guard down, and then it was only fractionally. Then he would touch his lips to her hair almost indulgently, and this would lull her into a sense of expectation which would invariably be smashed.

She wanted him to tell her about his day—to confide in her what his thoughts had been—just as if they were any normal newly-wed couple, but it was like drawing blood from a stone. They *weren't* a normal couple, nor ever would be. And he didn't seem to even want to try to be.

Gianferro was looking at her now, as she hovered uncertainly in the door of his study. It was a gaze laced with affection, it had to be said, but also with slight impatience—for his time was precious and she must never forget that.

'Yes, Millie?'

She laced her fingers together. 'You remember on our honeymoon I said that I wanted to learn French?'

'Yes. Yes.' He nodded impatiently.

'Well, I've changed my mind.' She could see his small smile of satisfaction. 'I think it should be Italian.'

'Really?' he questioned coolly.

'Well, yes. Italian is your first language.'

'I am fluent in four,' he said, with a touch of arrogance.

'It's your language of choice.' She looked at him. 'In bed,' she added boldly.

His eyes narrowed for just a second before his smile became dismissive. He loved her eagerness and her joy in sex—but did she really imagine that she could come in here at will and tempt him away from affairs of state? Very deliberately he put his pen down in a gesture of closing the subject. 'Very well. I shall speak to Alesso about selecting you a tutor.'

But something in the cold finality of his eyes made Millie rebel. She tried to imagine herself in one of the luxurious rooms of the Palace, with the finest tutor that money and privilege could provide, and realised it was just going to be more of the same. Isolation. 'But, if you recall, I said that I would like to learn in a class with other people.'

'And I think that, if *you* recall, I hinted that such a scenario would be inappropriate.' His eyes narrowed. 'What is wrong with taking your lessons here, *cara*?'

Take courage, Millie—he'll never know unless you tell him. 'Sometimes I feel a little…lonely, here at the Palace.' She saw his frown deepen and she hastily amended her words, not wanting him to think that she was spoilt or ungrateful. 'Oh, I know that you're busy—of course you are—but…' Her words tapered off, because she wasn't quite sure where she was going with them.

'You are still not with child?'

Millie stared at him and the nagging little feeling of guilt she had been doing her best to quash reared its mocking head. Perhaps a baby *was* the answer. Maybe she should throw her Pills away and no one would ever be the wiser. 'N-no.'

'You wish to consult the Palace obstetrician?'

There was something so chillingly matter-of-fact about his question that hot on the heels of her wavering came rebellion, and Millie bristled. As if a baby would solve everything! As if she was little more than a brood mare! 'I think it's early days yet, don't you?' she questioned, trying to keep her voice reasonable. 'We've only been married for six months.'

He quelled the oddly painful feeling of disappointment. She was right—it was early days indeed. Here was one thing he could *not* command. An heir would be his just as soon as nature—and fate—decreed it.

'Yes, that is so,' he agreed, and gave her a soft smile. 'What about your horses?' he questioned, for he had acquired for her two of the finest Andalusian mares that money could buy. 'Surely they provide adequate amusement for you?'

Millie bristled even more. 'It may have escaped your notice, but horses do not speak.'

'Yet the grooms tell me that you communicate with them almost as if they *could* speak.' His voice dipped with pride. 'That your enthusiasm for all things equine equals the energy you put in to your charity work.'

She knew that in his subtle way he was praising her—telling her that she made a good Queen and that there was plenty to occupy her without her trying to make a life for herself outside the rigid confines of the Palace. She could see that from *his* point of view it would be so much easier for a tutor to be brought in.

'And your English sisters-in-law,' he continued. 'You like Ella and Lucy, do you not?'

'Yes, I like them very much,' said Millie truthfully. But Ella and Lucy were different, and not just because they were mothers. Their relationships with their husbands were close and inclusive—and that wasn't just her imagining. She had seen them sometimes, at State Banquets, behaving with all the decorum expected of their position—but occasionally sneaking a small, shared look or a secret smile. Gianferro never did that with her.

She knew that comparisons were wrong, and could lead you nowhere except to dissatisfaction, and Millie wanted to be contented with her lot—or rather she wanted to make the best of what she had, not yearn for something which could never be hers.

But sometimes it was hard not to—especially when her sisters-in-law had genuine love-matches. Theirs had not been marriages of convenience, where the winning hand had been the bride-to-be's innocence and inexperience.

'I guess I don't really know them that well,' she said thoughtfully.

'Well, then?' said Gianferro impatiently. 'Invite them round for tea! Get to know them a little better!'

His arrogance and condescension took her breath away and strengthened her determination to fight for a little freedom.

'Very well, I will—but I should still like to go to a class,' she said quietly. 'What harm can it do?'

Gianferro drummed his fingers on the polished rosewood of his desk. He was not used to having his wishes thwarted, but he recognised a new light of purpose in his wife's eyes. 'It could...complicate things,' he murmured.

'How?'

Would she believe him if he told her? Or was this going to be one of the lessons she needed to learn for herself? He knew what she was trying to do—trying to dip into a 'normal' life once more—but she could not. Her life had changed in ways she had not even begun to comprehend. He felt a fleeting wave of regret that it should be so, which was swiftly followed by irritation that she would not be guided by his experience.

'It will not be as you imagine it to be,' he warned. 'Being Royal sets you apart.'

'I think I'd prefer to find that out for myself,' said Millie, but a smile was twitching at her lips, because suddenly this one small blow for freedom felt important. Tremendously important.

'Very well,' he said shortly. 'I will speak to Alesso.'

It was clear from his attitude that the usually sanguine Alesso disapproved of her request almost as much as Gianferro did, but Millie held firm and two weeks later she was allowed to go to an Italian class, accompanied by a bodyguard.

The class had been chosen by Alesso, and was held in a large room at the British Embassy. Millie was greeted by the Ambassador's wife, who dropped a deep curtsey before her. She wanted to say *Please don't make a fuss*, except that she knew her words would be redundant. People *did* make a fuss—indeed, they would be disappointed if they were not allowed to! But she had given Alesso prior warning that her participation in the class was not to be announced.

'I'd like to just slip in unnoticed,' said Millie softly. She had dressed as anonymously as possible—a knee-length skirt and a simple sweater, for while the Mardivinian winter was mild, there was a faint chill to the air.

Alesso had raised his eyebrows. 'Certainly, Your Majesty.'

She smiled. 'Loosen up,' she said softly. 'It's only an Italian class!'

The tutor had his back to her when she walked in— he was busy scrawling verbs on a blackboard—and as the door opened he turned round and frowned, pushing back the dark, shoulder-length hair which hung almost to his shoulders.

'You are late!' he admonished.

Clearly he didn't recognise her! Millie bit back a smile as she heard the slight inrush of breath from the Ambassador's wife, and almost imperceptibly shook her head in a silent *don't fuss* command. 'Sorry,' she said meekly, quickly making her way to a spare place at the back of the room. 'I'll just sit quietly and try to catch up.'

He nodded. 'Make sure you do.'

The next hour was spent busily trying to retain fact after fact and word after word. For a brief moment Millie realised how long it was since she had actually used her brain—not since school, and then not as much as she could have done.

But she found that she was enjoying herself, and soon lost herself in the challenge of learning something for the first time.

Her first faltering attempts at speaking aloud were greeted with smiles from the others, but she found herself smiling when *their* turn came. They were all in the same boat, and the sense of belonging she experienced filled her with a warm glow.

At the end of the class the others began to file out, and Millie was just gathering her books together when the tutor strolled down towards her and paused by her desk. He looked more like an artist than a teacher, she thought, with his long dark hair and jeans and T-shirt.

'You enjoyed my class?' he questioned.

Millie nodded. 'Very much. You made it seem… easy!'

'Ah! You should not say such things.' He laughed. 'Or the expectation for you to become my star pupil will be too high!'

'Okay, you made it seem really difficult!'

He was frowning now. It was not a frown of displeasure, but as if he was trying to place her, and Millie's heart sank.

'Don't I know you, *signora*?' he questioned softly.

'I don't think we've met.' Millie began to shuffle her books in order to put an end to a line of questioning which struck her as extremely inappropriate, but it seemed he was not to be deterred.

'Your face is…familiar.'

She guessed she couldn't have it both ways—she couldn't pull rank if she was trying to keep her identity secret! It was true that as she had been sitting at the back of the class only the tutor would have seen her face—but she couldn't do that week in, week out. And when she stopped to think about it hadn't she been living in cloud-cuckoo land even thinking that she could—with a dirty great bodyguard stationed outside the door?

'Is it?'

He gave a low laugh. 'You are the image of our new Queen!'

Millie sighed. 'That's because I am.'

'You are joking me?'

Millie laughed as his English deserted him in his confusion. 'Okay, I am!'

He gave a long, low whistle. 'I have the Queen in my class?' he questioned incredulously. 'The Queen of Mardivino?'

Millie smiled. 'Is that a problem for you?'

'For me, no! But perhaps for you?'

'I don't see why.' She allowed herself to believe the illusion and it was both heady and seductive.

His eyes narrowed. 'Why are you not being taught within the Palace?'

'Perhaps I want to experience life outside it,' she answered slowly.

'The caged bird?' he questioned thoughtfully. 'Who longs to break free?'

'You're being very impertinent!' she remonstrated.

'Am I?' He stared at her. 'You say you wish to experience life—and life outside the Palace means that people say what is on their minds.' He hesitated. 'What must I call you?'

She gave it only a split-second's thought. In this—if only in this—she would be like everyone else. 'My name is Millie,' she said firmly. 'You must call me Millie.'

'And I am Oliviero.' He smiled then, a genuine smile which made his eyes crinkle. 'Your secret is safe with me...Millie—though I doubt that it will remain so. But I can and will tell you this—while in my class, you are simply another pupil, and the others will respect that or they will be...' He shrugged and clicked his fingers in a dismissive gesture.

'Turfed out?' supplied Millie helpfully.

'Turfed out? Yes, it is just that!' His smile grew wider. 'I sometimes forget that it is the teacher who also learns!'

And Millie smiled back.

The challenge of studying added an extra dimension to her life, and she threw herself into her work with a new-found enthusiasm which was very gratifying.

She wasn't naïve enough to suppose that the rest of the class remained oblivious to her true identity, for their manner towards her was subtly deferential. But no one bothered her, or questioned her, or was intrusive.

She was always the last to leave—mainly to avoid being seen with her bodyguard, but also because she had grown to enjoy her little chats with Oliviero. He alone, of all people, treated her just as Millie. With him she felt like the person she knew she really was, deep inside. Not the Queen—a person who always led the conversation and was listened to with deference—but someone with whom she could have a genuine laugh. A small thing, but a precious and cherished one, and it reminded her of a very different life indeed.

Millie hadn't realised quite how much freedom she would lose when she married her Prince, but in a tiny way this compensated.

Her false paradise lasted for precisely one month, until the morning when Alesso knocked at the door of her sitting room. She had been sitting looking at an Italian newspaper. Oliviero had told her that she would understand almost none of it—and he had been right!—but that the best way to become fluent with a language was to familiarise yourself with it as much as possible. Each word she correctly identified felt as though she had found a nugget of gold!

'Come!' she called, and saw the tall, dark figure of Alesso, his face unsmiling. 'Oh, hello, Alesso!' she said brightly.

'Majesty.' He gave a deep bow.

'I'm just finishing up here.' She glanced at her watch, wondering what had prompted this rare and unheralded visit. 'I don't have to be at the Women's Refuge for another hour, do I?'

'The King wishes to speak with you.'

It was pointless to say, *Couldn't the King have come and told me that himself?* Because that wasn't how it worked. Millie rose to her feet. 'Very well. He is at work?'

'He awaits you in your suite, Majesty.'

'At this time of day?' she asked in surprise. But it was a rhetorical question and Alesso said nothing. Even if he had known the answer he would still have said nothing, for his first loyalty lay towards Gianferro. As did everyone else's.

Still unsmiling and unspeaking, Alesso accompanied her through the long portrait-lined corridors towards their suite of rooms, and Millie began to feel unaccountably nervous. 'I do know the way!' she joked.

'I gave His Majesty assurance that I would conduct you there myself,' he said formally.

The unwelcome thought flitted into her mind that it was like being led towards the gallows. A little knot of unknown fear at the pit of her stomach began to grow into a medium-sized ball, and by the time Alesso knocked and then opened the door her heart was racing.

It raced even harder when she saw Gianferro standing there, his face a study in anger, dark and brooding, and looking like she had never seen him look before.

'*Grazie*, Alesso,' he clipped out.

There was silence as she heard the door being closed behind his aide, and then Gianferro spoke, in a harsh voice she didn't recognise.

'I think you owe me some kind of explanation, don't you, Millie?'

CHAPTER NINE

MILLIE stared at the unfamiliar sight of a Gianferro whose face was contorted by fury. Normally it was implacable. Enigmatic. It wasn't just that he had been brought up to conceal his innermost feelings—Gianferro didn't *do* big emotions. She felt the shivering of apprehension suddenly tiptoeing over her skin as she stared at him.

'Explanation for what?'

The fury became transmuted into a look of icy disdain, and somehow that made her even *more* apprehensive. 'Oh, come, come, Millie,' he said silkily. 'I am not a stupid man.'

'Perhaps not,' she said shakily. 'But you are being a very confusing one right now. How can I give you an "explanation" when I don't have a clue what it is I'm supposed to have done!'

The black eyes narrowed and he regarded her silently, and Millie was reminded of some dark, jungle predator in that infinitesimal moment of stillness before it pounced.

'How is *Oliviero*?' he clipped out.

For a moment she had no idea what he was talking about—and when she did it made even less sense. Millie frowned. 'You mean my Italian teacher?'

'Or your lover?'

She stared at him. 'Are you...*crazy*?' she whispered.

'Maybe a little, but perhaps I am not the only one.' His mouth curved into a cruelly sarcastic smile. 'Does it feed your ego to make some poor little teacher fall in love with you?'

'What are you talking about?' she asked, in genuine confusion. 'Oliviero is not a "poor little" *anything*—he happens to be a brilliant linguist.'

'My, but how you defend him!' he mocked.

Millie felt as though someone had just exploded a bomb in the centre of her world, and she had no idea why. But Gianferro was angry—really, *really* angry—and the first thing she needed to do was to calm him down.

'Won't you tell me what this is all about?' she pleaded.

Gianferro's breathing was ragged, rarely could he remember feeling such an all-consuming rage, and yet her face betrayed nothing other than what seemed like genuine confusion. Unless she was a better actress than he had bargained for.

'Very well.' His dark eyes sparked accusation. 'The editor of the *Mardivino Times* rang Alesso this morning to ask whether anyone would like to comment on the rumours sweeping the capital about my wife.'

'R-rumours?' she stammered, in horror. 'What kind of rumours?'

He heard the faltering of her words with a grim

kind of understanding. Now, that—*that*—sounded like guilt. 'You don't know?'

'Of course I don't know—Gianferro, please tell me!'

He felt the acrid taste of jealousy and rage tainting his mouth with their poison as he glanced down at a piece of paper which was covered with Alesso's handwriting. 'Apparently you have grown *close* to—and I quote—''the devastatingly handsome young Italian who has broken hearts all over Solajoya''.' He looked at her trembling lips, cold to their appeal. 'Well?' he shot out. 'What have you to say?'

The accusation was so unjust and so unwarranted that part of her wanted to just tell him to go to hell and storm out of the room. But she couldn't do that—and not just because that wasn't the way queens behaved. She was his wife and this was a genuine misunderstanding.

'It isn't like that at all! He has just been…kind to me.'

His mouth twisted in scorn. 'I'll bet he has.'

'Gianferro, please.' Her voice gentled. 'Stop it.'

But he couldn't stop it, nor did he want to. It was as if he had stepped onto a rollercoaster with no idea of how to get off again. If she had obeyed his orders then she would never have found herself in this position! Black eyes bored into her. 'So you do not deny that you have spent time alone with him after every class?'

'That's one way of looking at it,' she said calmly. 'But that isn't how it—'

He sliced through her words. 'Just you and him? No one else?' If she denied this then he would know that she was lying, for had not her bodyguard been questioned just minutes earlier?

'Well…yes. But nothing has happened—'

'Yet.'

'How dare you?'

'No, Millie,' he said heavily. 'How dare *you*? How dare you be so thoughtless, so *naïve*?'

'I thought that what was one of the reasons you married me!' she retorted. 'I thought you liked that!'

He believed her now, but she must understand that he would not tolerate such behaviour. 'You'd better sit down,' he said heavily.

'I don't want to sit down. And certainly not if I'm going to be treated like a naughty child.'

'Don't you realise how people talk?' he demanded. 'How quickly rumours can gather force in a place like this?'

'And how quickly you believe them!'

'Then prove me wrong!' he challenged.

She had to convince him that she was completely innocent—and, more than that, didn't she owe him some kind of explanation for how this ridiculous misunderstanding had arisen? Shouldn't she try to make him understand why she'd acted the way she had? Dared she admit that Oliviero's attitude had been like a breath of fresh air blowing through the formal world of the Court?

'He made me feel like me,' she admitted slowly.

'Do *not* talk to me in riddles, Millie. Explain.'

'He seemed to like me just as a person. As me— *Millie*. Not because I was Queen.' Her blue eyes were full of appeal. 'He didn't even know for sure who I was. Not at first.'

His eyes were hard. 'Now you really *are* being naïve. Of *course* he knew!

'I didn't tell him.'

'The whole class knew.' He sighed. 'Do you not think that people might not have noticed the Royal crest on the car? The presence of a hulking great bodyguard outside? The fact that you were accompanied to the class by the Ambassador's wife herself? Did you not consider that people might recognise you from your photographs?'

'He may have known,' she said staunchly. 'They may all have known—but it didn't seem to matter. It made no difference to the way they treated me.'

'Oh, you little fool, Millie!' he retorted. 'How do you think I found out all this?'

She stared at him. 'From the bodyguard?'

'No, not from the bodyguard! From the Italian himself!' he snapped. 'Via the newspaper! He has been hawking your story round to the highest bidder!'

'But there is no story!' she protested.

He saw the hurt which clouded her big blue eyes and felt a momentary pang, knowing that he was about to disillusion her further, that this would shatter her trust completely. Could he do it? Had he not taken enough from her already in his quest for the perfect wife?

His mouth hardened. He had to.

'Maybe there isn't,' he agreed. 'But there was enough of a story for the editor to be interested. "A special closeness…"' His eyes narrowed. 'Do you deny there was that?'

'A closeness?' Millie rubbed at her eyes. 'Yes, probably. But special? Yes, probably that, too—if a person makes you feel something that other people can't.'

He flinched, for the barb was directed as much at him as at anyone. 'And what was that?' he asked quietly.

'He made me feel…' Millie shrugged as she struggled to find a word that didn't make her sound pathetic. Or ungrateful. 'Ordinary, I guess.'

'But you are not ordinary, Millie. You never have been and you certainly never will be now.'

It was a bit like having someone tell you that Father Christmas was not real—an unwelcome but necessary step into the world of grown-ups—and Millie recognised that Gianferro was right. She wasn't ordinary— she had bade farewell to the ease of an anonymous life on the day she had taken her wedding vows. She was Queen, and she must act accordingly.

She felt the sting of tears at the back of her eyes. 'I've been so stupid,' she whispered.

Inexplicably, her disillusionment hurt him more than her tears, and he went to her then, pulled her to her feet and gathered her into his arms and into his embrace. She was stiff and as awkward as a puppet, and maybe so was he—just a little—for to comfort a woman was a new experience for him. To touch without sensual intent was like walking on uncharted territory, but he began to stroke her hair and gradually she began to relax.

'Maybe I am the one who should be sorry,' he said softly, and for possibly the first time in his life he tried to see things from someone else's point of view. He frowned. 'You think that I neglect you?'

Was this part of being grown-up too—accepting her role completely—telling him that no, he didn't neglect her? 'You are a very busy man,' she said evasively.

He pushed her away a little, so that he could look down at her face. 'Which does not answer my question.'

'I think it does, Gianferro. There are only so many hours in the day, and yours are filled with work. So many demands on your time—and I don't want to become another burden when already you have so many.'

'Would it help if I made space in my diary once a week—so that we could have dinner alone together no matter what?'

They would never be *completely* alone, of course... there would always be servants and aides hovering in the background. But she recognised that he was making an effort, that the offer itself was an important gesture of trying to see things her way. And in response she must try to see things *his* way.

'That would be lovely,' she said evenly.

His eyes narrowed. He had softened the blow... now came the steel punch which lay behind it. 'You do realise that these lessons will have to stop?' he questioned softly. 'That you cannot be friends with this man any more?'

She nodded, determined not to let him see her hurt or her sinking realisation that in the end Gianferro had got his own way. Maybe he always did. 'Of course I do.' She must show him that she could be strong, that these things did not matter. 'It's just taking me a bit of time to make the adjustment,' she admitted with a smile.

He pulled her closer. 'And that is perfectly natural. Perhaps you are a little homesick? Would it help if I arranged for you to take a trip back to England?'

And be even further away from him?

She wasn't homesick at all. She was lovesick. Wanting to give so much more to him than he wanted, or needed. Wanting time to lie in his arms, to lazily trace her fingertips over the beautiful contours of his face. Wanting him not to be so frazzled with work that he would not fall into an instant sleep once they had made love. They were talking now in a way they rarely did, and it made her feel so close to him that she wanted to hang onto the feeling for ever, to imprint it on her mind.

She wound her arms around his neck and looked up into his face. 'Oh, Gianferro,' she sighed. 'Won't you just kiss me?'

Her parted lips were pure temptation, as was the buttercup tumble of her hair, and Gianferro hesitated only for a fraction of a moment before lowering his head, his lips touching hers in a kiss which was supposed to be fleeting. But then he felt them part, and the warm eagerness of her breath as it heated him. She was always so responsive! As a pupil, she had far surpassed all his expectations.

But the word *pupil* reminded him of her folly, and the brief tang of anger heated his blood, set it pulsing around his veins. His body responded with the age-old antidote to anger. The pressure of his lips hardened and he pulled her body against his almost roughly, feeling her instant response as her soft curves melted into his.

Millie felt the heated clamour of her breasts as they became swollen and hard, and opened her mouth eagerly as his tongue flicked in and out, tightening her grip on the broad shoulders, not daring to touch him anywhere else in case he stopped.

But he didn't stop. He touched her aching breasts, then slid his hand down to mould the contours of her hips, and she could scarcely believe it when it began to ruck up the hem of her dress, his fingertips finding the silken temptation of her inner thigh.

'Gianferro!' she gasped indistinctly against his mouth.

'What is it?' he drawled.

She was so on fire with need that she paid no heed to logic or good sense. To the fact that he had insulted and accused her—only to the knowledge that she wanted him so badly. 'Make love to me,' she said brokenly.

Dimly he was aware that he had about half an hour until his next appointment, and that this was sheer and utter madness—but what other feeling in the world could suck you so willingly down into its dark and erotic vortex and obliterate every other?

He stared down at her, at the pale upturned face and the parted lips, and he sucked in a hot and hungry breath as he forced himself to resist them. 'Do you want me and only me?' he demanded.

'Yes!' she gasped. 'You know I do!'

In one corner of the room was a chaise longue which was rarely used, and he pushed her towards it. She went willingly, unprotesting, not daring to speak in case that broke the spell, brought him to his senses.

For she had never seen Gianferro like this before— so fervent and intent, almost…not out of control, no—for that would be alien to his nature—but like a man who had for once given in to what he truly wanted rather than what was expected of him.

His face dark, his eyes almost unseeing, he pushed her down and slid her panties right off, brazenly touching the moist heat which seared him, a grim, hard smile curving his lips as she writhed in response. And then he unzipped himself and Millie watched him—the hunger of her body momentarily suspended by the unbelievable sight of Gianferro moving towards her—*in broad daylight*—to make love to her.

It all happened very quickly—but she guessed there was time for nothing else. There was no formality, no tenderness and no foreplay—but she didn't need it, and neither did he. God, she had never felt so on fire with need! A small cry of anguished pleasure formed on her lips, but he kissed it away with a hard and efficient kiss which muffled it as he thrust deep inside her.

Maybe it was the sheer incongruity of what they were doing in Gianferro's study in the middle of the day which heightened her senses to an almost unbearable pitch, but her appetite was so sharpened that her orgasm happened almost immediately, and she felt him give one hard, final thrust before he too followed, his dark head falling onto her shoulder.

They stayed like that for a moment—she could feel his breath, warm and rapid against her neck—and then he raised his head, his dark eyes glittering with a look she dared not analyse for fear of what she might read there.

'Does that make you feel better, Millie?' he questioned slowly, as he carefully eased himself out of her.

Her euphoria evaporated. He made it sound as if she had just been given a dose of medicine! But she wouldn't let her hurt show…indeed, wasn't she being a little precious to *feel* hurt? Gianferro had just done something extremely out of character—something they had both needed—and he had done it without a thought to propriety. She must be making some kind of progress, and she should seize on that and cherish it.

She wound her arms around his neck. 'Oh, yes,' she whispered. 'That was wonderful.'

Gianferro's eyes narrowed as he untangled her arms. 'You'd better straighten yourself up.'

Millie's cheeks grew pink as she reached down to find her crumpled panties, aware that she was all sticky and that it was miles back to her own office. 'Can you pass me some tissues?'

Gianferro stared, her matter-of-fact question making him feel slightly dazed. 'Can I *what*?' he echoed in disbelief.

'Well, I can hardly ring for a lady-in-waiting to help me.' She looked at him, biting her lip. He wasn't exactly making it easy for her. 'Can I?'

Without a word, he turned and did as she asked, grateful for the fact that his back was towards her and she would not see the look of disbelief in his eyes. It wasn't the thought that someone might have walked in which so nagged at his conscience—no one would have *dared*—but more the fact that what had just taken place had been so…so…

So utterly inappropriate.

Was that why she had broken out of the mould she

must know was expected of her? Had she deliberately flirted with the young Italian to get just this reaction—to make him jealous enough to behave in a manner more befitting a sex-starved teenager than a king? And it had worked, damn her! It had worked!

He adjusted his clothing and walked back to where she lay, her legs still splayed, her colour all rosy. 'Here,' he said tightly, thrusting the tissues at her. 'You'd better hurry.'

She saw the brief but unmistakable glance at his watch and her cheeks flushed scarlet. It wasn't until she felt halfway decent again that she dared to broach what had just happened—for surely they couldn't just ignore the fact that they had just had sex in the middle of the day and in the middle of Gianferro's busy diary? And what of the jealousy which had started it—shouldn't that be addressed, too?

'It's pretty obvious from the look on your face that you wish we hadn't done that,' she said quietly.

Gianferro heard the unspoken plea for reassurance, but he didn't respond. He didn't want to discuss it, but to forget it and wipe it from his mind. And not just because he had let his guard down in such an inappropriate way—for how else was he to concentrate on the matters of State which lay stacked up and waiting for his attention?

'It happened, Millie. Nothing we can do about it now,' he said flatly, and with an effort he flashed her a smile. 'Don't you have a reception to attend?'

So he didn't want to discuss the underlying jealousy either. In fact, from the look on his face, he didn't want to discuss anything. She wondered if her face showed her disappointment.

It reminded Millie of the times when her father had still been alive, when he had returned from one of his interminably long trips abroad and Caius Hall would be bustling with anticipation of his arrival. Millie would be so excited, and would want to wait up to see him, but when he finally *did* arrive he would tell her that it was late and that he would see her in the morning. The memory of all that quashed excitement had never really left her. He had effectively dismissed her—just as Gianferro was doing now—and maybe it wasn't some crazy coincidence.

Was that what had made her fall for him? Had she done what they said all girls did—married a man who was the image of her father, because that was the only relationship she knew, one she felt familiar with?

She stood up and tugged down her dress, giving him a cool smile.

'You're right,' she murmured. 'I'd better dash.'

But he did not like her brittle either. He watched her walk towards the door, knowing that he must make compromises if this was to work, and yet compromise did not come easily to him. 'Millie?'

Composing her face, she turned back to him. 'Yes, Gianferro?'

'I meant what I said—about time for the two of us. Let's put dinner in the diary and let's make it a regular date. I'll speak to my secretary and he will speak to yours.'

To anyone else it would have sounded mad, but to Millie it was a small victory won. Time with her husband. Just him. And her. 'How crazy that sounds.' She giggled.

He nodded. 'I know.'

'Have…have a good day, darling.'

But Gianferro barely heard her. He had made his small concession and now his dark head was bent. Already he was preoccupied. He didn't even look up as she opened the door—but then she doubted that he had even heard her leave.

CHAPTER TEN

THE small change to their schedule seemed to have a knock-on effect within the relationship itself—though at first Millie was still insecure enough to put that down to wishful thinking.

But time changed her mind for her. Their allotted time together was precious—she'd spend the whole day looking forward to it, and she suspected that Gianferro did, too. There seemed something decadent about dismissing all the servants, and the sight of the King strolling into their apartment and unbuttoning his shirt with a wicked smile seemed like the fulfilment of her wildest fantasy!

For other couples it would doubtless be a huge treat to dine off golden plates and drink rare vintage wine. For her and Gianferro the opposite was true—it was simple food eaten with their fingers, while lolling around on the silken cushions which they dragged out onto the starlit terrace.

'Oh, I just love this,' said Millie dreamily one night. Her head was on her husband's bare chest and they were lying naked on the floor, washed in the moonlight which flooded into the room. In the distance she could see the dark glitter of the sea. 'Just

143

love it!' she emphasised as his hand moved to her breast.

Gianferro traced over her puckered nipple with the tip of his finger. 'I know you do. You make that abundantly clear, *cara.*'

'You're supposed to say, *So do I*!'

'Ah, but you know that to be true.'

'Then say it!'

He gave a mock frown. 'But if I say things you already know, then surely that would waste time. And since you tell me that we never have enough of it—then why would I want to do that?'

'Because…oh, Gianferro!' she gasped. 'Wh-what are you doing now?'

'What do you think I'm doing?' he purred, as he touched the tip of his tongue against her skin. Her head fell back.

The moon was very bright by the time he had rolled off her, and the stars were looped in the sky like Christmas tree lights. If only you could capture a moment and put it in a bottle—then this was the one she would choose. When they were alone and at peace.

When for a few brief hours their world and all its privilege retreated. It was as close to normality as they were ever likely to come.

Millie had come to realise something else… That maybe she had been wrong about not wanting a baby.

Maybe that was what happened automatically with women—the stronger your feelings for your partner grew, so too did the urge to have his child. She no longer saw it as a trap—in fact, if she was hands-on with their baby, as she intended to be, then wouldn't that be an even more normalising experience for the two of them to share?

She knew that Gianferro had told her Royal children should be brought up in a certain way, but his mind might now be open to change—just as it was over these evenings together. His life was rigidly defined, and Millie had come to recognise that change could only be achieved gradually and subtly—ultimately this stalling device on her part would benefit them both as a couple.

She touched her fingertips to his olive cheek, suddenly seeing all kinds of possibilities being opened up by her having a baby. Perhaps the fleetingly soft side she occasionally saw of her husband might be liberated by the birth of his own flesh and blood. She could but hope…

He whispered his lips across her hair, lazily touching her breast. 'I wonder if you're pregnant now,' he mused, and his voice deepened with longing. 'I wonder if what we have just done is the beginning of it all?'

In a way, this was nothing more than a variation on what he had said to her on their honeymoon, but the words no longer scared her. The way he said them had profoundly changed. It no longer sounded like an arrogant exercise in acquisition, but a heartfelt longing to have a child together. And his attitude had changed *her* attitude—of course it had.

But how did she go about telling him that she had come round to his way of thinking? That she had just needed time and space to come to terms with her new life?

'Hmm?' he whispered sleepily. Was it wrong to let a woman closer than he had ever done in the past? When his defences were down—did that make a man weak? 'What do you think, *cara mia*?'

'I wish I was pregnant,' she whispered back, and that was the truth. But the pain of what she had done—or failed to do—tore at her—tore at her like a ragged knife.

He no longer mentioned consulting a doctor, and she sensed that the urgency had left him. Maybe that was a direct result of their growing closeness. But what was she going to do about it?

Leaving Gianferro dozing, Millie rose to her feet and walked through the sumptuous rooms to the bathroom, but she didn't bother putting the main light on.

There were mirrors everywhere, and the light was surreal and silvered. Her dim reflection looked troubled. And she *was* troubled.

If she told him that she wanted to get pregnant now, that would mean telling him about the Pill...

The Millie of now was a different person from the innocent bride who had been daunted by her new position. It was so easy to recognise that she should have discussed contraception with her husband—but back then they had not been in a place to discuss anything. Gianferro had been so dogmatic and dominant and all-powerful, and she had had to fight for her part in his world.

Now she had made her own space there—true, it wasn't a very big one, but at least she had a foothold, and surely it could only get better.

She unzipped her make-up bag and looked down at the foil strip with some of the little circles punched out, which lay underneath a clutch of lipsticks. She knew that she ought to tell him. But something stopped her—and it was not just the fact that she now felt ashamed of what she had done. Wouldn't Gianferro feel a tremendous sense of hurt that she had excluded him from such a big decision—and wouldn't that have a detrimental effect on their growing relationship?

If only she had had the courage at the time—to stand up for what she believed in. But she had been barely twenty—thrown into a strange new world and struggling to find her own feet.

She stared at herself in the mirror, aware that her face looked older and more serious. As far as she could see she had two choices. Either she went in there and told him everything, or she simply stopped taking it. Gianferro would never know and would never need to feel hurt that she hadn't told him—and she might become pregnant straight away.

But something about doing that troubled her. Her deepening relationship with her husband would be much healthier if she was upfront and honest. If she told him and he was furious with her—well, he would be furious, and she would deserve it, but he would get over it.

The sense of knowing that this was somehow the right thing was enough to make her act decisively, and her fingers curled round the packet of Pills.

A movement distracted her, and she glanced up into the mirror, her heart leaping with something very close to fear when she saw Gianferro reflected there. He was standing in the doorway, as still and as watchful as a dark and brooding statue.

Now her heart began to race. 'Gianferro!' she cried. 'You startled me!'

'So I see.' He reached up and snapped on the light-switch. The room was flooded with bright fluorescent light, like a stage-set. 'What are you doing, Millie?'

But his voice didn't sound like his voice, and his question was spoken like an actor saying a line. Asking it because he knew it must be said, but knowing the answer because he had already read the script.

'I was just…just getting something out of my make-up bag.'

'And what something is that?'

With a cold feeling of dread Millie realised that he knew. Her mouth felt so dry that it felt as if it was cracking inside. 'My P-pills,' she stumbled. She looked into his eyes and almost recoiled from the stony look she saw there. 'You saw?'

'Of course I saw,' he said icily.

'I know what it must look like,' she said quickly, 'but I was going to stop taking them. Tonight. I was just going to bring them into the sitting room to show you before I threw them away!'

'What an extraordinary coincidence!' he drawled sarcastically.

'I know what it must sound like, but it's true.'

'I don't believe you,' he said coldly.

She saw the light go out in his eyes, and something inside her began to scream with pain. And panic. 'It is. Honestly—'

'*Honestly?*' His mouth hardened into a look of utter disdain. 'How dare you use that word?' he raged. 'How *dare* you use it to me?'

'Gianferro—I realise how it must seem—'

'Oh, please, Millie.' The breath he sucked in felt as though it had been fired into his lungs by a flame-thrower. He had not known that it was possible to feel such a hot sense of injustice. 'I have had my suspicions—so please don't heap insult onto injury by attempting some kind of false apology.'

She stared at him. 'Your…*suspicions?*' she breathed. 'You mean you suspected?'

His eyes were like black ice. 'Of course I suspected—what kind of fool do you take me for?' he snapped. The kind of fool who had not wanted to frighten or to hurt her with his nebulous fears—when all the time it seemed he had been right to harbour them. Now he wanted to lash out. He wanted to hurt her back, as she had hurt him—and to salvage something of his pride, too, to show her that he was not a fool, and that she had badly underestimated him.

Oh, so very badly...

But he had let her, hadn't he? When questions had drifted into his mind he had chosen to ignore them... because he'd wanted to believe that his young wife was pure and sweet and true. Because the alternative had been unthinkable.

He had blithely ignored all the dangers of letting a woman get close and he had misjudged her. Just because a woman was a virgin that didn't mean that she couldn't also be a liar and a cheat. He had forgiven her for the understandable lapse with the Italian teacher, and yet all the time there had been this far greater sin of deception waiting in the wings.

'In some corner of my mind I have suspected for some time,' he said furiously, but part of his rage was directed at himself. For letting her innocence blind him to what was crashingly obvious. Well, *more fool you*, he told himself bitterly.

Millie's heart was breaking as she saw the look of contempt on his face—but worse than that was the fact that she had been deluding herself. She had thought that their relationship was deepening, that they were growing closer all the time. She had allowed herself to bask in the confidence that what they had between them would soon be strong enough to provide a secure base for a baby. But it seemed she had been wrong. How wrong?

She screwed up her eyes. 'But...but how? How on earth could you know?'

'Oh, come on, Millie! A woman who shares her

husband's desire to have a baby usually exhibits some
kind of disappointment each month when it does not
happen. But not you.' His eyes gleamed coldly as the
stealthy poison of betrayal began to seep in. 'Oh, no.
You used to answer my questions with the air of
someone who had always known what the answer
would be...because of course you damned well did!
You had already made certain what the answer would
be.'

Her lips trembled. 'Won't you please let me explain?'

'What's to explain? That you deceived me?' he bit
out, and he saw her flinch but didn't care. He didn't
care. For the first time in his life he had been guilty
of brushing a suspicion aside because he hadn't
wanted to believe it. And the fact that his judgement
had failed him wounded his ego and his pride as much
as anything else. 'Because, no matter how much you
try to dress it up, that is the truth of it,' he bit out.

But her words rushed out anyway, tumbling over
themselves in an effort to explain. To try and get him
to understand—even though deep down she feared
that it was too late for understanding. Oh, why had
she done it—and then, having done it, left it so long?
Because that was what happened sometimes. You
were troubled by a nagging fear and it just seemed
easier to brush it aside. Well, she was about to pay
for it.

With her marriage?

'I just felt that we were rushing into parenthood.

That it was too soon to have a child between us when we didn't really know each other as people. Gianferro—you wondered out loud on our *honeymoon* whether you had made me pregnant!'

'And how you must have laughed,' he said softly. 'Because presumably you were already on the Pill.'

'Yes! But I didn't laugh—of course I didn't. I was scared. And mixed-up, if you must know—because I had been to see my doctor and he had prescribed me the Pill as a matter of course. I understood that was what all brides-to-be did.'

'You didn't think of discussing it with *me* first?' he demanded.

'How could I—when the subject was so clearly off-limits? You married me because I fulfilled certain criteria, and the main one was my innocence! So you can hardly expect me to have brought up the subject of birth control with you before the wedding, can you? Even if I'd wanted to—or dared to—we were scarcely alone for a second!'

'How about afterwards, Millie? Huh? Once we had been…intimate? Couldn't you have told me then?'

She knew that it would muddy the waters still further to tell him that intimacy had been a long time in coming for her that only recently had she really felt they had finally reached it.

'You frightened me with your autocratic assurance that we should have a child straight away,' she admitted. 'I felt as though I would shrink for ever into the shadows if I did.'

'Oh, what is the point in all this?' he bit out impatiently. 'We could go round and round in circles for ever, and in the meantime I could use my time more usefully.'

'More *usefully*?' she echoed in disbelief.

He wanted to hurt her as badly as she had hurt him, and he lashed out now as only he could. Nothing so coarse as personal insults, but words dipped in the icy and distancing substance of Court protocol. 'If you will excuse me, Millie—I have matters which require my attention.'

'You still don't understand, do you?' she questioned slowly.

He gave her a look of imperial disdain and Millie almost shrank. 'Are you trying to suggest that I'm missing the point?' He raised his dark brows. 'Perhaps it was less a fear of pregnancy itself which was the problem—but concern about the identity of the father.'

'*What?*'

He shrugged. 'It is possible that your tutor's insinuations about the extent of your relationship were based on truth rather than fantasy.'

'Now you're just being ridiculous!'

'You think so?' He shook his head and raised his eyebrows in autocratic query. 'Everything suddenly looks very different when you discover that your partner has been living a lie. Tell me, Millie—did you imagine me to be such a tyrant that I would *insist* on you carrying a baby if the idea was so abhorrent to you?'

'N-no—but I didn't think you'd understand my fears.'

'Just your long-term deceit?' He shook his head as he opened the door. 'In that case, my dear—you have been a fool.'

Her head and her thoughts were spinning. Nothing seemed coherent or real any more, and the look of contempt in his black eyes told her that even if she did manage to explain how she had felt at the time he probably wouldn't believe her. He didn't *want* to believe her.

'Where are you going?' she asked him miserably.

'Out.'

'And when are you coming back?'

'I have no idea,' he snapped. 'And even if I did— it is none of your business.'

'Gianferro—please don't do this—please don't shut me out.'

His dark eyes were incredulous as they looked at her. 'How do you…*you*…have the nerve to say that to me, Millie?'

It was like when you dropped a leaf into a fast-flowing river as a child, and the current carried it far, far away, and you didn't know where—that was what was happening to them now. Her actions had prompted it, and he didn't want to fight it.

She wanted to ask him—was a person not allowed to make one mistake? But that might sound like begging, and in her heart she knew that he would despise that, too. If he wasn't going to forgive her, then she couldn't force him—but maybe if she put some space between them it might help him to try. Give him a chance for him to see how he really felt. And a chance for her, too, to come to terms with the fact that he might not want her any more.

'You once suggested that I might like to take a trip back to England?' she said slowly.

'Homesick, are you, Millie?' he scorned softly.

His attitude swung it. She was already isolated by her position and her age—but before she had always had the support of her husband. If he now withdrew it, she would be left with nothing.

Nothing.

'A little,' she agreed, wanting to save face and not to finish with a blazing row which would leave a bitter memory. 'Would that be possible?'

Her gaze was very steady as she looked at him. Was half of her praying that he would change his mind? Try to talk her out of it or come with her?

He stared at her. Outwardly she looked just as beautiful as when he had first met her—with her long blonde hair and blue eyes, and her skin which was as soft as silk-satin. But she had changed—he saw that now, as if for the first time.

She wore the air of a sexually confident woman, and he had liberated that in her. He had made her into his perfect lover, and supposedly his perfect wife as well—only now he had discovered that it had all been an elaborate sham. The girl of such simple tastes had gone for ever and he had been instrumental in making her that way. She had grown up.

And even if he could bring himself to forgive her—didn't her actions speak about more than simply the fear of having children? In a way, hadn't part of her been rejecting Royal life—because she had been in no position to reject it before, not until she had actually been exposed to it? And was that not her prerogative? Far better she did it when there was no child to complicate things even further?

But he was unprepared for the dark torrent of pain which swept over him. He was relieved when it passed and was replaced by the emptiness he was so familiar with. In a way he felt comfortable with that. He knew where he was with that feeling, for it had been with him all his life.

He stared at her as if he was looking at her for the first time. Or maybe the last. 'I will speak to Alesso about arranging a flight as soon as possible,' he said.

The anger had left his voice and been replaced with a kind of bleakness, and in a way that was much, much worse.

The last thing Millie saw before the door closed behind him were his shoulders, which had unconsciously girded themselves to face the prying eyes of the world outside, and she was left staring after him through a blur of tears, utterly heartbroken at what she had done to him.

CHAPTER ELEVEN

MILLIE stared out of the window at the familiar green landscape softened by water—a mixture of the steady rain which fell and the tears which were filling her eyes.

'It all looks exactly the same,' she said brokenly. 'Nothing changes.'

'But you've changed,' said Lulu, from behind her. 'You're almost unrecognisable.'

'Am I?' Millie turned round, her sense of surprise momentarily eclipsing the terrible pain she had felt since setting foot back in her old family home. 'But my hair is the same and my face is the same. The clothes are more expensive, and I may have lost a little weight—but that's about all.'

'Maybe the profound experience of marrying and becoming a queen almost simultaneously has altered you more than you realised? Oh, Millie—don't! Please don't start crying again!'

But Millie couldn't help it. She had bottled her feelings up—not wanting the servants to see her giving in to emotion—that had been one lesson which Gianferro had taught her so well. But once away from the closed environment of the Palace which had become her home the tears had begun to fall in earnest, and now they were splashing down onto her cashmere sweater, which she hugged close to her, like an animal seeking comfort.

'I just don't understand what the problem is.' Lulu stared at her in confusion. 'You didn't bother telling him you were on the Pill—is it really such a big deal?' she asked.

Millie bit her lip. She had thought that coming here might help put everything in perspective, but in a way it had only emphasised the gravity of what she had done. It was more than simply not telling her husband something—it was the severing of a trust which he gave to very few people.

But he suspected you, she reminded herself. He told you that himself. So he did not trust you at all.

'I just don't know what to do!' she whispered.

'Well, stop crying, for a start! Just calm down and take a deep breath.' Lulu's face was very fierce. 'It's not the end of the world.'

'But what if it's the end of my marriage?' questioned Millie shakily.

Lulu's eyes narrowed. 'Would that bother you?'

Millie scrubbed at her eyes with her fingers. 'Of course it would bother me!'

'Because you like being Queen?'

'No, you idiot—because I love him! How dare you suggest a thing like that?'

Lulu went quiet for a moment. 'Well, thank God for that. I just had to be sure, that's all. Sure you knew what you were fighting for.'

Millie turned her head to look at the rainwashed lawn. 'Maybe Gianferro doesn't want to be fought for. Maybe he's decided that it's over.'

'You're going to give in that easily? Whatever happened to the Millie who would never give up? Who got back on her horse again and again—no matter how many times she had fallen off?'

Millie listened to Lulu in silence and realised that her sister was right. That even if he *had* decided he didn't want her any more, she had to give it another chance. She had to. She would fight with every fibre of her being if that was what it took.

'I'm going to have to go back to Mardivino and sort it out,' she said slowly. 'Because he's certainly showing no sign of coming to England to find *me*.'

Lulu raised her eyebrows. 'Oh, come on!' she chided. 'How can he? What? Hop on a plane and arrive here unannounced? He's the *King*, Millie—and kings just don't do that kind of thing!'

He could, Millie thought—could have done it if he had wanted to. Because he had the power at his fingertips to do almost anything he wanted. The point was that he didn't want to—and who on earth could blame him?

She felt the cold, curling fingers of pain clamping themselves around her heart, but to stay in a state of confused ignorance would never help her heart to heal. Her marriage might be over, and the sooner she learned the truth about it, the better. And Lulu was right... Why should she give up when nothing in the

world had ever been so worth fighting for as this
man was?

Millie had travelled on a scheduled flight, but after
a week in England with no word at all from Gianferro
she was feeling tired and vulnerable. She couldn't
face the thought of returning to Mardivino by the
same route—with the VIP representatives fussing and
hovering round her at the airport, the inevitable lurking paparazzo photographer lurking around to snatch
a photo of the young Queen.

She had not anticipated how greedy the press
would be for images of her—or how carefully she
would need to plan her wardrobe for travelling. One
hint of a loose-fitting top and it would be announced
to the world that she was pregnant. Millie bit her lip.
How ironic.

She phoned the Palace, but Gianferro and Alesso
were not there.

Eventually Millie got through to Alesso on his cell-
phone. 'Is Gianferro there?' she asked him quietly.

'He is touring the new hospital.'

'I see. Well, I want to come home…' For a second
she was aware that she no longer considered England
as her home—it should have been a small victory of
her newly married life, but it tasted bitterly of defeat.
'Can you arrange for the King's flight to be sent for
me, Alesso?'

'Yes, of course, Your Majesty.'

'And Alesso? Will you tell him I rang?' she said

quietly and then her voice softened. 'And that I shall see him tomorrow evening.'

'Yes, Your Majesty.'

While Millie's lady-in-waiting packed for her, she and Lulu wandered down to the stables, and as they stood looking down at a brand-new foal Millie was overcome with a powerful wave of nostalgia for how things used to be—when life had seemed a whole lot simpler.

'Do you miss England?' asked Lulu suddenly, when they had walked back through the fields, splashing through the boggy puddles in their Wellington boots. The sun had emerged from behind a cloud and its brightness was drying all the leaves on the branches, like washing hung on a line.

Millie closed her eyes and breathed in the very Englishness of the air. Her senses could transport her back to other times and other places, and never more so than now, when her senses were so keenly alert. But nothing did stay the same—it might look the same on the outside, but the people who flitted in and out were growing and changing all the time. 'Sometimes.'

'But not the weather?' joked Lulu.

'No, not the weather.' Millie smiled.

'What, then?'

'Oh, the freedom. Yes, the freedom, mainly—being able to do what you want without consulting a diary or a secretary. Being able to wander off without men in bulky jackets never being very far away from you.

But that's life as a Royal—and I knew that when I married Gianferro.'

But in a way she had known it only on a purely intellectual level—she had been unprepared for the reality of almost complete loss of freedom. She had floundered in her new life, like a little squirming fish thrown into a mighty swirling ocean. And instead of turning to her husband for help and support she had pushed him away—driven a wedge between them with her stubbornness and the secret she had nursed.

Was it too late to try and get close to him again?

The private jet skated onto the runway at Solajoya airport the following day and Millie stared out of the window, hoping and praying for the sight of her husband come to meet her—but there was no sign of him.

Not even Alesso was there—just a couple of officials who Millie did not know terribly well. She had not wanted a fuss, but she had expected *some* kind of welcome—no matter how lukewarm. But this felt like…like what? As if she was being marginalised? As if a very definite message was being sent out to her?

Her feelings of insecurity grew all the way to the Palace, and once there things were no better, for there was no sign of the King. No note. Nothing.

Nothing.

Millie kicked the shoes off her aching feet and looked around the empty suite of rooms. Nor were there any flowers on the tables. The shutters were drawn as if nobody lived there any more, and she moved forward to open them so that golden sunlight poured like honey into the room, leaving her dazzled and confused as she turned to her dresser.

'Has there been any word on when the King might return, Flavia?'

'No, Your Majesty.'

She picked up the phone. Gianferro was not answering his mobile, but then he rarely did. It was Alesso that she got through to. As usual.

'You had a good flight, Your Majesty?' he enquired.

'Yes, yes,' answered Millie impatiently. 'Where are you?'

'In Soloroca—it is the anniversary of the opening of the Juan Lopez Gallery, remember?'

'Is Gianferro not there with you?'

'Unfortunately, no. He has taken the Spanish officials sailing.'

Millie scowled at her reflection in the mirror. 'And what time is he expected back at the Palace tonight?'

There was an almost infinitesimal pause. 'There is a reception which is not scheduled to end until late, Your Majesty. The King gave the instruction that he may be delayed and that you are not to wait up for him.'

There were a million things she wanted to say, but she could not. Alesso knew as well as she did that the King could leave any reception at any damned time he pleased—if he did not do so, it was because he had chosen not to. His wife had been away for over a week and he wasn't even going to bother to see her until the next day. Which told her in no uncertain terms just how much he cared.

Millie felt her heart plummet, as if someone had dropped it from the top of a very high building. She knew that so much in Royal life was never stated, that things were 'understood'. It saved embarrassment—and presumably little could be more embarrassing than having to tell your young wife that their brief marriage was over.

But was she going to sit back and accept that?

Millie stared at herself in the mirror and her scowl became a look of fierce determination, her blue eyes glinting and her chin held high. For sure she had made a mistake—but wasn't everybody allowed one mistake without it having such an irrevocable effect on their lives?

But she knew her husband's Achilles' heel—anything which threatened his strong sense of duty would be just that. He would not want his marriage to fail for the sake of his people—no matter what his personal feelings for her.

And Millie did not want her marriage to fail either—though her reasons were fundamentally different. So was she going to fight for him? To show him what he meant to her? That she loved him with a love that burned deep in her breast like an eternal flame?

Yes, she was!

The first thing she did was strip off all her travelling clothes and shower, soaping her body and her hair as if her life depended on it and then rubbing rich scented lotion into her skin afterwards, so that she was perfumed and gleaming. The faint golden colour she had acquired since living on the island made her eyes look very blue, and her hair was paler than it had been for a long time.

She chose her lingerie carefully, and a simple dress of lemon silk, and caught her hair back in a French twist—weaving into it a ribbon the colour of buttercups.

The next bit was the tricky part. She had to persuade her bodyguard to let her drive a car, unaccompanied and unannounced. She saw the furrowed lines of worry which creased his brow and sought to reassure him.

'I don't mean completely on my own! You can follow me,' she told him. 'I want to surprise my husband,' she finished, and gave him a smile which was tinged with genuine pleading.

And of course she got her way—short of refusing the Queen's command, what alternative did the bodyguard have? Millie rarely used the full power of her title, but this time it was vital.

If the purpose of the drive hadn't been so crucial to her future happiness then she might even have embraced the feeling of freedom and exhilaration as the zippy little car began to ascend the mountain roads outside the capital.

This was the kind of thing she never did—it was

always a big chauffeur-driven limousine with the
Royal crest on the front which conveyed her to and
from her Royal engagements. But this felt…

Normal.

Ordinary.

All those things Gianferro had reminded her that
she no longer was, nor ever would be again.

Maybe not. But the feelings she had were the same
as those experienced by ordinary people, weren't
they?

And right now the overwhelming one was fear.
That it might be too late. That she had messed it up.

Licking at lips so dry they felt like parchment,
Millie drove upwards. At least the way was well sign-
posted. Gianferro had told her that the road to
Soloroca had once been little more than a track, and
the village itself had been rundown and desolate—but
that had been before the works of the great artist Juan
Lopez had been housed there, and now people came
from all over the world to view them, bringing pros-
perity to the mountains of Mardivino.

She waited until she was on the outskirts of the
village and then she telephoned Alesso.

'I'm here,' she said.

'Here, Your Majesty?'

'Just down the road, in fact.' Millie drew a deep
breath. 'Alesso, I want the way cleared for me to
come to the reception, but I do not wish Gianferro
to know. I want to surprise him, so please don't
tell him.'

'But, Your Majesty—'

'*Please*, Alesso.'

There was a pause. 'Very well, Your Majesty.'

It was a mark of how much Royal life had seeped into her unconscious that her first thought had been to clear it with her husband's aide. For, while many would recognise her as the Queen, others might have considered her to be an impostor—there could have been an almighty fuss, and then the crucial element of surprise would have been lost.

And she wanted to see Gianferro's first instinctive reaction to her. Oh, he was a master at keeping his face poker-straight and expressionless, but surely his eyes would give *some* kind of reaction. Even if there was the tiniest bit of pleasure lurking in their black depths, then surely that was enough to build on?

And if there was no pleasure? What then?

Millie quickly smoothed her hair and straightened her back. She was not going to project an outcome.

Her way might have been prepared by Alesso—for all the guards bowed as if they had been expecting her—but that did not mean there were not curious eyes in the room. Older, predatory married women, who were always in evidence around the King, were fixing her with unwelcome eyes. Millie knew that many of them were just itching to step into her shoes. To provide the King with the physical comfort a man of his appetite needed—with no questions asked and no demands made.

Did he still want his foolish young wife? Millie

wondered, her eyes searching the high-domed white room whose walls were lined with the vibrant paintings of Lopez.

And then she saw him.

He was wearing a dark suit and looked both cool and formal. As usual, all heads were bent obsequiously towards him as people listened, and Millie knew that if he made a joke—however weak—people would fall about laughing. Because when you were King people told you what they thought you wanted to hear.

She knew then that her attempt at reconciliation must go no further than was necessary—for if she capitulated too much he would never respect her again.

He might be King, and she Queen, but the tussles within their marriage were not Royal ones—and unless they could find some real human ground on which to thrash them out then it would not be a marriage worth continuing with anyway.

Gianferro was listening to the Spanish Ambassador praising Mardivino's attitude to the arts when he became aware of a slight buzz in the room. His eyes narrowed as he saw heads turning in the direction of the door.

But he was already in the room! Who in the world could possibly be entering and capturing more attention than he could?

And then he saw her.

Her eyes were like a summer's sky and her hair as pale and gleaming as moonlight. She wore a yellow dress which made her look cool and composed, but he could see that her mouth was set and tense, though it wavered in a tentative attempt at a smile as she began to walk towards him.

Now the faces were turned towards him, watching for his reaction, the way they always did. They would be wondering what the Queen was doing here, for she was not expected—and members of the Royal family did not simply turn up out of the blue.

What the hell was she thinking of? he wondered angrily.

She moved towards him and the purely physical reaction which she always provoked in him kicked in—with a force and power which momentarily took his breath away. But then he remembered the ugly scene which had caused her departure, and he felt the faint flickering of a muscle at his cheek.

She came right up to him, her cheeks flushed and her eyelids dropping down to conceal the sapphire glitter of her eyes.

'Your Majesty,' she said, very softly.

And, breaking protocol for the first time in his life, Gianferro bent his mouth to her ear.

'What the hell are you doing here?' he breathed.

CHAPTER TWELVE

MILLIE felt faint and dizzy—her heart was beating so loudly that it threatened to deafen her as she looked into the cold and unwelcoming eyes of Gianferro— but somehow she managed to keep a small and non-committal smile pinned to her mouth. People were watching them—she dared not let her fragile emotions show.

'Are you not pleased to see me, Gianferro?'

With an equally non-committal smile, he placed his palm beneath her elbow.

'Surprised,' he murmured. And that was an understatement. The last thing he had expected was to see his beautiful blonde wife slinking across the reception room towards him, and for once he was unprepared. Fleetingly he allowed himself to wonder how a normal man might have dealt with such a situation, but the eyes of the room were fixed on them.

Damn her! Had she deliberately contrived to catch him off-guard? To slip beneath his defences as cunningly as she always managed to do in bed? When she made him feel like Samson after his hair had been shorn? Had he not spent the past week telling himself over and over that she must not be allowed to do so again?

'I will speak with you in private, my dear,' he continued. 'But first I must make my farewells.'

His voice was soft, but the words were undoubtedly a command, and something in the dark glitter of his eyes made Millie suddenly apprehensive.

'I didn't intend to drag you away,' she whispered.

'Really? Then just what *did* you intend, Millie? That you would flounce in here unannounced and everyone would just pretend not to notice?'

It was a reprimand, and one she knew she deserved. 'What do you want me to do?'

But at that moment, as if summoned by some unspoken order, Alesso appeared. Gianferro spoke to him rapidly and fiercely in Italian, and then he bent his head to her ear once more.

'Go now with Alesso,' he said, switching effortlessly to English. 'And wait for me. It will only complicate matters if formal introductions are made,' he added coolly. 'At least this way the Spanish Ambassador can be reliably informed that there is a family crisis.'

And was there? Millie wondered, as she followed Alesso from the room, pride making her smile at the people who bowed and curtsied as she passed. Of course there was…and by the time she and Gianferro were through maybe the Palace lawyers would have been instructed to draw up the papers announcing a formal separation.

In the corridor, she saw Alesso's look of resignation.

'I've got you into trouble, haven't I?' she guessed.

'He is not pleased.'

Millie bit her lip. 'I'm sorry, Alesso.'

He shook his head. 'No. It is for the best. I do not like to see the King miserable. He cannot rule with so much on his mind.'

'How has he been?' Millie asked breathlessly, wondering if Alesso would give her any inkling of the truth, or just be Gianferro's official mouthpiece.

'Distracted,' he admitted with a shrug.

And Millie wondered what he had been distracted with. Had he missed her? Or had he simply been working out the best and cleanest way to end the marriage? 'Is there somewhere very private we could go?'

He nodded. 'It is already arranged. The Cacciatore family own a house on the coastal road. He is taking you there. It is empty and—'

But at that moment Gianferro himself swept out, accompanied by a retinue of diplomats and servants. His black eyes gave little away as he looked at Millie other than faint displeasure, but he could not stem the sudden rush of blood to his groin. He found himself thinking how much more uncomplicated life was without a woman in it, and his mouth hardened.

'Come,' he said crisply.

As she slid into the back of the large unmarked car beside him she told herself that this was never going to be a romantic reunion. But his proximity sent her already raw senses into overdrive. She was achingly aware of him as a man—of the long, lean thrust of his legs and the muscular body so tightly coiled beside her. Could he not have touched her? At least reached out to squeeze the frozen fingers which looked so lifeless where they lay against the lemon silk dress.

Gianferro was aware of a mixture of powerlessness and frustration—of wanting to press her body hard against his and knowing that the presence of the driver ruled it out. But it was more than that. He still did not know why she was here—her very eagerness to confront him might spell her determination to seek a new life for herself.

Could he blame her if she did?

The silence between them grew as the powerful car ate up the miles, and Millie didn't know whether to be relieved or terrified when a pair of electric gates opened and their car was spotlighted by the security lighting which zapped on.

She wasn't really aware of the terse conversation going on between Gianferro and his head of security, only that it seemed to take endless negotiations before the two of them were finally alone in a rather formal-looking salon. It had the air of a room which had not been lived in for some time—although the furniture was very beautiful indeed.

Gianferro closed the door quietly and an immense silence seemed to swallow them up. He looked at her properly then, as if for the first time, but his face did not relax.

'So, Millie,' he said quietly, 'is there some kind of explanation for this extraordinary behaviour?'

She stared at him, bewildered and hurt. 'I wanted to see you.'

'And now you have.'

'You aren't going to make this easy for me, are you, Gianferro?'

He gave her the bland, formal smile she had seen him use at so many official functions. 'Make what easy?'

She wanted to drum her fists against his chest, to tell him that he couldn't hide behind that icy persona—except that she knew he could. Had she thought that simply because she had seen it melt from time to time it was gone for ever? Of course it wasn't.

She looked at him. 'I'm so sorry for what I did, my darling,' she whispered. 'And I wondered…' She swallowed down the lump in her throat and the salty taste of tears which tainted her mouth. 'Maybe I have no right to ask this—but do you think you can ever find it in your heart to forgive me?'

Her words touched him as he had not expected or wanted to be touched, and so did her stricken face, but he steeled his heart against her. 'I don't know,' he said tonelessly.

Millie felt as if he had struck her, but she remained strong. Maybe what had happened between them was too big to be cured with just a single word of apology. Maybe he didn't want it to be cured.

She bit her lip. 'Do you want to save our marriage?'

A cold and sardonic smile curved his lips. It had been his trademark smile as a bachelor, and he was discovering how easy it was to slip back into it. But this nagging ache in his heart had never been there in those days, which seemed so long ago now. 'Is it worth saving, do you think, Millie?'

She told herself that he was deliberately trying to hurt her, and that she must withstand his taunts. That this, in a way, was her punishment. And she *wanted* to suffer, for she had made him suffer, and then she wanted to be washed clean of all her pain and regret and to start all over again. But this might be one idealistic hope too far, it could only work if he wanted it, too.

'Yes,' she said, in a low, firm voice. 'Yes, I do. More than anything.'

And then she knew that she had to do something else, too. That it was foolish for her to wait for words of love from Gianferro. Even if he *did* feel love—which she doubted—he would be unable to show it, for nobody had shown him *how* to. This wasn't some quiz from a women's magazine. It didn't *matter* who said what and in what order. Just because some ancient code said that the man was supposed to declare his feelings first she didn't have to heed it! If it was just pride standing in the way of her telling him how she really felt—then what good was pride?

What good was anything if she didn't have her

man? And didn't she owe it to Gianferro to tell him how much he meant to her?

'I think it's worth saving because when I made my vows I meant them. I think it's worth saving because I have a duty both to you and to Mardivino, to provide emotional security and succour to their King.'

She swallowed down the last of her fears as she looked up into his face with very clear and bright blue eyes. 'But, most important of all, I think it's worth saving because I love you, Gianferro, even though you think I may not have shown it. I have loved you for a long, long time now, but I have never dared tell you. And now I am terrified that my stupid actions will prevent me from ever showing you just how much.'

He stilled. What she was offering was like a beacon glowing on a dark night. It was comfort from the storm and warmth in the depths of winter. It was like having walked in the desert for days and being tempted with the sight of an oasis shimmering on the horizon. But Gianferro had walked for too long alone to allow himself to give in to temptation. She was offering him an easier, softer option, and he didn't need one—he didn't *need her*.

He should tell her to go to hell. He should tell her that he could live without her. And he could. He had before and he would again.

His heart was pounding with the pumped-up feelings of a man about to enter battle. But as he looked at her he realised that he did not want to do battle with her. He continued to stare at her, remembering the slight figure and the fearlessness which had first so entranced him. Then she had been a tomboy, but today she looked regal and beautiful. In her eyes he could read that self-same fearlessness, but now there was doubt, too.

'You would recover if it ended,' he said harshly.

She shook her head. 'Not properly. Only on the surface.'

'And you would find another man.'

'But never like you,' she said simply. 'And you know that. You told me that once yourself, on the very day you proposed marriage to me.'

Gianferro's eyes narrowed as he remembered. So he had! Even on that day he had used an arrogant persuasion which could almost be defined as subtle force. He had been determined to have her and he had gone all out to get her. She hadn't stood a chance.

He had brought her here and then told her—*told* her—that she should have his child immediately, when she had still been so very young and inexperienced herself.

Was that the kind of tyrant he had become? So used to imposing his will that he didn't stop to think about whether it was appropriate to do so with his new wife?

Pain crossed his face as for the first time he acknowledged where his arrogance and pride could lead him if he let it. To a life alone. An empty life. A life without her. His life was one into which she had crept like a flame, bringing both warmth and light into it. Her absence had left a dull, aching gap behind—even though the independent side of him had resented that.

He had once seen her as a path to be taken in a hazy landscape, but now he could see very clearly the two paths which lay before him. He saw what being with his wife would mean, and more terrifyingly, he saw what being without her promised. A life which would be stark and empty and alone.

'Oh, Millie,' he said brokenly. 'Millie.'

The face she turned up to him was wreathed in anxiety and fear. 'Gianferro?' she breathed, in a voice she prayed would not dissolve into tears. Something in his expression gave her a tenuous hope, but she was too scared to hang onto it in case it was false. 'Just tell me—and if you really want it to be over then I will accept that. I will never like it, nor will I ever stop loving you, but I will do as you wish.'

Something in her words let the floodgates open, and feeling came flooding in to wash over the barren landscape of his heart. After a lifetime of being kept at bay it was sharp and bright and painful and warm, all at the same time, and Gianferro gave a small gasp of bewilderment—he who had never known a moment's doubt in his life.

He pulled her into his arms and looked down at her, not quite knowing where to begin. He had never had to say sorry to anyone in his life, and now he began to recognise that it had not done him any favours. He realised that he was more than just a symbol of power, a figurehead. Inside, his heart beat the same as that of any other man. And having feelings didn't make you weak, he realised—not if it could make you feel as alive as he felt right at that moment. Cut yourself adrift from them and you were not a complete person—and how could he rule unless he was?

'It is me who should be begging your forgiveness,' he said quietly. 'For living in the Dark Ages and refusing to make this a modern marriage. For thinking that I could impose my will on you as if you were simply one of my subjects, forgetting—or choosing to ignore—the fact that you are my wife. My partner. My Millie.'

'Oh, Gianferro!'

'I was a tyrant!' he whispered.

'Not all the time.'

He smiled. 'But some of the time?'

'Well, yes. But then, I have my own faults and failings that I must live with and deal with.' Shadows danced across her face, and then she looked up at him, her eyes clear and blue and questioning. 'What will we do?'

'We will begin again. What else can we do, *cara* Millie? As of today we will move forward, not back.'

Her heart felt as if it was going to burst with joy, and all the dark and terrible fantasies about what *could* have happened began to dissolve. Never again, she decided, was she going to take the coward's way out—of hiding her doubts and her fears and letting them grow. From this day forward there would be the transparency of true love. From her, at least. And she was not going to ask anything of Gianferro. Not push him or manipulate him into saying anything that he didn't mean. But she had to know something.

'Does that mean we can still be married, then?' she questioned shakily.

And Gianferro burst out laughing as he lifted her chin and allowed the love which blazed from her eyes to light him with its warmth. Why had she never looked at him that way before? *Because she was scared to.* He kissed the tip of her nose with lips which were tender. 'Oh, yes, my love,' he replied softly. 'Yes, we can still be married.'

She tightened her arms around his back. 'Kiss me.'

He grazed his lips against hers. 'Like this?'

'More.'

'Like this, perhaps?'

Millie gasped. 'Oh, yes. Yes. Just like that.'

He carried her upstairs and made love to her on the silken counterpane of some unknown bed, and it was better than anything she had ever known because now she was free to really show him how much she cared. She began to cry out in helpless wonder, and he gasped too, then bent his head to kiss her, until her cries were spent and her body had stopped shuddering in time with his.

Millie ran her fingertips down the side of his lean face, aware that her next words were going to remind him of what she had done—or failed to do—but she was never going to shrink from the difficult things in life again.

'I'm going to chuck my Pills away—'

'No.' He shook his head. 'No, that is precisely what you are not going to do, *cara*.'

In the moonlight, she stared at him in confusion. 'But, Gianferro, you want an heir—'

'So I do,' he agreed gently. 'But you are only twenty, Millie, and I want us to have time together first. To learn about each other. To learn to love one another.'

To *learn* to love. If she had heard that only hours ago it would have hurt, but Millie had done a lot of growing up in those hours. She had had to—her marriage had depended on it. And life wasn't always like the fairy story you longed it to be. Love didn't always strike you like a thunderbolt—though lust did! Sometimes it had its basis in all kinds of things you didn't understand. Two people could instinctively reach out for one another on a level which would confound common sense—and that was what had happened to her and Gianferro—but after that you had to work at it.

It was like riding. You could love horses with a mad passion, but you couldn't possibly learn to ride without being thrown off!

'We will have a baby when it is time to have a baby,' he said, and bent his lips to brush them over hers. 'And in the meantime—what is it that they say?'

His eyes glittered with mischief. 'We will have fun…
practising.'

Oh, yes, she thought, as he pulled her against him
once more. You can say that again.

EPILOGUE

MILLIE learned the hard way that babies were not something that could be ordered up—like strawberries on a summer menu.

She and Gianferro had a year to themselves before they ceremonially threw her Pills away while he wiped her tears of regret with soft and healing kisses. A year of exploring and learning about each other, learning how to live as husband and wife. And how to love. But that bit came more easily than either of them had expected—especially where Gianferro was concerned. It was as though, having given himself permission, he entered into loving with the true zeal of the convert. Passion had always come easily to him, and so now did love.

Millie was having formal language lessons, and she got her husband to speak to her in French and Spanish, and Alesso in Italian, and gradually she was picking up a smattering of all three.

It helped that she had nephews and nieces who were fluent in all the languages spoken on Mardivino—and she had made a big effort to befriend their mothers. Their slight diffidence towards her had quickly worn off, and once they'd seen that she wasn't just going through the motions of friendship Ella and

183

Lucy had welcomed her into their families with open arms. And for the first time since he had been a little boy Gianferro had begun to get to know his two brothers properly.

In fact, everything was absolutely perfect except on the baby front—because nothing had happened. After months of trying, she still wasn't pregnant, and Millie didn't know what to do about it. She didn't dare ask anyone else about *their* experiences—not even her sisters-in-law—because she didn't want anyone else to know. It was too big a deal for everyone concerned. She wasn't like other women. Once she went to the doctor it would be on record, and then…

But what if…?

'Why are you frowning so?' Gianferro asked one night, as they were getting dressed for dinner.

Millie had once made a vow to herself that she would not shirk responsibility, but she was unprepared for the pain of voicing *these* fears—and even more concerned about the possible consequences if they happened to be true.

'I'm not pregnant,' she said.

'I'd rather guessed that.'

Her head shot up. 'How?' And then she saw the silent laughter in his black eyes, and blushed. 'Gianferro—it's not funny—what if…what if…?'

'What if you can't have a baby?'

'Well, yes!' She put her hairbrush down with trembling fingers. 'You'll have to divorce me!'

'Millie, stop it,' he said gently.

'But you will!'

'How long has it been now?'

'Nearly four months!' she wailed, and to her fury he burst out laughing. 'Don't!'

'Come here,' he said tenderly. 'What does that book you've got say?'

Millie sniffed. She hadn't realised he'd noticed her reading it. 'Not to worry until it's been at least a year.'

'Or not to worry at all, more like it,' he said sternly.

'Why aren't *you* worried about it?' Millie questioned.

'What if I told you that I was having too good a time just the way things are?' he said simply.

'*Are* you?' she asked softly, in delight.

'Yes, *cara*. I am. Now, come over here and have a look at the designs for the statue.'

She walked over to him and leaned over his shoulder, looking down at the plans. 'Oh, Gianferro,' she breathed. 'It looks beautiful.'

'Doesn't it?' he agreed, with a smile of satisfaction.

All three brothers had decided that it was high time that their mother should have a monument erected in her honour, and a prestigious Mardivinian sculptor had been given the precious commission. It was to stand just outside the capital, in stunning landscaped gardens with a small lake and tinkling fountain. It would be a place where families could picnic and children could play, and lovers could lie and look at the rare trees and shrubs.

*   *   *

The statue was unveiled six months later, on a beautiful, sunny spring day, and Millie sat with her sisters-in-law—their faces all soppy with pride and love as they watched their three dark husbands bow before the marble image of their mother.

Prince Nicolo. The Daredevil Prince.

Prince Guido. The Playboy Prince.

And King Gianferro. The Mighty.

As the three men walked towards their wives Ella laid a hand on Millie's arm, her face concerned.

'Are you all right, Millie?' she questioned anxiously. 'You look awfully pale today.'

Millie shook her head, and then wished she hadn't as a wave of nausea hit her. 'No, I'm just feeling a bit…under the weather,' she said weakly as a shadow fell over her. She looked up with relief when she saw it was her husband.

'You're not sick, are you?'

Millie met Gianferro's eyes, which were filled with love, as they always were, and some new emotion, too.

Pride.

She raised her eyebrows at him in question.

'No, Ella,' he said softly. 'The Queen is not ill.' Tenderly, he touched his hand to her blonde hair and smiled. 'Shall I tell them, *cara*, or will you?'

LIMERICK
COUNTY LIBRARY

MILLS & BOON®
*Super*ROMANCE

Enjoy the drama, explore the emotions, experience the relationships

A Child's Wish
Tara Taylor Quinn

A Man of Duty
Linda Warren

*Super*ROMANCE

*Super*ROMANCE

4 brand-new titles each month

Available on the third Friday of every month
from WHSmith, ASDA, Tesco
and all good bookshops
www.millsandboon.co.uk

GEN/38/RTL11

0208/05a

**On sale
7th March 2008**

MILLS & BOON
BY REQUEST
3
NOVELS ONLY
£4.99

*In March 2008
Mills & Boon present
two spectacular
collections, each featuring
wonderful romances by
bestselling authors...*

Brides by Blackmail

Featuring

The Blackmail Marriage by Penny Jordan
The Greek's Blackmailed Wife by Sarah Morgan
The Blackmail Pregnancy by Melanie Milburne

Available at WHSmith, Tesco, ASDA, and all good bookshops
www.millsandboon.co.uk

0208/05b

**On sale
7th March 2008**

MILLS & BOON
BY REQUEST
3
NOVELS ONLY
£4.99

Don't miss
out on these
fabulous
stories!

Spanish Affairs

Featuring

A Spanish Vengeance by Diana Hamilton
A Spanish Honeymoon by Anne Weale
His Brother's Son by Jennifer Taylor

Available at WHSmith, Tesco, ASDA, and all good bookshops
www.millsandboon.co.uk

MILLS & BOON®
MODERN™

...International affairs, seduction and passion guaranteed

The Greek Tycoon's Pregnant Wife
Anne Mather

Miranda Lee
Blackmailed into the Italian's Bed

MILLS & BOON
MODERN™

MILLS & BOON
MODERN™

8 brand-new titles each month

Available on the first Friday of every month
from WHSmith, ASDA, Tesco
and all good bookshops
www.millsandboon.co.uk

GEN/01/RTL11

0108/06/MB131

Coming in January 2008

MILLS & BOON

MODERN™
Heat

If you like Mills & Boon® Modern™ you'll love Modern Heat!

Strong, sexy alpha heroes, sizzling storylines
and exotic locations from around the world —
what more could you want?

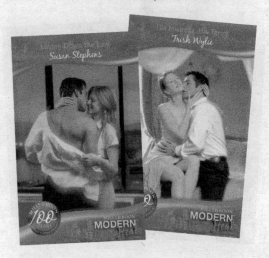

2 new books available every month
Starting 4th January 2008

Available at WHSmith, Tesco, ASDA, and all good bookshops
www.millsandboon.co.uk

MILLS & BOON®
Desire™ 2-*in*-1

2 passionate, dramatic love stories in each book

3 brand-new titles to choose from each month

Available on the third Friday of every month
from WHSmith, ASDA, Tesco
and all good bookshops
www.millsandboon.co.uk

GEN/51/RTL11

MILLS & BOON®

Blaze®

Scorching hot sexy reads...

4 brand-new titles each month

Available on the first Friday of every month
from WHSmith, ASDA, Tesco
and all good bookshops
www.millsandboon.co.uk

GEN/14/RTL11

MILLS & BOON®
INTRIGUE
Breathtaking romance & adventure

8 brand-new titles each month

Available on the third Friday of every month
from WHSmith, ASDA, Tesco
and all good bookshops
www.millsandboon.co.uk

GEN/46/RTL11

0208/46/MB132

MILLS & BOON

INTRIGUE

proudly presents:

Nocturne

A sensual tapestry of spine-tingling passion with heroes and heroines guaranteed to be out of the ordinary

Coming in February 2008 starting with

The Raintree Trilogy

As an ancient foe rises once more, the rejoined battle will measure the endurance of the Raintree clan...

Raintree: Inferno by Linda Howard – **on sale February 2008**
Raintree: Haunted by Linda Winstead Jones – **on sale March 2008**
Raintree: Sanctuary by Beverly Barton – **on sale April 2008**

Available at WHSmith, Tesco, ASDA, and all good bookshops
www.millsandboon.co.uk

Celebrate 100 years of pure reading pleasure with Mills & Boon®

To mark our centenary, each month we're publishing a special 100th Birthday Edition. These celebratory editions are packed with extra features and include a FREE bonus story.

Now that's worth celebrating!

4th January 2008

The Vanishing Viscountess by Diane Gaston
With FREE story The Mysterious Miss M
This award-winning tale of the Regency Underworld launched Diane Gaston's writing career.

1st February 2008

Cattle Rancher, Secret Son by Margaret Way
With FREE story His Heiress Wife
Margaret Way excels at rugged Outback heroes...

15th February 2008

Raintree: Inferno by Linda Howard
With FREE story Loving Evangeline
A double dose of Linda Howard's heady mix of passion and adventure.

Don't miss out! From February you'll have the chance to enter our fabulous monthly prize draw. See special 100th Birthday Editions for details.

www.millsandboon.co.uk

0108/CENTENARY_2-IN-1